THE PATH TO VENGEANCE

BOOK 3

I0586886

BY
PHILLIP TUCKER

www.philliptucker.com.au

ACKNOWLEDGEMENT

Thank you to my friends and family, for putting up with me while I wrote this book. A special thanks to Aaron and Lindsey, for their hard work in turning hundreds of pages of writing into a readable book.

CONTENTS

LOVERS

The bike's steering handled like a soggy marshmallow as its overconfident rider screamed into the corner. Leaning into the curve, the rider's knee fleetingly skimmed the road's surface as he tried to stabilise his bike through the turn. Fear and adrenaline both coursed through his veins, sharpening his reflexes, giving him the impression that time had slowed. He became aware of every stone and rut on the road's shoulder, as he tried to avert the disaster he'd created. Skidding sideways and feeling the cycle drift, he gunned the accelerator on the crumbling bitumen's edge, praying. The bike straightened as it won its fight with gravity, the relieved rider chuckled to himself.

'That was close," The rider confessed to himself from inside his jet-black helmet, his bike's Speedo nudging a little over one hundred and forty.

"Go Ninja go." A female voice squealed behind him, unaware of the averted calamity. Her arms gripped him tightly around his waist, enjoying the thrill. "That cabin better not be too far!" Her husky voice screamed as he felt her pelvis rub up against his arse. He was about to shout a reply, when a rusty old sign, marking the turnoff, came into view. Slamming on the brakes, he felt the woman's body compress against his back, as at the same time she expelled air from her lungs. Groaning with both fear and pleasure her grip became a bear hug, as adrenalin surged through her.

Gunning the bike, he turned down the dirt side road, the tacho going into the red, as the wheels fought for traction. Dodging a multitude of potholes and poultry, he accelerated up the decaying and forgotten road. Coming to an entrance of what appeared to be an abandoned farm, with a large farm stay sign, he slammed on the brakes. Mentally checking the number of it, he concluded that they'd reached their secluded weekend getaway.

Rather than dismount and open the gate, he guided the bike between two posts of a walking track beside it, driving on. Arriving at what appeared to be two derelict buildings, he again applied the brakes, standing the bike on its nose. Looking around, he saw the door of an old barn ajar. Accelerating, he drove into the decrepit turn of the century structure, before simultaneously slamming on the brakes and turning the bike sideways. This catapulted both the rider and his passenger onto a large pile of freshly turned hay.

Reacting first, Peter reaches for the woman, who was trying to get to her feet. Tripping her, he rolled on top of her, pinning her down by his knees. Pulling off his helmet and then hers, he tried unsuccessfully to kiss her as his captive fought for dominance. With practised simplicity, she slammed him backwards, onto the dirt floor.

"Do you think I'm that easy?" She giggled, stripping off her leather jacket, taking up a fighter's stance.

"I know you're easy Marlise or I wouldn't have brought you here." He answered, as launching himself forward, he attempted to tackle her. Without seeming to exert herself, she raised her left arm, gripping his collar. Twisting, letting his charge supply the energy, she flung him over her shoulder. Unprepared Peter landed heavily beside the pile of hay, grunting at the impact. Marlise sniggering at his awkward landing, waited for him to recover and try again. Several seconds passed, as silence dominated the room his failure to rise, becoming ominous.

"Peter, are you okay?" She asked with a slight tremor of concern in her voice, as he continued to lay face down. Moving forward, she grabbed his left arm feeling for a pulse. Concerned, she felt guilty for using her new assault training to throw him, from a course she'd just completed. Up until this point of their sexually charged romance, Peter usually won these fanciful matches. It appeared not anymore. Frightened, she bent down next to him, her face next to his.

"Can you hear me, Peter?" She asked, slapping his face lightly, trying to bring him around.

"Marlise. I can't move my legs." He whimpered, sounding vague. Marlise, leaned in close, as Peter's voice became a whisper. The realisation came to her that she might have severely hurt him. This caused a sob to escape her lips.

"I'm so sorry Peter I didn't mean it." She sputtered out, as Peter without warning pulled her to him, kissing her.

"Got ya." He chuckled.

"You're a fucking arsehole." She snarled, getting up and walking away, his laughter following her. Getting to his feet, seeing her walk towards the farmhouse, he sensed he'd gone too far. Following her, he watched her flop down on the veranda next to the front door.

"Hey, I was only foxing soldier girl. Didn't they teach you to watch for that?" He pointed out, walking over and sitting down beside her.

"You're not funny. I thought I'd hurt you." She confessed, angry at his horseplay.

"What? A French Paratrooper hurt me, no way." He mocked, knowing what was coming. One minute she was sitting looking upset, the next she was at his throat. It became a beautiful, yet deadly dance as two elite soldiers battled it out for an apology. Peter was by far the more muscular and the fittest combatant. Marlise, on the other hand, was a martial arts pro, with an athlete's physique. Both took blows that would have crippled an untrained civilian, as they pivoted around each other, searching for an opening to deliver the killer blow.

As if the enormity of their conflict's conclusion broke through to their subconscious, the two wearily parted. Knowing someone would be severely hurt if they continued, Peter dropped his hands to his sides, suing for peace.

"I'm sorry Marlise; it was a stupid thing to do." He confessed, watching her. For several seconds she stood as if in a daze, her blood up, preparing for her next move. In the

6

end without warning, she turned away, walking back to the barn and the bike.

"I suppose this dump, is the romantic hideaway you promised me." She barked, detaching her gear from the discarded machine.

"Yes, it is. Although the ads for it, made it seem a lot more romantic." He admitted, trying to win her back.

"For your stunt, you can make dinner. I'm having a shower." She told him, moving towards the hut. Grabbing his gear, Peter then stood the bike up, checking it over. His stunt had cost him not only Marlise's anger but also an ugly dent in the fuel tank on his brand new Kawasaki Ninja.

"You're an arse." He told himself, knowing tonight that unless there was a miracle, he'd be sleeping on the sofa if the hut had one. Marlise, reaching the hut tried the door. It was unlocked.

"No surprise there!" She yelled back to him, still displeased. Walking through the hut looking for the bedroom, she idly glanced out through a crack in the lounge room window's curtain. Coming to a complete stop, she stared at the immense valley that fell away to a magical deep blue lake in the valley below.

"My God. Who would've thought?" She said out loud, captivated by the view. She found it hard to believe, that such a view could be concealed behind a broken down farmhouse and an old shed. Moving to the window Marlise opened the curtain, taking it all in.

"It's beautiful Marlise. But it doesn't hold a candle to you." Peter whispered, coming up behind her. Standing there enjoying the moment the young couple stood silently, both held captive by nature's beauty. Seizing the opportunity, Peter placed his hand around her waist holding her. Feeling her move into him, rubbing up against his side, Peter smiling kissed her neck.

"See, I can fake it too. Now piss off and cook dinner." She erupted, pushing him away. Walking across the lounge room to the door opposite, which she guessed was the bedroom; she entered, slamming the door behind her. This left Peter staring forlornly at the view, wondering what he'd cook. Inside the bedroom, Marlise concealed a giggle as she stripped off for her shower.

'That will make him think next time' she smiled, walking into the bathroom. He had scared her, although her reaction was more from her intense training over the past two-months than his boyish prank. Something big was coming she mused, and her unit would be in the thick of it. She'd been given this weekend off as a reward, knowing when she returned that they'd be moving out. Where they were going was top secret, rumours hinted at Africa.

Up until now, she'd always confided in Peter. This one was different. Peter was part of the Swiss Special forces, while she was a member of an elite French paratrooper regiment. Security on this mission was tight, meaning no one could know, especially a soldier from another country. Switzerland and France were close allies and neighbours, but when national interests were at stake, some secrets had to be kept.

Peter, breaking away from his thoughts of Marlise, wandered towards the kitchen. Part of Peter's farm stay included a well-stocked pantry. Walking into it, Peter tried to orientate himself, working out where everything was. As advertised, the fridge was well stocked with food and a sizable selection of alcohol.

"This might help the situation." He grinned, moving to what appeared to be the pantry.

Gathering a mixed bag of vegetables, he swiftly cut them up, deciding to bake them. Once they were in the oven, he found a slab of venison. Cutting it into small pieces, he decided on stewing it, adding seasoning and herbs. He then made something special, a thick sauce that his mother used and had taught him how to cook. He was no chef, but he thought Marlise would be impressed.

His mother had taught him basic cooking when he was young. At the time, they were in hiding, and his father was on the run. His mother was adamant that he be anything but a soldier. She'd hoped he would become a chef; unfortunately, he didn't have the gift. Instead, she taught him 'Kiss cooking,' as she'd called it. 'Keep It Simple Stupid', was what the initials stood for. Smiling, remembering those days of cloak and dagger, Peter poured two glasses of wine moving into the lounge area to await Marlise.

Ten minutes and no show, made Peter recheck his meal. Finding it had at least another twenty minutes to cook, he moved through the lounge room, opening the rear door to the valley. Walking outside, he stared down towards the lake, seeing movement in the trees. A small herd of deer were grazing as the shade of the coming night crept over them. It was a good tactic to come out now he thought. With the light failing, it would make using a scope impractical.

The deer had adapted he smiled. Feeding at dusk, hiding from the danger during the light of day, had become part of their evolution of survival. The animals awakened memories of his first hunting trip near here, where he first met Marlise. She had become his addiction, and from that first moment, Peter had become hooked. It was also for the first time; he saw the ugliness of his father's past life. Assassins had tried by capturing him, to kill his father and his friend Aaron. They'd been lucky and had come out of it alive, if not changed. He'd lost his bloodlust for deer hunting soon after that, finding the killing of an endangered animal foolish.

"Now I hunt men." He smiled, seeing the mockery in choosing to hunt a more dangerous, if not prevalent animal. Hearing a noise behind him, Peter turned, looking into the main bedroom's window. Marlise stood naked, combing her wet hair unaware of his presence. Her skin was ebony white from her breast to her thighs. This with her dark tanned head, shoulders, and limbs made her appear tantalisingly camouflaged, like a nimble African gazelle.

Despite her intense military training, she was still a full-bodied woman, athletic yes and in his eyes, wildly erotic. As if she sensed his desire or primaeval animal hunger, she turned to the window, facing him. A small smile appeared in the corner of her lips as she continued to comb her hair, brazenly showing him what had been denied him. Dinner was forgotten, as he moved to the bedroom door.

Marlise watched him draw closer, his smooth, effortless stride, reminding her of the hunting approach of a savage lion, moving in for the kill. The shower had inflamed her need, and despite their fight, she wanted him. Marlise crossed to the door she unlocked it, opening herself to him with this gesture. Without a word spoken, he lifted her. Carrying her to the bed, he lowered her upon it, kissing her lightly on the shoulder.

Surrendering to his male domination, she lay back as he grabbed a handful of her hair. Brutally pulling her head back, he stared into her eyes, before savagely crushing her lips with a kiss. Moaning, she, in turn, raked his back with her fingernails, feeling him tense at this small show of force. It served a purpose though; reminding him she too had claws.

Standing, Peter swiftly undressed, his eyes never leaving hers, as Marlise beyond waiting, aggressively sat up, pulling him onto the bed. Mounting him, she released a loud moan of satisfaction, as they began their weekend together, the fight forgotten.

Dinner of course was ruined. Taking solace in why Peter promptly cleaned up the mess and repeated his meal preparations. Putting it again in the oven, he moved back into the lounge area, finding Marlise at the window. Their valley view was now covered in a blanket of darkness; the only lights visible were the stars that filled the sky.

"Full marks Peter. This place is magic."

"Yes it's beautiful spot, and it's also the perfect location, being on the border with your France and my Switzerland." Peter pointed out, holding her.

"How's your family? You don't talk about them much like you used too."

"Since the trouble with Michelle and her husband, we have become a little withdrawn."

"She's still with him then?"

"Yes, amazingly she forgave him, although I don't think dad ever will."

"He's just a doctor Peter; they believe that they're bulletproof, you should cut him some slack." Dodging an answer, Peter poured two glasses of wine handing her one. Seeing he wasn't going to talk further about his sister, she moved on.

"How are your Mum and Dad then?"

"Good. When I left, they were packing up to go skiing in Germany with Aaron and Petra."

"Do they all still ski?"

"Yes, although since Libya, Aaron has a limp. Over long distances, like doing cross-country, he has trouble, although he'd never admit it. Dad told Aarons still a devil on the downhill slopes though. It appears that despite what happened to him, he refuses to let it slow him down. Mind you, the two of them like nothing better than to just sit around the bar with a drink and relax. It's one thing most of their lives they've had trouble doing."

"What about their other two friends? The one from Australia, named Steve and his wife the journalist?"

"Steve and Natasha were coming on this ski trip as well. Natasha came down with the flu and was bed ridden. Steve was upset about not coming."

"He scares me and not many men do, even at his age," Marlise admitted, remembering Libya as well.

"That was three years ago; the guy's nearly sixty."

"You know what I mean Peter. No one moves like that."

"Anyway, how's your Dad?" Peter changed the subject.

"Still running the hunting lodge although most people now, shoot with a camera. He doesn't care as long as they keep coming. Old age won't kill him, the drinking of schnapps will," she giggled. Peter had always had a little trouble with Marlise's dad. On that first hunting trip when he'd met Marlise, they'd spent the night on the run together. They'd been forced to camp in a secluded valley in the mountains to throw off the people hunting them. One thing had led to another, and they'd ended up making love.

Her father must've guessed something went on, and since then, he hadn't been exactly thrilled to see Peter with Marlise when she'd visited him.

"Are we ever going to talk about Libya Peter?"

"No Marlise, Better to keep that part of our lives buried forever," Peter softly answered, kissing her cheek, before moving back to the kitchen.

Like most weekends they'd spent together this one ended with many questions left unanswered. Travelling back to Marlise's army base outside Marseilles, Peter considered many times to stop and ask Marlise a question he wanted her to answer. Pulling up near the front gates, Marlise sensing something was wrong, unloaded her bags before reaching across and turning his bike off.

"What's wrong? You haven't stopped or said anything since we left."

"Is this all there is? Do you want something more than just these weekends? I love you Marlise and want you with me, like getting married or at least living together." Peter confessed, tired of not being with her.

"Would you give up your life in the army for me?" Seeing Peter hesitate, she continued. "There is something big going on at the moment, and like you, I am needed here. My time to re-enlist happens in six months, why don't we talk about it then?" She suggested, stopping a reply from Peter by kissing him.

"Okay Marlise, if you leave so will I. Dad wants me to take a position in running his bank, so I can take over when he retires. It's just I need you with me," he admitted his feelings for her exposed.

"Till then?" She smiled, kissing him again, before picking up her gear and walking through the gates.

"Well at least she didn't say no," Peter reassured himself, starting his bike and heading for home.

The drive back through the Alps always made Peter thankful that he was lucky enough to live here. Looking down into the valleys from the road that followed the mountain pass that towered over him, Peter felt what he called the presence of God. Like his father, he was a devoted Muslim, although he didn't let it rule him like many of his once friends. A moderate they called him as if it was an insult. Slowing the bike, he turned up a side road and stopped. Taking out his prayer mat, he faced Mecca and prayed.

Like his father, he thought their religion's connection with violence was obscene. People in time would come to their own conclusions on Islam; these so called fanatics only confused the issue, turning many against them. Praying for peace always brought a small smile to his face, as being a soldier seemed contradictory to his thoughts.

"God works in mysterious ways," he said out loud smiling, before standing and moving back to his bike. Looking back down the road he had travelled, he thought again about Marlise's fixation with the trouble they'd had in Libya. He decided one day soon they should talk about it and his father's past.

Arriving at his family's home, Peter pressed his remote, opening the property's front gate. Driving up the tree-lined driveway, Peter turned into the entrance to the front door to find two police cars parked there. Hesitantly getting off his bike, he saw a young woman, her back to him, talking to the police. It was Michelle, his sister. By the rise and fall of her shoulders, he surmised she was upset and sobbing. One of the Officers must have pointed out his arrival to her, as with one fluid motion she turned.

"Peter!" She screamed collapsing onto the ground, as Peter already off his bike, ran to her.

"Michelle, what's wrong?" He asked, fear in his guts as he saw the look of bad news on the faces of the police.

"They're dead Peter. Mum and Dad are dead." She groaned, her eyes rolling back in her head, as she collapsed onto the driveway. Carrying her inside, Peter was just about to call an ambulance when Michelle's husband, Hussein, arrived. Assuring Peter she'd be all right, Hussein stayed with her, while Peter accompanied the police to the lounge room. Here the police explained what had occurred.

On their ski trip, they'd left the main ski circuit, to do some cross-country skiing into the mountain ranges. They'd been caught in an avalanche, its cause unknown. Peter's parents and another couple named Aaron and Petra Gambian, had been killed. There were no signs of foul play, so the cops were putting it down to death by misadventure, as the area they were in, was sign posted out of bounds by the local authorities. Grief stricken, Peter thanked the police for coming and informing him, showing them out. He then broke down and cried.

ANSWERS

The funeral was a big affair. Peters parents, although reclusive, were popular. Marlise having taken some time off, stayed with him helping arrange the funeral. Afterwards, Peter provided food and drinks, many shared moments they'd spent with his parents and him. Only one thing worried Peter, Steve Robert's absence. He'd personally rung Steve's home four times, getting his answering machine every time. It wasn't like Steve. He'd just lost four of his closest friends, yet he was a no show, why?

Peter could think of only three things that would stop Steve coming. One, Natasha was far worse than first thought. Two, Steve thought the avalanche was no accident or three he was dead. After the last guest had left, Peter sat with Michelle, Hussein and Marlise discussing what happened next. Hussein being wealthy himself, went along with everything Peter suggested, his only concern was for Michelle. Peter had to admit he was impressed with Michelle's husband seeing him in a different light.

Marlise, now the funeral was finished, seemed uncomfortable with knowing Peter's family's goings on, excusing herself. Michelle through all the business talk had remained silent, with Marlise's departure she came to life.

"You're a fool not to marry that woman Peter."

"It's complicated sister. If it makes you feel any better, I asked her to marry me or live with me. She isn't going to re-enlist, so in six months something might happen."

"Dad would've loved to have seen you two marry. God, I miss them. Since Libya I felt a void with Dad, it upset me." She whimpered, Hussein, reaching across and holding her hand.

"He was just scared for you and Hussein. You two aren't like Dad or me."

"I don't know if your father told you, but he came to visit me at my hospital several weeks ago. He apologised to me for mistreating me; I couldn't believe it after the danger I put Michelle in when we went to Libya," Hussein sobbed.

"You're a good man Hussein, and I am glad dad made peace with you." He was also proud of his Dad for putting that business behind him.

"Why wasn't Steve here?" Michelle suddenly asked.

"I don't know sis, but I judge by your tone you think something's wrong?"

"The three of them were like brothers. Even with Natasha sick, he still would've come."

"There could be any number of reasons sis, although you have a point. Till I find out more, I suggest you both take a break and go somewhere quiet. Hussein, you have family in the hills above Beirut in Lebanon. Maybe now is a good time for a visit?"

"It can't hurt. I will make arrangements Peter, while you make enquiries into Steve's no show. We will not return until we hear from you," Hussein told him, as Michelle broke down crying.

"It has started again, hasn't it?"

"I'm not sure sis. It could be anything. Let's see what I find out first before we panic."

The next morning Peter said goodbye to Marlise. Whatever her unit was doing or where it was deploying remained a mystery, as she remained tight lipped. Steve's no show he kept to himself, letting her leave without worrying her about what he was up to. Once she'd departed, he went back into the house grabbing a bag he'd packed the night before. Steve Roberts was one thing; his parent's death was another. Jumping on his bike, he headed for Germany.

Three hours later, found a frozen Peter alighting from his bike at a roadhouse in the German Alps region. Hiring a cheap rental car, he continued, leaving his bike at the rental shop. This whole trip could be a waste of time Peter thought, knowing he hadn't mentioned it to Marlise because of that very reason. Driving up to the ski resort of Garmisch, he realised that staying there overnight would be near impossible.

It was the height of the ski season, and with the snow thick on the ground, the village was packed to capacity with skiers. Being already close to lunchtime, he gave himself four hours to investigate, before he would have to leave.

"So where do I start?" He whispered, spotting the lodge where his parents always stayed when skiing here. "As good a place as any," he concluded, locking his car.

Reaching the lodge, he saw the Swiss and French flags, flying at half-mast beside the main entrance doors. He figured they were there to honour his father and mother from Switzerland and Aaron and Petra from France. They had stayed here every year, and it seemed they had made friends, judging by the numerous floral wreaths hanging on the doors, in remembrance of their loss.

Walking inside, he engaged members of the staff, candidly asking if they knew what had occurred. Most knew the same story he'd heard from the police; only one had a variant. The staffer remembered seeing the group talking to a ski patrol member. He was sure that the man had told them that the trail they wanted to travel along was safe. He'd told the police during the investigation and had even given a brief description of the Ski patrol member.

He believed his information hadn't been taken seriously, because he'd been drinking the night before. His description was a man of medium height and light brown hair, with a bushy moustache. The only distinguishable feature was a scar on the left side of his chin. Thanking the man for his help, Peter moved on. His next stop was the Ski patrol headquarters. Asking around, he found most either hadn't seen signs marking the trail closed or hadn't taken any notice. One reported the signs in place around the morning break, which was about ten-thirty, but not before.

The actual avalanche was believed to have been triggered, by a muffled explosion, maybe a gun. It wasn't uncommon for hunters to sneak up into the hills to try for a local deer, which moved down close to the village during the winter. When he asked about a ski patrol member with a moustache and a scar on his chin, he came up empty. It appeared no one knew of anyone fitting that description. The next stop was the Hospital, where he asked directions to the Morgue.

The attendant was strange, to say the least. Then again anyone who worked with dead people all day couldn't be completely sane Peter thought. Although he had a good memory of what occurred that day, he told Peter it worked better if he received a reward. Slipping him a hundred Euros, made his memory crystal clear. There were four bodies brought in that day, all having received injuries associated with an avalanche. The only thing out of the ordinary was they were all found lying near each other, and no one had skis.

"I suppose they all could've tried standing behind the same tree in a line, after taking off their skis. That way they may have avoided being hit and that would explain not having skis. Otherwise, we usually find their bodies scattered over a wide area." The attendant pointed out.

"Any sign of drugs in their systems?" Peter asked.

"They weren't tested. Why would we, when they were obviously killed by the avalanche." The attendant smiled, not understanding.

"Yeah, you're right, just thinking out loud," Peter replied. Thanking him, he left for the police station.

The police, like everyone else, considered it an open and shut case. Asking about the mysterious ski patrol member the police had just chuckled, putting it down to many drinks. Peter, seeing his time was up, thanked them for their assistance and made ready to leave. Approaching the door, he saw a skier across from the police station talking on his phone, when he saw Peter he ended the call.

Moving through the ski resort, Peter occasionally stopped looking in different shops. At one he entered buying several items. Glancing out the window, he saw the same skier with the phone across the street from him.

"He's still watching me, but why?" He murmured to himself, having used the shopping as a way of observing his unexpected tail.

Up till this point, he'd thought the trip a waste of time. Now the staff member's recollection of the mysterious ski patrol member came back to him. Leaving the shop, he walked to his car. Unlocking it, he climbed in and swiftly started it. Driving casually out of the resort, he looked in the rear view mirror. There he saw the man tailing him, hop into a waiting car.

After ten minutes driving, the car same car his tail had climbed into, appeared behind him. Peter now knew without any doubt, that his parent's death was no accident. Reaching the car hire shop, Peter exchanged his rental car for his bike. Complaining of the slippery road, Peter asked the owner for some weights he could put in his saddle bags to give him some traction. The owner, thinking him a novice rider gave him two old dumbbell weights he'd used for exercise, before giving fitness away.

Thanking him, telling him they were perfect for what he needed, Peter mounted his bike and headed for home. His tail of course appeared behind him again, even though several times he had to slow down so they could catch up. Turning up a side road, he watched them turn, before roaring away red lining the bike. Coming to a dangerous hairpin corner, Peter slowed, using the snow on the hillside to stop his bike. Moving the bike further down the road, Peter then carried the two weights back to the corner.

Climbing the hillside opposite the drop, he waited. He'd just lowered the weights to the ground, when he heard the sound of a car coming towards him at speed. It was his tail, and by the way, they were driving, they'd realised they'd lost him. Reaching the corner the vehicle crossed onto the wrong side of the road, to straighten out the corner, so as not to slow down.

Peter seeing his chance lobbed the two weights down in front of the charging vehicle. One missed, the other did the job, impacting with the windscreen. Reacting out of fear of the unknown, the driver tried to slam on the brakes. On an ice-covered road, it was the wrong thing to do, as the car rammed the side barrier, going over the edge. The drop was about twenty metres down sloping terrain.

Peter watched the vehicle rollover at least four times before stopping on its roof. Reaching into his pocket, Peter withdrew the gift he'd bought at the resort, which was small decorated hunting knife. Moving to the car, Peter found both men hanging upside down, but still alive. One he noticed had a scar on the side of his face. Cutting him free first, he used the safety belt to tie his hands and feet, before repeating it on his friend. Confident both men couldn't free themselves, he began.

"You two made a big mistake back there. If you'd kept out of sight and not followed me, I'd have believed the story of the avalanche and been none the wiser. Instead, you convinced me that my parents were murdered. That's going to cost you both dearly."

"So you spotted us, big deal. Best let us go before the law turns up." Scarface spat out.

"You killed my parent's arsehole. Now you're going to tell me why?" Peter growled shoving his knife deeply into Scarface's left leg.

"We will tell you nothing," Scarface chuckled taking the pain, his friend remaining silent. Leaning forward, Peter cut Scarface's throat, his blood spraying over his companion.

"How about now?" Peter asked Scarface's friend, who on cue, started talking, telling everything he knew.

His friend Scarface had with three companions ambushed Ali, his mother and the other couple after they left the lodge. Threatening to kill the women, they'd forced Ali and his male friend to drink a sedative. Knocked out, Ali and Aaron collapsed onto the ground, at which stage they'd repeated the threat, making the women drink as well. Closing the trail with a sign, they triggered an avalanche, letting nature do the rest.

"So Scarface and three other men, killed my parents and their friends for money?" Peter asked his talkative companion, keeping his emotions controlled.

"Yes. I was brought in to watch for you, on the off chance you turned up. We were told to follow you back to your home and wait for the others. I am only a watcher, the killing done by professionals," He told Peter, secretly loosening the bindings on his hands.

"Your friend was no pro I can assure you. If he had of been, he wouldn't have let you be seen tailing me."

"Spotting me would make no difference to them. You are a target like your parents." the watcher warned him, his hands now free. Peter at first was surprised by this admission. Deciding he needed more information, he moved on.

"I'll handle your friends when they come. Now are you sure this is the address of the man who hired you?"

"Under the circumstances, I doubt anyone would lie to you." He answered as grabbing a handful of dirt he flung it at Peter with his free hands. Closing his eyes, Peter sprang backwards. Clear of the dirt spray, he opened his eyes to see his prisoner leap for his knife hand. Having no time to try and capture him again, Peter stabbed him in the right eye killing him.

"You fool. You weren't involved in the killing, like your friend here; I was going to let you go!" Peter yelled at the corpse.

Getting up, Peter dragged the two bodies back to the car. Tossing them inside, he used his knife to puncture the fuel tank. Shoving a rag into the escaping fuel, he soaked it, before walking up towards the road. Lighting the rag, he tossed it back down onto the ground beside the car. With a loud thud, the car burst into flames, sending a cloud of black smoke into the air. Checking, making sure no one else was following, he mounted his bike and rode away.

After several miles, he stopped looking back behind him. He observed a thin veil of smoke blanketing the valley he just cleared. Looking for any signs of pursuit and finding nothing, he rejoined the main road heading home.

Reaching his parent's home as the sun was setting, he found Hussein waiting. Seeing traces of what looked like blood on Peter's clothing, he hurried to him.

"Are you okay?" Hussein asked concerned. Checking him, he discovered it wasn't Peter's blood.

"Hussein I'm sorry."

"Don't say anymore, Peter. Your sister and I will leave tomorrow. Good luck my brother," Hussein told him, moving towards the house. Peter was just about to follow, when Hussein turned. "Make them pay Peter. I loved your mum and dad," He whimpered, turning away to hide his tears.

"That my brother, I can assure you."

HUNTED

Peter didn't sleep at all that night. Worrying that the two men he'd killed, might have friends arriving at any moment, kept him awake. He'd as a precaution, even activated the external security system, installed by his dad. The night, fortunately, passed without incident, so after turning off the security system, he had a quick shower. Trying not to panic his sister in the morning, Peter had a leisurely breakfast with them.

"Are you sure you don't want us to stay Peter?" His sister Michelle asked. Luckily she appeared unaware of his meeting with Hussein the previous night.

"Thanks, sis, but it's better if you and Hussein take a break until I'm sure everything's okay. Just to be safe." Michelle relieved, gave him a kiss on the cheek as she hugged him. Promising to call them when he was sure everything was okay, Peter walked with them out onto the driveway. Waving goodbye, he watched them drive through the front gates. Making sure it closed, Peter walked back inside, his happy mood gone.

"What now?" He asked himself, as entering the house he activated the external security again.

Having taken an extended leave from his unit; Peter sat down planning his next move. He was sure that despite the trouble at the car, he had the correct address of the contract killer's office in Paris. They were the key to find out who had hired the men to kill his parents. The question was would they try for him now?

They must know their two men weren't coming back by now, so he thought their next step was to take care of him. His talkative prisoner had said they were after him already, so he suspected they were aware of where he lived. Yawning reminded him that he hadn't slept, so checking the house to make sure it was secured, he went to his room and slept.

Two o'clock in the afternoon found Peter stirring from an uneasy sleep. A constant distant beeping made his mind abruptly become alerted. It was the external security system. Someone had triggered an outside sensor. Ali, his father, had installed the system more for his wife Julie than himself. It was state of the art, with a network of beams and movement sensors throughout the surrounding property.

Listening and hearing no movement, Peter ghosted down the hallway to his father's office. Pressing a hidden button under his father's desk, opened a door disguised as a bookshelf. Peter knew it led into a panic room his father had built for his family. Pulling the secret door open, he entered. Inside was a double bunk on one wall with the other wall lined with weapons.

Peter's eyes were immediately drawn to the Heckler and Koch sniper rifle. It was the one his father had let him borrow when Aaron had taken him deer shooting for the first time. Instead, he'd used it to defend himself as assassins tried for Aaron. It was also the first time Peter had made love to Marlise. Smiling at the memory, he returned to the present, his smile fading. Running his eyes along the rack of weapons, he took down a Mac10. How his father had got it, was a mystery, as except for its use in the odd old American gangster movie, the automatic submachine gun, had disappeared into collectors vaults.

The gun was famous, for its incredible rate of fire, but over distance, it was useless. Peter knew whoever was out there was going to get up close and personal. At that range, the little bastard was brilliant. Taking several mags, he was moving back to the door, when something on the top bunk, caught his eye. Under the pillow, he saw the butt of a pistol. Pulling it out, he found a Gunmetal grey Glock fitted with a silencer.

Tucking it in the back of his pants, he moved to the window. Sneaking a glance outside nearly cost him his life, as the glass shattered, a bullet missing his head by a fraction of an inch. Diving to the floor, Peter crawled along the corridor as bullets peppered the hallway. The sound of a door being forced open, made him freeze, as he tried to locate where the noise had originated.

Unlike most of the houses in this area, Peter's family's home was on one level. His father had told him, that he'd purchased it because of the extensive grounds and the view of the lake at the rear. His mother, on the other hand, told him she had fallen in love with it, as it reminded her of her home back in Australia. Peter leant towards his mother's explanation, as where they lived was usually up to her.

Their first home had been two storeys, with a view of the lake like this one. Peter as he lay on the floor, wished his father had stayed there. On one level, there was no choke point, which in a two-storey house would've been caused by the stairs. A defender could just hold the stairs, watching just one approach route. Here they could come out of any room, either behind him or in front. Lying flat in the corridor served no purpose, so rather than wait for something to happen, Peter decided to go on the offensive.

Knowing the sniper was on the driveway side of the house near the front gate, made him keep away from that area. Ghosting through the dining room, he made his way out towards the back of the house. Entering into the lounge room, which faced the lake, he closed the door behind him. He then moved to a corner with a view of both the windows to the outside and the doorway he'd come through. Knowing it was now their move, he waited.

Five minutes crawled past and still no movement. Once in a while Peter thought he heard the noise of doors opening, but not where. 'Stay calm' he told himself, as a shadow crept past the window, next to him. The guy dressed in a casual sports jacket and black pants didn't quite fit with the silenced assault rifle he was carrying. Stopping opposite each window, he scanned each room before moving on.

Unlike the gentlemen with the scar, this guy knew his business. Peter thanked God that they'd come for him in the daytime, as trying to spot them at night would've been fatal. Lowering his Mac10 to the floor, he pulled out his silenced pistol. Moving to the window the pro had just left; he aimed and squeezed off two rounds. The first deflected through the glass, just grazing his target. The second, travelled through the now broken glass pane hitting the man in the back. Screaming in pain, he fell to the ground. Peter, taking no chances, shot him in the head, stopping the screams. Sure he was dead, he returned to his corner and waited.

The sound of running feet in the hallway made him turn towards the interior door. As swiftly as the noise started, it stopped, as Peter picked up the discarded Mac 10. Steadying his breathing, he aimed at the door. The slight movement of the door handle was enough. Opening fire, he emptied the magazine into the doorway. Reloading, he waited, as tense seconds passed. In the distance, Peter heard the sound of a siren approaching.

'The security company must have rung the police' he mused, wondering what his friends outside would do. If the man he'd persuaded to talk had told the truth, there were three hitters out there.

The one with the assault rifle was down, the second outside this doorway had either joined him or was injured, that left the sniper. Five minutes passed with no movement or noise. The siren, loud now, came to a stop outside the front gate with a scream of tyres. It was followed, by the sound of two pistols firing before silence returned. Several minutes passed before the sound of boots could be heard in the house.

"This is the police. Come out with your hands in the air!" a voice shouted out. Peter unsure remained hidden. "If you can hear us, Peter, don't be alarmed, we have killed the remaining assassins." the voice reassured him. Peter breathing a sigh of relief was just about to stand, when a red light came on in his brain. They might know his first name was Peter, but they wouldn't know the three men were assassins?

They could've been just thieves for all the security company knew, why call them assassins? Taking a chance Peter moved to the window, opening it, he turned back to face the interior door.

"I'm coming out don't shoot!" He then jumped out the window. Behind him, the room he'd just left erupted, as the shaped charge that had been thrown into it, exploded. Running towards the lake, Peter a little deaf from the explosion, raced into the boathouse. Opening the lakeside doors, he jumped onto his jet ski, starting it. With a roar, the jet ski burst into life. Not waiting, Peter cannoned out of the boathouse onto the lake.

Knowing that travelling in a straight line was near fatal; he turned along the shoreline as the first bullets whipped past him. For over twenty minutes he continued along the lake heading for a small town to the east. Looking back several times, he saw no pursuit. He was just about to congratulate himself when he saw for a brief second the rotor blades of a chopper behind the forested shoreline.

Cursing himself for not thinking of how fast they'd got there, he swerved towards the shore. Not slowing down, he hit the beach hard, driving the Jet Ski up into the brush next to the lake. Thinking to cover the Jet Ski with branches, became a waste of time, as the chopper charged in, overflying him. It was accompanied by the impact of rounds, as his pursuers, sprayed the lake and bushes around him.

"Fuck! I'm in for it now!" he cursed, as the chopper turned, coming back. Running, he headed for the safety of the trees, as an explosion behind him sent him spinning to the ground. Turning, he saw the helicopter that was pursuing him, become a giant fireball. Staring opened mouthed; Peter watched the wreckage of the chopper fall from the sky. Now in its place by another helicopter, with the Swiss flag on its side, it hovered above the shoreline.

"Need a hand Captain?" A familiar voice echoed over a megaphone. Peter relaxing knew the voice well; it was his commanding Officer, Colonel Briaze. As the chopper landed, Peter waited until the Colonel had disembarked, before approaching.

"That was great timing Sir. Thank you."

"You were lucky Captain that Private Hinder was monitoring the local police net. He picked up a 'shots being fired' from one of your old man's neighbours. That plus the security alarm company's call alerted us."

"Was anyone hurt?"

"Two cops were shot, though both will recover. Care to fill us in on what's going on?" His commander asked although it sounded more like an order. For the next twenty minutes, Peter gave a brief background report on what he thought was going on. His commander stayed silent, paying attention, till Peter had finished.

"Look, Peter, you're one of my best men, but I can't protect you or help you. As you said, your family has made a lot of enemies, not Switzerland. This attack we'll put down as a robbery gone wrong, but that's it. I know it's hard, but I want your resignation on my table tomorrow." Peter stood there feeling gutted. He knew he'd planned to leave anyway, but to be asked to resign was gut wrenching. Then again, he realised that a Captain in the Swiss Special Forces couldn't just go around killing people.

"I understand Sir. I'll do the paperwork tonight, and thanks again for your help boss, you saved my bacon today."

"Nonsense you'd have worked out something. Just be careful Peter, whoever these guys are, they're pro's and well-funded," the Colonel pointed out offering his hand, which Peter shook. "Oh and another thing, we weren't here, so you better get your Jet Ski going," he grinned, hopping back aboard his helicopter. Peter watched till the chopper had disappeared, before checking his ride. Starting it, sure it would work; he manhandled the Jet Ski back to the water's edge. Starting it again, he drove leisurely back along the lake.

Motoring back to his father's home, he found the police waiting for him as he came in beside the boathouse. Having been briefed on what occurred, the police gave him the 'get out of town for a while speech' and left. Calling some maintenance specialists and cleaners, Peter did his best to return the house to its original state, before the invasion. Two weeks and happy with the house's repairs, Peter made ready to leave. Wanting to make sure his parent's house was safe until he returned, he employed four guards.

They were retired Swiss soldiers, recommended by Colonel Briaze. Peter knew his parents' home would be safe until he returned. Finding a hotel in Zurich to stay in, he sat down to plan his next move. By now, the Assassin's failure would be known. A second attempt was possible, although Peter doubted it would occur for a while. The fact they had loss of all the five men involved, meant whoever had hired them, would want more Intel on the target before they tried again.

The increase in the number of assassins worried him. The chopper and five good men cost money and lots of it. Who hated them that much that they'd pay hired killers to go after them? He remembered one of Steve Robert's daughters, had married an American FBI agent. Thinking to start there, he went through his father's old contact numbers. He finally found one marked Agent Nigel Chamberlain. Next to it was scribbled Steve's son-in-law.

Looking at the clock, he saw it was close to two in the afternoon, meaning it was mid-morning in America. Dialling the number, he waited.

Nigel was having a shitty day. After ten years with the FBI, he had been recruited into the CIA, in Counter

Intelligence. Many had wondered about his switch, although his close friends knew his talents were being wasted at the FBI. His new boss was all over him about wire intercepts, being jammed, from the Middle East, being jammed. He, like his boss, didn't understand it, as the Arabs didn't have the know how to interfere with their transmissions. His boss was convinced, it was a hacker, Nigel wasn't so sure.

He leaned towards another countries' intelligence group, but who'd have the balls to block their signals? His phone ringing made him lose focus.

"Agent Chamberlain, who is it?"

"My name is Peter. You knew my father as Ali Moustaffer."

"That was a long time ago Peter. So why the call now and why did you say knew your father?" Nigel asked.

"My parents were killed, along with Aaron and his wife while skiing. Do you know where Steve Roberts is?" Nigel for a few seconds remained silent. He felt his world sliding, as he remembered Aaron from the hospital in England. He and Ali had been outside Steve's hospital, watching over him.

He'd been shot, stopping a madman pulling the trigger on an Atomic bomb. Nigel was visiting Steve to tell him one of his daughters was moving in with him. Aaron sharpening a knife had warned him they'd be watching him. It had scared the shit out of him.

"Steve and his wife Natasha are feared dead. Their boat blew up off the West Australian coast," Nigel told him.

"What are the chances of the three remaining men of an elite unit, dying within days of each other?" Peter growled.

"It could still be a coincidence Peter?"

"Do you believe that?"

"No, not for a minute," Nigel replied, fear making him look at the picture of his wife and child.

"Two nights ago, five pro's in a helicopter tried for me. That was after I visited the ski resort where my parents supposedly got caught in an avalanche."

"God, are you alright?"

"Yes, luckily I had help. Is your wife with you?"

"No, she went to Australia a couple of days ago to find out what occurred. She took our son with her," Nigel confessed, sounding worried.

"She will be okay as long as she doesn't go digging. Best warn her and anyone else connected to Steve. I'll go after the men who contracted these killers."

"I'll do that and thank you, Peter, for the heads up," Nigel said before stopping. "How do you know who hired them, Peter?"

"I have a gift for making people talk, like my father. We'll leave it at that," Peter told him, Nigel deciding not to push it.

"Look, I'll do some digging here after I make sure my wife and son are safe. Give me a week and ring back okay?"

"Thank you, Agent Chamberlain. I'll ring back at around this time next week."

"Okay, Peter and one other thing. I work for the CIA now."

"It doesn't matter Nigel. This is family."

"Yes you're right it is. And call me Nigel, Peter. I have a feeling we'll be talking a lot." Looking at his phone for several seconds Nigel angry, started calling in favours.

CONTRACTORS

Paris, the city of love, was also Peter knew, the home to the people who'd been hired to kill his parents. Rather than drive, he opted to fly there, even though it presented him with a problem, he needed a gun. The underworld of illegal weapons in Paris was a cutthroat business where rip-offs occurred consistently. He decided instead to go in a different direction. Upon arriving Peter caught a taxi to a seedy part of the city. Because of the high crime rate the city of love was awash with, police travelled in twos. For their protection, they were armed, with not only pistols but also stub-nosed automatic submachine guns.

Waiting at the entrance to an alley, Peter faked a robbery attempt. Lying down, he screamed for help, as two police officers were passing. Alerted to his screams the two officers entered the alley warily. One officer checked Peter, the other standing guard. Waiting for the right moment, Peter standing up pretended to fall. The officer standing guard, of course, moved in to steady him. It was over quickly, with both officers down, knocked unconscious.

Peter took one pistol and one machine gun and their spare ammo, leaving the officers with some protection. Waiting until they started to stir, knowing they'd be safe now, he hurried away. Armed now, he headed for the address, given to him by Scarface's friend.

The contractor, who had hired the men to kill his parents, had an impressive terraced apartment. Located on the Left bank, in an up market section of Paris, it was impressive. Peter looking across the street saw the top of the Eifel Tower looming above the apartments opposite the contractor's home, meaning it was close. Number four was one of a row of thirty identical three-storey terraces that followed the tree-lined road towards the Latin Quarter.

At street level, the ground floor of most terraces were either coffee shops or boutiques, which sold a wide variety of expensive clothing and merchandise. The second floor on some had been converted to offices, leaving just the top floor for the living quarters. Number four was one of the few, which was used as a home, a huge home, but one just the same.

Wandering along the street, Peter tried to look as casual as he could, before sitting down in a coffee shop opposite number four. Ordering a coffee and a small cake, he settled in, enjoying the morning sun. The contractor, of course, knew his assassins were not coming back and had taken precautions. Peter noticed that every time the front door opened, two men could be seen standing inside. After sitting there for over an hour, Peter spotted at least six different men in the ground floor level of the terrace. Knowing he wasn't going in through the front door, he moved on.

Paying for his coffee, he window-shopped his way down the street. Turning left then left again; he entered a small walkway behind the terraces. This part of town was built before the motor vehicle came along, or vehicles would've had access to this lane for the residents to park at the rear of their homes. Instead, a pathway bordered by high fences ran down the middle of the backyards of houses from two different parallel streets. Garbage bins randomly sat outside gates at the rear of terraces, giving an untidy slum like appearance to the pathway.

Peter cautiously approached the back entrance of number four looking for any signs of guards. Spotting no guards, he stopped outside the rear gate. Peered through the crack where the gate opened, he looked at the house's back door. Cursing, Peter saw a camera facing directly at him beside the door. Ducking out of sight, not waiting to see if he'd been spotted, he retraced his steps drowning himself in the people shopping on the main street.

Looking back, Peter saw four men rush out of the back lane he'd just left. Moments later four men took up positions where they could scan the crowd.

"They know I exited this end," Peter whispered to himself, as watching them, he saw one talk into a radio, before looking, straight at him.

"Shit they've got surveillance in the streets as well?" Peter spoke out loud this time, spotting a dome shaped camera opposite where he was standing. "Calm down," he told himself, as turning away from the men, he entered a small shop selling souvenirs. Moving to the back, he turned watching the front. The men had disappeared.

"They're there alright, just waiting for me to poke my stupid head out," Peter cursed, knowing he'd trapped himself.

"Can I help monsieur?" A voice sounded from across the room, as a female shop assistant, with a typical French woman's hourglass figure approached.

"Just looking at the moment." Peter shot back in passable French, slightly rattled, by the situation he found himself in.

"Okay. I will leave you to browse. Call me if you need anything." Her voice sang in his ears, as with a smile, she gave him a quick once over, before moving back to her cash register. Peter impressed, watched her tight dress retreat to her desk, as with a smile, he came up with an idea.

"There is something you can help me with madam."

"Have you found something that you want or desire?" She playfully replied, watching him as a small smile crept onto her lips. If Peter had the time and Marlise didn't find out, he would've been tempted to ask her out. With her long black hair and an incredible figure, she was striking. But what attracted Peter more was that she liked to flirt and that turned him on. Unfortunately being hunted took priority.

"I was wondering if you had a back door? I have a small problem?"

"We do indeed Sir. That will be a hundred Euros."

"For using your back door, you're going to charge me a hundred Euros'?"

"I have to make a living Monsieur. And you don't have to pay; you can walk out the front door. But I'd say for some reason you don't want to go out there. Do you?" She smiled, pointing out front.

"You are not only beautiful, but you're smart." Peter chuckled. Handing over the hundred Euros, the woman grinning from ear to ear, guided him out back through a series of curtains. Coming to a small-disused wooden door, she pried it open, turning sideways so he could get past. Squeezing past her to leave she pulled him to her, giving him a seductive kiss on the lips, before letting him out.

"Next time you're in Paris, come visit me. Then I will show you my front door," She purred, giggling softly, as she closed the door behind him.

"God French women are hot." Peter chuckled, thinking of Marlise, as he cautiously moved away from the area.

Merging with the afternoon crowd, Peter bought a hat at a roadside stall. At another, he purchased an old ski jacket always moving. Jumping on a tourist bus at the last moment, he found a seat at the back. Sitting down he watched the bus fill up before the doors closed and the bus, shaking badly, moved off. Discreetly pulling out the police pistol he'd borrowed, he placed it on his lap under his second-hand ski jacket, which needed a serious clean he noted by the smell.

Of the passengers on the bus about a third were male. Most were old in their late sixties; only five were of age, which made them a potential enemy.

"Could be any one of them?" Peter whispered, the lady in the seat in front of him turning at his muffled speech. Nodding, and saying a soft good morning, appeased the lady, who with a nod turned back around. 'Keep control' he told himself watching his fellow travellers. A block from his hotel, Peter alighted from the bus moving casually along the footpath. Checking for tails, he saw one man from the bus window-shopping behind him. It could be just a coincidence, but from experience, Peter knew, to always look on the dark side, and expect the worst.

When he'd arrived in Paris, the first thing he'd done was find a good hotel with multiple exits. The Hotel du Louvre suited his criteria. Standing on a triangle like corner block, with the main entrance right at the corner itself, made it perfect. Lined with shops on two sides following the streets with internal doors to the hotel, gave multiple of exit points. It was also reasonably priced, and comfortable, something he'd learned to appreciate, as he grew older.

Entering the main door, he went to the front desk, picking up his key. He then went up in the lift to the fourth floor. Exiting on the fourth floor, he waited near the lift checking for his tail. Ten minutes and no show allowed him to proceed up another two flights of stairs to the sixth floor. He'd picked a room at the end of a long hallway so that he could look through his door's spy-hole down the corridor. Outside his window, had a fire escape, just in case.

He could still remember the secretive smile on the manager's face when he'd asked for a room with a fire escape. The guy apparently thought he had issues, but true to his profession he took the request seriously and did his best. Quickly showering, Peter changed. Moving a heavy set of drawers, he blockaded the door and placed his weapons in easy reach on his bed. Lying down, he thought about what a cock-up he'd made of his hunt so far to find his parent's killers. He hoped tonight to get some answers.

At the moment he knew because of his stupidity today, the next move was no longer his. Now he was again the hunted, something he didn't like.

Back at the number four, Matthew Jefferies sat eating his late evening meal. Jefferies when he travelled, usually liked to eat alone. Unfortunately, the contract his firm had accepted, had come back to bite him.

"So Pierre, you send two men to follow him, and they disappear, so without proper Intel, you go after him at his home. That cost us another five men and a helicopter, and now he has found his way here? Have I got it right so far?"

"Yes that about sums it up," answered Pierre DeGrope, who sat eating his entree of oysters. Despite his obvious mistakes, Pierre enjoyed the cooking of Jefferies private chef. This surprised the two men standing at the door behind Pierre, as both thought he was a dead man for his failures.

"You don't seem too worried by your dismal failures?" Jefferies pointed out, voicing what his two bodyguards thought.

"I know at the moment the situation is fluid, then again the primary targets have been taken care of, and the men contracted to carry out the assignments, now don't need to be paid. The helicopter lost was unfortunate, but it was stolen anyway, so all we lost was its further use. There is also the lucrative contract fee for this job, we knew when we took it there would be problems," Pierre explained, wiping his mouth on his serviette, preparing for his main meal.

Jefferies stared at his second in command. He remembered Pierre as the unstoppable little paratrooper in his unit over twenty years ago. Then in Algiers, he had shown his loyalty in capturing and interrogating so called freedom fighters. The man was ruthless, smart and unpredictable; Jefferies suspected he had a plan if things went wrong at this dinner. They had both been members of the French Legion, the ruthless legionnaires.

Finishing his steak, Jefferies like his business associate, wiped his mouth. He had opted for just a piece of sirloin steak, flown in that day from South Africa.

"I judge you made arrangements if this meeting didn't go well?" Jefferies grinned, his two guards going on alert as if someone had goosed them. "Relax men," he added, his men still on guard.

"Yes. When I sat down, I pulled the pin on the grenade I have in my pocket. The pressure of me sitting here keeps the lever down." Jefferies security men moved back a fraction.

"I always like that about you Pierre, you think ahead. So what do we know about this Peter Moustaffer?"

"He is a Captain in the Swiss Special Forces. He keeps to himself mostly, although he has a girlfriend in the French Army, which we already knew. My contact told me he is more than just a soldier; they believe he was trained as a small boy by his father to look after himself. That aside, my men have tracked him to a hotel in the inner city. Tonight four of my best are paying him a visit."

"And if that fails?"

"We pack up the terrace and leave. This is, after all, the only lead he has."

"Okay, Pierre I will leave you to clean up this mess. No more mistakes or the grenade will be pointless." Jefferies getting up, left without a backwards glance. Pierre sitting there made no move until he heard the front door close. Getting up with his hand in his pocket, he walked to the front window looking down into the street. Jefferies could be seen hopping into his limo before the car drove away.

"That was close," Pierre whispered, pulling out the grenade from his pocket. With a slightly shaking hand, he reinserted the pin. He survived he smiled, having thought he was having his last meal. Feet approaching warned him Jefferies' chef was bringing his main meal. The Chinese style barbecued duck was his favourite, having got a taste for it while working in the orient.

"Your meal Pierre." The chief informed him, placing it professionally on the table.

"Dobie. Your entrée tonight was worth dying for."

"Thank you, Sir. Coming from you that is high praise." Dobie smiled, backing away. "Would you like a dessert later with your coffee Sir?"

"No this meal is more than enough. Thank you anyway." Pierre responded feeling good. Relaxing, Pierre thought about the problem with Ali's son. Usually, he planned these hits to perfection; this was the first one where there had been a complication. Was he getting too old he wondered.

He'd had a very prosperous life and had substantial investments maybe it was time to retire he mused. Taking a bite of his duck, he felt the beautiful aroma hit him, marvelling at the taste. Tonight he smelt something else, something bitter. He knew that smell from somewhere, he just couldn't quite remember. Choking reaching for his wine, the burning in his throat grew, making him reach for the jug of water instead.

Drinking deeply, he threw it up, as the burning in his guts grew. Gulping more water, taking as much as he could, his brain suddenly registered where he'd smelt that aroma.

In Africa, he had come up with a way of stopping the movement of freedom fighters, around the desert areas on their flanks. He'd poisoned several key wells, severely limiting their water supply and stemming their movement. He used cyanide he remembered, as his body broke into uncontrollable convulsing before he ceased breathing and stilled.

Matthew Jeffries walked sat in the first class lounge waiting for his flight when his phone rang. Looking at the ID, he answered.

"Dobie. How goes the meal?"

"Mr Jefferies, your partner, has been retired," Dobie informed his boss, as he walked swiftly along a street away from Pierre's terrace.

"Very well Dobie. Did you make sure the terrace was properly taken care of?"

"Yes, Sir. I left the fire going on the third floor and turned the gas on in the basement. Shouldn't be long now." Dobie pointed out, rounding a corner two blocks from the terrace. Behind him, the sky flashed white, as an explosion echoed over Paris. "The job is now complete Sir."

In his room, Peter woke to a distant explosion. Looking at the clock beside his bed, he saw it was just past nine o'clock. Getting up, he walked to the front door, peering out through the peephole. Nothing out of the norm was visible, just a maid's trolley halfway down the corridor towards the lift.

"Bit late to be cleaning." He whispered to himself. Something not seeming right made him look again. There beside the trolley, Peter could see the tip of a brown discarded shoe. 'The cleaner saw something and paid for it'. Peter's mind screamed as he rushed to the window. Looking down the fire escape, he saw two shadows taking up position.

"Shit, Shit, Shit," he cursed, as in the distance he heard sirens. "Good Idea," he smiled running to the bathroom.

Grabbing a roll of toilet paper, he pulled out a cigarette lighter he carried for such a situation. Hopping on a chair, he reached up placing the now burning paper against the fire detector. Instantly he heard the building fire alarm come to life. Tossing the paper in the bath, he threw anything combustible in with the burning toilet paper. In no time the apartment had filled with thick smoke. Placing a wet cloth over his face, he retreated into the lounge area and lay on the floor.

Seconds later, the front door became a sieve, as round after round of automatic fire ripped through it. From the window, a smashing of glass heralded the arrival of a stun grenade. The large bang and flash had little effect on Peter, as he lay with his eyes closed and his hands over his ears, having expected it. As the people in the hallway tried to force their way in, Peter concentrated on the window, as two sets of feet jumped into the room. Armed with similar stub nose weapons as his own, they scanned the room searching for him.

Without warning, Peter sprayed the two men with a full clip. Both men were practically cut in half, as Peter reloaded. The thumping on the door had ceased, since his firing, so he sent another mag into the door for good measure. Standing, he moved to the window and climbed out onto the fire stairs, starting down. He'd covered three floors, when a storm of metal hitting metal from above, made him dive through a window.

The young couple in bed were seriously involved in some horizontal dancing, as he crashed down beside them. Both screamed in terror, the guy louder, as without even a sorry, Peter rushed to their door. Running out into the corridor crowded with people using the fire escapes to flee, Peter found another room not closed, in its occupants rush to leave. Moving inside, he locked the door and waited.

Renewed screams from the young couples room, heralded the arrival of two men. Peter saw one had a bandage over his bloody shoulder, as they moved cautiously down the hallway, past his door. The sight of men with guns, one bloody, brought a tidal wave of screaming from the hotel guests. Panic ensued, as the evacuation of the building became a stampede. The people fearing a terrorist attack fled.

This stopped the two men, who after a brief chat turned around and headed back to the room of the screaming young couple and out onto the fire escape.

Peter waited long enough to see the young couple half naked run past before retracing his steps.

Moving to the fire escape he found the men had departed, so he with great care, followed them down to safety. Standing in the shadows at the bottom, he checked the street in both directions, before moving to an old fiat parked in an area for the staff. Jimmying the door, he hotwired the ignition. With several backfires, the old car burst into life, as Peter throwing caution to the wind, accelerated away from the area.

He hadn't gone five kilometres when he noticed the tail. Turning several corners at random he saw the tailing vehicle do the same. Whoever they were they were good, to get back on to him so quickly, having anticipated his movements. Thinking about his situation, Peter, concluded that he could salvage some of this mess with these men.

Turning swiftly onto a freeway, Peter planted the accelerator flat to the floor, pushing the car to its limit. The vehicle behind him, although more powerful, did not attempt to overtake him, preferring to follow him.

'The bastards are calling in backup,' he surmised, knowing he had to make his move soon. Up ahead he saw a large semi trailer hauling a load of pipes in the middle lane. Driving past it on the overtaking side, he turned in front of it, before swerving into the slow lane next to the curve. Slamming on the brakes, he ended up behind it, as his tailers passed the semi in the overtaking lane. Getting behind the semi, he saw the tail do his same trick, slamming on his brakes. Peter waiting until they were nearly back beside him, before ramming their car.

Both cars hitting the dirt slammed into the side railing, ending up a twisted mess off the road. Peter having been ready, was first out of the cars, firing a burst into the passenger who was trying to do the same thing. The driver pinned in the car by Peter's fiat put his hands in the air. At that moment, a Good Samaritan, who had stopped to help, came running back to them.

"Is everyone okay?" he shouted, carrying a first aid kit.

"No. One is dead and the passengers trapped. Can you help me get this man out," Peter cried out. Hiding his gun under his coat, where the wounded man could still see it, Peter with the Good Samaritan, wrenched the door open. Freeing him, Peter moved in close.

"Make one sound, and you both die," Peter whispered to the tailer, nodded he understood.

"I'll go check on his friend; you get this one to my car."
The Samaritan suggested.

Thank you." Peter replied as he nudged his friend along
the road to the man's car.

"He's been shot!" the Good Samaritan yelled out, as
Peter produced his gun. The Samaritan, taking in the
situation, quickly fled into the bushland.

"Thank you anyway," Peter shouted after him, as he
opened the boot of the car and indicated to his captive to get
in. "Well, that went okay," Peter smirked, slamming the boot,
before hopping into the Good Samaritan's Mercedes and
driving away.

Checking behind him regularly, Peter drove for several
hours, before pulling over into a roadside stop. Seeing it was
empty, he walked to the boot opening it.

"I suppose this is where it ends for me?" The tailer
smiled. Peter took in the shoulder wound the man had,
realising he was one of the men from the hotel.

"That depends on you, my friend. How much are you
being paid for this hit?"

"Not that it's any of your business, but 20 thousand
American dollars. Pity I won't get to spend it."

"Did they already transfer the money?"

"Only half, the rest was after you'd been retired."

"You've got guts, my friend. I'll give you that. So, who
hired you?"

"Do you really expect me to tell you? Even if you don't kill
me, I'd be on the run for the rest of my life."

"Not if you give me their names. I can promise you they
won't be coming after you." The tail took in what Peter was
saying; still, Peter could see he was scared of these men. He
knew he would have to sweeten the deal. "How about I add
thirty thousand to the ten you already have?" The tail looked
at him as if he was bullshitting him.

"Where would you get that type of money from?"

"My father, who your friends killed in Germany, while skiing, was a banker. I'm what you would call loaded now." Peter smiled, taking the grin off his tail's face.

"Make it forty and we've got a deal?" Peter looked at the man wondering how much he could be trusted. The tail sensing Peter's uncertainty started talking.

"The guy who hired me was an old Legionnaire paratrooper. After the failed hit on you, we phoned him to find he was forcibly retired, along with half the street where his terrace was. Are you interested now?"

"Go on it sounds believable."

"For this to work we both have to trust each other. How about we drive to a bank, and you show me the money." The Tail smiled.

"Okay. The name's Peter."

"Mine's Bartholomew. I'm named after a saint."

"Well Bartholomew, saint or not, you're going back in the boot?"

"That's okay you can hold this for me?" He chuckled, revealing a small pistol he had in his bandaged hand. Peter looked at the gun knowing he could've shot him.

"You just earned the front seat Bartholomew."

"Thanks. As much as I would've ridden in the boot, my shoulder's killing me." He groaned, moving to the passenger door.

Bartholomew or Bart as his friends called him had been in the American Rangers. He'd come home to find his wife shacked up with another man. Not seeing the funny side, he'd broken the guy's legs and one of his arms. It was towards the end of this beating; his police ID had fallen out of his pocket. Deciding the chances were he'd not get a fair hearing, he'd taken the first plane out of the country. A month later he was broke.

Hearing that a private security firm was hiring ex-soldiers, he'd fallen in with Pierre's group. At first, he'd just been given boring jobs from babysitting spoilt rich kids to foreign dignitaries who had made enemies. As his employers grew more trusting of him, he received more important assignments and an unexpected perk. For doing special work for Pierre, he received a genuine set of fake ID papers.

All of Pierre's long-term employees became residents of Spain. How they managed it, Bart had no idea, but the passport he carried stood up to any check. Of course, this perk had conditions attached to it, meaning from time to time he would have to accept a few less than honest assignments, including the odd hit. Most were just scumbags, people who owed money to the wrong people or drug mules who had decided to skip town with their load of goods.

At first, Bart had been reluctant to go down that path, but without the ID he was dead, so he swallowed his moral code and got on with it. After a year, he'd made a name in the firm for getting the job done, which had brought him to the attention of their real boss. He'd been called into Pierre's office one day and been given an assignment by Pierre in person. This surprised him, as the assignments always came by coded emails.

He was to go on a raid into Egypt with ten of Pierre's best men. On that raid, he for the first time met Pierre's boss. This was a shock, as he thought Pierre was the boss. Getting over it, he readily agreed, knowing that the job must be big. Known only as Mr Jefferies, he had met him in the country, planning the raid himself. He was a tall, well-built man, similar in age to Pierre. He spoke with a strong English accent, although he could speak fluent French like a local Parisian.

Rumours were he had served in the Legion with Pierre. They'd both been canned for conduct unbecoming the Legion. Something to do with torture in Algiers was all Bart knew. The raid in Egypt was in Cairo's main Museum during the 'Arab Spring' revolution. While the authorities were busy trying to restore order in the streets, Jefferies' team went in removing a selected number of pieces for one of his clients. Twelve guards at the Museum were killed, during the raid.

Jefferies seemed impressed with Bart's skills, giving him a bonus for his part in the raid. It was at this stage Bart knew he was in too deep to get out. After this raid, he was leaned on to do some freelance hits on people who weren't criminals, just targets. There weren't any direct threats, but he got the impression his fake passport papers, would suddenly be leaked to the authorities if he didn't play ball. He had been on one of these assignments in America when he heard about the German ski resort bungle. Pierre worried the son of one of the targets might come after him, ordered Bart to be ready at a moments notice to return.

When the raid on the son's house went pear-shaped as well, Pierre had recalled all his men to Paris. This stopped a relieved Bart from carrying out a hit on some Libyan, living there in hiding in New York. When he'd arrived back, he found the son was in Paris and had eluded Pierre's security team at his office. Bart and three others were immediately sent to Peter's hotel, as one of Pierre's men had at least managed to follow him there. The rest Peter knew.

"Again Libya is involved," Peter whispered, thinking of the hit Bart was on in America. "Bart, do you know who the target was in New York?"

"It was sketchy. All I know was he was part of one of the revolution groups, trying to overthrow Gaddafi. Why ask about that?"

"My sister and her husband were held hostage by one of the freedom groups. I went in with my father and rescued them. I was wondering if there was a connection to the hit on my parents." Peter explained, knowing he had told this stranger more than he'd told anyone else.

"I judge there's more to the story than just walking into Libya and walking out again with your family?" Bart smiled, at Peter's skimming of the story.

"Yes, quite a bit, it got bloody."

"Yeah, there's a surprise. From what I've seen you can handle yourself. I judge your old man could too?"

"He and his two friends, even at their age, made me seem like an amateur," Peter confessed, remembering their last escapade.

"Where are we going anyway?" Bart asked, seeing they entered the business district of Paris. Bart to Peter seemed overly worried.

"Relax Bart. I'm going to a subsidiary of my father's bank in Switzerland. It's called the Bank De Rue. Luckily it's got a branch here in Paris. I can transfer funds from there. It should be in the next block." Peter informed him, as Bart came to life.

"Keep going, don't slow down!" Bart ordered, his eyes scanning the footpaths.

"What's wrong?" Peter continued past the bank and around the corner.

"When I rung Pierre to tell him we were in place at the hotel, I was part of a conference call with one of the men on the fire escape. He was in charge and wanted to lead the hit on you. After getting my instructions, Pierre told him if you escaped, this was a logical place to reacquire you. I didn't think you'd come here."

"Where did you think we were going?"

"I figured, you had the money stashed somewhere. I didn't think for a moment you'd approach such an obvious location."

"You're right; I should've thought this Pierre guy would check into my background. I can take you to an ATM, but I can only take out a thousand Euros at a time. Would you take a cheque?" Bart just stared at Peter thinking he was joking.

"Fuck you might be a shit hot soldier, but you're about as street wise as a priest. Give me a cheque, and I'll put it in my account. Until it clears, we are twins, and I want interest." Bart replied, trying to look serious and not laugh at Peter's blunder. Peter thought about it for a while as they drove. He was putting his life in the hands of a hit man, on the run from the law and employed by his target. As stupid as it seemed Peter liked the guy. "I won't betray you, Peter. You're the only way I can get out of this mess," Bart admitted when Peter hadn't spoken.

"Okay, Bart I'll trust you, but remember, I'm a hard man to kill."

"Good, now stop at a pharmacy and get me a couple of bandages and some painkillers. Then let's find somewhere to eat and sleep, while we plan our next move. You're paying of course." Settling back, Bart promptly went to sleep. Peter looking at his dubious partner in crime couldn't help smiling. An hour ago he was going to kill him; now they were off to dinner. God, what would his father had said.

A Continent away, Nigel, frantically called in favours, friends and fellow agents. Others he leaned on, wanting as much Intel as he could get. Since his call with Peter, he'd called his wife warning her. Andrew, Steve's brother-in-law, and an ex Australian Federal Police officer had been his second call. To say he was shocked and angry was an understatement.

He'd immediately called one of his friends named Jeff, who was still the Commissioner of the Federal Police in Australia. Pointing out the new information, Jeff promised to look into Natasha and Steve's reported accidental deaths on the Western Australian coast near Perth. Andrew then called his wife, to tell her after mourning her brother's and sister–in–law's death, that it might be much more.

Considering his family and his extended family were safe, Nigel had started digging. Making a list of who could've been after them, proved to be a long one. From Drug Cartels to Foreign Governments, Steve and his merry bunch of Ex CIA special op's friends had just about pissed off everyone. Most of that was in the past and even the CIA who had wanted them dead the most had moved on.

The two Directors of the CIA at the time were both still locked up in a funny farm, partly due to Steve's unit. Thinking back, Nigel remembered visiting Natasha and Steve about a year ago.

It had been for a month, and they'd stayed with them at their home North of Perth, on the coast. Steve had been overwhelmed at meeting his granddaughter, even getting over his daughter getting married pregnant. Nigel and Steve had a strained relationship, over past issues. Nigel's daughter had bridged the gap. While there, Natasha during a small spat with Steve had mentioned how old men should stay at home with their families, instead of risking their lives overseas.

At the time Nigel thought she was talking about his past, when he'd been shot in England, saving London from a terrorist attack. Now he wondered if Steve had done something else in the not too distant past. Making a note of the timeline from when he'd been in England with him, he decided to have a friend in migration see if he could check Steve's movements. It occurred to him that if Steve had been somewhere, the chances were after what had happened, that Ali and Aaron were also involved. Picking up his phone, he decided to check with Interpol, knowing that after England, Aaron and Ali had been under light surveillance

VISITING THE EX BOSS

Dumping the stolen car, Peter and Bart after an expensive dinner and a night at a good hotel, got moving. Hiring a Range Rover 4WD, they drove north from Paris, entering the English Channel tunnel. Jefferies, unlike Pierre, lived in a secluded area of Northern England, separating business from pleasure. Jefferies had interviewed Bart before the job in Cairo, at his office in London.

Either he or Pierre, before giving a new man his first special assignment gave them a little talk.At this meeting, the new man was made aware of the penalties for failure or trying to get out of their obligations. While there, Bart noticed two photos on Jefferies' desk of a country mansion. Jefferies bragging had gone into detail describing the views over the countryside north of Newcastle. Bart was sure if they drove through the countryside, he would recognise the home when he saw it.

Peter, on the other hand, thought a real-estate agent would be a better way of locating it, rather than driving aimlessly around the countryside.

Showing their passports at the England end of the tunnel received only a precursory look, as turning north, they proceeded towards Newcastle. Arriving on the outskirts, Peter turned off the motorway driving up into the hills. Stopping at a small village, Bart like usual, suggested a quick bite at the local inn. Sitting there enjoying a hearty lunch, Bart described to the serving girl the country manor their friend lived owned. To both their surprise, the girl pointed to a series of photos on the wall, showing a group of country homes.

As a tourist promotion, the local castles and the odd manor locations were displayed, showing the best spots for a holiday snaps to be taken. Getting up his meal, Bart studied the photos, before returning to the table.

"It's the third from the left. What a stroke of luck. Now not only do we know it's here, but we have its address!"

"And if we go to the place advertised, we can take as many photos as we like, without arousing suspicion," Peter pointed out.

"Well, it's just after two. I suggest we finish eating Peter and head there now for a quick look around. Then find somewhere to set up for the night and plan our visit. You're paying of course."

"My pleasure, Bart."

The drive out to the manor lookout was in silence, as both men thought about this mission. To Bart, it was a step into the unknown. The target this time would be his employer for the last two years. Sure, he'd been led down a slippery slope into the world of killing for money, but it had been his fault, as much as theirs. In the Rangers, he'd killed under orders, sometimes on dubious targets. He'd always been assured it was for the greater good, but the killing had taken a toll on him. Now he killed for no other reason than to exist.

If he helped Peter to succeed here, he'd be free to move on. If they failed, he would be a hunted man with, a painful, bloody death ahead of him. Even if he got lucky, they'd just inform the authorities, and he'd spend the rest of his of life in prison. Looking across at Peter, he saw a man who only days ago had been his target, so what was he now? Sure he could be using him just to get to his boss, but he didn't think so. It had been a long time since Bart had trusted someone; he hoped the man beside him was worthy of that trust.

For Peter, it was the time for answers. Who had ordered the killing his parents and their friends? Failure didn't worry him, as he would just try again; it was being on the run forever like his father, which he feared. Bart beside him was the weak link. He tried to gauge from their time together, how much he could count on him? Betrayal now would probably cost him his life. Somehow he sensed this wouldn't happen.

His father, although ruthless, had admitted that at times in his life when on the run, he'd trusted people who most would've considered liabilities.

'Sometimes in life, you make decisions with your heart, not your mind,' his father used to say. Usually, this would be followed by a secretive smile or snigger, as he thought back to a time when it had paid off. Now as they approached the Jefferies home, Peter's indecision grew.

"You know Bart, I can drop you off, and you can stay out of this. Let's face it; this is nothing to do with you."

"When I told you where he lived I crossed over Peter. If you fail here and escape or get caught, they will know it was me who squealed. Now it's in my best interest to follow through and back you up. I've got to get out Peter, and this is my only chance at doing that." Silence followed, as Peter pulled over and the Manor appeared around the corner.

"Well let's have a look shall we?" With the decision made both men got out.

After a casual walk or recon, the two men had a rough idea of the countryside, and the man made obstacles that surrounded the target. At no time did they approach closer than half a kilometre, as cameras were visible, at several vantage points around the rambling country estate. Built, in the early seventeenth century, the house in many respects was designed like a castle, dominating the surrounding landscape.

With its back to a sheer cliff and side walls over four metres high, the only straight forward approach, was over a large flat area at the front of the manor. It was also where the only approach road entered, along a hedge-lined road. To approach the front of the manor would be over grazing land with no cover. The walls at the side would surely be protected with sensors and manpower. The heights above the manor seemed the obvious choice to Bart.

"What do you think?" Peter asked, seeing Bart looking over the manor.

"The heights seem the obvious choice, that's what worries me. Jefferies is an ex-Legionnaire, he too would know that."

"Then what do you suggest Bart?"

"We go right to the front door. It's so stupid an approach that no one will suspect it, let alone be ready for it."

"Any ideas, on how we get to the door in the first place?" Peter sounded sceptical.

"No, we'll have to think about it, as well as how we get weapons. England's as tight as a fish's arsehole, when it comes to illegal guns."

"Does your ex-boss keep weapons anywhere?"

"Maybe at his office, back in London. It's on the first floor, over an old warehouse he owns. He always supplies all our weapons on assignments, so if they're anywhere, they'd be there."

"Right, we'll go there first. If we come up empty, we'll try to purchase them through the London underworld."

"Good idea and I know a fantastic place to stay. It's expensive, but not far from the warehouse."

"Then let's get moving. You can drive for a change. It will make up for me paying for your expensive hotel there," Peter smiled, as they both walked back to their car.

"No problem, as long as you pay for the fuel."

After a good night's sleep, at the hotel Bart had recommended, Peter with Bart, took an early morning stroll. Passing Jefferies' warehouse, Bart and Peter both snapped off an impressive amount of pictures to study later. Peter looking at the structure knew it wouldn't be simple. Jefferies' office was situated on top of the warehouse; although it looked more like a prison than an office.

Barbed wire encircled the building and guards could be seen patrolling inside. The warehouse also had plenty of guards some armed, although the office seemed the area most heavily protected.

"Well, we can always take their weapons?" Bart suggested, his eyes watching for danger, as they walked back to their hotel. Once inside they put their collection of photos onto the room's flat screen television, giving them a much better look. After studying the structure for several minutes, Bart put forward an idea.

"Power is the key here. If we take out the electricity during the night, they'll go to backup, which lowers their security to manpower."

"Someone will still man the surveillance system."

"Yes, but the cameras without light will be a lot easier to defeat. Most of the ones I can see in the photos cover the office area and the outside street areas. If we climb over the rear fence area and keep to the shadows, we should be able to gain entry."

"It won't be that easy Bart. As you said, these men are pro's, and they'll be on alert if the power goes."

"Have you another idea?"

"Yes, it's just as crazy, but with a twist."

For the next ten minutes, Peter laid out his plan; Bart's eyes going wide open with surprise.

"And you said my idea of hitting Jefferies' front door was wild."

"So are you in?"

"Yeah, I'm in. Although if we are lucky and end up in a cell together, you're picking up the soap." Bart grinned, as both men compiled a list of equipment they'd need.

Bart drove the old cement truck, down the winding road, towards the warehouse. He'd stolen it from a building site after knock off time, hoping it wouldn't be missed, till the following day. Increasing speed as he rounded a corner, spotting the warehouse in the distance. Bart then tried to find Peter who was supposed to be near the warehouse entry door. He was nowhere in sight, but that didn't surprise him, having been surprised by him before. Gunning the truck, he grabbed a bottle of whisky from the seat beside him upending it on his clothes, before taking a swig.

"Here goes nothing?" He laughed, crossing onto the wrong side of the road, slamming into a power pole beside the warehouse entry. The hideous crunch of impact was replaced by a high pitch bang, as the power shorted with a blinding flash. Bart recovering from the sudden stop put on his rubber gloves before opening his door. Springing clear of the truck, he ended up in the gutter beside the sidewalk. Standing unsteadily, he found two security guards towering over him.

"Holly shit! He smells like a brewery." One of the guards observed, as the other guard informed his advisor on his walkie talkie, bring them up to speed. Bart looking around moved onto the sidewalk to find a hand blocking his way.

"Stay where you are chum. You aren't going anywhere till the flatfoots get here." The second guard warned, as Bart, watched a shadow appear behind the guards. Two muffled thuds rang out as both guards dropped to the ground at Bart's feet.

"I wondered where you'd got to," Bart whispered, as both he and Peter searched the downed guards. Finding two automatic pistols plus a couple of spare mags, they put Peter's plan into action. Splitting up, Bart walked to the corner, while Peter entered the warehouse. By this time, the guard's boss was approaching through the warehouse with two more men, to see what had occurred out front. Glancing towards the front door, he saw a shadow raise a weapon.

"Get down!" He screamed to his men, as toggling his radio, he called for backup. He'd just hit the ground when an avalanche of shots echoed through the warehouse.

At the next corner across from a traditional pub, Bart stopped. Many of the patrons who had heard the crash had come outside. They had also witnessed the downing of the guards, as they stood momentarily frozen, as Bart approached.

"Die, infidels!" He screamed out, firing wildly at the pub. Pandemonium broke out, as the crowd screamed as one. Scattering, many of the crowd scrambled back into the pub, causing hysteria. Those with phones contacted the police, informing them of a terrorist attack. The police bombarded by reports of the shots being fired, sent everything available unit, including a swat unit.

Inside the warehouse, the guards unaware of the shooting at the pub armed themselves. Rushing towards the front of the warehouse to aid their companions, many dived for cover as bullets ricocheted off the steel walls. Peter, seeing the number of guards would soon overcome him, retreated across the road, Bart finished at the pub joining him.

"Time to go," Bart warned him, as sending what ammo they had left into the warehouse, they retreated up a side street. They'd just left when the scream of sirens announced the police's arrival. Securing the pub, seeing casualties were mainly from being trampled rather than shots, the police moved towards the warehouse. Many of the injured patrons pointed out most of the shooting came from there.

Inside the warehouse, the sirens signalled the end of hostilities. With the mysterious snipers gone, the guard's boss instructed his men to lose their weapons, knowing the police would soon enter. As he had predicted the Swat team soon approached the warehouse shouting out for everyone to get down. The boss complying ordered his men to the ground.

The police were no fools. The weapons might have been missing, but the smell of cordite from firing them hung ominously in the air. A thorough search soon revealed the rather large amount of weapons and ammunitions, all illegal. Questions started to be asked about the shooting, like were the shooters' weapon's purchased from this warehouse? The guards and their boss' silence, refusing to answer any questions, lead to the arrest of them all.

Two hours and a wagonload of police barrier tape had the whole area secured. Leaving, two uniformed police officers, to keep the area secured, the Swat team escorted the guards back to their station. It was only after the police did a roll call, that they discovered, they'd left two police who didn't exist, to secure the warehouse.

Back at the warehouse, Peter and Bart in their hired police costumes started looking around. The police had cleaned out the obvious weapons. Peter believed the more exotic weapons would be harder to find. With time being their enemy, they decided to split up so they could search twice as fast. The warehouse was far larger than Peter had calculated, full from top to bottom with crates. After an hour he became worried. Bart arriving from his side signalled he had no luck either.

"What now?" Bart whispered, seeing guards still in Jefferies office. For some reason, the police considered both areas separate.

"Why are they still there?"

"Jefferies has powerful friends, and he may have the warehouse in another name, to keep himself safe."

"Well they might see us, but we're just cops snooping around as far as they're concerned. Let's give it another hour?" Peter suggested, both men separating again. It was Bart who in the end got lucky.

After searching for twenty minutes, Bart sat down on a bench to think. Sitting there, he rocked back on the bench, stretching when he heard a loud crack. Looking at the wall, he wondered why such a solid wall would creak. Looking down, he saw scratch marks where the bench had moved. Behind the bench was a plain timber wall, with several knots or holes where the timbers had broken down over the years. Gripping the bench, Bart put his fingers in the knots and pulled. Despite its age, the wall moved smoothly, opening to reveal a small room. Barely larger than a bathroom, it was full of weapon and ammo boxes.

Bart excitedly turned to shout to Peter, when he stopped himself. Cursing softly, he went in search of him. Peter by this stage, had given up, he was in the process of looking for Bart and leaving. When Bart approached him, he didn't have to ask if he'd found something, his evident joy, making him grin madly. Bart seeing he knew, waved for him to follow. Arriving at the room, Bart elatedly explained what had occurred as Peter stared at a stack of crates inside. They were just about to enter when Bart's hand flew across in front of Peter stopping him.

"Trip wire," Bart warned, bending down. Reaching around the corner, he followed the wire finding a grenade at the end. Taking out a small knife, he cut the wire, tied to the pin. "Lucky the cops didn't find this room." He added as they moved to the crates. The top two boxes contained a selection of silenced pistols and extra clips. The two larger ones underneath were filled, with a beautiful collection of assault rifles and their ammo. Bart being American went for a Browning pistol and a cut down version of an M16.

Peter chose's a Glock pistol, and a newer version of an AK47, with a folding stock. Gathering up their loot they were just about to leave when Peter glanced into the corner behind the now open door. There, leaning against the wall, were four RPGs.

"You carry the weapons, I'll carry these," Peter instructed, as they hurried through the warehouse to the front door.

"Wait, Peter. We can't just walk outside carrying this lot," Bart warned. Peter nodding his understanding looked for something to hide the weapons. In a cupboard beside the front door, he found some tarpaulins. Wrapping their haul up, they carried them to their hired Range Rover. Behind them, two police cars ground to a halt out front of the warehouse, as four officers hurried to the front entrance. Waiting till they'd moved inside, Peter started up their vehicle and drove away.

"Well, that turned out okay?"

"Yes. Although now Jefferies knows we're here, he'll be ready," Peter pointed out.

"Not for what's coming," Bart sniggered, checking his stolen pistol, as Peter drove north.

Jefferies stood with his wife at the front door saying goodnight to their guests. His wife radiant in her latest thousand dollar purchase from Paris, gaily smiled to friends and business associates alike, the perfect hostess. Twenty years his junior, she had been an up and coming model. Jefferies regarded her as one of his most precious possessions. Her father was a Minister's assistant in the French Government and an addicted gambler. Running up a huge debt to the wrong people, he had come to the attention of Jefferies. Accepting the assignment to reclaim the debt, Jefferies had sent two of his men to convince him to pay.

Gerardo, the Minister of Finance assistant, was broke, having lost everything. Jefferies saw threatening him wouldn't work, so he came up with an arrangement. For the clearing of his debts and a hefty monthly payment, the Minister would from time to time help Jefferies in his business dealing. This had led to many favours, including the passports in different countries' names for his men.

As a guarantee, Jefferies also took his daughter as insurance. At first, she'd been, to say the least, disgusted with her father, hating the very idea of living with Jefferies. Knowing in the end that her father would be killed, Gina reluctantly agreed. Over time they had come to an agreement, she even willingly slept with him as long as she could continue her career. His powerful connection helped her become not only a high priced model but also one of the leading fashion divas in Europe.

She loved the attention that money gave her, accepting her enforced whoring, as she called it. True, Gina had a discreet affair once in a while, but no one could lavish gifts on her like Jefferies. As the last guest left the smiles left their faces, glad the charity event was over.

"I'm going for a shower; I'll meet you in bed," Gina whispered, kissing him seductively on the chin, before walking to the staircase. Jefferies watched her walk up the stairs his eyes hypnotised by the sway of her hips. 'She was his best investment ever,' he smiled. Sure he knew Gina strayed from time to time, but a friendly visit from a couple of his men to her suitors always ended these problems. As she disappeared onto the next level, Jefferies' mind flicked to more pressing matters.

His warehouse had been violated. Tonight Jefferies had been reminded of the fact that he was a low-life. Maybe a rich, well dressed successful low-life, but still a thug to the upper crust of society. The local police inspector, who was at his charity drive for orphan children, had asked him for a word in private. He had told him of the raid on the warehouse where his office was located. Of course, he had pretended to be shocked, pointing out he knew nothing of the warehouse's business dealing.

The inspector, believing him had still warned him he'd be asked to come into the station for questioning. Smiling, telling the chief he'd come in the next day, he'd continued with the party not a care in the world. Behind closed doors, he'd called the office wanting to know why he hadn't been informed. Promising his men there that heads would roll, he had one of his men alert the guards around his home.

He also arranged for his top men to come straight here for a meeting. It would start once this stupid publicity stunt for a bunch of dropkick hungry kids was over. Looking at the stairs, he knew screwing his prize would have to wait for a little while longer. The sound of a helicopter on the front lawn heralded the arrival of his lieutenants. Having a drink to steady himself Jefferies watched as his ten men shuffled into his study seating themselves. Having his butler serve them drinks, they sat around talking until the butler had left. Now the room grew quiet.

"What the fuck is going on?" He growled, his eyes searching each man's face for a sign of betrayal.

"Joseph at the warehouse fucked up!" Bobby Vance, one of his up and coming lieutenant answered. Bobby had dead eyes giving away nothing Jefferies noticed, as some of the others squirmed. They all knew friends' lives hung in the balance and Bobby had just sentenced Joseph to death.

"And how did he do that?" Jefferies barked making even Bobby hesitate.

"He reacted to a set-up and fell right into a trap. Instead of taking in the situation, he armed his men and charged in firing. He should've just called the police," Bobby answered.

"You weren't there. It's easy to judge from a distance," Jamison, one of Jefferies' oldest employees interjected defending Joseph. Jefferies, giving him the floor had him continue. "I went to the office before coming here. The whole thing was a well-organised raid, carried out by pro's."

"Who were they?" Jefferies asked, his voice sounding more controlled.

"Video of the warehouse although compromised by the power being out, showed two cops searching the warehouse after the others had left. One is the target from Paris; the other was Bart." This brought a gasp from the gathered group of men. One of their own had switched sides helping the target.

"This Peter Moustaffer, what have we got on him?" Bobby enquired. Jefferies looked to Jamison who pulled out a file and started reading.

"He is the son of Ali Moustaffer a CIA trained black ops specialist. He and his team carried out assignments for the CIA for some years before the CIA tried to eliminate them. The CIA failed, although what happened or what they did to be left alone remains a secret. On and off, his father was a killer for over forty years. He is even rumoured to have lead a raid in Libya several years ago. Peter, was trained by him, and a guy named Steve Roberts, whose nickname was the Ghost." This caused several sideways looks, the name was known.

"Anyway Peter was a Captain in the Swiss Military's Special Operations group, inside sources tell us he's one of their best men. Why he left was caused by this company targeting his parents. His boss a Colonel thought it best they part company, so he couldn't be linked to them if his revenge got messy."

"Why did Pierre take such a dangerous contract?" Bobby asked, knowing their company tried to avoid military targets.

"Because like me, he thought his men were up to it," Jefferies snarled, being the actual one who'd accepted it. Bobby like most there didn't look at him. The hit on both Ali and Aaron, and the separate one on Steve Roberts, had been well planned. The follow up of watching Peter was the part that was bungled. The silence stretched out, as Jefferies waited for someone to say something, in the end, he continued.

"Look, this collection of hits is part of a much bigger move for this firm. The client has promised a contract adding up to hundreds of millions, which we will benefit all of us. That is why we broke tradition and went after military personnel. The problem is how do we clean it up?"

"We could tell him who the client is. That would make him back off," Jamison suggested. He knew this option wouldn't be accepted, with so much money involved.

"I had considered it, but it's gone too far to shake hands and walk away as friends. This guy is going to keep coming, recruiting Bart shows that he is willing to take chances to get what he wants," Jefferies answered, watching Jamison. Up until now he always backed him no matter what. 'He was getting too old, he's lost his edge,' he thought deciding after this crisis was dealt with, to retire him.

"Boss, did Bart know you lived here?" Craig Border asked, looking at his watch. All through this discussion, he'd stayed in the background like the others just listening. Now he put forward his thoughts.

"He's never been here, although I once told him about the picture in my office, being my home in the north of England."

"Then they're coming here. The raid on your warehouse was I'd say for weapons, as they are hard to come by in England. How many men are here?" Craig asked.

"Enough, plus of course this group."

"I suggest you take the helicopter and get out now. We can all stay and handle this situation," Craig put forward, looking casually towards the window.

"I think you're underestimating our forces here?" Bobby chuckled.

"How long since the raid on the warehouse took place?" Craig asked Jefferies, ignoring Bobby.

"About four hours. Why?"

"To drive here let's give them three hours. A quick recon, would take another two hours. If they're as good as I think they are, they'll hit this house first thing in the morning, at about five when we're half asleep. I suggest if you're not leaving boss you get ready," Craig warned them, many now looking towards the windows.

"You're full of shit!" Bobby piped in standing up, unhappy at Craig's handling of him.

"Sit down!" Jefferies ordered thinking, as Bobby showing suppressed anger, collapsed back into his seat. "There is a large supply of weapons, stored in the basement. Bobby, take Jim and Henry and a couple of my guards and retrieve them. The rest of you check the grounds for weaknesses and report back here. In the mean time, I'll have the chopper fly Gina to safety. We'll meet back here in three hours," Jefferies ordered, the room emptying.

Jamison watched the others scramble out trying to look like they knew what was going to occur. Like the others, he had always been the hunter, never the target. The role reversal worried him, as he moved outside. Craig watched Jamison walk out onto the open grounds at the front of the manor, where the vehicles were parked. Trotting he caught up to Jamison.

"What are your thoughts my friend," Craig asked. The two men had been close friends for years.

"It's over Craig. We've become sheep, and this Moustaffer and Bart are now the lions."

"There are only two of them."

"It doesn't matter. This place is both a fortress and a trap. Who knows what they took from the warehouse. It could be anything, remember we had some RPGs there."

"They were well hidden, although you're right they could have them. Even so, we have a responsibility to stay and defend Jefferies."

"Like we had a responsibility to Pierre? Look, Craig, you want to stay then go ahead, I'm finished."

"Jefferies will see you dead for this?"

"You've got to be alive for that. Goodbye, my friend." Jamison added, starting up and driving away. Craig watched him go, and the urge to join him crossed his mind. Turning back to the manor, he saw Bobby standing there watching him.

"You should've stopped him, Craig."

"He's too old, best let him run away and hide," Craig forced a smile, as Bobby chuckled.

"Yeah, even though Jefferies will want him dead for chickening out."

"We'll worry about him after we take care of these other two problems," Craig suggested, walking the perimeter, watched by Bobby.

Jamison felt a weight lifted from him as he drove through the gates on the property's boundary. Craig could've put a bullet in him for running and would probably suffer for letting him go.

'That's if he survives till tomorrow,' Jamison mused seeing a cop standing in the roadway, waving a light for him to stop. Pulling up, he saw it was two police, not one.

"What can I do for you officers?" He asked seeing their car was a Range Rover. He knew then that the two problems had arrived early. "I judge your Peter Moustaffer and our ex-employee Bart?" He chuckled, as a gun equipped with a silencer appeared at his window.

"You're Jamison one of Jefferies' team leaders aren't you?" Bart accused, having seen him once at a meeting.

"Yeah, I was, now I'm on the run. Be warned, they know you're both coming and are ready. Jefferies has his usual guards plus nine of his ten top men. It won't be easy."

"Why leave then?" Bart asked.

"I got old Bart, and I don't like being hunted. It's better if I try and retire."

"A wise move, anything else we should know?" Peter asked, his smile hidden by the darkness.

"Jefferies isn't going to run even though he has a chopper. He intends to fly his wife out, so try not to target the chopper, she's a beautiful woman, married to a bad man. Oh and they've got a heap of weapons," He added, waiting for the bullet that would end his life.

"Thank you for your help, Jamison. You can go." Peter told him, causing Bart to look sideways at him. Jamison at first thinking it was a sick joke before he bought it, hesitated. Instead, he saw Peter Moustaffer turn his attention back to the manor. Shocked he put his car in gear, addressing Bart

"Good luck Bart. Like you I'm glad to be out." Jamison stammered out, letting out the breath he was holding. Happy, he drove away feeling reborn, realising this man wasn't the type he was used to dealing with.

Once the car had left, Bart turned to Peter.

"Why'd you let him go? He could still warn them," Bart exclaimed, forgetting to keep his voice down.

"The guy's trying to get out, as you did. If he helps them against us, we'll deal with him later. Let's stick to only killing the ones who mean us harm; it's better that way," Peter explained, moving cautiously towards the house.

Jamison leaving, was taken as a bad omen. Many started to think he was the only thinker there, wishing they'd gone too. Jefferies after an hour of pleasure decided to keep the chopper in reserve. Gina was a handful in bed and beautiful, but to a man with money, they were plentiful. Instead, he moved her downstairs into the basement, locking her in a storeroom. She didn't complain. After, seeing armed men preparing to make war on someone outside, she decided being locked up wasn't so bad.

Jefferies, meeting again with his men was furious at Jamison's defection.

"I want that coward dead. First thing tomorrow Bobby, I want you to take two men and kill him and his whole family. No one runs! Is that understood?" He bellowed, everyone, nodding their understanding. "Right take up your positions. Anyone see any weaknesses?"

"The cliffs above your home could cause a problem." Bobby pointed out.

"It's covered by four of my men already. Anything else?" He asked. Receiving no replies, he spread his men around his home, even leaving a couple near the front, just in case.

Peter and Bart after their meeting with Jamison realised the Range Rover just didn't look like a cop car. Going back down into the village where they'd first started recon, they found a small police station. Walking around the back, they located a garage, with a police vehicle inside. Opening the garage doors, they opened the car's door releasing the brake and pushing it down the road. At a safe distance, Bart started to hot-wire it when they noticed the key in the ignition.

"Who'd pinch a cop car?" Bart sniggered, starting it.

Driving back to the entrance to Jefferies' property, Peter stopped, and Bart jumped out. Unloading the four RPGs and his weapons, he carried them to the boundary wall. Finding a suitable location where he could see the whole area surrounding the manor, he prepared the first missile. In the meantime, Peter, adjusting his copper's hat, drove up to the front door. It was three o'clock in the morning when the blue light of the police car was spotted approaching.

"What now?" Jefferies asked, wondering what the local cops were coming to tell him. "All you men except Bobby, stay out of sight," He warned, not wanting any trouble. "Bobby you cover me from just inside."

It was pitch dark outside, too dark even with the outside light on, to see properly. Jefferies waited as the police officer hopped out of his car, adjusting his hat.

"Sorry to disturb you Mr Jefferies," The officer nervously started, having turned up at three in the morning.

"What's the problem Officer? You're lucky I was up working and saw your approach."

"Yes again I'm sorry about that Sir, but we just had a report of two heavily armed men being involved in an accident down the road towards the village. Both men are badly hurt and under guard in the local hospital. They had rough maps of your manor. The chief thought one of us should come out and make sure you were okay?"

Bobby inside couldn't help grinning knowing Jamison had run for nothing. Relaxing, he left his position and walked back through the manor. Finding Craig in the kitchen, he told him what was going on. It brought an unexpected reaction.

Having been checking security at the back of the manor, Craig hadn't been informed of the arrival of the police officer. He was preparing a cup of tea when Bobby came into the kitchen. He immediately started mouthing off, about a police officer, coming here to tell Jefferies that Bart and Peter Moustaffer had been hurt.

Craig throwing his tea in the sink, exploded from his chair.

"It's them, you fucking idiot. The cop's a fake like at the warehouse!" He screamed grabbing his gun and running towards the front door, followed by the others.

Jefferies unaware of what was happening inside walked the officer back to his car, relieved the coming attack wouldn't materialise.

"Thanks for the warning constable, I'll be sure to ring your boss tomorrow and thank him as well," Jefferies chuckled finding it hard to hide his obvious joy. Even so, with all this good news, something about the cop worried him. Reaching the police car, Jefferies as if struck by lightning, became aware what it was. The guy was too fit and spoke too clearly for a local hillbilly cop. Looking at him, he saw the slightly Arab complexion making him freeze.

It was too late as a pistol struck him across the face, knocking him against the car. Opening the door, Peter shoved the unconscious Jefferies into the back seat. He was just moving to his door when the front door of the house burst open.

"Stop!" Craig shouted, as five men including Bobby, levelled their weapons at Peter. Instead of complying, Peter pointed towards the front gate. There standing in the light of the right-hand gatepost, fired the first RPG.

"Back inside!" Craig screamed, already moving, as the rocket sped towards the house. He'd just cleared the door, jumping behind the stone sidewalls, when the rocket hit. Designed originally, for stopping tanks, the explosion was spectacular. Through a room full of accrued smoke, Craig injured, thanked God he was still alive. Bobby and the others weren't so lucky.

Bobby, unlike Craig, wanted to save his boss above all else. Instead of running with the others, he fired at the now moving police car. Peppering it with rounds he hadn't even got through the magazine when the rocket arrived. Like the other men following Craig, he took the full force of the explosion. When the police turned up four hours later, they'd find what was left of his shredded body first.

Five minutes of absolute confusion found all the men that remained at the front door. Looking for leadership, they got Craig to his feet, asking him what they should do. Telling them what had occurred, he ordered them to give chase and bring back Jefferies. Without a backwards look, they all charged outside jumping into their cars. Starting up, the first car's driver gunned the engine, charging down the driveway. Two more vehicles followed moments behind.

Craig having recovered enough, hobbled outside to find all the men gone.

"Who's going to guard the house you stupid fools?" He screamed out at his departing men, as the second RPG roared out of the forest next to the front gate. It turned the first vehicle into a melting candle, as the other two cars slammed on their brakes. "No you fools keep going. Get off the road!" he screamed out, knowing it was a waste of time, as two more rockets roared out of the trees, finding the two stationary vehicles.

Standing, at what was left of the front door, Craig watched the police car return across the lawn. Stopping, two heavily armed men climbed out, moving with caution towards him.

"That was well done!" was all Craig could say, as they swiftly searched him.

"Thank you, anyone, else around?" Peter enquired, placing a field dressing from his pocket against Craig's leg, where a large diagonal cut was creating a puddle.

"No, I think you retired most of them."

"What about his wife?" Bart cut in, sounding worried.

"She's in the basement. He locked her in and left the chopper for back up. What an arsehole," Craig replied, as Bart left them, rushing inside.

"So, do you know who hired your firm to go after my parents?" Peter asked.

"Unfortunately I have no idea. I recruit the teams for the missions; I don't have much to do with the running of the firm. I judge you're this Moustaffer guy?"

"Yes, your firm picked the wrong targets this time."

"I said the same thing to Jamison last night before he left, I should've gone with him."

"We intercepted him at the gate last night."

"Is he okay?" Craig blurted out, thinking they'd killed him, as he sat back down.

"Yes. I'm not a hired killer like you people. I only kill when it's necessary."

"Well you've got Jefferies; I'd say he'll sing like a canary to save his arse."

"Unfortunately no. One of your men at the front door fired a clip into the vehicle. He had shocking aim, missing me by inches, but spraying his boss repeatedly. He won't be saying anything." Craig sitting down couldn't help starting to laugh.

"Holy shit what a cock up. That mess on the ground beside you was a guy named Bobby who did the shooting. He had a big mouth, but not much behind it. As for the contract, I suppose you could check his private office here. Otherwise, the main office back at the warehouse is the only place I can think of."

"Are you alright to travel then?"

"What? You're going back there? Are you kidding?"

"Would you prefer to be shot here?"

"On second thoughts, it sounds like a great plan." Craig chuckled, getting slowly back up.

While Peter convinced Craig to come back to London, Bart freed Gina. The basement being concrete had weathered the explosion with no damage, although the noise had rattled her. Unlocking the door, Bart entered to find Gina face down on a small single bed. Turning her over, he waited for her to recover. Gina, suffering from shock, tried to focus on her rescuer.

"Bart, what are you doing here?" She cried out, hugging him.

"It's been a while, Gina, how are you?"

"I thought he'd killed you after Amsterdam."

"No, but he was onto us. If I hadn't stayed away, your life would've been at risk."

Pulling him down onto her, she kissed him hungrily, as caught up in the moment, he returned the kiss. Feeling his need rising, he pulled away. "Look we've got to get away. Jefferies is dead, and we're both in danger. I'm here with a dangerous man and one of Jefferies men named Craig. Don't let them know, that we know each other," he warned her, helping her up.

Reaching the ground floor, Bart steered her towards Jefferies' office, looking for any information on the client. After rifling around for twenty minutes, as he feared nothing of Jefferies' other life was here. Moving back to the front door area, they found Peter and Craig waiting.

"I came up empty in his office Peter."

"Yeah, I was afraid of that."

"What now?" Bart enquired pushing Gina ahead of him.

"We take the chopper." Peter pointed towards where it sat on the front lawn.

"Can you fly it?" Bart choked, worried.

"Of course, my dad taught me," Peter assured him, as he turned to Gina. "You can go if you want too. I know you had no part of this."

"For now, I'll stay with you. I'd rather not be here when the police arrive." She replied, moving towards the chopper with Bart. Peter saw her hand momentarily squeeze Bart's, as they climbed into the back seat.

"There's a surprise," Craig whispered, as he and Peter followed them.

"Why would you say that?"

"Bart was once given the task of tracking down one of her mystery boyfriends. Jefferies knew someone was bonking her, but not who. Bart tracked him down and took care of him in secret."

"How do you know that he got the right man if no one knew who it was?"

"Her happiness stopped. Either he got the right man, or scared him off, the first is more likely." Craig watched Bart take a seat beside her. "The guy's heartless to sit there next to her after what he did," Craig growled, as Peter secretly smiled, adding up her touching of his hand to the unknown lover.

"Yes he's certainly full of surprises," Peter agreed, hopping into the chopper's pilot seat, as Craig reluctantly sat beside him.

Landing on the outskirts of London, they borrowed a vehicle. As before, they drove by the warehouse, checking out who was still on guard there after the police raid. Despite the warehouse being deserted, the office section still had plenty of men on watch. Peter pulling over thought about the best way to enter the office section.

"Why go there at all? You've got the man responsible for your family's murder Peter." Gina asked from the back seat. Since the flight down she'd stayed with them, much to Craig's surprise.

"I never wanted your husband dead, even though I won't shed any tears. The reason I kidnapped him, was to find out who paid for the hit, that's the man I want." Peter smiled. All in the car felt no joy from that smile.

"They'll fight Peter. It isn't going to be easy?" Bart in the back added. Unlike at Jefferies' manor, Bart knew the men here. Some were friends.

"It makes no difference Bart. If there were a hundred soldiers in there, I'd still go in. It's my only way of finding the people responsible."

"Can I suggest something else?" Gina put in, as Peter surprised nodded for her to continue. "They don't know my husband's gone yet. When they do, they'll realise they're all out of a job. Drive back to the front gate and let me tell them. Let's face it; I am the only one now who can pay them, being the widow." Gina pointed out, appearing far from unhappy with her husband's demise.

"She's right. Jefferies didn't have a will. Once the shooting at his Manor becomes known, the police will seize all his assets. I'm owed money too." Craig informed them.

"Then let's go?" Gina suggested, taking control, as Peter put the car into gear.

Walking through the entry gate, Bart felt his heart hammering in his chest, as except for a pistol he was defenceless. They'd left their assault rifles and assorted other weapons in the land rover, rather than appear hostile. Gina out front with Peter walked along without a care in the world. Bart smiled, thinking that now Jefferies had departed, it was pretty true. Watching her walk, he thought back to the affair he'd had with her. How it had begun, he could still remember, as if it happened yesterday.

He'd been in Paris after fulfilling a contract on a drug mule that had skipped town with the merchandise. Jefferies had in person congratulated him on a sensitive contract. The target had been a relative of another firm's director in the same business as Jefferies. Rather than start a war, Jefferies had insisted Bart make it look like an accident after recovering the goods. Tracking down the target, he found him on a train between Paris and Berlin. Watching him, he saw him get involved in an argument over seating, with several skinheads on their way to a Nazi rally in Berlin.

His bravery facing down three of these thugs impressed the other passengers and Bart until he caught sight of a pistol. It was concealed, in the target's pants belt, where the other passengers couldn't see it. The skinheads, of course, could see it and sensed the man was willing to use it. This danger seemed to shake the skinheads' bravado, who after threatening vengeance, hastily retreated. The target smirking at the so called bravery of these supposed supermen sat back down, getting claps from the other passengers.

The weapon worried Bart, as he hadn't been told that the target was carrying. Of course, this was something he should've suspected of anyone stupid enough to rip off a drug cartel. His boss had made it clear it couldn't look like a hit, and the gun made it harder to achieve. Coming up with a loose plan, Bart moved into the carriage, sitting down across from the target. The target's side of the carriage had small double seats, while Bart's side had more roomy doubles, bordering on triples.

Watching him, he saw the front of a briefcase tucked under his seat. As if feeling his close scrutiny, the target looked sideways fixing him with a hostile stare.

"What the fuck are you looking at?"

"I like the way you handled those Nazis, that was brave," Bart answered, looking slightly uneasy.

"Find another seat. I don't like the look of you," the target growled, suspicious of Bart. Getting up, without another word, Bart moved, sitting behind him. Taking out a knife, keeping it covered with his coat, he cut out the lower rear section of the target's seat, revealing the case. Leaving his coat on his seat to cover the damage, Bart moved through the carriage into the compartment in front of him. There, having a heated discussion, he found the skinheads.

"We should go back there and do him." One of the crew-cut brawlers with a scar on his chin spat out, giving away his cocky English accent.

"He's got a gun remember." Another put in, sobering them.

"Can I make a suggestion?" Bart said from behind them, making them turn towards him.

"What's it to do with you arsehole?" Several asked, staring at him.

"Not all of the Aryan brotherhood shave their heads, brothers. I too am attending the rally in Berlin," Bart stared back, daring them to doubt him.

"What do you suggest then?" Scarface said softly, noticing they were attracting the attention from the other passengers.

"I'm sitting behind him. When you are ready, hit the emergency stop button. Once the train slams its brakes on, I will disable him. You can then take him somewhere private for a chat." The skinheads breaking out in grins of pleasure told Bart he had them sold.

"Okay we'll do it your way, but you better not betray us," Scarface warned, showing Bart he was carrying a flick knife.

"For fuck's sake! If he's not knock out, you keep walking. So you want to do this or not?" The skinheads including Scarface all nodded yes.

Good. Now give me ten minutes to get back to my seat." Bart growled leaving.

Bart, hiding a smile at how gullible people could be, headed back towards his seat. Passing the target he received an irritated look, before sitting down, he returned to his magazine. Bart then braced himself and waited. Time drifted by as Bart wondered what was keeping them. He was just about to go and find out when the train suddenly jumped from over a hundred and ten miles an hour to a shuddering halt.

The passengers caught completely unprepared were catapulted forward. Screams filled the air, as Bart joined the others crashing into the seat of the target. Luckily he was better prepared than most, as reacting he steadied himself.

The target was not as lucky. Caught completely by surprise he slammed into the seat in front of him. Reaching over Bart grabbed the semi unconscious man.

Twisting his neck sideways in a vicious sharp movement, brought an audible cracking sound as the target's life left him. Looking up, he saw the skinheads rush into the carriage.

"He's knocked out get rid of him," Bart whispered, as the group sharing a communal grin, grabbed the dead target dragging him away. Looking around seeing the passengers coming to terms with what had occurred; he grabbed the target's briefcase, moving to help the downed passengers. When sanity returned, some of the unhurt asked where the brave young man had gone? At this question, Bart softly told them how the skinheads had taken him.

Horror replaced pain as the passengers concluded that the skinheads were responsible for this disaster. Many grabbed their phones calling the police as the rescue crews arrived. Bart, his assignment finished, left the train disappearing into the confusion. The skinheads caught with the corpse were arrested. Their defence that a well-dressed man, who no one could quite remember, had helped them, fell on deaf ears. Each one received an eight-year jail sentence.

Jefferies overjoyed with the professional way Bart had handled it, inviting him to a private dinner where Dobie had cooked for them. Dobie was well known to Bart having been on an assignment with him. Together they had silenced a consortium of drug suppliers. Bart had the job of getting Dobie into a restaurant, where posing as a chef he had poisoned the group of men. Bart had then taken care of the survivors.

Later Dobie had admitted to him, that he liked killing as much as he liked cooking, so he'd combined them both. A short time after this joint assignment, Jeffries made him his cook. Bart suspected Jefferies' also used him as his private assassin. Bart aware of this, let Jefferies start eating first. His hesitation was not lost on Dobie, who smiled at Bart's hesitation.

"Is everything to your liking?" Dobie asked.

"It's the best meal I've ever had. I just hope it's not my last?" Bart grinned, causing both Dobie and Jefferies to chuckle.

"You'll go far, Bart. In this business knowing what's going on around you can be the difference between life and death." Jefferies concluded, knowing Bart had found out about Dobie. Bart's reply was cut off as Gina entered. She'd been held up at a photo shoot causing her to miss dinner. Bart tried not to take too much notice of her, having heard through the grapevine that it could be terminal.

Giving Jefferies a peck on the cheek, she glanced at Bart, before explaining she was tired and going upstairs to retire. To Bart, Jefferies seemed hostile at her late appearance and then retiring. Excusing himself, he followed her upstairs, while Bart finished his meal. The raised voice of Jefferies could be heard soon after, followed by an audible slap and a thump on the floor.

Dobie dutifully stood beside Bart replenishing his glass. Both men looked at each other waiting for the other to comment. Bart in the end spoke.

"It's none of our business Dobie," he said, wiping his face with his napkin, preparing to leave.

"That's the right answer, Bart," Dobie smiled with those dead eyes as if warning him.

"Can you thank Mr Jefferies for a great meal, I enjoyed it." Bart faked a smile, heading for the door. He was just about to leave when Jefferies appeared on the stairs hurrying down.

"Before you go, Bart, I have a problem. Someone has been coming on to my wife?"

"No problem Boss. What's his name, I'll go straight there?"

"No, this I must take care of myself. All I ask is you stay here and make sure no one enters, and my wife stays put until I return."

"Whatever you order Mr Jefferies. Are you sure you'd rather not I go? I can be discreet?"

"Dobie will take care of any unpleasantness, just remain here," Jefferies said firmly, the discussion over.

With a slam of the door, Dobie and Jefferies departed, leaving Bart to lock the door. The house became deadly quiet, as Bart checked the lower level making sure the house was secure. Sitting down in the lounge area, Bart picked up a paper intent on reading. The sound of someone sobbing, whispered through the room making concentrating on reading impossible. He knew of course who it was, as he sat there ignoring the crying.

Ten minutes of listening, had him pacing back and forwards. 'Don't do it,' his mind screamed as he looked at the staircase.

"It's none of my business," he said out loud, feeling a little fear at what his sub-conscience wanted him to do. "Fuck I'm cursed," Bart groaned, heading up the stairs.

Gina lay face down on the floor crying, her only clothing a towel wrapped around her waist. Her sobs were the sobs of someone not just in pain, but broken hearted. Bart unsure, grabbed a blanket from the bed covering her. Rolling her over, he carried her to the bed, lying her down. Neither had said a word, as he pulled the coverings up over her, sitting down on the edge of the bed beside her. Hiding her face humiliated Gina continued to cry.

Bart knew he was in unknown territory as he held her hand sitting motionless not sure what to do. After about fifteen minutes Gina stopped crying. Wiping her eyes, she looked at Bart, who had his head turned away as if giving her some privacy while holding her hand supporting her.

"Thank you," she croaked out, releasing his hand.

"Are you okay?"

"Yes, until the next time?"

"Does this occur often?"

"Only when he suspects me of being unfaithful." Bart at this answer didn't reply. Gina seeing the uncertainty in Bart at her answer poured out her life's story, about being forced into this marriage. In the end, the couple sat together again holding hands.

"Why don't you just run away?"

"He would find me. He'd send men like you or worse. Even if he didn't find me, he would kill my family for revenge. No, I am trapped here, the only escape is my affairs with men brave enough to risk being caught."

"He's gone after one of them tonight."

"There is no one. He thinks because I am late that there must be someone. He is wrong; I was just late as he will find out."

"Then he won't be long? I must leave," Bart admitted, sensing danger in just being here.

"What is your name?"

"Bartholomew, but my friends call me Bart."

"I am Gina, Bart. Would you risk seeing me again as a friend?" She asked, her eyes locked on his. Bart stared back, lost in those sad eyes. His mind warned him to say no, it was deadly to be this girl's friend. As if seeing it in his eyes she let go of his hand. "You'd better go."

"How about we have coffee next week? Where can I meet you?" He asked, watching her for the first time smile.

"I have a photo shoot at the Betrou Gallery in Amsterdam next Tuesday. You could meet me at the back door at eleven. No one will be watching me, but just in case."

"Until then," he smiled, moving towards the door. Stopping, he turned back. Reaching down, he pulled Gina to him, kissing her lightly on the cheek.

"Thank you," she cried, as he hurried out.

Reaching the lower level, he was doing a quick check of the doors and windows, when a movement behind him made him turn swiftly, drawing his weapon.

"Relax Bart; it's just me!" Dobie warned, seeing Bart was about to fire.

"You fucking idiot! I nearly shot you!" Bart barked, replacing his pistol in its holster.

"That was impressive Bart. No one usually hears Dobie approaching." Jefferies in the doorway chuckled.

"Don't ever test me, Boss. It's a good way of dying."

"What were you doing?" Dobie asked as if miffed at his approach being detected.

"Checking the windows and doors for the fourth time, you can never be too careful. How did you two go?"

"Our visit was successful. There will be no more threats to my wife. By the way, is she still here?"

"I heard what sounded like sobs upstairs and some moving around a while ago. She hasn't come down, so she's still up there," Bart answered his face emotionless.

"Good. Thanks for your help Bart. I'll be in touch," Jefferies smiled, as Bart left.

Outside Bart cursed himself for being such an idiot. He was putting his life on the line for a woman he had only seen for a couple of minutes. True she was beautiful, but the world was full of beautiful women. Why had she got under his skin? Was it because she was vulnerable or because of her treatment at the hands of Jefferies.

"I will stay away; I won't go near her!" He growled, seeing it as his way out. Walking on, he thought again of Gina. "You'll go alright. Like a moth to the flame, you can't help it you romantic idiot," Bart chuckled, walking home.

THE AFFAIR

As planned, he waited at the rear door, for her to arrive. He'd hired an unremarkable Fiat, hoping to blend in and avoid attention. Checking his rear view mirror for the tenth time, Bart started to wonder where she was. Doubt crept into his mind as the thought that she may have been forced to confess to Jefferies about their arrangement to meet. He envisioned Dobie moving in on him as he sat like a clay pigeon waiting to splattered with buckshot. Feeling down beside his door, he felt the reassuring butt of his pistol as a shadow flashed by him, making him jump. Next to him, stood Gina.

"Sorry I didn't mean to scare you." Looking at her, he could see she was happy to see him.

"Just a little jumpy," He smiled back, getting out. "What would you like to do Gina?"

"Can we just walk and talk a little?"

"Whatever you like Gina. As long as I get a coffee somewhere." He joked offering her his hand. Looking at it, she shyly reached out gripping his hand with hers.

"I know just the place." She answered, wrapping a scarf around her head. With her sunglasses on as well, Gina's face disappeared from view.

"You won't need a disguise here surely."

"I'm not worried about Jefferies men being here. It's the press and some of my fans, snapping a photo of us, which ended up in the papers could be a problem."

"You're right. I forgot about your other life. It must be hard to be in both your worlds?"

"Yes, on the catwalk I'm happy and surrounded by adoring fans. At home, I'm a prisoner afraid to breathe." Her beautiful smile Bart noticed had gone.

"Cheer up we've got this day," he reassured her, seeing the smile creep back onto her face.

For three hours they walked hand in hand talking about anything except their lives. True to her word, Gina found a coffee shop with the smoothest coffee Bart had ever tasted. Walking back to his car, he now held Gina around the waist, walking like an old married couple along the sidewalk. Stopping, both wanted to prolong saying goodbye.

"Am I worth another date?" Gina asked her face emotionless. Instead of answering, Bart pulled her closer, kissing her lightly on the cheek. "I'll take that as a yes," she replied, kissing him back on the lips.

"Here take this, and memorise it. If you want me, I'm on that number."

"Thank you, Bart, Most men I've known, just took me to a hotel for a quick romp before leaving me. Today with you was special, I'll remember it always."

"Yes it was special Gina, but still one day I'd like a romp as you put it." He answered, Gina, breaking into an accustomed laugh.

"Till then." She smiled, disappearing swiftly back into the rear entrance of the building, leaving Bart staring at the door. She was everything he had dreamed she would be he thought. Thinking of the risk he was taking, he smiled, slowly climbing into his car.

"I would risk everything to be with her again," he said to himself, as he happily drove away.

After several more brief encounters, Bart knew he needed more.

"I want to be with you, Gina. I want more than having a coffee or stealing a secretive kiss."

"I know Bart. I have a solution, although it's risky."

"Let's hear it." He softly replied, caught up in the conspiracy to be together.

"Come to the house?"

"You're joking?"

"No, I'm not. Of all the places I go, it is the last place he would watch."

"I can't just walk in the front door?"

"There's a secret entrance from our main bedroom, to a hidden door in the alleyway, behind the apartment block. I wasn't supposed to know about it, but by chance I found a piece of my husband's clothing caught in it one day. My husband must've used it for some reason and hadn't returned. A day later when he was out, I searched the room finding a hidden switch beside the secret doorway. It comes out beside a large rubbish bin. There you'll find a loose brick at waist height when you press it twice, the wall opens."

"Okay, just ring me when you want to meet. If it's humanly possible, I'll be there." Kissing her, always fearing it would be the last, the lovers departed.

A week of quiet reflection on the enormity of this extension of their relationship, found Bart in the alley. Walking its complete length, Bart looked for any security surveillance. Sure there was none; he walked back to the bin. Unless you were looking for it, you would never have guessed the doorway was there. Bart, of course, knew the entrance was there and by studying the brick wall, he saw the unmistakeable outline of a door. Feeling the bricks beside it, he on the fourth attempt found the loose one. As Gina had told him, pushing it twice, caused the wall to crack open. Pulling it found the doorway sliding silently open, allowing him to enter.

Closing the door behind him, he climbed a long thin staircase made of steel making his way upwards. Reaching a flat section, he walked along a short narrow corridor with several doors off it. Wondering what Jefferies kept here, he looked into one of the rooms. He found a storeroom filled with filing cabinets. Bart surmised Jefferies kept his private 'off the books' business dealings here. Moving further down the passage, he came to a plaster wall with an engraved handle in it.

Looking closer, he saw Jefferies' supposed coat of arms on it. He was just about to open it when raised voices made him freeze. When Gina had called him, she'd told him Jefferies was about to leave, travelling to his country manor in England. He was supposed to have left that afternoon. Looking at his watch, he saw it was close to eight in the evening, why was he still here?

"He might have discovered Gina, and I are having an affair?" Bart whispered, pulling out his pistol. Preparing to enter, he grabbed hold of the door handle. Hesitating, he considered that Gina might have been forced to tell them he was coming through the secret passage tonight. Wondering if Dobie was waiting for him on the other side of the door, Bart taking several deep breaths, slowly opened it. Finding the bedroom empty, he advanced into the room, leaving the secret door open. Hearing the voices downstairs, he walked out onto the landing.

"Don't leave the apartment my dear or you will regret it." Jefferies threatened Gina, who could be heard sobbing below him near the front door.

"Don't you trust me?" Gina answered as Bart heard a loud slap followed by a short yelp and more sobbing from Gina.

"Not for a second my dear. You are nothing but entertainment Gina, but you are my property. Stray again, and it will be your last darling." He warned, putting on his coat. Bart filled with black rage, walked to the staircase railing above them. Pointing his weapon down at Jefferies, he was about to squeeze the trigger, when Dobie's voice sounded from outside the front door entrance, making Bart duck back out of sight.

"The car's here boss," Dobie called from the doorway, as his eyes if sensing someone was upstairs, momentarily drifted upwards to the landing. Spotting nothing, thinking he was overreacting, he moved back outside. Bart for a second thought about taking them both out, but with Gina down there amongst them, the chances were she'd take a hit. Feeling a coward, he put his pistol away.

"Just remember what I told you, Gina. Although I'm away one of my men will be watching this place." Jefferies told her, leaving with a slam of the door. Gina sobbing collapsed onto a chair. Cautiously coming down the staircase, Bart approached her.

"Are you okay Gina?" Bart whispered as Gina shocked turned towards him. Standing, she ran into his arms.

"Thank God he didn't catch us. He came back deliberately to check on me. I was so scared you'd turn up while he was still here."

"Well, he didn't. So let's forget about him shall we." Gina wiping her eyes took hold of his hand, leading him back upstairs. It was so quiet Bart mused, as they both silently watched each other take off their clothes and climb onto the bed.

"You're beautiful Gina," Bart smiled, kissing her. The kiss seemed to awaken them from their enforced silence, as they both came together on the bed. Gina moaning with pent up hunger raked Bart's back with her fingernails making him groan in pain and ecstasy. Pinning her onto the bed, he savagely entered her, both of them screaming out, their twin passions igniting, daring the world to try and stop them. It was a night that they both would remember as the moment they committed themselves to each other.

Afterwards, they went downstairs naked having a brief meal together, before returning. Dawn breaking through the windows, awoke Bart. Gina still lay with one of her legs over his. Watching her chest rise and fall with each breath, Bart knew he was head over heels in love with her. As if she sensed him watching her, Gina's eyes slowly opened locking on his. Climbing on top of him, they made love again, until

Bart knowing time was against them, climbed reluctantly out of bed and reluctantly dressed.

"Can't you stay longer?" Gina's voice begged as Bart pulled her to him kissing her.

"I can't Gina; you know that. Leaving now is dangerous enough, in full daylight someone might see me in the alley." He warned, before going to the secret door. Looking back, closing it, he saw her watching him as if her life was somehow leaving her. Coming to the alley door, he slowly opened it, checking the alley. Two men, cleaners by their clothing, passed the doorway, luckily not seeing him. Fear made him hesitate, reminding him of the risk both of them were taking.

"Fuck it; it's worth every minute." He said out loud, walking away.

Their affair continued for over six months. Many times he stayed over at the apartment, each time his fear of discovery growing. Gina sensed it too, although to have Bart with her, she'd risk anything. Then it all came crashing down. Bart staying in a unit south of Paris received a summons from Jefferies. He wanted to discuss something with him, at his apartment at two in the afternoon. Bart worried that he knew, loaded up.

Placing a stiletto on his left leg and a small pistol on his right leg in special holsters, he then cleaned his pistol. The Glock he carried had a porcelain frame, making it hard to detect with a metal detector. Tucking it in the back of his pants, he then tucked a stun grenade in his left pants pocket. Checking that nothing showed in the mirror, he left for the meeting confident that if there was a falling out, he'd be ready.

Arriving at the apartment Bart was relieved to see no sign of Gina. Dobie like usual waited just inside the front door.

"Are you carrying?" He asked, his dead pan face staring at Bart.

"Of course I fucking am Dobie. The boss sounded like he had a problem." Bart replied as Jefferies appeared.

"Forget that Dobie. Bart's proved himself." Jefferies ordered, Dobie his eyes emotionless, nodded for Bart to enter. Waving Bart into his study, Jefferies offered him a drink. Declining it, seemed to please Jefferies who himself didn't drink.

"I have an assignment for you which requires a large amount of discretion. You have seen my wife, Gina?"

"Yes, briefly on my last visit here," Bart answered, keeping his voice neutral.

"It seems that despite my love and support, my wife may have taken a lover. I'm not completely sure though, but by her moods, I'd say it's been going on for several months."

"That's a shit deal boss. Any ideas who it is?"

"No. As I said it could be just my over cautious mind, but I need someone to follow her and take care of the problem."

"If I find someone, how far do you want me to go in making him stop?"

"That, I will leave to you Bart. Just get it done."

"No problems. If you give me her itinerary for the next two weeks, I'll make sure if there's a problem, it goes away."

"Thank you, Bart, and keep this quiet."

"No one will find out Mr Jefferies. That, I can assure you." Bart promised, walking back to the door. Turning, he saw Dobie following.

"Is there a problem Dobie?" Bart asked his voice clouded with anger.

"Why the attitude Bart? I was just going to give you a copy of her movements for the coming week." Dobie replied, standing neutrally beside him. Bart knew despite Dobie's friendly appearance; he was ready for Bart if he attacked.

"I don't like seeing the boss upset that's all. I can't believe she's cheating on him." He lied. Dobie beside him smiled.

"Well, for once we're in agreement Bart. I too don't understand why he puts up with her."

"Love is blind they say, Dobie. Tell him not to worry; the problem will be gone soon."

"See that it is," Dobie answered going back inside. Bart continued around the corner at the end of the block. Stopping beside a waste bin, he threw up.

"What do I do now?" Bart sobbed, wiping his mouth and walking on, entering a pub.

Three hours later, Bart was still at the pub.

"He's onto us because Gina's happy!" Bart cursed, downing yet another drink, attracting the attention of several patrons at the bar. One glare silenced their hostility, making them turn away. Knowing he'd drunk too much, he stumbled outside onto the street, walking home. Once there he sat down trying to think of a way out of his predicament.

What could he do, was the question?

He could pretend to kill someone, but Gina would still be happy. Thinking about it, Bart sadly concluded that he would have to break off his relationship with her. Angry, he tried to think of anything other than that. He thought seriously of eliminating both Jefferies and Dobie in one well-planned hit. Taking them by surprise would be easy, as he could go to his unit to tell Jefferies he'd got Gina's lover.

The problem was it wouldn't achieve anything, as Pierre, Jefferies' partner, would come after them. Looking at Gina's schedule, he decided to wait until he saw her, hoping by then he'd have another plan.

Following her, for a week Bart had plenty of times where he could've approached her. Each time he backed off, knowing he would have to tell her. In the end, he found a time when she was alone at the apartment. Using the secret entrance, Gina was surprised when he appeared.

"My God Bart you scared me." She smiled, coming into his arms. His lack of response warned her something was wrong. "What is it?"

"He's onto us. I've been hired to find your lover."

"Then lie to him, say you ran him off."

"He will know by your reaction. While we're together, you are too happy. Faking getting rid of someone won't work, we have to end it."

"No, you can't be serious. You said you loved me!"

"I do love you, Gina, that's why I must leave. If I don't we're both dead," he confessed, as tears ran down his face. Sobbing Gina broke down collapsing face down on the bed.

"Gina, look at me," Bart begged as Gina continued to cry. Knowing staying there was useless, Bart left. Outside Bart wiped his face, shaking with suppressed rage.

"What had he done?" He asked himself, his heart broken. Taking out his phone, he dialled Jefferies.

"How did it go, Bart?"

"The problem has gone Boss."

"Good work Bart. Now take a break you sound worn out."

"Yeah this one was hard, a break is just what I need. I'll call the office in two weeks," Bart replied, severing the call and his happiness.

LONDON OFFICE

"Gina, Craig, what are you two doing here?' A voice challenged.

"It's Dobie, Gina, be careful," Bart warned.

"Dobie is that you?" She asked in a loud voice.

"Yes, it is. Where is Jefferies?"

"He's dead, along with all his men," Bart answered, as Dobie came into view, backed up by four men.

"Well, well, well. If it isn't our missing action man Bartholomew? I thought that Peter Moustaffer had got you?"

"No, I let him live in return for Jefferies' life," Peter told them, as the men visibly became alerted.

"You're dead meat," Dobie growled, raising his pistol.

"Put your weapon down Dobie. With my husband dead, I now run this firm. If you men want to be paid before the police completely close us down, you'll do as you're told." She ordered, walking past the surprised men. As the others moved to follow, Dobie shoved his gun into Peter's stomach. Dobie was just about to say something poignant when he saw Peter had his gun out pointing at his chest. Bart also had his weapon out pointing at Dobie's head.

"I've heard a lot about you Dobie, none of it good," Peter snarled. Dobie looking for support saw his backup melt away, following Gina.

"How about backing me?" He spat out, as one of the men turned around.

"We all knew how badly Jefferies treated his wife, Dobie. Let's get paid and leave. Killing someone now makes no sense." He stated, walking inside. Dobie, in the end, lowered his weapon, before pushing past them and leaving.

Gina was more than generous with her ex-husband's money. To the gathered men's surprise, she paid all his men six month's severance pay, including the ones arrested. Happy, the men abandoned their weapons left. Peter, while this was going on, went to Jefferies' office. There he was greeted by a long line of locked filing cabinets. After an hour of searching and finding nothing, Bart and Gina joined him. Craig having been paid said his goodbyes and left with the others.

"Any luck?" Gina asked, openly now holding Bart's hand.

"No, he wouldn't leave it here I don't think, it's just too easy."

"There must be something more. At our home in Paris, he had a secret escape passage. Maybe there's something the same here?" Bart put forward, looking at Gina and remembering.

Looking around it didn't take long to find one of the end rooms was shorter than the rest. Not bothering to look for an entrance, Peter kicked a hole in the plaster wall. Large enough to climb through, found the three in a corridor. At the end was a ladder going down. Descending carefully down the rungs, they came to a square room on the ground floor. Stacked against the wall were shelves full of money.

"Holy hell! There are millions here," Bart chuckled.

"Enough for a good life for the two of you," Peter added, seeing them look at each other.

"We only just met," Gina stuttered out, caught by surprise.

"Yeah, sure you have," Peter smirked, seeing them both go red. Bart was just about to explain when he saw contract folder sitting on a shelf. Opening it, he saw a group of names including Peters.

"Is this it?" Peter taking it from Bart read through it.

"This is it." He gasped seeing the contractor's name.

"My God! Why would they be after you Peter?" Bart asked seeing the clients name as well.

"This makes no sense? Why would they be after my parents and me? We have done nothing to them."

"I've no idea Peter, but this is the end of the line for me. As much as I would like to help, I've had enough. I'm taking Gina and getting away from here; she deserves something better." Bart told him, as Gina held his hand squeezing it.

"Thank you for everything Bart. I hope you both find happiness." He smiled. "I suggest you load up and follow me out this way. The front might soon be full of police." With that, he left through the hidden back door.

This advice saved all their lives, as Dobie had camped out front, waiting for his chance to finish them all.

To him, they had killed his only friend and benefactor, and he wanted them all dead. Unlike the others, Dobie killed for the fun of it, not the money and now his reason for living was gone. When they hadn't exited the building in two hours, Dobie livid, had entered. Finding the hole Peter had made in the wall, he knew they'd outsmarted him and left through the secret passageway.

Hearing the police approaching, he left the same way, promising vengeance on the three of them.

When Gina and Bart had gathered up all the money, they went out through the rear as Peter had. Thinking Peter had taken the car, they hot-wired an old Volvo, driving into the city. Finding a hotel, they booked a room under a bogus name, spending the night together. The following morning, they went to the railway station, leaving their money in three lockers, they then went London police headquarters.

Walking in together, Gina walked up to the front desk and gave her name to the constable on duty. Several seconds passed before three plainclothes detectives rushed into the room and detained them both. Two hours later they walked out, the police shocked by their story. One of England's shining lights in finance was nothing more than a contract killer. The true story wouldn't be told, sighting the damage it would cause.

Instead, the story that terrorists had attacked Jefferies' home in an attempt to kidnap him was adopted. Gina wasn't happy wanting the truth known. The fact that she was free to go in the end convinced her to go along with the fabrication.

Arriving back at their hotel room with their money, Gina suggested they hire a car. They could then travel back to their apartment in Paris. She told Bart that Jeffries had stored money in one of the storage rooms hidden in the escape route from their apartment's bedroom. Bart was at first against it, but Gina reminded him of the last time he stayed over there. Remembering, Bart merrily agreed.

Six hours after they'd walked out of the police station, the lovers back at Gina's apartment. Walking in the front door, Bart carried Gina upstairs tickling her making her giggle hysterically. Kicking open the bedroom door Bart nearly dropped her when he saw Dobie sitting on the bed watching them. In his hand, pointing at Gina was an old Walther PPK pistol. The pistol was the type used by James Bond in many of the 007 movies. Although old, Bart was sure it would still fire.

"What do you want Dobie?" Bart snapped, letting Gina down and moving her slightly behind him.

"You killed my boss, what do you think I want?"

"We have money. Do you need some?" Gina asked, her voice squeaking with fear.

"Both of you lay down on the floor."

"Forget reasoning with him, Gina. He kills for the fun of it, without it, he's a waste of space." Bart smiled, hoping to get Dobie to move closer.

"I said get on the floor Bart. Or would you rather I shoot your girlfriend in the guts?" Complying, both Gina and Bart lay down. Moving behind them, Dobie swiftly secured their hands with wire ties then Bart's feet. Finished he kicked Bart hard in the kidneys. Trying not to cry out, Bart wore the pain, as Gina beside him sobbed.

"It's going to be a long night Bart. First I'm going to rape this bitch and then I'm going to torture her. When I'm finished, it will be your turn." He sniggered insanely, moving to Gina.

Ripping her clothes off, he manhandled her onto the bed, while Gina begged for their lives. Slapping her, he looked over at Bart seeing his eyes black with anger.

"Nothing to say to me, hero? It's never too late to beg?"

"You're less than a man Dobie. What was your relationship with Jefferies, was he the father you never had, you sicko bastard." Bart answered, his anger making his voice shake, as Dobie broke into laughter. He knew he was goading him, trying to get him to react. Unfortunately, it hadn't worked.

Lying there, Bart silently groaned, knowing he'd failed to save Gina. He'd hoped by egging Dobie on; he might kill him first. He thought if he did that Dobie would be happy just to rape Gina, leaving her alive. It was a shitty deal for her, but at least she'd be alive. It hadn't worked, and now he was powerless to stop him.

"This is going to be fun." Dobie grinned, his eyes looking over Gina as his hand went to his belt. He was in the process of undoing it, when a strange look appeared on his face. For several seconds he seemed to be frozen as if trying to figure out some problem. Bart lay on the floor wondering what was going on when he saw his neck gushing blood. Toppling over, Bart saw a knife protruding from the back of his neck. Gina having closed her eyes opened them to see Dobie slump on top of her. Screaming, seeing the blood, her eyes went to Bart.

"What's happening?" She sobbed, as a shadow moved across the room. Pulling Dobie off the bed, it dumped him on the floor, before covering Gina with a blanket.

"Who are you?" Bart asked the shadow, which was just a man dressed in black from head to toe.

"I'll ask the questions, and I can assure you, you'll answer them." A deep voice commanded. "Where did Peter Moustaffer go? And did he find out who killed his parents? Lie to me, and you will both join this piece of trash."

"He was returning home, and yes he knows who ordered the hit," Bart truthfully answered, knowing Peter could handle himself.

"Who was it?"

"The French Government," Bart replied, hearing the intake of breath from the man. Momentarily the man seemed frozen as if it was working out a complex problem.

"Thank you." Was all the shadow said, before cutting the bindings on Gina's hands and walking out the door.

"Gina massaged her arms, worked some movement back into them. Moving to her dresser, she took out a pair of scissors. Cutting Bart's bindings, they both moved to the bed, sitting down.

"Who the hell was that?" Gina asked, still crying from their brush with death.

"Who knows, but I'm glad he came along when he did."

"Do you think he's after Peter?"

"Yes, and I feel bad that I gave him the information, although we have one ace up our sleeves. Peter gave you his mobile number; we can at least warn him." Bart smiled, rushing to retrieve Gina's phone.

While Gina rang Peter's number, Bart checked the house making sure this time they were alone. Sure they were, he barricaded the bedroom door just in case. Gina by the time he returned had passed on the warning to Peter. He had thanked her and told them not to worry about giving him up. Clearly, they had no choice. When Bart finished the securing of the room, she told him of the conversation, Bart looked relieved.

One last job thing to take care of." Bart told her, pointing to Dobie. Wrapping him in a blanket, they opened the secret doorway and dragged him inside. Although the passageway was thin, they managed to drag him down the stairs to the alley. Opening the door, making sure the coast was clear, they dumped him into the garbage bin. Positive no one had seen them; they locked the outside door and proceeded back to the bedroom.

"Not exactly the night I'd expected." Gina mused, holding Bart.

"No, it wasn't. I know you like it here Gina, but tomorrow we leave, and we won't return."

"I don't care where we go as long as we're together," Gina answered, kissing him.

Peter looked at the phone wondering what this man wanted. From what Gina had told him, he'd saved their lives, so he had some sort of moral compass. Chances were, he was hired by the French government to stop Peter going further. It could also be someone Nigel Chamberlain had sent to help him, for all he knew. The one thing he was certain of, was the French Government had paid for the hit, and he wanted to know why. Taking out his pistol, he quickly cleaned it. Knowing trouble was coming, he'd told the men watching his father's home to stay away until he called. He knew there would be no running this time; he needed to know what this man knew.

NIGEL DOWN UNDER

In America, Nigel battled bureaucracy to get something moving. The Whitehouse seemed relieved Ali's group was finally gone, unwilling to investigate further. Realising he was getting nowhere, Nigel took two months leave, sighting family problems. Thinking it better to have Nigel out of their hair, his boss granted it. Ringing his wife, he arranged for her to meet his flight that he'd just booked to Perth, Western Australia.

After a twenty-hour flight, a crumpled Nigel disembarked in Perth. His wife greeted him with a kiss, bundling him into a car. She left their son with his uncle in Sydney before flying here. Edward, although getting on, had been an Australian Federal Policeman and the brother-in-law of Steve Roberts. He was also a man who could look after himself. Steve's demise, which now appeared to be a deliberate act, unfortunately, came as no surprise to him.

He'd been worried for some time that Steve would meet his maker by a hostile act. There'd been many attempts over the years to make him go away; it appeared this one had been successful.

Clearing customs, Nigel moved outside to the pickup point. He had no sooner placed his bag on the ground, when a red rental car, screeched to a halt in front of him. His wife signalling for him to jump in made him wary.

"What's wrong?" He asked looking into the rear view mirror as his wife drove off.

"I got the feeling, I'm being watched." She replied, as she too stole glances into the mirrors.

"You're a beautiful woman Lindsey of course men look at you." He smiled, seeing a small smile appear on her lips.

"You always were smooth."

"It's worked so far."

"No it's just since I went and inquired about the loss of the boat, I've had a feeling someone's watching me." Nigel for some time kept quiet digesting what she had said. Not wanting to worry her he changed tack.

"Did you get in touch with Mary?"

"Yes, that's where we're headed now. I told her you were suspicious of the accident."

"How'd she take it?"

"Not well. She broke into another language and started talking to someone else. I'd say it was her husband by the tone. He sounded angry."

"His name's Omar. Both of them are from Afghanistan. Steve introduced me last time we were here. They live up the road from Steve and Natasha's place. I heard her father was Steve's sergeant major in the SAS; they were close. He died a couple of years ago, too many smokes."

"Did you tell them about Aaron and Ali?"

"No, not yet, I thought it best we see them first."

"Good thinking, I'll make an agent out of you yet." He joked, his wife smiling.

A lot had changed since Steve moved here with his first wife, Michelle. The coastline was wall to wall units, except in Steve's street where native bush still covered both sides of the road. Mary's parent's house was the only other building in an area of prime real estate.

"Your dad made the right decision holding onto this land. It's beautiful here. Have you talked to Robin about the place?"

"Yes, she is like me and wants it left as it is. She suggested making the bushland a state park, to keep it natural."

"Good idea. Someday I'd like to come and live here; I'm over New York."

"My God, after the fuss you made with my dad about taking me there to live forever." She smiled, before losing the smile remembering her father was now dead.

"I always rated that as the bravest thing I ever did. I thought he might kill me for living in sin with his daughter."

"Anyway, we better go in and talk to Mary. I have the feeling they're watching us?" Lindsey warned, seeing the curtains on the window move.

"Yeah, good idea," Nigel replied, seeing the same thing. Walking up to the door, Nigel was just about to knock when the door swung open. In the door, way stood a man with an olive complexion. He had a blunt 'don't give me shit,' look about him, as Nigel cleared his throat.

"I'm Nigel, and this is my wife, Lindsey," Nigel said waiting.

"I know who you are; I remember Steve introducing us."

"Let them in Omar. Give them a break." A female voice echoed from inside the house. As if unsure, but wanting to please his wife the man relented, letting them in. Walking silently in front of them, the man led them to a kitchen dining area, overlooking the beach. There they found a woman with the same olive skin feeding a small baby in a highchair.

"You're Lindsey, Steve's oldest girl and I judge this is your husband Nigel, the FBI agent. Steve was very proud of his girls and their husbands; he used to brag about you two all the time. I am Mary; you've met my brooding husband Omar already. This is John, named after my foster father."

"It is a pleasure to meet you all, but unfortunately we have a problem."

"You think Natasha and Steve's death was not an accident," Omar stated.

"Yes. Can we all sit down?" Nigel asked, as knowing something was coming they took his advice and sat down. Seeing he had their attention, Nigel started.

"I was rung nearly a week ago now by Ali's son Peter. Ali was Steve's unit commander when he worked for the CIA. His father and the other remaining unit member, Aaron, were killed in a skiing accident along with both their wives. At first, I thought it might just be a coincidence that three members of an elite unit could die at the same time. The fact that there was then an attempt on Peter's life for looking into it makes it no coincidence. I came here looking for clues as to who is responsible."

"We loved Steve like a father Nigel, we too would like to help, but the child makes us hesitate," Omar confessed.

"I understand Omar. Like you, we also have a child, he is with his uncle while we are here," Lindsey answered, understanding.

"Then I have the solution. Lindsey, me and the baby can disappear until you call us. That way Omar can help with the locals, he has become well known as an avid fisherman," Mary smiled, seeing Omar bristle at the off-handed compliment.

"That sounds good to me Nigel. Let's face it Omar would be more help than me." Lindsey put in, happy to spend time with Mary and the child.

"Is it okay with you Omar?" Nigel noticed he'd remained silent. Getting a reluctant yes in the form of a nod, Nigel moved on. "Okay, tomorrow we'll visit the marina, where Steve's boat was berthed. We can find out if anyone showed an interest in it?" Nigel suggested.

"We can also enquire about the man who witnessed the accident." Omar put in.

"I didn't know there was a witness?" Nigel answered surprised.

"It didn't make the main news channels, just the local ones. He supposedly saw them working on the engine, before the explosion." Mary explained.

"Yes. He could be very handy." Nigel answered, wondering about the witness.

The next morning Omar and Nigel waved goodbye to their wives and Omar's son. Once they'd departed, they loaded some fishing gear into Nigel's hire car and drove north along the coast. Omar didn't say much until they neared the marina.

"Nigel, I have had my fill of killing. I want you to know that."

"We're only here to ask questions, Omar, there should be no problems." Omar looked at him for a few seconds before answering.

"Your Government turned Steve and his team into the elite killers that they were, then tried to kill them. After the trouble in England, your Government pardoned Steve, and he returned here with Natasha and left that life behind him. He found peace here Nigel, and we became good friends. A couple of years ago, he returned from a supposed holiday with Ali, Aaron, and their wives; he was badly shaken. I know that look from Afghanistan Peter, you call it shell shocked. I asked him what had occurred, but he refused to tell me, for our own safety he confessed.

It drove a wedge between us as I feared for my wife and child. The day they died he asked me to come fishing with them, but I refused wanting to keep my distance. If I had gone, this might not have happened. It fills me with shame. I have not told Mary any of this, but if I find out your Government is still causing him trouble, I will go to the authorities and tell them everything."

"I know nothing of this Omar. I didn't even know about the holiday, even though I remember Natasha turning up alone two years ago in June. She told us she was meeting him in Switzerland, that's where Ali lives." Nigel confessed, as something stirred in the back of his mind. Omar saw the look.

"You remember something?"

"Yes, I remember Natasha seemed edgy. I thought Steve and her had argued at the time. Now I wonder if she was indeed scared."

"Let's go see the man who witnessed it. Then you have much to check on." Omar suggested. Nigel nodded, that he would, as they walked towards the dock.

The marina was in full swing as they walked along one of the many floating docks out towards the witnesses' boat. Omar remembered it from the news clip. It was a professional fishing boat, with a distinctive fly bridge and a large aerial above it. Seeing no one near it, Omar strolled over to a cabin cruiser moored next to it. On its deck, doing a good job of cleaning it stood an old guy of about seventy.

"Good morning, have you seen the owner of the fishing boat?" Omar asked.

"Why what's it to you?" The guy was taking in Omar's casual dress and Nigel's cop like suit.

"He was the local who saw the accident here about two weeks ago. I want to ask him some questions, that's all." Nigel replied.

"You look like a cop?" The old man snapped back.

"That's because I am, so where is he?" Nigel asked bluntly.

"Well he might've seen the accident, but he's no local. My name's Jim, and I've been around here for thirty years, and I haven't seen him before. Another thing, he's got a pommy accent, he must have brought his boat here just before the accident." The old man told them, before spitting with great gusto, into the water. Both Omar and Nigel digested this information before continuing.

"Did you know Steve Roberts then Jim?" Omar asked.

"He was a good man, and his wife was a peach. I find it hard to believe he was messing around with his boat. He had me service it for him for some extra spending money. I was a diesel mechanic before I hit the bottle after my kid died. There was nothing wrong with that engine." Jim exclaimed, getting angry.

"Did you tell the police that?"

"They didn't bother asking me. Took the word, of that so called witness, that he'd been tinkering with the engine." Nigel was about to ask another question when he saw Jim glance behind them.

"Here they come copper. The other man was here that day as well." Jim whispered, making himself scarce.

As the two men neared, Nigel saw them glance from Omar to him, one dropping back slightly. Nigel knew from his training this was a method used when you knew a confrontation was coming. Beside him Omar although he hadn't said anything moved a little away from Nigel.

"Good morning. My name's Omar. I understand you witnessed an accident a couple of weeks ago?" Omar asked, addressing the man from the interview.

"What's it to you raghead?" The man retorted, recognising Omar's complexion. Omar for a few seconds paused then continued.

"The man killed supposedly by accident was a friend of mine. You were supposed to be local, but I haven't seen you here before, and I come here quite a lot."

"Yeah, I've seen you hanging around here fishing from the wharf. But then again you stick out. If that's it we've got some work to do." The man smiled, his friend remaining silent.

"I've never been here before, why did you lie?" Omar growled, moving towards the witness. His friend seeing the gesture moved his hand behind his back, producing a gun. Several people on their near by boats who were watching what was going on, either fled or hid on their boats.

"Well that didn't take much did it?" Omar smiled to Nigel, who was trying to hide the state of shock he was in, at how a simple interview had escalated. Coming to life he intervened.

"I am a Federal agent, drop your weapon or my snipers will open fire." He ordered, producing his badge. Both men froze, before quickly looking around. Seeing nothing, they both chuckled.

"Good bluff. If you had brought backup, they would have fired by now. Finish them Rob," was all he got out, as a 'twang' like noise sounded behind Nigel. A split second later, a spear appeared in the man with the gun's chest, making him stagger backwards, falling off the jetty. The fake witness seeing his friend go down went for his gun. He just grabbed hold of his weapon, when Omar set upon him. Head butting him; the witness staggered backwards collapsing onto the jetty. Moving forward, Omar relieved him of his weapon, before kicking him in the head.

"That's for the raghead comment." Omar snarled, as in the distance sirens could be heard approaching.

"Well, I'm glad you warned me about avoiding shooting?" Nigel pointed out to Omar, as Jim emerged from his boat carrying an empty spear gun.

"Thank you, Jim. You saved us both."

"No problems. Who are they?"

"I'd say they were the men paid to kill Steve and Natasha. They were most probably ordered to stay here and make sure no one nosed around."

"I judge Omar set them up, as I've seen him fishing here too." Jim chuckled.

"Yes. Although their reaction was not what I expected." Omar admitted as the police swarmed onto the wharf.

At the station Nigel being an FBI agent from America, didn't cut him any slack. Nigel, Jim and Omar found themselves in cells opposite the witness.

"Fuck! Some thanks I get for saving you two?" Jim smirked, spitting through the bars at the witness opposite.

"You killed some nice people arsehole; you're going to rot in prison for this."

"Save your threats, old man. I'll be walking out that door any minute; they've got nothing on me." The witness spat out, looking confident.

"You're wrong there Mr Bennett's." A voice sounded from the door, as four men in business suits walked in.

"Fuck, more coppers?" Jim sniggered, Omar, nudging him to be quiet.

"Yes, we're coppers, Australian Federal police officers to be exact. I'm the Commissioner of the Federal Police in Australia and was visiting near here when Andrew, Steve Robert's brother-in-law and my friend, contacted me. Scotland Yard has told us that Mr Bennett's here was part of an organisation running out of England and Paris. Someone took them down a couple of nights ago; most are dead or on the run. Their records have been seized, and your name came up after we fingerprinted you Mr Bennett's."

"You're bluffing; I'm in the clear," Bennett answered, but his bravado was gone.

"The Russians want you for a murder you carried out there a couple of years ago. They have the death penalty there my friend, care to make a statement?" The Commissioner smiled.

"It was just a job, nothing personal." Bennett's answered as the room grew deadly quiet.

"You fucker. I hope the Russians fry you!" Jim shouted out, tears in his eyes.

The Commissioner had Nigel, Omar and Jim released soon afterwards.

"You're a good man Jim. I hear there's a position for a diesel mechanic to service our vehicle fleet in Perth. Think you can handle it?" The Commissioner asked.

"Yes Sir, I'd be honoured." Jim softly replied.

"You might have to curve the swearing." The Commissioner added.

"I'll try." Was all Jim said, as walked off, wiping his eyes. The Commissioner then turned to Nigel and Omar.

"Now, you two keep your noses clean is that understood?"

"Yes Sir and thanks again," Nigel answered, Omar, nodding his agreement.

"Just as a matter of interest, who do you think wiped out their organisation?" The Commissioner whispered.

"Steve's remaining unit members were all been wiped out a couple of weeks ago. Ali, the leader of the unit, had a son named Peter. He is a special ops soldier in the Swiss army. He's on leave at the moment, that's all I'll say," Nigel informed him.

"God it runs in the families. I'm glad Steve had daughters," the Commissioner answered, hurrying away to a waiting car.

"Well, that's the end of it?" Omar half smiled, seeing the wives arrive to pick them up.

"Here it is. For Peter, I'm sure it's no," Nigel whispered, trying to smile and wave happily to his wife.

THE MISSION

Marlise like the rest of her ten-man team members, prepared to jump. Why they were parachuting into the southern backcountry of Libya, she had no idea, other than it was in France's best interest. Chad and Niger to the south of Libya had been plagued with Islamic tribal raids since Libya to the north had in the Arab Spring, ousted President Gaddafi. There'd been some bloody fighting, with horrific casualties, now tribal leaders ruled there.

The Bedouin tribes, having gained massive supplies of weapons and ammunitions, had pushed south into Niger and Chad. The French, having a treaty with Chad had sent troops there, while the Americans assisted Niger. They had launched joint offensives, with both Niger and Chad troops, driven the militia units back north to the border, inflicting heavy casualties. Libya's coalitions of tribal leaders had been less than impressed with France, which curtailed any shipments of oil from Libya to France.

Marlise had been there briefly with Peter and his father a couple of years ago; it had been intense. Of course, no one here knew that which was the way she would like to keep it. It had been the first time she'd seen action, and she'd felt like a green recruit next to Peter's father and his friends. The Ghost had been there, and even long past his prime, he was deadly.

She'd heard the term 'born killers', but until she'd seen him, she thought it was just a myth. Peter refused to talk about the whole thing, which she could understand, as it involved his family. She, on the other hand, wanted to know more about this Steve Roberts, like how he had become such a professional soldier.

A flashing green light above the jump door, indicating it was time to go. Forgetting the past, Marlise concentrated on her jump. Three seconds found the whole team out the door. The mission, although vague, was an Intelligence gathering operation. They were here to observe and remain hidden, passing on info to the military forces to their rear. Why they couldn't get their information from satellites and drones, she had no idea, like they said it was in the national interest, so they were deployed.

Glancing down Marlise saw the ground coming up fast. Dropping her pack onto a long piece of rope below her, she hoped it would lessen the impact, as with a thump she hit. Getting up swiftly, she gathered her gear, burying the chute. Looking around, she saw the others doing the same, as a series of thud like noises echoed around them.

"Mortars!" Someone screamed, as round after round impacted near two of the team members to Marlise's right. Both went down, as the others lay on the ground till the bombardment stopped. After the initial plastering, Marlise's team rushed to the downed men. It was a waste of time as both were dead.

"Gather their gear and weapons." Captain Lenore ordered, as another round of thuds was heard. Diving for cover the round impacted in the area they had just left, this time causing no casualties.

"Everyone down in the gully and head north until we've cleared this hot zone." The Captain shouted, as his team now two members down, moved off at a trot. Dodging mortars for the rest of the day, found two more team members slightly injured. Moving into the mountains which formed part of the border, they dug in.

"Marlise come here for a minute," Lenore whispered, as night started to fall. Moving cautiously across to his foxhole, she waited for him to talk. "What is your take on the situation Sergeant?"

"Is the radio still off the air?"

"Yes. It's working, but the frequency we're using appears not to be monitored.

"Then we've been set up Sir. Stumbling upon us while we are jumping is one thing, having a mortar set up and dropping right on us is more than luck. Now the radio's frequencies are useless? Someone's fucked us over."

"I was thinking the same thing, but who would do such a thing and why?" Lenore asked confused.

"I suggest we go back and find out. We could all use a good walk."

"Yes although going back to the south, is out of the question. It's the first place they'll block. I thought we could go east and cross into Niger? The border is more porous there and our lines, are closer to the actual border."

"Sounds good Sir, although it's going to be a good hump across a lot of desert."

"Well like you said Marlise, we need a good walk."

Not waiting till morning Marlise's team started out at 3 am. Still, pitch dark, they moved through the dark countryside on guard for movement. The squeal of machinery, made them all freeze, as back behind them near where they had camped, came the roar of heavy weapons fire, backed by tanks. Knowing moving was too dangerous they headed again into the high country, looking for a safe hideout. By accident one of the men found a small canyon, that was heading in the direction they were travelling.

Finding no way down into the steep sided gully, Lenore asked for all the rope his men were carrying. For emergencies most carried some rope, so once he had it all, he tied it together, making it to the bottom. The problem was they might need it again, so it had to be looped around a large rock, to allow them to pull it down after they'd used it. This halved its length, making the rope twenty metres short, meaning once you came to the end of the rope, you had to climb hand over hand to reach the bottom. Captain Lenore insisted on being last and paid the penalty.

Climbing down to the end of the rope, his job was to disconnect from the rope, and pull it down. He managed to disconnect the rope; only to have it entangled his leg. This caused him to fall the last twenty metres. A loud snap when he hit left no doubt in the team's minds that he'd broken something. Checking him, their first aid specialist found his left leg had a compound fracture, the broken bone visible. Having no time to look at it, he quickly bandaged it, as the others put together a rough stretcher.

Making sure no one was following, they moved out at a reduced pace, taking turns carrying the stretcher. The Gully had an unexpected bonus, not only was it cooler in the shaded gorge, in several places they found water. Refilling at one of these small seeps in the rock surface, the group on guard, rested. Marlise now checked the Captain's leg. With the help of the medic and a shitload of morphine, they cut the Captain's leg enough to move the broken bone inside and set it.

As the Medic stitched the wound up, Marlise washed and cleaned it, to avoid infection. Finished, two of the men made a pair of splints out of the two spare rifle barrels of their fallen team members.

"Thanks, Marlise. You're in charge until I'm back on my feet." Lenore told her, collapsing back onto the stretcher.

"We'll be back in France in no time, drinking too much. Just take it easy, the others need the exercise anyway," she added, getting light-hearted abuse from the others. Rested, feeling better, the team again moved off, wondering what had happened to their enemy.

Mahomet Jundela looked from his smoking barrel to his now dead Colonel. His job had been simple; capture the French dogs once they'd landed. Instead, he'd decided it was safer to fire mortars and then make them surrender. His stupidity had resulted in their escape into the mountains. Jundela didn't handle failure well, thus the Colonel's permanent removal.

"Captain Bursa, you are now in command until you fail. Where are they?" Jundela asked.

"I have over two hundred men combing the mountains Sir. Other than that, I have no idea." Jundela stood looking at his new field commander. He had guts to answer like that he thought, giving a rare smile.

"Very well Captain. Keep me informed," he ordered, stepping into his jeep. Signalling his driver to leave, he saw the Captain move to his radioman, most probably threatening his men, as Jundela had threatened him.

"Fear has always worked amongst our people," He smiled, looking at the silent companion sitting beside him. "We will soon have her brother. Then the fun can begin." He chuckled, as his brother remained silent, his eyes the only thing showing he'd heard. They were black with hate.

Crossing the border back into Libya, the jeep, continued north, entering Jundela's tribal lands. For all intents and purposes, the thousands of miles his people controlled, was nothing but barren deserts, with a sprinkling of mountains. His people didn't work the land; they were Bedouin slave traders and had been for over a thousand years. Leaving a primitive tribal existence, they had survived for centuries, by plundering the coastal towns, for food and slaves. When threatened, they retreated into their tribal lands ambushing the enemy and depriving them of water. Most retreated unable to stand the heat and sand that was until General Gaddafi came along.

Brutal and intelligent with a modern army, he had waged war on Jundela's tribe nearly wiping them out. They had fought bravely, but Gaddafi had tanks and aircraft, making the desert barrier useless and ineffective. Forced to yield they, like all the other tribes, waited their time growing stronger. Still, they lacked the ability to buy weapons and equipment. Slavery having been outlawed, saw their income dropped.

Many had to serve in Gaddafi's army to support their families; something their leaders thought was an unbearable insult. That all changed, when in the late eighty's a Russian company found black gold in their deserts. Oil, millions of barrels of oil lay under the barren wasteland they called home. Gaddafi was no fool and immediately called their tribal leaders in for a discussion on sharing the wealth. Many tribes overjoyed attended, Jundela's father the sheikh, sent his cousin instead.

He was told to pretend he was the tribal leader and attend the conference, then return and tell them what he'd learned. They were massacred, not one leader escaping. Guerrilla warfare broke out, with Jundela's tribe taking the commanding position. Where before Gaddafi's air force could bomb their villages, this time his aircraft found nothing. Buried beneath the dunes or hidden in caverns in the mountains, Jundela's people survived.

As casualties rose amongst Gaddafi's forces and the oil revenue stopped flowing, Gaddafi called a truce, bending to the tribe's conditions for the oil wealth to be shared. Half for Gaddafi and half for the tribes sounded grossly unfair; to the tribes, it was more money than they'd ever dreamed of.

From near poverty, they became the richest people on earth. Still, it would never be enough, as long as Gaddafi controlled their lives. Jundela's tribes, unlike the others, followed a brutal, unforgiving religion. Reaching out to their brothers in Iran they secretly flew trainers in to teach their men the way of the terrorist. Extreme Muslim groups found sanctuary and training in the mountains of Jundela's people, forming a close association with these hard people. The Arab Spring became their chance to dominate all of Libya and beyond.

Joining the uprising they used their new skills to take over a large section of the inland country, while freedom fighters battled over the coastal towns. Through their contacts, they had allowed Gaddafi's officers and men to join them, promising them untold riches if they changed sides. Soon their forces equalled Gaddafi's; all they had to do was wait and let the freedom fighters wear Gaddafi forces down. Then his brother had made a mistake, which cost them dearly.

Jundela at the time had been leading their forces in Chad and Niger when the news of the disaster reached him. His father the Sheik and many loyal supporters had been slaughtered, and his brother shot in the spine. Jundela had cried like a baby when his brother was returned to their fortress in the centre of their tribal lands. Unable to walk or do anything other than sit, was his punishment. He couldn't talk or even be a man with a woman; all he could do was see. His eyes became his outlet, his way of showing his emotions when not filled with hate, as they were now.

"You should never have taken the hostages, my brother. Better to have killed them all?" Jundela whispered, his brother's eyes blinking rapidity as if he was indicating he remembered. "It is in the past, my brother. Soon we will have our revenge and honour our father's memory, little brother. Then we can turn all of Africa into an Islamic state."

THE VISITOR

Peter sat in the dark watching the outside window. Several minutes ago, a shadow had moved past it, continuing around the back of his father's home. Whoever it was, knew enough to know where he lived and Gina had confirmed that he hadn't asked for his address. Peter felt a touch of fear, for whoever he was, he moved well, as despite him seeing the shadow, he'd heard nothing. After watching for ten minutes, Peter started to relax thinking the stranger had gone.

Moving to the window, he flirted with the idea of climbing outside. This thought was swiftly squashed, when the floor creaked in the hallway outside his room. Turning to face the door, Peter took aim, releasing the safety catch.

"I judge you're in there Peter?" A deep male voice asked from outside. Peter's mouth opened remembered that voice, although it made no sense.

"Steve, is that you?"

"Yes, it is. Although I suppose someone could mimic me?" Steve replied slowly opening the door and walking in, hands raised in the air.

"They said you were dead?" Peter stammered out, his grief at the loss of his parents bubbling to the surface. Moving to Peter, Steve embraced him.

"They came for me to Peter. I was careless and had let my guard down. I didn't check my boat before letting Natasha onboard. The bastards planted a bomb on it, Natasha, took the full impact. I was thrown clear."

"They killed both my parents and Aaron and his wife." Peter sobbed, both men sharing their grief. "When I went to check on their deaths they came after me, otherwise I'd have believed it." Finished they broke apart their shared emotions ended, as they turned on a light and sat down.

"Your friend Bart said it was the French Government, is that true?"

"Yes, they paid a bunch of assassins a lot of money to wipe your unit out. The question is why?"

"I judge you took care of the assassins?"

"They won't be doing any more contracts."

"I find it hard to believe the French Government is behind this. Although it's got to be some high up official to have this much clout and money."

"Jeffries, the leader of this group, had someone on the inside who supplied passports for the group. He's got to be the link?"

"Would Gina know?" Steve asked.

"Let's find out."

Bart and Gina had just finished packing when Gina's phone rang.

"Don't answer it. Let's go," Bart warned her, sounding scared.

"Only Peter knows this number. He could be hurt?" Gina replied, answering the phone.

"Is that you Peter?"

"Yes, Gina and I'm okay," Peter answered, as Bart took the phone.

"Peter its Bart, did you take care of the problem?" Bart in a round about way asked.

"Yes, the problem turned out to be an ally. We're working together now."

"What do you want Peter we're leaving, and the phone's not going with us?"

"Does Gina know who Jeffries had inside the French Government?" Peter asked. Turning to Gina, Bart repeated the question.

"I'm not sure. He used my father a lot, but he hasn't got that much power. Wait a minute. He's been spending a lot of time with the Foreign Affairs Minister Fredrick Genet lately. They have a shared interest in helping the poor, which is bullshit."

"She says he spent a lot of time with Frederick Genet the Foreign Minister," Bart told Peter, who in turn told Steve. Steve nodding signalled for Peter to end the call.

"Good luck Bart. Look after Gina," Peter told him.

"You too Peter. I'd say keep out of trouble, but better to tell you to keep your head down." Bart smiled, as the line went dead. Bart staring at the phone dropped it on the ground and smashed it.

"Let's get out of here love." He smiled, grabbing the last bag.

"Will Peter be alright?"

"I don't know. Although he seems to have a professional friend with him now?"

"That man saved our lives, Bart?"

"Yeah, the guy moved like a ghost," Bart said then stopped. "Well, I'll be fucked he's not dead."

"Who isn't?" Gina asked.

"Best you don't know love. Let's go." He smiled as hand in hand they left the apartment for the last time.

Two days after the attack on Jeffries' business, Frederick Genet sat in his office reading a report from French Intelligence. Jeffries and a substantial number of his associates were either dead or in prison. He'd seen the story on the news the day before, although he didn't know what had occurred. Even with this intelligence report handed on from British Intelligence MI5, no one could be sure what exactly happened. It would appear from several witnesses who luckily survived, that it was surprisingly the work of two men.

Some sort of vendetta the report suggested. Gina, Jeffries' wife had fled fearing for her life the report also mentioned. Genet knew from talking to Jeffries that Ali's son Peter had been seen in Paris when Jeffries' organisation, was first hit. Like his father the kid was ruthless. It hadn't taken him long to find out about his parent's death and who was responsible.

"What a fuck up?" Genet said out loud.

"I judge we have a problem?" A voice announced from the lone chair across from Genet's desk.

"Yes. The son of one of the original targets has become a nuisance."

"My benefactor paid you and Mr Jeffries a lot of money to make all the targets go away, except the girl of course. He won't be happy if his plans are upset by your failure." The voice answered, laced with menace.

"Do not come into my office and threaten me. You might be Libya's new Ambassador Makalu, but to me, you're just another dirty Arab with oil. I'll take care of my end of the deal; you'd better deliver yours. Now get out." Genet ordered, as two plainclothes security men entered his office.

"Escort the Ambassador out thank you, men," Genet told his security, as the Ambassador stood up.

"I know where the door is Genet. You have two weeks." He warned, before leaving. Genet stared after him until the door closed. Once it had, he wiped his forehead feeling the sweat. He was shit scared, and he feared the upstart Ambassador knew it. Pacing the floor, he thought about a way out of his problem. When this operation began, he had at first thought to use the French Intelligence service to take care of the targets.

Wanting secrecy, he had instead used his old friend Jeffries. He had failed miserably. Genet knew France needed Libya's oil. With world supplies dropping and the price of a barrel of oil rising drastically, French industries needed a dependable, cost effective supply. Makalu's guarantee of cheap fuel had persuaded him to accept the secret conditions, which at first had seemed easy. Now he had real doubts that all the targets could be neutralised.

There was also another problem, Jeffries link to him. Although there was no paper trail, this Peter Moustaffer may through other means, mainly torture, find the connection. Knowing it was too late for secrecy, he decided to have the French Intelligence community, take care of the problem. Looking at the clock above the door, he saw it was just on nine thirty in the morning, in other words, morning tea time. Pushing the intercom button he called to his aide to send his coffee in. Receiving no answer, he walked to the closed office door and opened it.

To his shock, he found his aide, his two security guards and the Libyan Ambassador, lying on the floor their arms and legs tied.

"What is the meaning of this?" He shouted in fear, as a gun appeared beside his head. Turning to his left, he found two masked men standing against the wall beside the door.

"The Foreign Minister I presume?" A mature voice mocked.

"How dare you come," was all he got out as the gun flashed towards his face breaking his nose. Overwhelmed with pain, he dropped to the floor.

"You killed my parents you piece of shit!" a younger voice growled as a boot-covered foot, crashed into his side. Rolling in agony Genet tried to think of a way out of an excruciating death at the hands of these madmen.

"I am a patriot," he announced as the gun pushed into the side of his head again.

"Bullshit you are. You took money to kill innocent people you murderer," the young voice snapped.

"How about you ambassador? Are you going to shed some light on what's going on?"

"I will tell you nothing. My master will have his revenge. Already he has your woman." He laughed. This caused both masked men to look at each other.

"Yes, the tramp who shot our Sheik and his son will feel a thousand blades before she begs for death."

"Who is your master?" The older voice demanded, placing a knife against the Ambassador's throat.

"I will tell you nothing," he reiterated, as the knife moved away from is neck, plunging into his left shoulder. Groaning the Ambassador started saying his prays.

"Waste of time," the older voice said as the knife withdrew from the shoulder wound, slashing his throat. Gurgling, the Ambassador in shock, reached for his throat to try and stem the flow of blood. Collapsing face first onto the floor, he thrashed about like a chicken with its neck broken, before going still. The two guards and the aide stared at the dead man in absolute horror, as Genet kept his eyes closed, too frightened to look.

"Who's next Genet? You or one of your guards?" The older man stated, his knife touching Genet's throat.

"Wait please, I'll tell you."

"Why were we targeted?" Peter, the young one asked.

"It was your own fault. You left witnesses when you went on your little raid to Libya," he told them. "The Sheik you killed, eldest son, was away at the time and now controls a large part of Libya. He paid for the hits and the delivering of your girlfriend," he smiled seeing his words hit home. The barrel of a pistol striking his face took the smile away.

"What is this new sheikh's name?" Steve asked.

"Mahomet Jundela and unlike his brother who you left a cripple, Jundela is a professional."

"Why does he want the girl alive?" Peter asked.

"She shot his brother. He wants to torture her then kill her in front of him, to ease his pain."

"Where is his base?" Peter whispered.

"No one knows. It's hidden in the desert about three hundred miles south of Tripoli somewhere," Genet confessed.

"How much were you paid?" Steve growled.

"Twenty million and the supply of France's future oil needs. You must admit it is a good deal for this country?"

"How and where did you deploy Marlise's unit?" Peter asked stepping in close. Genet felt a touch of fear by Peter's proximity.

"I asked for her elite unit to patrol just north of the Libyan border to check on the movement of terrorists along the border. Jundela was informed of their drop zone. Once they were on the ground, I had the radio link severed."

"Do you know the radio frequencies?" Steve barked, his face blank.

"No, but my assistant does." Genet smiled, just before Peter cut his throat. A shocked look came over Genet, as pain momentarily replaced surprise. Gurgling he tried to speak, before joining the Ambassador in hell. The assistant, of course, was only too glad to give them the frequencies. Having gained all they needed they made to leave. The relieved assistant and the two guards bound on the floor had thought they'd join their boss.

"Thank you." The assistant murmured his eyes full of tears.

"You three were just doing your jobs; we have no quarrel with you," Peter told them from the door.

"If it's any help I think Jundela's men failed to capture the paratroopers sent. I heard the Minister arguing yesterday with someone about it." He told Peter. To Peter, this was more than just good news.

"Thank you. You're a better man than your employer." Peter told him, dropping a knife on the floor next to him so he could untie himself. Once the two masked men had closed the door, the assistant cuts his bindings then moved to the two guards cutting theirs. All three realised their boss was in league with the Libyans, and none of them gave a second thought to trying to stop the two masked men leaving the building.

Clear of the Foreign Minister's building, Peter and Steve took off their masks and drove out of Paris heading back towards Switzerland.

"I'm so sorry Steve. My family's problem in Libya is why we were all targeted." Peter broke down, as Steve pulled over.

"Your father was a good man Peter. He saved me more than once, and I don't blame you for Natasha's death. I knew when your father called, that rescuing your sister and her husband would be risky. That said your sister was well worth the risk. If anyone is to blame it's this Jundela, the remaining son of the sheikh. A wise man would've moved on knowing they brought it on themselves."

"Would you have?" Peter asked.

"No. Like Jundela, I'm not a wise man," Steve smiled. Looking at the motorway, Peter saw Steve veer to the right and head south.

"I thought we were going back to my place?"

"You're never going back home, Peter. I'm sorry my friend, but you killed a Minister of the French Government. If he were evil or not, the Government would want you taken care of. It's best if you keep away from your home and your family. Like your father and the rest of our unit, moving, never staying in one place too long, is the best option for you."

"You are probably right. That aside, I judge you have a plan?"

"We'll see. I'm going on a hunch." Steve confessed, as Peter put his head back and slept while Steve drove. Sleeping, he thought back to Libya and his sister.

MISTAKES IN THE PAST

Ali sat, eating his breakfast in his office looking at the phone. It had been three weeks since his daughter and her righteous husband, had travelled to Libya. They had gone to help with the humanitarian situation gripping the country, caused by the Arab Spring. Hussein, a surgeon fresh out of University had volunteered to work in a United Nation's field hospital in supposedly neutral territory. Michelle, his daughter, was a trained nurse and had decided to go with him. Despite Ali's warnings not to go, that it was too dangerous, two young lovers had journeyed to Libya, as if it was a holiday.

"Call me every week or at least send an email daily." Ali had begged them before they left. Getting a, 'you worry too much' look, they, in the end, had promised to at least send emails. Now, after spasmodic calls and messages over the last few weeks, he found he hadn't received one for five days. Staring at the phone, he thought of the trouble he'd be in with his daughter if it were just that they had been too busy. His gut feeling, in the end, made him pick it up and dial.

Contacting the United Nation first, he received a 'we'll check if we get time' answer, from a like-minded young person like his son-in-law, who thought the United Nations was untouchable. Not happy, he used his bank connection ringing the Swiss Foreign Office. Speaking to the Minister who had several accounts at their bank, some unknown to his wife, he got some action. By seven that night his worst fears were realised.

The foreign affairs office confirmed there had been a raid by a tribal group on the hospital. The patients had been slaughtered, the hospital staff taken for ransom. With limited resources the Swiss could tell him little, so he rang Peter. Being in the Swiss Special Forces gave him access to a higher level of Intel. Through a back-door the Swiss kept with the American's CIA, he received up to date satellite surveillance of not only the raid on the hospital but real time photos of where the hospital staff, were imprisoned.

Breaking a few rules, Peter downloaded the data to his laptop, bringing it home for his father. Taking extended leave, Peter, arrived home to find Aaron, one of his father's closest friends, there as well. After comforting his mother who took her daughter's kidnapping badly, Peter left her with Petra, Aaron's wife, while the men, went over the Intel. One look at Aaron's face told Peter everything.

"This is bad Ali. This old army headquarters is a fortress; we will need a few more men to breach their defences."

"Hey, you aren't thinking of going yourselves are you?" Peter blurted out.

"Why wouldn't we?" Ali asked, as Aaron knowing what Peter was referring to chuckled.

"Dad you're both in your late fifties. That's old for soldiers." If Peter was trying to be subtle, it didn't work.

"We're not marching through Libya Peter. I'd say there'd only be a little actual walking." Ali answered, his eyes daring his son to say more.

"He's right Ali. We're getting on, we need new blood," Aaron interrupted. Ali seemed disappointed Aaron hadn't backed him, as he sat silently thinking, before he answered.

"What do you suggest Peter?"

"I could ask some of my men."

"You'd never get permission, and the Swiss Government would never stand for it," Ali pointed out. Stumped Peter remained quiet.

"How about Mercenaries Ali?" Aaron suggested.

"Soldiers for hire are a security risk. There's serious money in play here, and we don't want anyone changing sides. It's too risky."

"How about Marlise? She's good soldier." Peter put forward.

"Yes she is Peter, and she is also your girlfriend. Do you really want to put her in danger?" Aaron warned.

"She's a paratrooper in an elite French unit, and her speciality is as a sniper. She could be our cover?" Ali looked at Aaron who nodded his acceptance.

"Okay, that's one, who else?" Ali asked.

"Ring Steve, Ali," Aaron suggested, watching Ali bristle.

"That is unfair Aaron. He is out of it," Ali snapped. Peter sat there remembering the old Australian SAS soldier. Like the others, he was past it, although Peter knew from his father that Steve was special.

"Call him Ali. We need him," Aaron pleaded.

"Even if he comes, that's only five of us," Ali pointed out.

"Look, whoever these terrorists are, they must have enemies?" Peter put in.

"You're right son. Let's get to Libya and find out where these murderers are live. They left a lot of people dead at that hospital, and someone will want justice."

"I know a few people over there; I'll make some calls," Aaron suggested, as Ali nodding his acceptance, picked up his phone.

It was the hardest call Ali had ever made. Steve had found peace, which he deserved. How could he ask him to come back to a life he hated? Wiping his eyes Ali listened to the phone ring, hoping he wasn't home. A crackle as it answered, made him groan. The voice on the other end hearing the groan hesitated.

"Steve Roberts, who is it?"

"It's Ali Steve. I need your help," Ali got out, his voice cracking.

"What's wrong my friend?"

"They have kidnapped my baby girl and her husband," Ali sobbed.

"I'm on my way," Steve answered hanging up. Ali sat there looking at the phone. He didn't ask why or where or what the danger was waiting there, he was just coming. Aaron and Peter sat across from him wondering what was said.

"What did he say?" Peter in the end asked.

"He's coming."

Three days of planning and waiting found Ali and Aaron at the Zurich airport. Steve had informed them of his flight time, so together, they stood silently waiting. Checking his watch, Aaron, saw they had another twenty minutes, when a tap on his shoulder made him turn. Behind him stood Steve Roberts.

"God Steve where'd you come from?" Aaron said out loud, first in French having been surprised, then in English.

"I took an earlier flight, Aaron. Some habits die hard.

"Thank you, Steve for coming. I had no right to ask you." Ali apologised, quickly wiping his eyes.

"You would've done the same for me, my friend," Steve replied, hugging first Ali, then Aaron.

"I should've known you'd come on a different flight?" Aaron smiled, grabbing one of Steve's bags, as they left the airport. Once inside Ali's vehicle the three friends for several minutes sat in silence as Ali negotiated the roadway out of the airport. Once free of the heavy traffic Steve broke the silence.

"What happened?"

"My son-in-law is a surgeon. He and my daughter volunteered to travel to Libya to help with the Red Cross treating casualties from the fighting. I warned them of the danger, but they went anyway, I feel such a fool for letting them go." Ali stopped talking holding back tears. "They'd been there for five weeks when they stopped emailing me, so I made a few calls. It appears one of the tribal groups opposing Gaddafi, attacked the hospital without warning. They massacred the patients and staff, taking all the westerners for ransom."

"Do we know where they're being held?" Steve asked, his voice emotionless.

"Yes. There's an abandoned fort in the desert to the south of Benghazi. It was one of Gaddafi's fortified positions, used during the tribal wars about twenty years ago. Despite its age, it's an impressive stronghold." Aaron told him, handing him several pictures. Steve one by one examined them.

"How many men have we got?" Steve asked.

"Peter, his girlfriend and the three of us. I thought once we got to Libya we'd find allies," Ali replied. Even he thought it sounded lame.

"Piece of cake," Steve responded, as the other two turned momentarily to look at him before Steve burst into laughter.

"It's not funny Steve." Ali rebuked him, Aaron beside him trying not to laugh.

"Can you put together the money for the ransom Ali?" Steve asked.

"You think we have that little chance?"

"We have two barely trained, but fit soldiers and three mean, yet old men. There is also our phantom army of Libyan patriots, willing to lay down their lives for westerners. Pay the ransom. We can tag along to make sure it goes smoothly," Steve suggested.

"The Bedouin tribe involved, have a history of taking hostages for money, then killing them once the money is paid. They're fanatical in their religious beliefs Steve there will be no exchange." Ali admitted, his voice taking on a frail sound, something no one had ever heard from Ali before. Steve, like Aaron, sat there in silence taking in this new information.

"Then let's go get them. How long till the ransom's due?" Steve asked.

"One month, that's all we've got," Ali confessed.

"Like I said, a piece of cake," Steve replied. This time they all laughed.

Arriving at Ali's home found Julie, Ali's wife, a mess. Petra, Aaron's wife, was comforting her. At Steve's arrival, she fell to pieces, sobbing. Pulling herself together, she hugged him.

"I'm sorry Steve, it's just you being here means Ali thinks the ransom won't work, doesn't it?" Julie asked, her voice a whisper.

"Don't give up hope Julie. You know me, I don't fail." Steve assured her, his eyes misting up too. Ali stood in the background crestfallen as Aaron talked to Petra who then came forward and led Julie away. Once Julie was out of sight, Ali led the others into his home and to his study, where Peter and Marlise were waiting. Greetings were exchanged, with the minimum of speaking, all there felt the gravity of the situation overhanging them.

"Alright Ali, you're our Captain, what have you planned?" Steve asked as he stared at a mock up of the Libyan fort.

"The operation I have worked out is quite simple. We give them what they want. We deliver the ransom, right through the front gate." Ali exclaimed leaving everyone stunned. "Of course ours will be slightly different," Ali added, as he laid out his idea. When he had finished his outline of the mission, he looked at the faces around the study.

"Anyone got any questions?" He asked as a silence gripped the room, broken by Marlise.

"You're kidding aren't you?"

THE MISSION

Phase one of the plan, 'getting there' proved easier than expected. Aaron, who lived near the Mediterranean in the south of France, volunteered for this assignment. Ali after seeing air travel was too dangerous, asked him to locate a suitable vessel to cross to Libya. Travelling along the coast, Aaron with the help of a local contact, found a high-speed cruiser belonging to a rich, but absent American owner.

Moored at his seafront mansion south of Monaco all they had to do was pacify the house staff, while they borrowed it.

Two nights after their meeting, they turned up at the house at seven in the evening. Dressed in black and armed to the teeth, made the rental security guards and housemaids very accommodating. Securely tied up, Ali's team loaded up the boat and set sail. At a top speed of fifty knots, the sixty-foot boat practically flew south. By the time the theft and the staff had been discovered the next day, they were halfway across the Mediterranean. By early morning on the following night, they had reached their demarcation point south of Benghazi.

Landing on a supposedly deserted beach, they were met by one of Aaron's associates, who had also arranged passage for forty people going in the opposite direction on their borrowed boat. Once the craft was refuelled, Aaron did some quick handshakes in the dark, before they were escorted to a vehicle. While the car weaved its way into town, Aaron talked freely to the driver, as if they were best friends.

Steve wasn't the only one who wondered if wine growing was all Aaron was into. Handed on to another shadowy associate the group found themselves on a secluded estate on the southern desert side of town. Despite being away from the fighting, damage around the city was widespread, meaning that at this stage of the war; Gaddafi's air force still ruled the skies. After a swift but diligent sweep of the area, the group set up inside, while Peter and Marlise kept watch, outside.

"Well we're here, that's a start." Ali pointed out, as Steve silently looked over some up to date photos of the target.

"How are your friends going in the search for volunteers?" Steve absentmindedly asked Aaron, while studying the photos.

"Slow. My contacts here are limited." Aaron divulged, getting a raised eyebrow from both his friends. "Hey I know people," Aaron added, sensing their looks.

"They buy wine from you do they?" Ali asked, Steve, hiding a smile.

"A little, although on occasions I've helped them purchase other goods."

"Weapons I judge?" Steve suggested.

"They're fighting for their lives here against a well-armed enemy. Someone who can help with modern weaponry could be considered a necessity and an ally." Aaron defended himself.

"So, you do it for love?" Ali asked, hiding a grin as Aaron became flustered.

"I make a small profit that's all." He confessed, looking embarrassed, making his friends grin at each other.

"Well, your friends here have proved invaluable so far Aaron. I suggest we move to phase three and contact these kidnappers," Ali put forward, as their smiles faded.

"What if the UN or the Red Cross have already been there to negotiate the prisoner's release?" Steve asked Ali.

"Then it's all over, and we've come here for nothing. We have to go on the belief that the UN or the Red Cross thinking they are untouchable and will drag their feet over paying millions of dollars to terrorists. My contacts in the Swiss Government tell me nothing has been planned yet, as they both think the terrorists won't go through with their threats."

"Did he tell you how many staff members are they are holding Ali?" Aaron enquired.

"Forty-three, including my daughter and her husband."

"They are fools to doubt these monsters' threats. The Bedouin are nothing more than murderous thugs, out to make a living off the death's of the innocent." Aaron warned as Ali's face betrayed his fear for his child.

"Then let's not delay another minute. Time is everything now. Let's go meet these tribesmen?" Steve proposed, Ali and Aaron, nodding their support.

As per the video that the United Nations had received, the terrorists asked for a representative to meet them at a crossroad thirty miles south of Benghazi, after first leaving a white flag at the city's southern gate. Steve and Aaron would negotiate, while Peter, Marlise and Ali covered them. Ali, of course, wasn't happy at not doing the negotiations. Steve warned him that he was too emotional to handle it.

Looking at Steve about to argue, Ali looked at the other's faces. He saw worry on them for him. Going silent, he nodded that he understood letting it slide.

"Okay let's do it tomorrow morning. Everyone check your gear, we can't have any stuff ups," Steve warned, as the meeting broke up.

Leaving at six in the morning, Steve and Aaron arrived at the southern gates at eight. Aaron hopping out of their jeep planted a white flag in the ground before jumping back in. Steve sitting in the jeep looking in the rear vision mirror saw a Bedouin tribesman behind them raise a phone to his ear.

"Couldn't see anyone?" Aaron admitted, as Steve put the jeep into gear and drove off.

"They saw you, that's all that matters." Steve pointed out, seeing an old truck drive out of a side road behind him.

"I hope Ali's isn't delayed?" Aaron answered, watching the truck take station about one hundred yards behind them.

"Yeah, I'd hate to join the other forty-three hostages."

Behind them, in the truck, Mohammed Jundela's younger brother Miguel, watched the vehicle in front cruise along as if it was sightseeing in the country.

"Do you think they know we are following Miguel?" One of his men asked.

"I'd say they have known that since we left the town." Miguel smiled.

"They don't appear to be concerned?" Bazra, Miguel's friend and right-hand man, pointed out.

"Yes. That in itself is a problem." Miguel smiled.

"Why do you say that?" Bazra asked.

"They're driving through a war zone to discuss the payment of ransom to a group of terrorists, yet they show no fear. That leads me to believe that these men are no strangers to violence."

"Do you think it's a trap?" Another man asked from the rear.

"No, I just think whoever has organised this meeting, knows his stuff and has employed either ex-soldiers or mercenaries. Either way, I would suggest being very careful when we arrive at the meeting place." Miguel warned, smiling slightly at his men's apparent nervousness.

In front of them, Steve spotted the burnt out tank, indicating the meeting place. Pulling over, he turned the truck around facing back the way they'd come. Next, to him, Aaron fingered one of the two AK47s they'd brought with them.

"Stay in the truck and be ready. I'll do the talking." Steve suggested. Not waiting for an answer, he opened his door and jumped out. Adjusting his pistol in the back of his pants, Steve leaned against the tank as the old truck approached. Pulling up on the opposite side of the road, eight men jumped out. Six immediately took cover around and behind the truck, as the two remaining men walked out into the middle of the road. Steve without a backwards glance joined them.

"I hope you speak English?"

"Yes, I do, from my time at Oxford." The younger one answered with an arrogant smirk. Steve looked at the young man's stance, sensing by his attitude to be either in charge or close to it. The thought of holding him hostage and exchanging him for the people kidnapped crossed his mind. Taking out the other men Steve considered could be tricky, so he let it slide.

"Good. You have two hostages I want." Steve began, as the young man stopped him.

"Aren't you here on behalf of the UN for all the hostages?" Miguel, the arrogant one, asked surprised.

"I couldn't give a shit about them, I'm being paid to retrieve just two of them."

"Then how did you know to meet here? Only the UN knows about this meeting place?" Miguel growled.

"My employer has immense power and wealth; I'd say he bribed someone." Steve smiled.

"This meeting is over," Miguel announced, turning to leave.

"He will pay twenty million for the two." Steve barked, stopping Miguel in his tracks.

"That is nearly half what we wanted for the forty we hold. Why so much for those two." Miguel asked.

"I cannot divulge that information, only that they are family to my benefactor."

"Why not just wait for the UN to pay?" Miguel asked.

"My benefactor believes you won't hand over anyone, even if you get the money. That is why he hired us to negotiate."

"He knows us?"

"He knows of your reputation, Miguel." At Miguel's name being mentioned Miguel and Bazra tensed.

"You know my name?"

"Yes and your tribe Miguel. Like I said my employer knows a great deal about your group," Drawing his pistol, Bazra pointed it at Steve, as Miguel's men near the truck, aimed.

"You sure you want to do that?" Steve asked as Bazra's pistol exploded in his hand. Screaming with pain Bazra gripped his bleeding hand, as Miguel's men took cover behind their truck. Steve moving forward took out his handkerchief. Wrapping it around Bazra's hand, he tied it off. Reaching into a side pocket, he retrieved a bandage and wrapped it around the handkerchief.

"That should hold it. You were lucky you didn't lose any fingers?" Steve smiled, as a slightly frightened Miguel, signalled to his men to relax.

"I judge you at some time in your past were Special Forces or something?" Miguel calmly asked. Looking around at the surrounding hills, he saw nothing.

"Something like that. Well, Miguel do we have a deal?"

"What are the hostages' names?"

"Look if I tell you that, you might single them out for special treatment. Better when we bring the money, that we'll pick them out of the crowd."

"You think we'd spirit them away and ask for more money. That's not very trusting?" Miguel pointed out.

"Is it a deal?" Steve was blunt.

"In a week's time, you will meet one of my men here. If you have the money, he will guide you to where we're holding the hospital staff. Once there you can pick out your employer's family members. Do you find the conditions agreeable?"

"Yes, Miguel. But be warned, trying to deceive us will go badly for you." Steve warned, before walking back to their vehicle and jumping in. Aaron, waiting, immediately started up and drove away.

Miguel stood in the road watching Steve and Aaron drive off. Cursing, he spat in the direction they were travelling. Walking across to their men, Miguel, examined Bazra's hand.

"You were right Miguel they were professionals." Bazra groaned as Miguel looked over the dressing Steve had applied.

"It isn't serious Bazra you were indeed lucky."

"Do you intend to go through with the meeting?"

"Yes, they will get to see the two hostages they want, just before I butcher them."

"Is that wise? They could be a danger to us."

"My thoughts exactly Bazra. That is why I cannot afford to let them go. Better to kill them all than have to worry about them in the future," Miguel chuckled his men laughing on queue.

Back at the estate, Ali led the debriefing.
"How did it go?" Ali asked Steve.
"As expected, you were right Ali; they will not honour the agreement.
"So the bug worked?" Ali asked.
"Yeah. After Marlise, shot Miguel's second in command, I dressed his wound and planted a bug on him. When we were driving back, we heard them discussing our demise."
"Planting that bug was good thinking Aaron. Until Miguel's man washes his pants, we should pick up some more Intel." Steve smiled.
"Shows us old guys still know something."
"Yeah, but it was one of the young ones that shot the gun out of that guy's hand. Could you have done that?" Peter interjected.
"Let's stop comparing dick sizes and get on with it," Marlise snapped, silencing the men. Steve beside her grinned momentarily, before becoming serious.
"Well we know where we stand now, do we proceed to the next step?" Steve asked.
"Yes. We all know what to expect from these people now, so we'll give them what they want," Ali smiled as a knock came from the front door. Looking towards it, Ali saw the others grab their weapons and move to their pre-determined positions. Happy with their professionalism, he walked casually to the front door. Standing outside were at least twenty men and women, some bearing arms.
Surprised, Ali for the first time since arriving in the country, reached for his pistol. It was then that he spotted one of Aaron's friends who had driven them from the beach, standing at the rear. Seeing Ali, he came forward.
"Good afternoon Mr Moustaffer." He called out in English.

"Tori! You nearly gave me a heart attack." Ali exclaimed, making some of the men and women outside smile. "Who are your friends?"

"I am sorry Mr Moustaffer, but you asked for help, in let's say your coming adventure. These men are related one way or another to the people taken or killed. They have been waiting for someone who could help them right this wrong." Ali looked at the gathered men and women. Some looked fit, others not so.

"Put up your hand if you speak English," Ali ordered. Nearly half complied. "That is good as one of us speaks only a little French." Steve embarrassed shrugged his shoulders.

"Hey, no one said the French language was compulsory."

"Anyway, you people will buddy up with the ones that don't. Do that now and know that the man you pick must watch your back." Ali warned, seeing a slight uneasiness amongst the crowd. Pulling Aaron's friend to the side, he spoke softly. "Have you done any checks on our recruits?"

"Yes, Mr. Moustaffer. All are indeed related to the hostages or are friends. Although some could be plants."

"Thank you, Tori; we'll take it from here," Ali told him walking him to his car.

"One other thing Mr Moustaffer. There are men in town looking for you. They belong to a Bedouin tribe called the Youstisy. They are no friends of the west I can assure you," Tori warned, before climbing into his car.

"We will keep watch Tori don't worry. And call me Ali, I'm old enough already."

"I know a bit of Aaron's and your background Ali. I won't worry too much." Tori grinned driving off. For the hundredth time since he'd arrived here, Ali wondered what Aaron had been up to?

Walking back to the gathered men and women, Ali led them around the back where now his team was gathered. Both groups were silent as they weighed up the opposite group. Aaron, who had a grasp of their language, introduced everyone, before telling them all to change into their field gear. The training he told them, started immediately. Steve watching the group, looked for anything out of the ordinary, so far he found nothing worrying.

"What do you think Steve?" Ali asked, in a low voice coming up beside him.

"They're a mixed bunch all right. Although so are we."

"Can we trust them?" Ali whispered.

"That's something we'll find out in time. For now, let's confiscate all communication devices and then divide them into groups for training."

"Do you think there is a spy?" Ali asked.

"Without doubt Ali. Related to the victims or not, the kidnappers had good Intel when they raided the hospital. Someone told them, and they could be here now," Steve warned, his eyes still watching the recruits.

After their initial training that day, Ali taking stock broke the group into set squads. Marlise's group would be the cover squad, trained to lay down cover fire and snipe at the enemy forces. She received most of the least fit men and women, who would have trouble with the assault. Their only quality was their ability to hit targets at long range. Peter and Steve who would lead the assault, had the pick of the most promising men and women. Although training a group for an attack in under a week was, to say the least optimistic. Most had some military training; several were ex-soldiers trained in the army of their now enemy Gaddafi.

Ali and Aaron, on the other hand, trained the squad that would go in the front door with the money. Fitness, although needed, was not as important as working as a team. In their role, close in fighting in a tight knit group, would either kill them or win the day. That night after an exhausting day, they all gathered after a quick meal for a briefing. Ali explained the mission, getting shocked looks from the new members. Going into details seemed to placate their growing pessimism, some looking slightly relieved. Showing them a mud map of the position, brought a gasp from one of the recruits.

"What's wrong?" Ali asked Nadal, one of Steve's new squad members.

"I was stationed there once, when I was a trainee in Gaddafi's army."

"Is our map accurate?" Ali asked.

"Mostly, but it doesn't show the tunnels."

"Where are they?" Ali asked, the whole group moving closer to see.

"It was ten years ago, but I remember Gaddafi at one stage thought to make this into a retreat for him and his family. In case of trouble, he had the recruits, including me, build a series of tunnels in case they needed to hide or escape. Gaddafi has always been a cautious man." Nadal smiled, as the other laughed, thinking they were now at war with this cautious man. Drawing another outline of the fort, Nadal roughly sketched in a bunker system under the fort with two escape passages.

"It is not exact, but it is close," Nadal warned, as Steve looked hard at the tunnels.

"This is where I'd keep the hostages Ali."

"The exit from these tunnels, how are they secured?" Ali asked Nadal.

"The doors are steel and well camouflaged. Inside they have a booby-trap. If the door is opened from the outside without disconnecting it, it will explode."

"This is good news although they don't help us much. We will have to think about how this affects our original plan?" Peter pointed out.

"Let's sleep on it. Tomorrow we'll go over it again." Ali suggested as the group broke up. The twenty recruits, were sleeping in two outside areas. One held fourteen men, the other the six women. Like most Arab men there was a little hostility at having women in the ranks. Marlise had most of these women with her covering force, pointing out that covering the men gave them a little personal satisfaction. Most had husbands killed, or close family members taken and were willing to do anything to see justice done.

Already Marlise had singled out one as her second in command. Jasmine showed not only a good grasp of English, more importantly, she was also skilled with a sniper rifle. As the women turned in, Marlise put Jasmine in charge of the first watch.

"Watch for any sign of movement on the perimeter and make sure none of the men get frisky for a woman," Marlise warned.

"If they come to our tent they will leave without their manhood," Jasmine promised, her eyes dark.

"Good. At one, have Japora relieve you." Marlise ordered, moving towards the house, leaving Jasmine just a shape in the darkness. Jasmine, taking no chances, decided to do a swift check of the perimeter. Moving towards the men's' section, she found Aaron had instructed the men to post a guard as well. It was Turk, a rather tough looking man with a scar on the left side of his face.

He'd been helping fire an old mortar when a round had cooked off in the barrel. It had killed two other men, leaving Turk with a scarred face and body. She'd briefly seen his chest during training. It was crisscrossed with ugly scars. Approaching him, she made her presence known by stamping her foot.

"Scare" Turk challenged. She could see he had already lined her up with his weapon, showing he had been aware of her approach.

"Crow." She answered as Turk lowered his weapon.

"So little fighter you drew the first watch also." He smiled, his teeth visible in the darkness.

"Who else would keep watch over you?" She smiled back, hearing his suppressed laughter.

"Some day I will smack your bottom," He replied, his voice reflecting his interest in her.

"I look forward to it," She giggled, "But now, we have work to do." She sniggered moving on. Rounding the front of the house where the road came in, she either heard or sensed movement. Freezing she stood looking into the darkness as a hand wrapped around her mouth, making her struggle.

"Be silent Jasmine." Marlise's voice warned. "Get down on the ground and cover the road." As she complied, she watched Marlise move a little to her left and copy her, lying down. Jasmine for the first time in two years felt her fear return.

At the time, she had been part of a militia unit for only two months when it had occurred. She was with an odd collection of fellow civilian soldiers out to prove themselves against Gaddafi 's finest. Dug in along a back road, to shield an attack on the coast, a Bedouin unit had moved up to cover their flanks.

A sense of uneasiness had run through her group at the presence of these silent allies. This premonition of doom increased, as darkness slowly descended over the desert. To the west shells bursting and huge fires marked where another militia unit was positioned in front of theirs. The unease with their allies' proximity and the failure of their advance unit to the west was soon forgotten, as artillery started falling in front of their position. It continued for ten minutes before abruptly stopping.

A deadly silence developed as track vehicles could be heard approaching. Many considered joining the other militia unit, when five tanks supported by at least two hundred troops, crested the rise to their west. Even in the gathering darkness, the silhouettes of these victorious enemy forces could be seen against the fires burning behind them as they rushed towards their positions. Lacking heavy weapons made their position precarious, as to their surprise, the Bedouin tribesmen let loose with a barrage of rounds from several anti tank weapons.

The tanks caught in the open, were swiftly dealt with, as Jasmine's unit came to life, pouring round after round into the demoralised enemy troops. Gaddafi's force severely beaten, retreated over the rise, running for their lives. Cheering broke out from her victorious unit at the rout of their enemy. They had met the enemy and humiliated them with the help of the Bedouin. Leaving their prepared positions, they danced with each other drinking in the fact that they had survived their first battle. As one they approached the Bedouin fighters to thank them for their help.

To a man, they were cut down. Caught in the open, many having left their weapons behind, they were shot like dogs. Jasmine having been left behind to attend the casualties, watched in horror, as the Bedouin finished off the living, before advancing on their position. Terrified, knowing what these men did to women, she hid in a trench caving it in on top of herself. Leaving only a narrow slit for breathing she waited.

Fear gripped her, as she heard the screams of the wounded, the Bedouin taking their time with them. She lay in that hole for the rest of the night, fear paralysing her, every sound triggering a panic attack, as she lay frozen.

At daybreak, she had cautiously dug her head out enough to look around. The desert appeared devoid of life as she slowly crawled out of her hole, moving to a rise. Scanning the surrounding countryside, she saw her unit laid out in a line, all of them grossly disfigured. Vomiting she cried for her fellow soldiers ashamed she had survived. Finding a discarded rifle, she picked it up and started walking east towards their reserve battalion.

Halfway to safety, she was intercepted by a jeep like vehicle. Crying with relief, she waved her arms at the vehicle, as it roared towards her. Her relief swiftly turned to disbelief, as the vehicle with three Bedouin soldiers stopped beside her. All dressed in black they stared with eyes full of hatred at

Jasmine. Getting over the shock, she reacted. Aiming her rifle, she shot the driver point blank in the chest, as the other two leapt upon her.

"You will pay for the killing of our brother." One of them screamed, as drawing their knives, they swiftly cut her clothing from her body.

Staring at her athletic firm body, they both giggled insanely, before pinning her to the ground. Taking turns raping her, they seemed to get enjoyment from her every scream, rather than the actual rape itself. Finished with their entertainment, they staked her to the ground, as the suns heat burnt into her exposed body. Turning their vehicle around, they stared down upon their victim.

"The Prophet says it is unseemly for a woman to fight like a man. Have you got any words of forgiveness for your sins against Allah?"

Burn in hell, you cowards. If God wishes it, I will track you all down and kill every one of you," Jasmine screamed, as in answer to her prayer, a rocket propelled grenade impacted on the jeep. Both men were shredded, as the vehicle burst into flame. Jasmine finding her pegs securing her, had been blown from the ground, rolled away from the flames. Finding a weapon, she sheltered behind the burning jeep knowing whoever had killed her torturers could still be watching.

The sound of a vehicle moving off in the distance meant her presence had gone unnoticed as she hesitantly stood up. Naked, she searched for something to wear. Finding the driver she'd shot, she stripped him, donning his black clothing. Covered, she felt the heat leave her exposed skin. Badly burnt and barely able to walk from her abuse, she staggered on towards her battalion's position. With no water and severe burns, she only made two miles before she collapsed exhausted. The next thing she remembered was waking up in hospital a month later.

Her story of the Bedouin's treachery was hushed up, for fear of open warfare between the freedom fighters' coalition.

Instead, she was suspended from duty fearing reprisals from the Bedouin men she'd killed. Thankful to the hospital staff she had tagged along with them helping tend the wounded. She had struck up a friendship with a tall, good-looking doctor named Douglas who hailed from Scotland.

He knew her background and slowly built up her trust in men again. She had not slept with him fearing the intimacy of making love but had come to love him in her own way. Worried that she would lose him if she didn't sort out her problem, she had visited a local Mosque, praying for a solution. Meeting many women who had also been raped in this vile war, she realised it was silly to avoid the issue. Promising herself, she would make love with Douglas that night; she had hurried back to the hospital.

All she found was the tortured bodies of the ones not worth ransoming. Guiltily she in a way relieved, knowing Douglas, as a foreigner would have been taken, not killed. Going to the hospital's accommodation section, she hoped to find some clue as to where they'd been taken. One burnt body in the doorway halted her in her tracks.

Bending down her worst fears were confirmed as she saw the remains of a stethoscope, around the body's neck. At first, she prayed that it was just a medical staff member, not her beloved Douglas. Looking at the body, she took in its height, knowing only Douglas, was above average height in the group. Collapsing onto the ground beside him, she sobbed, until one of the survivors of the massacre approached her.

"He died because he fought them, allowing many including myself to escape," she told her crying. "I only returned to see if anyone else escaped," she sobbed, before running away, not wanting to stay longer. Jasmine recovering ran after her. Getting a description of the attackers, she found it matched the Bedouin of her nightmares. Burning with anger, she armed herself, searching for them. After a month she had found nothing.

It was then that she heard whispers through the grapevine of a group planning an attempt to rescue the hostages. She had immediately sought out the group, hoping to get her revenge. Now as she lay in the dirt, the vision of her abuse crashed against her sanity. Frightened beyond belief, she looked for a place to hide.

Turning towards Marlise, she saw her pull out a grenade, and then point in front of them. Jasmine turned to see five shadowy figures moving towards them. Coming back to reality, Jasmine, likewise pulled a grenade from her pocket. Focusing on the shadows, while watching Marlise for orders.

"Scare!" Marlise challenged, as the five figures turned to statues. When after several seconds no answer came, Marlise hurled the grenade towards the figures, followed by Jasmine. Screams in Arabic filled the night as both grenades exploded, with a brilliant flash of light. The five figures dropped to the ground either dead or wounded, as, behind them, another wave of figures could be seen advancing. Both women opened fire spraying the first five before concentrating on the others.

For a short time, Marlise and Jasmine held the upper hand inflicting casualties on the advancing phantoms. Unfortunately laying in the open soon found them running for cover. Hiding behind an old well, Jasmine felt the advantage slipping away as the enemy split, advancing from two different directions.

"What should we do Marlise? They will soon have us in a crossfire?" Jasmine shouted as Marlise signalled her to stay put. By now Jasmine could hear firing all around them, as Marlise, beside her, communicated with the others on her radio.

"Our teams are coming in from the sides," Marlise informed her, seeming unworried, she concentrated on the enemy troops in front of her. Jasmine, trusting her, continued to fire as well.

Marlise beside her although not showing it was indeed worried. Firing could be heard from all over the estate. She estimated that there could be a force of at least a hundred enemy fighters out there, slowly closing in on their positions. For now, the enemy seemed to be consolidating their gains, using their weight of numbers to wear down the defenders. 'Where was Peter?' she asked herself, worried for her lover.

Feeling the start of panic she focussed on the enemy, trying to pick them off by their weapon's flashes. Blinking, she watched several on the right side stop flashing, indicating they'd stopped firing. As she watched, she saw more flashes stop, as the darkness spread from right to left across the enemy positions. Soon there were no flashes, as the enemy weapons grew silent. Jasmine beside her looked to her for advice, as she too wondered what was going on.

"Marlise are you there?" Peter's voice sounded in the dark.

"Over here near the well." She answered as Peter and Turk appeared. Dropping down beside her, he gave her a quick hug before scanning the area in front of them.

"You two have been busy." Peter pointed out, looking at the bodies around the perimeter.

"Not really, just a little practice," Marlise answered, although her voice seemed to tremble slightly.

"Let's go out and do a sweep for any still alive?" Peter suggested.

"Is that a good idea? They all stopped shooting for some reason. They could be preparing an ambush." Marlise barked, thinking Peter was overconfident.

"Before the trouble started, Steve, Ali and Aaron made their way secretly outside the perimeter. I'd say the enemy is either dead or running?" Peter explained, leaving Marlise and Jasmine stunned. They had both believed that the older men were just the employers on this mission.

"They've been doing this for a long time," he explained, having seen their looks.

"He's right." A voice sounded in front of them, making them all jump. Not ten feet away stood a lump of grass holding a weapon.

"Stop showing off Steve." Aaron's voice resonated through the dark, as another lump of grass materialised beside the first, followed by another.

"Fuck Steve. We could've shot you!" Peter exclaimed. As Ali, Aaron and Steve walked past them.

"Fat chance of that, the way you four were shooting," Steve replied, as Ali and Aaron burst into laughter.

Inside Steve and the others removed their Gillis suits, as they were now called.

"Jesus Steve, you could have gotten us all shot sneaking up on those young ones." Ali erupted.

"Yeah, I didn't even see them till I was right on top of them. Can't believe my eyesight is that bad?"

"Well, you can still ghost along. You scared the shit out of them." Ali sniggered as the three separate units crowded into the lounge area. After a thorough search, forty-two bodies had been found. All were now confirmed dead.

"Does this mean the mission is scrubbed?" Peter asked, everyone, turning towards Ali.

"No the exchange is still going ahead. These men were not Bedouin fighters. My guess is they were friends of someone here, hoping to grab the ransom." At this statement, everyone went quiet.

"Are you sure? Everyone tonight did their best?" Peter pointed out, having done a round of the perimeter during the firefight.

"How many of our personnel were killed or injured Peter?" Ali asked.

"Two were killed another two received light injuries."

"Are all our volunteers here now?" Aaron asked. As the crowd looked around, Peter did a quick headcount.

"With the two dead, there should be eighteen; there are sixteen, plus our original group." Peter pointed out.

"Who is missing?"

"Jampora and Cade. They volunteered to stand watch." Jasmine told the others, meaning everyone was present.

"Did anyone see those two fighting?" Ali asked, his voice sounding as hard as steel. Blank looks came back. "Okay, no one saw them fight. Well did anyone see them resupply their ammo, before going on guard duty? He continued. Still, blank looks answered his questions. "Turk. Take two men and go check to see if they're still out there patrolling." Turk pointing to two men rushed outside. Two minutes had passed before they returned.

"They're gone, Commander!" Turk shouted angrily, as he entered.

"Right everyone. I want the three units to do a sweep towards the town. Marlise takes the right side of the roadway, Peter you take yours down the other. Steve and I will drive my unit towards town and backtrack. Get moving everyone. It is my opinion that either one or both ratted on us, before we took away their phones. If they make it to town with what they now know, it's all over," Ali snapped, as the room rapidly emptied.

"How do you know they didn't grab one of the attacker's vehicles?" Peter whispered.

"We disabled them before we mopped them up. No, they're on foot so we must hurry" Ali insisted, moving to the door.

Daylight was coming up as Ali's group swept back towards the estate. Gunfire earlier, meant one of their units had taken care of either one or both of the traitors. Until they met up with the two other units, they would continue searching. Steve out on the wing was the first to see movement. It was Jampora, and she was running wildly, scared to death. Steve raised his weapon and took aim, only to hesitate. He'd always had a blind spot for women. Even though he knew what was at stake, he couldn't shoot.

Jampora rushing towards him suddenly froze as she saw him.

"They will kill my husband if I don't help them," she cried out, making Steve signal her to stand still. Walking towards him, she collapsed onto the ground in front of him. "Don't kill me, Captain Roberts," she begged as a shot rang out. Jampora in front of him folded spinning along the ground. Jasmine then appeared behind her, cradling her sniper rifle.

"She was going to surrender Jasmine," Steve whispered, as Jasmine approached the body. Turning her over Jasmine pulled a pistol from her hand.

"For a warrior, you have much to learn about women."

"Yes, it's always been a failing with me," Steve whispered sadly, as between them they carried her body to the road.

News of the fighting on the outskirts of town, did reach Miguel. Most put it down to rogue soldiers looting some wealthy family. The exchange was now four days away, and as yet there hadn't been a whisper of what the mercenaries were up to. Miguel, when he had returned from his meeting with Steve, had told his father Sheik Abdul Hardaire of the meeting. Unlike his son, the Sheik felt the involvement of these mercenaries could mean trouble.

"You worry too much father. I have it in hand."

"Worrying is what has kept me alive when others died," his father replied.

"The exchange will be made outside the front gates of this fort. With a hundred of our best fighters here, the place is impregnable." Miguel retorted upset with his father's lack of trust in him.

"I wish your brother was here Miguel. He has a better understanding of these westerners." His father added, angering Miguel.

"My brother leads a fruitless campaign outside of Libya to the south, when he should be here father. I am quite confident I can handle this."

"He does the work of God my son. Never forget the importance of conquering the unbelievers. He also warned us against taking hostages in the middle of war Miguel. Now I wish we had heeded his advice."

"The money we receive for the hostages, helps fuel the overthrow of not only Gaddafi but these so called freedom fighters from the coastal cities. Jundela has lost sight of the true fight. Only by conquering the disbelievers here, can we consolidate our gains in the south." He angrily replied, his father raising his hand to silence him.

"Okay my son, we will do it your way on one condition. At the end of this week, I want the hostages taken care of, as well as these so called representatives of the two unknown hostages. There are to be no witnesses Miguel, kill them all."

"As you wish father?" Miguel smiled, thinking for once he had turned the tables on his brother.

"Bazra to me!" Miguel shouted watching the dust cloud to the north.

"Yes, Miguel what is it?" He asked as he reached him.

"My man at the crossroads reports that six men with the money have arrived there."

"All is ready Miguel. The men are in position."

"Remember. I don't want anyone to fire until I give the signal," Miguel told him. Bazra, nodding his understanding, moved back to the fort's front gates.

In the last two days before the exchange, Miguel had instructed his men to prepare their ambush. They had dug a series of trenches opposite the gate, which would cut down the westerners before they had time to dismount from their vehicle. Forty men manned the walls above the gate, with another twenty in the trenches. Forty others patrolled the rest of the fort, including the bunker where the hostages were being held.

At first, Miguel nervousness had made him opt to open fire, as soon as the vehicle stopped. Now, confident of his plan, he had decided to teach these westerners a lesson. Once he'd checked the money, he'd have one of them accompany two of his men to pick out the two hostages to be released. Once they had returned to the vehicle, he'd have the two prisoners' throats cut in front of their would be rescuers. He would then either, shoot the westerners or if possible disarm them.

If this happened, he'd have them staked out in the sun and watch them burn, while they slaughtered the other hostages in front of them. To his Bedouin tribe, this was their trademark punishment for all who opposed them. Happy thinking of the money which was about to flow into their coffers, he ordered his man at the crossroads to lead them to the fort.

At the crossroads Ali watched the Bedouin tribesmen gawk at the stack of dollar notes in the rear of their truck. Twenty million dollars took up a lot of room, leaving the minimum room for Ali's men. Swiftly he counted several stacks trying to work out if the correct amount was there. In the end, confident Miguel would check it too; he phoned Miguel. Smiling, Ali had one of his men translate to the tribesmen how happy he was to get the exchange completed. The tribesmen, in turn, grinned back, knowing their fate.

After the tribesmen's phone rang the second time, Ali knew they'd been given the green light to proceed. This was confirmed, when the tribesmen in a flurry of hand gestures pointed to the road to their left, which led to the fort. As the tribesmen gave them permission to drive, Ali signalled to Turk. Turk nodding his understanding used his radio contacting the other two teams. Getting two 'in position' in return signals from them, Turk gave Ali the thumbs up, as the truck started moving.

The tribesmen sitting next to the money in the back of the truck watched the exchange between Ali and Turk, sensed something was wrong. Looking again at the money, he watched as hitting a bump; a crack appeared on the side of the stack. Reaching down, he pulled at the crack, watching the top piles of money fall off. Shock made him stare into the steel box inside. The money only lined the outside with bundles on the top. Shock turned to terror as he saw the steel box was filled with ball bearings. Pushing his hands into the ball bearings, he pushed them aside to see slabs of C4 explosive filling the centre.

Reacting, he reached for his phone. Looking up, as he made ready to dial, he saw Ali beside him raise a silenced pistol. The tribesman without any thought for his own safety pressed the call button, as two coughs sounded from Ali's weapon, smashing the phone and sending the surprised tribesman onto the floor of the truck. Still alive, shot in the hand and chest, the tribesman looked up at Ali.

"You're a brave man. Miguel does not deserve you." Ali told him, before shooting him in the head. Climbing down from the truck, Ali moved to its front.

"Are we all ready?" Ali shouted out, to the men in the front cabin.

"Yes, commander." They both answered as the truck stopped. Jumping to the roadside, Ali's team ran to a gully beside the road, returning with six shop front-dummies, dressed as soldiers. Positioning them around the truck with two in the front, one of the men from the cabin handed Ali what looked like an overgrown model plane controller. Their truck, to all intents and purposes, was nothing more than a remote control model.

Peter had come up with the idea, having worked with the bomb squad in Switzerland. They had built a decoy truck for the Special Forces there, for use as target practice and simulated hostage situations. Aaron like usual had found an associate in the country, who had helped procure the necessary equipment. Ali came to the conclusion that except for Aaron's army of friends, this whole enterprise may never have gotten off the ground.

Finished with the deception, Ali's men armed themselves. Clinging to the side, they hung on, as Ali sitting on the front bonnet, drove the vehicle with the remote. Ten minutes found them on the rise overlooking the fort. Dust camouflaged them, as jumping from the vehicle, they moved into a ravine bordering the road. Here Ali found a spot where he could guide the truck to the fort's front gate. Signalling for his men to move down the hill towards the fort, Ali contacted the other two groups telling them the mission was a go.

On a ridge opposite the front gate, Marlise and her group looked down onto the enemies' ambush. She was lying next to one of her team members in a shell scrap dug out the night before. Sheltering under sand-coloured tarpaulins from the unrelenting heat, they were all but invisible. The ambush position she noticed had been well thought out, heavily camouflaged in the same manner as theirs was. The Bedouin's only mistake was not being regular soldiers and overconfident in their fortifications, they hadn't bothered to patrol the surrounding area.

Looking to the north, she saw no sign yet of Ali's truck, the road to the fort empty. Looking at her hands, she saw them tremble slightly, as the battle grew closer.

"Where is Steve Roberts?" She asked herself, knowing the new improvised plan, now rested on him. As if sensing her concern, Jasmine heavily camouflaged, slid in between her and Habra. Habra, Marlise had chosen to be with her, because he was by far, the best shot.

"Any word from Captain Roberts? " Jasmine whispered.

"No, although he did say his radio would be his fallback only," Marlise told her.

"If he had been caught, we would know by now." Jasmine pointed out.

"Yes, the fact we've heard nothing means he is still out there somewhere," Marlise replied.

"He is despite his age, deadly. The night of the attack, I nearly died when he appeared next to us." Jasmine confessed.

"In his day he must've been unstoppable?" Habra whispered. All the men had trained with Steve.

"Let us hope he still is?" Jasmine said softly crawling out of their dugout. Marlise after she'd left, thought about Steve, Ali and Aaron. Peter had told her only a brief history about their unit. Still, from other sources, she had gleaned a little insight into this elite unit. All reports said 'The Ghost' Steve Roberts was a silent ruthless killer, the likes of which had never been seen before. She'd smiled when she heard these stories thinking them nothing but fairy tales. Now as she lay in her dugout, she hoped to God they were true.

Aaron lay with Peter with the rest of their men. After spending the night looking for the elusive hidden entrances to the tunnels, they had found one in a dry creek bed. Aaron had originally been in Ali's team. With the discovery of the tunnel system, Ali had decided to send Steve in to find the hidden door from the inside. It was a major change in the plan, although if successful greatly improved their chances of minimising casualties.

Peter had been against Steve going alone, thinking the plan needed two men. Ali had overruled him, pointing out that one man had a better chance of infiltrating the bunker. If Steve failed, Ali would go with his original plan and detonate his surprise. Peter and Aaron's group hearing the explosion, would rush the rears lightly defended wall, while Marlise's group, would help Ali's gain entry at the front. Casualties would be high in this kind of assault, so everything hung on gaining entry to the tunnels. Like Marlise, Aaron prayed silently for Steve's success.

Steve looked towards the bunker entrance for the tenth time trying to gain entry. During the night he had scaled the rear wall undetected, making his way to the bunker's entry point. That was two hours ago, and still, he lay hidden beside a disused armoured vehicle. Long ago, the old armoured car had been stripped of anything useful, leaving it a reminder of times past. Over the years many names had been carved in it making it somehow a historical part of the fort.

At the bunker doorway, Steve watched as two Bedouin soldiers approached. He had expected some sort of code to be used to pass by the sentries; instead, they shoved their way passed the guards, without saying a word. Surprised, Steve studying the guards and saw they were not as tanned as the two Bedouin who had entered.

"They're not Bedouin of the same tribe." He murmured, seeing, at last, a way to get inside. Moving to the rear of the armoured car he approached a line of tents where the Bedouin slept. Moving outside one, he heard the tell tale sound of snoring. Opening the tent flap, he stole inside, finding three men asleep. Drawing his combat knife, he made sure they didn't wake.

Walking from the tent, now dressed as a Bedouin soldier, he approached the bunker. The two guards spoke to him, but Steve not knowing their language anyway, pushed past. One said something softly, clearly an insult, as Steve spinning placed his knife against his throat. Staring at the man through the slit in his headgear, he then turned and walked inside. The guards he heard spat in his direction, but he made no move to follow Steve as he continued into the tunnel, ignoring them.

His excitement at breaching the entrance was soon lost, as he walked down a half lit hallway. Hearing muffled moans and pleads coming from up ahead, he suspected he'd reached the bunker area where the hostages were being held. From Nadal's map, Steve knew to his left was a branch in the tunnel, which led out under the wall to where Aaron and Peter were waiting. Twenty paces further along the passage, he reached it. Across the entrance to this side, tunnel was a sign, which had a skull and crossbones picture on it.

Steve didn't have to know the language, to know it meant there was trouble waiting down the tunnel. Entering, Steve walked along the passage for a couple of minutes until the lighting ran out. Looking back, knowing no one would see the light; he pulled out a small torch. Carefully making his way along the tunnel, he found his way blocked by a steel door. Moving towards it, he immediately stopped. On the floor, his torch momentarily showed a black piece of wire stretching across the tunnel. Following the wire, he found a grenade embedded in a cavity in the sidewall.

Cutting the wire, he made sure the pin was securely in place, before moving to the door. Here an old satchel charge was wired to the door. Steve figured it was powerful enough to bring down half the fort on top of them if he made a mistake. Looking over the charge he carefully disconnected the trip wire from the wall. Sure there were no hidden backup trip-switches, he slowly turned the handle on the door. Opening it just a little, Steve looked out, as the barrel of a gun appeared in the crack.

"I judge that's you, Peter?"

"Who the fuck else would it be." Peter's voice softly answered, sounding on edge. "Where the hell have you been?" He asked as Steve pushed the door wide open.

"I didn't stop for a bloody ice cream Peter," Steve told him softly, as voices could be heard trying not to laugh.

"Sorry it's just we'd just about given up," Peter apologised, as Steve moved back down the tunnel. Nearing the lit section of the tunnel, Steve stopped. Crowding together, their heads close, Steve, walked them through what was waiting. Making sure they all knew what he intended, he in his Bedouin clothing moved ahead. Screwing a silencer on his pistol, he turned to where the prisoners were being held.

Sneaking a quick look around the corner, he saw the hostages all tied up on the floor, while four guards gleefully examined the women. With the coming executions, they must've decided the time was right to pick out a partner for special treatment. Steve horrified saw one of the women being manhandled was Michelle, named after his first wife. The rip of clothing from another woman meant things were getting out of hand, as Steve walked casually into the room his gun hidden in the fold of his black robe.

Strong Arabic voices challenged him, as he, in turn, pointed at a blonde nurse in the corner. The four men seeing where he pointed smiled, as one shouted a warning, pointing at his arm. His white arm now visible gave away his nationality. Reaching for their weapons they saw Steve raise his pistol firing two handed at them. One managed to scream a warning, before all of them crashed to the floor.

The sound of two sets of running feet could be heard approaching, before as if hitting a wall, they stopped. Looking outside the door, Steve saw the two guards from the door, lying in the hallway near the passageway to the escape door. In the side passage, Peter and Aaron stood wiping their knives. Moving back into the room, Steve reached Michelle.

Cutting her bonds and removing the rag from her mouth brought her panicky voice. Placing his hand over her mouth, he whispered for her to be quiet as Peter entered with the other men. The hostages awake to what was happening remained quiet as their bonds were released. Peter approached his sister and hugged her, before telling her to follow two of his men. Waving their understanding, the hostages hurried down the side passage escorted by several of Peter's men.

Moving back in front, Steve led the way to the tunnel's entrance. Looking secretively outside, he saw several Bedouin gathered there. Wondering whether to wait for Ali before exiting, Peter pulling him back, whispered in his ear. Steve smiling and nodding yes, stripped out of the Bedouin clothing he was wearing, handing them to Turk. Once he put it on, he moved outside.

Yelling at the gathered men brought laughter from the tribesmen who moved off, as another one of Peter's men appeared dressed in Bedouin clothing. Taking their positions either side of the door, made the Bedouin outside disperse.

"What did Turk say?" Steve whispered to Aaron.

"He told them the guards in the room were enjoying the women. The shots were caused by one of the men hostages trying to stop them. He told them their turn was coming soon."

"He's got that right. How about we go out and thin their numbers down a bit?" Steve suggested.

"That mightn't be a bad idea. It will be light soon the hostages will be visible from the rear wall shortly. By my watch, Ali will be here in less than half an hour, so don't get caught." Peter warned.

"I'll take Turk and Aaron; the rest can stay with you. I suggest you at least warn the others that the hostages are safe." Steve told him, moving outside followed silently by Turk and Aaron. Peter watched them go; secretly wishing he was going with them. Looking at the time again, he decided to at least tell Marlise of the situation, as Ali would be listening anyway. Switching on his headset's mic, he spoke into it.

"Marlise are you there?"

Marlise in her dugout jumped as her headset broke its imposed silence.

"Yes. I read you, Peter."

"The hostages are free; they're being led away as we speak." He told her, cutting the connection. Marlise overjoyed softly, told Habra.

"As I said, Captain Roberts is unstoppable." Habra smiled, as pushing his rifle butt into his shoulder, he lined up his first target. Ali in the ravine also heard the message. Wiping a tear from his eyes, he pushed forward the control lever, as the truck cleared the rise heading down towards the fort. He then told the others the mission was a go.

Miguel on the wall was one of the first to see the truck.

"Alert the men!" he shouted to Bazra, who shouted to one of his men. The soldier ran to an old bell and pulled the cord summoning their men to their stations. The Sheik inside the main fort's office area, heard the alarm too. He admitted to himself, that despite his misgivings, Miguel had handled the hostage situation like a professional. Dressing in his finest robe, he strode to the room's front door, deciding to watch his youngest son in action. Opening it, he found a Bedouin soldier there about to enter.

"What do you want?" He asked the tribesmen.

"Revenge," Turk answered, stabbing the Sheik in the heart, as he covered his mouth to prevent him screaming.

"Nice work Turk," Steve said, as he and Aaron, moved past him, searching the room.

As the truck neared the front gate, Miguel feeling the tension, forgot his plan for revenge and ordered his men to open fire. Opening up with everything they had, the truck began to disintegrate under the relentless pounding. Smiling to Bazra, he looked at the ambush trenches to see men dropping like flies. Above on the ridge, he saw the flash of weapons fire, along with puffs of sand from hidden snipers there.

"Bazra look." He shouted, as Bazra looking towards the ridge, saw what was going on as well. Bazra knowing it was a trap, shouted to the man with the bell, who rang it loudly. This was the signal for the ambush position to retreat inside. With ten men down already, the other thirty tribesmen rose from the trenches. Rushing across the road, they used Ali's truck for cover as they sought the safety of the fort.

Ali in the ravine seeing this triggered the explosives. Miguel frightened by the sudden loss of control, fled the wall. He had just descended and was moving to the gate, when the truck exploded. It was like a sickle through wheat, as the thirty men from the trenches, were sliced to pieces by a wall of metal fragments.

The fort's front wall and gate area having stood for over fifty years collapsed, causing mass confusion inside. Miguel thrown to the ground saw nothing through the debris, as he held his head trying to cushion himself from the deafening roar. Bazra looking around wiped his bleeding nose, before clearing his vision. He'd luckily, been thrown clear of the wall landing on a pile of sandbags. Running to four of his men, he had them gather their remaining forces. Telling them to deploy a heavy machine-gun to sweep the hills in front of the fort, he then ran towards Miguel.

"Are you okay?"

"Yes, Bazra. Can you get the men from the rear wall, while I hold here?" Miguel asked, his face showing his despair at being deceived by the enemy.

"Do not doubt yourself, Miguel. We will punish these infidels. I have ordered my men to bring a machine-gun to the front gate. We will teach them a lesson!" He promised, gripping Miguel's arm.

"You are right brother. We are not dead, yet he smiled, as Bazra ran towards the rear of the fort. Miguel fuelled by anger gathered twenty men, as the machine-gun arrived.

"Set it up and take care of those dogs hiding in those hills." He ordered, as his men rallied, taking up positions to cover the breaches in the wall.

Marlise, with the rest of her team; lay waiting for the dust to settle. Their part in the plan had gone off without a hitch. When the Bedouin had opened fire, they had picked off at least ten of the men in the trenches and another five on the walls. Just before the men in the ditches had broken cover and ran for the fort, she'd been watching two tribesmen talking on the wall. These she now knew were part of the command structure of the enemy, maybe even the leaders.

Aiming for the older one, she was just about to shoot when the man left. Targeting the younger one, who seemed to be in charge, she was just about to fire, when he too ducked down some stairs. Cursing, she lined up another tribesman, when Ali's truck exploded. Like the others she had dived down in her hole, riding out the storm of metal and body parts, which rained down around them.

Once the initial blast had passed, they found a massive cloud of dust and debris shrouding the entire fort.

"I can't see anything Habra. How about you?" She asked as round after round of weapon fire hit her position. The shooting continued for several minutes before it moved along the ridge to her right. Shaking herself, finding no injuries she turned towards Habra. He was lying silently next to her as if he was asleep.

"Habra are you okay!" She shouted, shaking him. Feeling wetness, she looked at her hands; they were covered in blood. His stomach she saw was gone, his internal organs spattered along the trench underneath him. Crying, she took out her ground sheet placing it over him. Scooping sand from underneath her, she buried the sides of the groundsheet securing it over him.

"You bastards!" She yelled out loud, moving back to her weapon. Through the dust, she saw the tribesmen had moved a heavy weapon up to the collapsed wall beside the front gate. Around it, she could see two men lying face down the gun not firing. This meant her team had successfully silenced it. As she looked through her scope, she saw the same young man from the wall, pull a body off the gun before manning it himself. Seconds later the gun resumed its search for her team members.

Miguel with a borrowed pair of binoculars searched for enemy positions while the gun beside him, hammered away. His men were regaining the upper hand as a group of enemy soldiers appeared in a ravine beside the road to their south.

"Get those westerners!" he shouted, as several tribesmen behind the collapsed wall, began shooting at them. Watching he saw two drop, the others take cover. "Good work men!" he yelled, feeling the odds were swinging back in his favour. It was then that the two-man crew of the machine-gun were hit. Knowing time was everything he jumped over one of the dead crewmen, and pulled the other crew-member off the gun. Aiming, remembering where the shots had come from, he opened fire on the hills again.

"No, you don't arsehole!" Marlise shouted, taking aim and pulling the trigger. She was rewarded as the gun stopped firing. Looking again through her scope, she saw the young man lying on his back staring at the sky. The tribesman at the gate stopped firing at the loss of the young man. Marlise smiling was just about to fire at another tribesman, when smoke grenades exploded at the fort's entrance, the area immediately filling with thick white smoke.

Bazra, while the gun was firing, had reached the rear wall. He found dead tribesmen everywhere. Finding a group of ten holding an old warehouse, he waved them to him. They immediately left their position, joining him.

"Bazra we have been deceived," one wept, ashamed at their defeat.

"There will be another day brothers. Gather what you can, we must leave," he ordered, the men calling out as they moved towards the front wall, searching for others. It was during this move that they found the sheikh. Bazra overwhelmed with grief, had two men carry him. His ten men were now twenty moved towards the front. Approaching the gate, Bazra wondered how he would tell Miguel of his father's death, when he saw him lying on his back beside the gun.

"Throw any smoke grenades you have towards the gate," he ordered as four tribesmen complied. Once the area was bathed in smoke, he moved to Miguel finding him still alive. "Careful men. Let's move him to our vehicles," Bazra commanded, as gathering up any remaining men, they fled to the eastern wall. Here behind a disused building sat four trucks and a jeep.

"Doran, to me!" Bazra shouted as a tall tribesmen rushed to him.

"Yes, Bazra."

Take Miguel and our leader back to their home. I will remain behind with two volunteers to cover you." Bazra ordered, as without a word the dead Bedouin leader and his son were loaded onto a truck. This completed, the others climbed aboard the other trucks, as two tribesmen moved to stand beside Bazra.

"We are honoured to stand with you Bazra." One of the two black-garbed men told him, as the trucks started up. Moving in front of them, Bazra opened a small gate just wide enough for the trucks to travel through. With fist raised in the air, the surviving tribesmen drove out into the desert. Behind them, Bazra secured the gates.

"Be ready brothers our enemies will be coming soon," Bazra warned, as they moved towards cover behind the abandoned jeep.

Aaron, Steve and Turk had just been readying themselves to attack the ten tribesmen when Bazra had appeared. Hiding, they watched the Bedouin retreat to the front gate. Following waiting their chance, they'd seen the tribesmen numbers grow making attacking them risky. When the smoke grenades had exploded, the three of them had charged into the smoke hoping to take out a few in the confusion. Instead, they found nothing, the tribesmen having retreated.

"Where did they go?" Aaron asked as the smoke started to clear.

"Get down!" Steve shouted as he suddenly realised Marlise's group would fire on them dressed as Bedouin. Radioing Marlise, Steve explained the situation as Marlise coming out of her dugout yelled to her group to stop shooting. Steve getting the all clear rose from the ground quietly discarding his disguise.

"Shit I forgot about that?" Aaron smiled, as Peter's remaining members arrived from the bunker.

"They have retreated to the eastern corner," Peter told them as Marlise and Ali's groups arrived. Many noticed a third of the two groups were gone.

"What's in the east corner that would make them head there?" Steve asked Peter, as the sound of engines starting, could be heard.

"Their transport must be hidden there!" Aaron yelled as they all charged towards the truck noise. As the solitary jeep came into view, Steve yelled a warning to take cover. Everyone dived for cover, as the three Bedouin fighters opened fire. It was a one-sided firefight as the three tribesmen were quickly killed. Looking around for any more surprises, Steve saw Aaron on the ground.

"Aaron!" Steve screamed out, running to his friend. His left leg was lying at an acute angle. A bullet had smashed his knee and blood flowed freely. Pulling a bandage and a field dressing from his leg pocket, Steve swiftly wrapped the field dressing over the wound securing it with the bandage. "He needs a doctor now!" Steve warned as Ali came running up.

"My daughter's husband is a surgeon. We must get Aaron to him," Ali ordered, running to the jeep. It was full of holes from the fire-fight. Ali, praying nothing vital was hit, hot-wired it. On the second time, it fired, as Steve with Peter's help carried Aaron to the jeep. Once Aaron was in, Steve climbed in behind him, as Ali put it into gear. Turning around, he drove to the rear gate. Steve climbing out opened it as Ali drove through, not waiting for him. Steve knowing where Ali was heading followed on foot.

Two hours with the sun directly overhead found Ali's teams all gathered with the hostages. Most needed medical attention, as well as four of their team members. Handing out what water they had, several members went back through the tunnels, getting more water from the fort. The arrival of their transport consisting of ten army trucks driven by Aaron's associates brought cheers from the group, as they all climbed aboard.

Driving back to their estate, Ali cleared the lounge area making it into a field hospital. Four of the hostages were doctors, which proved invaluable. While Aaron and the others received treatment, Steve and Marlise supervised the evacuation of the hospital staff. Most needed transport out of the country, which started immediately, organised by Aaron's associates of course.

When told Aaron had been wounded, his associates showed shock and concern promising to help him. Two hours after they had arrived, a Libyan Air Force helicopter with rebel markings on it, dropped down next to their villa. Many gathered weapons as Turk shouted for everyone to be calm. Moments later, General Tombie the rebel commander himself climbed out.

Turk greeted him with a salute, before talking to him briefly. He then led him inside. The General after a brief look around headed straight for Aaron. Steve and the others gathered as Aaron groggy from his surgery conversed with the General. After a ten-minute talk, he left for his chopper, asking Turk to walk with him.

"What was that about?" Peter asked Jasmine.

"It seems Captain Aaron is well known here." She smiled, as Turk moved away from the chopper as it ascended. Seeing them watching him, he walked over.

"What did he want Turk?" Ali asked.

"The General heard Captain Aaron was hurt. I gather they are close friends. It seems Aaron for some time has been helping the rebels procure weapons," Turk smiled.

"I knew he was up to something here; I just didn't know it was this big," Ali replied.

"Did he want anything else?"

"Not from you Commander. He wants the hospital staff to relocate to the rear of his army, where they will be safe. He also wants all the Libyan fighters here, like me, to join him. He seems impressed with our little raid on the Bedouin; they have been causing him a lot of problems. The bloody nose we gave them should keep them out of the rebel alliance and trouble for some time."

"Will you join him?" Marlise asked.

"Yes. The man is a good leader and has the support of all the rebel groups. Until Libya is free, he will keep us fighting Gaddafi, instead of each other." Turk answered, looking towards Jasmine. "Will you come with me?" He asked conveying to her, more than just fighting.

"Yes, Turk. With you in a dugout with me, the enemy will never hit me."

"You confused me, Jasmine," Turk answered, moving away, although he seemed happy she'd said yes.

By the next morning, most of their volunteer fighters and the hostages from the hospital had left. Many took up the General's offer, some having had enough had left by boat. Everything the rebels could use had gone including all the vehicles. Michelle and Hussein had, of course, stayed with Ali although they weren't speaking.

"They could've left us a jeep to move Aaron," Peter pointed out.

"Let them have it. Aaron had me contact Tori. He will pick us up this morning." Steve informed him. By seven everyone was out front waiting. Aaron on a stretcher lay sleeping to the side.

"Someone's coming," Steve announced, a pistol appearing in his hand. Peter turning strained his eyes spotting dust. Beside him, Marlise looked again at Steve.

"How did he know that? I can barely hear or see the car?" She whispered.

"Dad said he was called the Ghost by his unit. I believe it, the guy's uncanny." Peter replied, as Steve hearing, looked towards them. Both looking embarrassed turned their attention to the approaching vehicle. The noise, turned out to be two vehicles, approaching from the direction of the town. Steve with his binoculars signalled it was two of Aaron's associates.

"Tori! How are you?" Ali called out, as the two cars stopped.

"Somehow I knew you'd pull it off Mr Mustaffer; I mean Ali." Tori chuckled. "This is my son Benga. He will help me drive you all to the beach. Is Aaron better?"

"Yes he is doing well, but his days of chasing women are over."

"Many will weep at that news," Tori answered, the group laughing.

"I can hear you two you know." Aaron groaned from his stretcher, as Ali bent down next to his friend.

"Someday you can tell me the story of General Tombie?" Ali grinned.

"Never heard of him," he answered, trying not to smile.

"Load up everyone. It's time to go home." Steve ordered, tossing his bag in the rear of the first car.

They had travelled back across the Mediterranean in the same boat, although it had changed colour and appearance slightly. Reaching the Italian coast this time, they had travelled by train back to Zurich. Aaron, now walking again with a cane, insisted on coming with the others to see Steve off at the Airport. The others after saying goodbye to Steve stood back, as the three friends walked towards the departure gates. There they stood silently before Ali first, then Aaron, hugged Steve.

"We couldn't have done it without you old friend," Ali confessed, his eyes misty.

"Of course you could've. Aaron could have raised an army out of his associates over there." Steve smiled, his friends grinning. Stuck for words Steve looking at the clock broke the silence. "I am bringing Natasha here to ski next year. How about we all go together?"

"That sounds great. Just ring with the date, and we'll be waiting." Ali promised.

"Yes, we can ski and drink and talk about old times?" Aaron suggested.

"No, we won't my friends," Steve replied, forcing a smile, before disappearing into the crowd near the gate.

"I'm sorry Ali, I just got carried away." Aaron apologised, as Ali continued to look for Steve. Like usual he was gone.

"Forget it, Aaron. I for one will have many tales to tell, just not of war," He smiled, as grabbing Aaron around the shoulder, they walked back together to the others.

BACK TO THE PRESENT

Peter yawned, before looking out of the window at a Marina. Snapping wide-awake, he looked sideways seeing the driver seat was empty. Feeling for the comfort of his pistol, he opened the door stepping out into the pre-morning light. His watch showed it was four in the morning, which explained why there was no one in sight. Making sure the car was secured he casually walked across to the entrance of the marina. The gate he could see had been forced, so he walked through it onto the jetty area.

"Why had Steve brought him here?" He asked himself, as he walked onto and along a floating walkway. Cruisers and yacht's lined the narrow floating passageway; many he noticed were well over sixty feet in length.

"Over here Peter." a voice whispered to his far right. Recognising it, he turned in that direction onto another floating pathway. Twelve boats up, he found Steve on a cruiser. "Sorry I didn't wake you, but you were sleeping soundly, and I wasn't sure it would still be here." Peter looking around remembered.

"Shit is this the same boat we went to Libya on?"

"Yeah. Aaron once told me he kept it here in case of an emergency."

"You're not thinking of crossing the Mediterranean in this again are you?" Peter asked thinking of the time it would take.

"No, not this time. Aaron told me that he kept it full of weapons, so we'll take what we need and take that instead." Steve pointed towards the back of the boat. There, tied to the rear of the boat, sat a seaplane.

"Fuck that Aaron thought of everything didn't he?" Peter smiled, before losing it, remembering he was dead.

"Aaron was one of a kind. He was one of the bravest men, with the biggest heart I knew. He helped those rebels in Libya, knowing he might never even get paid. In the end, he made nothing, Ali even said he lost on the deal."

"He made a lot of friends though?"

"Yes, he did that. Anyway, let's see what he's got?" Steve changed the subject as he started to pry open the cabin door. As if remembering something, he stopped. Dropping the crowbar, he felt along the doorframe.

"Shit, I nearly forgot that?" Steve chuckled, showing Peter a wire running from the door to the frame. "We used to do this where we stored weapons in Singapore. You didn't need a key if the door was booby trapped," Steve explained, as reaching for the door, he pulled it open, showing it wasn't locked.

"I'm glad you remembered." Peter sniggered, as Steve turned on the inside light. Hesitating, Steve looked back along the dock.

"What's wrong?"

"The light is very bright; it should be dull as no one should've been here for some time."

"Maybe he has it serviced?"

"Not with a booby trap in place. That's a good way of costing you a serviceman." Steve replied. "Watch the walkway Peter; I'll look around."

Minutes passed as Peter stood watch. The noise of Steve dragging boxes frequently came to him, as he kept his eyes glued on the pathway. Twenty minutes and Steve appeared beside him.

"Did you get what you wanted?"

'Yes. Now get aboard the plane we've got company," Steve warned, as Peter stared back along the dock.

"Are you sure?" Peter started to say; when three silhouettes passed a brilliant white cruiser's bow one hundred metres away.

"Stay here Peter and fire at anything that moves, unless I call out," Steve told him, as he slipped into the water. Peter drawing his pistol aimed as the three silhouettes vanished.

"They must have seen me?" He told himself, waiting for the inevitable charge to start. Instead, he heard splashing then laughter.

"Peter, it's Steve, come here?" Steve's voice echoed over the water. Peter for a few seconds hesitated thinking they might be holding Steve captive. Remembering Libya and doubting it, he walked back along the pathway, gun out in front. Arriving at the corner he found Steve and two figures dressed in black, helping another black robed figure out of the water. Lowering his gun, he moved closer. Suppressed laughter came from the men as the third one sputtered and stood up.

"I cannot believe it is you, Captain Roberts." A gruff voice with a heavy accent erupted into the night.

"Keep it down Turk. What are you doing here anyway?" Steve asked as Peter opened-mouthed came to a stop.

"I don't believe it." Peter stammered out, as the group burst into laughter.

"Let's move back up to my office. We can talk there," Turk suggested, Peter, following in a daze.

"Why are you here Turk?" Peter asked sitting down with Steve and the others as towels and bottles were passed around.

"I should be asking that question. Peter isn't it?" Turk replied.

"Yes, it is. So what are you doing here?" Peter began again.

"Aaron got us all jobs here, after things in Libya became uncertain. He owns this Marina or did. When we heard he'd been killed, we found he had left it to us." Turk answered sadly.

"He was murdered." Peter corrected him, his eyes misting up.

"We feared as much. Since the Arab Spring, much has happened." Turk said sadly, the others nodding, showing their feelings.

"Turk we have come for weapons and the plane to avenge our friends. The Bedouin we defeated at the fort are the ones responsible; they are now after Marlise, Peter's girlfriend on the southern border with Libya

"You didn't marry her? You are a fool." Turk pointed out. Peter nodded agreeing. "They control most of Libya and influence the countries around them, Peter. Going after them won't be easy." Turk warned.

"Marlise's safe return is our main priority at the moment. Revenge can wait." Steve put in.

"I would suggest you fly south across Libya to Chad. The French have some influence there and could be of help?" Turk suggested as Steve looked at Peter.

"It might be best if we kept our search between ourselves. The French are in league with the Bedouin's leader, a Mahomet Jundela. He was to supply oil to them in exchange for our deaths and Marlise's capture.

"Then we have something in common. Jundela has a price on my head for killing his father." Turk told them.

"How could they know all this? It is one thing to know Marlise shot Jundela's brother, but both? Someone has talked who was on the raid." Steve pointed out.

"Nadal!" Turk's friends answered.

"Do you mean the Libyan who told us about the tunnels?" Peter asked.

"Yes. I'm afraid my brother Tamal here is right, it must've been him, although he may have had no choice." Turk admitted, before continuing. "After you left, Nadal and his wife, who was a nurse at the hospital left too. We heard he travelled to Chad to escape the fighting. The fool, to make money, wrote an article on the raid to humiliate the Bedouin. We heard they put a bounty on his head. He and his wife disappeared soon after. It is only as rumour, but it is said he and his wife were staked out in the desert as revenge.

They say to get his wife free; he told them I killed the Sheik. It was several months later when they tried for me. Luckily I was away at the time, and they missed me. To my shame, I fled rather than die. I didn't know they knew about the rest of you, or I would have warned you."

"Forget it, Turk. We have all made mistakes," Steve answered, as silence descended over the room, broken by Peter.

"What happened to that pretty girl named Jasmine you left with?"

"I am still here Peter." The friend of Turk who went in the water answered, taking off her mask.

"You haven't changed a bit, Jasmine," Steve told her, causing her to smile.

"And you are just as sneaky Captain Roberts. I now owe you for the swim you gave me."

"I apologise, but unlike the other two, you spotted me."

"There is that." She grinned, as Turk looked offended.

"You will be the death of me wife," Turk smiled, before becoming serious.

"Look, Peter, if it weren't for my situation here I would help. To come with you would lead the enemy here to my wife and brother. I must stay out of it."

"My husband forgets one thing, we both will come with him then he worries about leaving no one." Jasmine put in.

"I will not hear of it woman. It is too dangerous." Turk exploded.

"He is right Jasmine. This is our fight." Peter answered, backing Turk.

"They are hunting you my husband, and the French are helping. How long till they come here if we don't do something?" She replied.

"She has a point brother, and if these men fail, they will only grow stronger, making finding us easier." Tamal, his brother answered.

"Jasmine I can't," Was all Turk got out, his eyes wet with tears.

"You will not lose me, husband. Like before, my gift is with a sniper rifle, not close up." She pointed out, gripping his hand. Turk seemed torn as he weighed up what he had to lose against doing nothing.

"Okay we will help, but I still say we chance Chad, it is the safest option.

"Okay, then Chad it is and thanks for coming with us." Peter smiled, as the group moved back to the boat. Looking at what Steve had selected Peter gasped.

"Where did he get them?"

"Who knows Peter, although Aaron would've had a reason," Steve explained, as Turk, Jasmine and Tamal, added their own selections. Steve at this point pulled Peter to him.

"I need you to do me a favour?"

"Anything. What is it?" Peter answered, surprised by Steve's nervousness.

"I want you to ring Nigel and tell him what you have done and what you're up to. But you mustn't mention me."

"They should know you're alive Steve."

"No, best I remain dead Peter. On this mission, we could fail badly. No, I don't want their hopes lifted, only to be crushed again. Do this for me, Peter." Peter looked at Steve, seeing he was worried for their safety.

"Okay Steve, I'll do it before we leave," Peter promised, as they started loading supplies aboard the seaplane.

The following night they were ready. Steve and Peter wanted to leave earlier, but as Turk explained, they couldn't just up and leave, or questions would be asked. Having a friend look after the marina and spreading word that they'd gone hunting in South Africa, they set out at midnight.

Flying across the Mediterranean took just under six hours.

Angling toward Egypt, they at the last minute dived to the floor.

Flying southwest they angled along the Libya, Egypt border, keeping low, as the sun came up. Once they reached Chad, they followed the border with Libya, keeping as low as possible. Several times they were hailed, although no one tried to intercept them. Coming up on the point where Chad, Niger and Libya met, they took the seaplane down.

Amazingly being near the end of the wet season, they found a small river big enough to land on and more importantly, take off from. Landing, they drove the seaplane up onto the shore. Mindful of crocodiles, they secured it, before throwing branches over the wings to conceal it. Unloading the equipment, Steve discussed with Turk how to find a suitable vehicle for them and the equipment.

Looking at a map of the area, he pointed out to Steve the location of a couple of villages marked on it, upstream towards the border with Libya.

"We will try there tomorrow at first light. For now, we will check the equipment and get some sleep. Tomorrow will be a big day." Steve told them all, before adding something. "And make sure you all sleep well away from the water." He warned, pointing to the water. There the tail of a reptilian creature broke the surface behind where the plane was moored. As if sensing they were watching it, the creature submerged below the surface.

"Sounds like a good idea," Peter replied, checking his weapon.

At first light, Peter, lying next to Tamal and Jasmine, stirred. Putting on his boots, he quietly got up before going in search of Steve. He had the pre-morning watch and Peter had no doubt he was somewhere close watching over them. Climbing a small rise that would give a good view of the surrounding area, he found Steve and Turk. Both seemed frozen, as they looked north towards the distant village on their map and Libya.

"You two are up early," Peter said softly, as Steve raised his hand warning him to be quiet. For several minutes he stood with them in silence as they stared out over the harsh dry countryside. Even though the wet season had just passed, this area was mostly desert, the only source of water was the river they had landed on.

"Do you hear anything?" Turk whispered to Peter, who took a moment to listen before answering.

"No nothing, except the wind." Hand signalling for them all to move back to their position, Steve stood as stone for a moment longer, before following. Reaching their position, they woke the others.

"What is wrong?" Jasmine asked, swiftly putting on her boots, as did Tamal.

"We're not sure yet, although we both feel uneasy," Steve told them.

"It's too quiet isn't it?" Peter put forward, now understanding why they were like stones on the rise when he went up there.

"Yes. The village although distant is not small and should produce a lot of noise. The sun is now up, and by rights, we should be able to hear at least an engine starting or someone yelling by now." Turk pointed out.

"Okay, full battle dress and personal weapons. We'll leave the heavy gear here until we find out what's going on." Steve ordered as they all made ready.

Moving in an extended line with a twenty-metre spacing, the five walked towards the outskirts of the village. Seeing the first signs of man in an old broken down fence, Steve had the line move in closer together as they approached the village. Now with just a four-metre gap between them, they advanced slowly as Steve in the centre became tense. Five minutes of sweeping right to left, found them approaching the village centre. A large market area dominated the town square, where like most African towns, bartering for goods took place.

"Where is everyone?" Jasmine whispered, her voice thunderous in the quiet.

"Search a few huts, Peter. We'll cover you." Steve suggested as Peter rushed to the closest one, before moving on to the next. After five he stopped.

"There is no one here; the whole place has been abandoned," Peter yelled to them, his voice echoing.

"Maybe with the raids from the north they moved further south," Turk suggested, as Steve telling them to remain here, ghosted through the town to the river. In his absence, Peter and the others searched for anything that would give them an idea of what had taken place. They found nothing, but Jasmine located an old truck behind a mud brick building.

The building turned out to be the village service station, complete with fuel bowser. By the time Steve had returned, they had the old vehicle running and filled with fuel. Steve seemed to be in a hurry, as coming up to them, he examined the vehicle.

"This will do. Everyone climb on now, we've got to leave."

"Is there a problem Steve?" Turk asked as they all boarded.

"The villagers did not leave." He announced, as Peter at the wheel, drove out of town. No one talked; no one said anything, as they drove back to the plane. Once there, they loaded up the truck, before taking a break for lunch.

"What happened back there, Steve?" Peter softly asked.

"Best finish eating," Steve replied, remaining silent, causing the others to follow suit. Jasmine watching Steve saw how tired he looked.

"Too much bloodshed." She unconsciously said out loud, as the group looked at her, then at Steve. Steve acknowledged what she had said with a shrug; it was no good denying it. Finished his meal; he wiped his face before telling them what he'd found.

"Like I told you I went through the village to the river. I started to see drag marks on the ground. At first, I thought the villagers had taken what belongings they could gather and travelled by boat downstream away from the trouble at the border. What was left of the villagers was floating in the river? It explained why we saw so few croc's where we stopped yesterday."

"Why would they kill them all? Surely it is better to keep them as slave labour?" Jasmine pointed out.

"I saw a Catholic church burnt down near the wharf. I'd say that was their religion and the rebel force took affront to it," Steve explained, being the only one there that wasn't a Muslim.

"This is not the teaching of the Prophet Steve. These fighters are just scum here to murder," Peter pointed out, the others voicing their support.

"Okay, we're all rested. I think we should leave this area and head towards the border," Steve suggested packing up, ending the conversations.

"How will we find Marlese? She could be anywhere?" Peter asked as they climbed aboard.

"We'll find some of these rebels and ask them," Steve answered, a small smile on his lips. The others knew there was no warmth in that smile.

CIA HEADQUARTERS
LANGLEY, VIRGINIA

Nigel stared at the phone before dropping it back in its cradle. He had just finished talking to Peter having recorded it all. He had arrived back from Australia two days earlier, to find on his desk a pile of please explain letters and emails from his boss and several other department heads. He hadn't lied and had told them what had occurred pacifying most of them, now this. Peter's murderous romp across Europe had up till now remained a series of confusing killings. Now Peter had the key to certain problems the Agency was having.

The jamming of their transmissions now became clear. France trying to secure oil had been helping the Bedouin leader Jundela. Showing his boss what he'd uncovered brought a gasp of surprise.

"Those fuckers! All the time we thought the French were just holding back in Chad. Now we find they have been helping that butcher cement his claim on Libya.

"Then why fight them in Chad at all?" Nigel asked.

"Keeps us out of it. Sure we help in Niger, but the French are in charge over there. They are probably having a two-way bet. If Jundela doublecrosses them, they can hit him from the south through Chad. If he plays ball, they can let him have Niger and push us out."

"Maybe it's over now their Foreign Minister has been killed?"

"No, oils everything to those frogs. They'll play ball with Jundela and hope no one finds out." His boss growled.

"Well, we know now. Maybe they'll back off?"

"We've got no proof, and our only witness has been killing people all over Europe, and in Africa soon I'd say by the sounds. No, we'll have to keep digging and wait for our chance. How long until this crazy friend of yours rings again?"

"Peter said he would contact me once he finds his girlfriend."

"Shit, he's either in love with her, or she's a handful. To risk this little adventure, it's got to be love. Tell me immediately when he contacts you. In the meantime, I'll bring the other Department heads up to speed on our French Allies loyalties." His boss barked, as Nigel headed back to his desk.

'Had he betrayed Peter?' he wondered, thinking about the mess Peter had caused in Europe that his bosses now knew about. On the other hand, Peter had revealed a major operation by a supposed ally against America's interests. In the end that was more important to his bosses than just about anything.

LIBYA'S SECRETS

Travelling north, along the only track marked on the map, Steve became more and more uneasy. The track appeared well used, causing Steve to halt the truck regularly and sweep the track ahead on foot. This slowed the trip to a crawl, as they reached a crossroad. Pulling up short, Steve signalled for everyone to dismount, as taking his weapon, he once again scouted ahead. He was only gone a short time when he reappeared.

"Jasmine. Get behind the wheel. The rest of you, help me push the truck off the road into that scrub area." He whispered. No one bothered to ask why Jasmine couldn't just drive the truck into the scrub. They all knew someone was ahead and would hear it if they started it. Five minutes found the vehicle off the road and hidden from all but an aerial search. Once the truck move was completed, he signalled them to follow him, telling them to take off their safeties.

With Steve somewhere ahead of them they silently crossed the intersection where tracks could be seen going right to left. As they approached a rise, Steve showed himself, signalling for them to get down, as they all crawled forward, stopping just short of the rise. Steve signalling to Peter, led him forward as the others remained flat on the ground. In the silence, the distant sound of voices floated on the wind, as the smell of cooking fires came to them.

Peter, crawling up beside the now stationary Steve, looked down into a small depression below the rise. There sat four armoured troop carriers, with about forty soldiers sitting around their cook fires eating a meal, while several others put up tents. What drew his attention, was tied to the fronts of the vehicles, were eight unfortunate naked women. Peter felt bile build in his throat forcing him to duck back down behind the rise, for fear of vomiting. Steve seeing his retreat came down next to him.

"I was going to let them go to sleep and then sneak past them. I think instead we should take a few prisoners." Steve softly told him, his eyes black.

"There are a lot of them?" Peter warned, keeping his voice down.

"As darkness approaches, most will be asleep. We will only have to take care of the guards and make sure no one gets aboard the vehicles." Steve pointed out, his voice cold. Peter at first made to complain, to point out they weren't here to fight. The words died in his mouth as he looked into Steve's eyes.

"Let's go tell the others?" He whispered as Steve grabbed his arm.

"What do you think Peter? Be honest with me."

"I think this is a rash move. You've based it more on punishing those men for what they're doing to those captives down there."

"You are dead right about me wanting to punish those animals, Peter, although that is only a part of the reason for attacking them. Firstly, I want prisoners so I can find out where Marlise is. I also want two of their vehicles, so we can travel around this area safely, as the Bedouin forces hold sway here. Don't be afraid to ask me why Peter. I might once have been a shit hot soldier, but I'm getting old. Always question me when you're not sure of my plan. Understood?"

"Okay, I understand now, why we're doing this. It's just the numbers worry me."

"Good, now work on a plan to minimise the risk before we reach the others," Steve told him, moving back towards the others.

Steering the group into a brush-covered depression, Steve made them all break for a meal, while he discussed with Peter how they'd carry out the raid. Peter, sitting with Steve, made several suggestions about the coming raid as they ate their rations. Steve listened silently, while he continued to eat, giving nothing away. Once everyone had finished eating, Steve outlined the mission. Explaining the plan, Steve gave them all clear instructions on their roles in the coming raid. Peter, who thought Steve hadn't paid too much attention to what he'd suggested, found the plan based around what he'd put forward.

Once the first shot was fired, Jasmine and Tamal would lay down cover fire from a small hill above the enemy's position. Peter and Turk would accompany Steve and secure the end two armoured vehicles. Steve of course while they did this, would take care of the sentries. Jasmine's only problem with the plan was the darkness. She was worried about shooting blindly when friend and foe would be just shadows. Steve assured her that once the sentries were down, he'd make sure there was plenty of light.

"How are you going to do that?" She said out loud, before going quiet.

"By making the enemy board the two vehicles in the centre. There will be a surprise waiting in there for them." He smiled, making them all shudder.

"What about the hostages?" Peter warned.

"Unfortunately by tonight, they will be either dead or with the soldiers. We can't save them." He confessed, as the group now resolved to the raid, broke away to rest till dark.

Four in the morning, the worst time of the night to be a sentry, approached. The six soldiers on guard took turns yawning as they sleepwalked around the perimeter, stopping for the compulsory piss. If any of them had been listening, instead of fighting off sleep, they would've heard the silence grow as one by one their fellow guards lay down never to rise again. Peter, from his position on the forward armoured vehicle, slowly raised the rear door using the vehicle's electric power.

He had already mined the vehicle forty paces behind his and didn't want the door down when it went up. Turk, to the rear, had done the same. Laying a mine in the vehicle in front, he had entered the rear vehicle, to find the driver asleep at the wheel. Cutting his throat, he laid him on the floor, before closing the rear door as well. The noise of the two doors closing did stir several soldiers, but except for a few words to keep the noise down, no one approached.

Why would they anyway, Peter mused. Who would be stupid enough to take on four armoured vehicles and forty soldiers? Smiling to himself, he suddenly saw the brilliance of Steve's plan based on the absurd.

Jasmine sat in the dark with Tamal, thinking of all the things that could go wrong. Lying there listening to the odd snoring and occasional moan of pain from one of the luckless women held by the men below, Jasmine felt again, the comforting metallic feel of the trigger on her Saw automatic assault rifle. The Saw had never been overly popular with soldiers around the world, as it was heavy, holding hundreds of rounds in its magazine.

Stationary, as she was now, was a whole different proposition. Its rate of fire and the damage it could inflict made it the perfect support weapon. Beside her, unaware of her concerns, lay Tamal. This was his first engagement, and unlike her, he looked forward to the coming fight. Since Turk, had been made a target by the Bedouin, he had been on the run with him, unable to fight back at these monsters.

Now as he lay waiting, he hoped in a small way to prove himself as a warrior. Despite this, he was no fool and would not leave his position next to Jasmine. Like Turk had told him many times, 'you have to survive to prove you were right, better to let the enemy die for his ill-fated cause.

Steve lying in the dark amongst the enemy troops thought of nothing. His every sense was alive, listening and watching, waiting for any sign of moment. The sentries were now all taken care of, all that remained was to trigger panic. Pulling three grenades, he tucked them under sleeping fools, pulling the pins and moving on. Finding a spot where he could watch the whole area from, he pulled his rifle from his back strap. Lining up several sleeping figures close by, he took a deep breath. Screaming at the top of his voice, he opened fire.

Pandemonium broke out, as the soldiers bewildered all jumped to their feet as the three grenades rolled free. They were just starting to look in Steve's direction when the grenades ignited. Three explosions one on top of the other lit the area, as Jasmine and Tamal on the rise, opened up on the shadows in the flashes. Confusion, gave way to discipline, as their remaining officers ordered them into the vehicles. Many dropped hit by the fire from Jasmine and Tamal as they clamoured towards the false safety of the armoured vehicles.

Finding the first and last vehicles' doors closed up, they rushed to the centre two. Rushing aboard, they triggered the claymore mines planted there. The explosions caused the whole area to be bathed in white light, as the two vehicles blew sky high. Metal fragments from the two mines and the vehicles accounted for nearly all the remaining soldiers. Those left, either fled or lay injured, as the rattle of gunfire stopped, punctuated by crackles of metal from the burning vehicles. As the fires ebbed, the moans of the dying enveloped the area, as Steve standing up, called for everyone to cease fire.

Knowing the clever ones would remain silent on the ground waiting their chance, he moved forward. Shooting all the bodies through the head, he let three wounded soldiers live. Peter and Turk left the vehicles and joined him, only to be told to return to them immediately, while he kept searching. Jasmine and Tamal on the hill above remained stationary, waiting for Steve to give the all clear.

"Are you okay Tamal?" She whispered.

"Yes, is it over?" He softly asked as the noise of something running towards them erupted in front of them.

Tamal frightened hesitated, while Jasmine opened fire dropping two figures, which were almost upon them.

"Good shooting Jasmine." Steve's voice sounded out of the darkness to their right.

"Is that all of them Captain Roberts?" Jasmine asked, her voice sounding like a cannon in the night.

"Yes, that's all of them. Pack up your gear and move to the vehicles."

"Let's get moving Tamal," Jasmine told Tamal, who had remained stationary.

"Jasmine. How could you be sure they were the enemy and not Captain Roberts just then?" Tamal asked, his voice trembling in the dark.

"They made noise." She answered, helping him up.

For the rest of the night, they stayed where they were. Steve having secured the prisoners swept the area again, making sure there were no surprises. Once they had enough light to see, Steve with Turk checked over the two undamaged armoured vehicles. Both had received burn and shrapnel impact marks from the explosion of the other two vehicles. Starting them up, making sure they would run, Steve signalled for the three prisoners to be brought over to the first vehicle.

"Right Turk, see if they speak Arabic?" Steve asked. Turk getting Tamal's assistance dragged them to the vehicle asking them questions as they went.

"They won't answer." Turk angrily told Steve.

"Tell Tamal in Arabic to cut one of their arms off," Steve answered, as Turk talking to Tamal pulled out his knife. Two of the soldiers pulled their arms in close.

"Always works." Steve chuckled, shooting the one who hadn't moved in the head. "Now tell them if one of them tells us about the hunt for the paratroopers, he will live while the other one joins his friends. Warn them if they lie, they both die."

Turk spoke to them in Arabic, before both soldiers exploded, talking simultaneously.

"It appears both soldiers want to live Captain," Tamal replied.

"Ask them about the French paratroopers. See if they know about a search for them." Steve asked as Turk translated. Both soldiers looked at each other as if trying to glean some information from the other's face. One in the end spoke. Turk waited for him to finish then told Steve.

"He admits he knows nothing of French paratroops, but the Bedouin tribe who they serve, have moved many of its tribesmen to the border with Chad and Niger to the west. Why he wasn't sure, but they heard mortar fire several days ago in that direction." As Turk finished, the other soldier started squawking. Once he had finished, Turk excitedly translated. "This one knows nothing about paratroops or fighting, but he heard two Bedouin discussing their leader's obsession with a woman. They say he is searching for her now."

"It's got to be her, and they're close, maybe fifty miles?" Peter interrupted, as Steve raised his hand for silence.

"Ask them if they were part of the raid on that village by the river?" Steve told Turk. Everyone went silent as Turk asked the question. Both soldiers looked around at the faces before both answered. Turk, giving nothing away, waited till they stopped rambling.

"They say they were part of the guard detail, covering the road. The Bedouin tribesmen themselves carried out the raid.

"Thank them for their help, and release them," Steve ordered. Turk translated, seeing their faces light up as he cut the ropes securing them.

"Okay everyone climb abroad. We'll take these two vehicles and transfer our gear from the truck. It can be left here hidden in reserve." He told them moving to the prisoners. Holding out two canteens of water, he let them drink. Seeing everyone was aboard he pulled out his silenced pistol and shot each one in the head. The others shocked, watched, as Steve climbed onto the first vehicle signalling for it to go as if nothing had happened. Reaching the truck Peter, pulled Steve aside.

"Why did you kill those two soldiers? They told us what they knew?" Peter was angry, as the others too stood there, also wanting an answer.

"I said they wouldn't be harmed, if they didn't lie," Steve saw they all seemed confused, so he continued. "There were no track marks on the road near the village, so they weren't guarding it. There were, however, track marks down near the river. The road from the river comes to this crossroad from the right, where we saw this group's track marks enter. The Bedouin also love to torture their victims. The village's men were all shot then thrown into the river. The women raped then shot before joining the others, not the usual mark of the Bedouin."

The explanation changed the group's worries. They all nodded their support for his actions, before commencing unloading the truck into the two armoured vehicles. Peter, feeling he'd slighted Steve made to apologise.

"I'm sorry for," Was all Peter got out before Steve stopped him.

"You were right to ask Peter. I should have explained why I killed them; I know that now." Steve smiled. "I'll check the area." He continued moving into the scrub that surrounded them. Steve walking out of sight from the group sat down. Looking at his hands, he saw them shaking.

"I'm getting old?" He concluded remembering the faces of the others. Ten years ago he wouldn't have bothered explaining anything, as it wouldn't have worried him or his team. They'd been killing for so long; they did it without a second thought. No one then would've bothered to query his decision, knowing he would've had a reason. Now he felt the butcher's bill for his life of killing clouding his thereafter.

He'd never thought of dying before, but now as old age crept up on him, he felt soon he might be standing before the creator and having to explain himself.

"Was his cause always just," He asked himself. He hoped it was, although he had his doubts God would see it his way? Was he going to the cloudland or was he going where he wouldn't need a jumper? Shaking himself, Steve looked around at the desolate country and thought again of the reason why he was here now. He was here to save Ali's son's girlfriend from an evil group of sadistic zealots, if nothing was more just than that he didn't know it.

"If I die on this one. I will know I died doing something good." He chuckled. Getting up from his bout of depression, he noticed his hands had stopped shaking. Finishing his patrol, he rejoined the others.

The armoured troop carriers although slower than the truck, gave the group a little more protection from their enemies. Marked as they were with the Bedouin tribe's insignia, gave them the added bonus of invisibility while travelling through the border area of Libya. Of course, soon the massacre of the soldiers belonging to these vehicles would be found, Steve hoped it wasn't for at least another day. Maps found in the lead vehicle showed the Bedouin didn't exactly trust these recruits from other countries. Sure they believed in their Hard line Islamic cause, but maybe not to the death.

Peter, was first to notice, that the maps were divided into sectors. Each area was assigned to different groups of fighters. Only the Bedouin tribes own men could enter another's sector, without permission. This gave them all hope that until someone crossed into the sector, they were in to check on the soldiers, their disappearance would remain unknown.

Crossing into Niger was a non-event. The river crossing wasn't even manned by guards, as the Niger army had long since retreated south. Moving west, they found that not everything was going in the Bedouin's favour. Coming over a rise, they found the remains of a burnt out armoured column. Twenty vehicles, half of them tanks had been pulverised. Turk dismounting with Steve walked ahead on foot, checking the wreckage.

"Air attack. Most probably American I'd say," Turk whispered, looking skywards.

"Why American and not French?" Steve asked.

"Not many misses. The Americans and English, have much better smart missiles," Turk explained, with a smile. Moving back to the others, who had all dismounted, Steve explained what had occurred.

"At least they aren't after us?" Tamal beamed, till Turk smacked him lightly across the back of the head.

"Whose vehicles are we travelling in you idiot?" Turk exclaimed as Tamal embarrassed looked at the ground, the others trying not to laugh.

"I forgot that. Should we cover the vehicle markings then?" Tamal put forward, as they all walked back to the vehicles.

"No. There's more chance of meeting the forces of this Mahomet Dundela than the French. We'll just have to watch the sky and pray we spot them before they spot us." Steve answered, as climbing aboard, they continued.

Marlise lay two-thirds buried in the side of a mountain pass looking out on the open ground to the east.

"Fuck it's flat as your chest?" Captain Lenore chuckled silently beside her. He too lay buried keeping the heat and hostile eyes away from them.

"Captain, you've been looking?"

"And that's all I'll do with that boyfriend you've got." He smirked, as Marlise laughed softly.

"I wish he was here now?"

For over two weeks, they'd sneaked across the rough mountainous country avoiding the hundreds if not thousands of soldiers searching for them. Four times they'd shot it out always escaping into the surrounding hills. When they'd first found the gully where Lenore had broken his leg, they'd thought they'd given the enemy the slip. Four nights after seeing nothing, they had decided to rest and took refuge in a small cave in the side of the gully. Marlise had been on guard duty at around four, when Sergeant Perry had silently nudged her.

He had the next shift; so having a quick look around, she made ready to leave. It was then, out of the corner of her eye, she saw movement. Putting her mouth next to his ear, she told him she'd just seen something move from the direction they'd come. Perry looking spotted the movement as well. Whispering, he said he'd wake the others, she gave him the thumbs up and continued watching. No more than two minutes had passed, when she heard the rustle of movement as her team joined her. Captain Lenore managed to crawl up beside her even with his splinted leg.

"How many are out there?" He whispered, next to her ear.

"Six and a dog. It must be muted to stop it from barking." She whispered back. By now the dog was nearly to the point where they turned and made their way to the cave.

"Fire when I do," Lenore ordered, aiming. Marlise beside him tensed her sniper rifle in the dark was near useless. Instead, she reached into her ammo bag on her belt, pulling out a grenade. Lenore beside her, seeing the gesture, signalled no, making her put the grenade away.

"Too much noise," He whispered aiming.

Below them, in the middle of the gully, the six men and the dog reached the turn-off. The dog sniffing turned towards their position as the six tribesmen stopped dead. Looking at each other, one suddenly shouted out a warning, as the others either dived to the ground or ran for it. It was futile as Captain Lenore opened fire, followed by the others.

"Cease fire!" Lenore yelled. "Go check them, Sergeant." He ordered as Perry and the other men moved forward. Marlise made to go as well when Lenore stopped her.

"Stay with me Marlise. Your sniper rifle is no good in the dark." He told her, keeping his rifle trained on the area where the tribesmen had gone to ground.

"They are all dead. Including the dog." Sergeant Perry's voice echoed across to them, as his men returned. After a quick sweep of the area had found no other soldiers, Lenore had a debriefing. Although no one had been hit, a fare amount of ammo had been used. Making a decision, Captain Lenore had two men hand over their spare ammo to the other members of the squad, before going down to the tribesmen and gathering their weapons. All six had AK47's plus several grenades. The two men without ammo broke down their weapons, and loaded them into their packs, taking two AKs and ammo for their use.

The other squad members broke down the spare AKs and packed them, with any extra ammo they had gathered. It increased their load, but gave them added firepower and ammo in any coming skirmishes. Twice more the Bedouin had intercepted them during the night, which was the only time Marlise's squad was able to move, the day being too dangerous. Both of these incidents caused only minor injuries on both sides; the last skirmish was different.

As the squad came closer and closer to the border with Niger, the soldiers chasing them became more ardent in their attempt to capture them. Knowing their destination, made working out their route easier. Captain Bursa, who had at first been confident of capturing them, now saw his firing squad, drawing closer. Looking at the map, he saw the mountain range narrowed before turning into desert. He knew they couldn't cross the open ground without being spotted, so the logical thing to do was wait till they tried to cross.

Unfortunately, his leader wanted results now, or else he would be killed. Seeing there were only four valleys of any worth, he concentrated his units ahead of the paratroopers blocking the valleys. Bursa was throwing the dice, knowing his head would roll if they got past. To push his point with his men, he joined one of the blocking groups.

The first warning they received to the presence of the blocking force, was when Sergeant Perry, was catapulted from his feet by a shot to the head. Marlise was taking her turn helping carry Captain Lenore when Perry died.

"Everyone down!" She screamed as the squad dropped to the ground. Looking around for the sniper, Marlise ordered everyone back behind a rocky outcrop they'd just passed. It was twenty metres to the outcrop. They lost another man reaching it.

"Can you see them, Sergeant?" Lenore shouted out, showing his fear in calling her Sergeant.

"Give me a minute Sir," Marlise replied, crawling to a break in the outcrop. A ricochet beside her made her duck back. "He's good whoever he is," Marlise called to Lenore sneaking another look. This time the round nicked her beret, making her yelp in fright if not pain.

"Are you okay?" Captain Lenore shouted.

"Yeah. I just got a bit cocky; I'll try somewhere else." She yelled back. Moving away from the gap, she looked of a better position. Crawling continuously for ten minutes, she reached a point where scrub trees covered the slope. Finding a good hide, she scanned the distant three peaks. From the angle of his shots, she knew he was on either the left one or the centre. Catching Lenore's eye, she signalled for him to make a diversion. Marlise watched as he signalled one of their men to put one of their berets on the end of a rifle and show it. Marlise smiling watched the peaks.

As the hat appeared, a shot rang out from the peak to the left. Looking through her scope, Marlise worked her way backwards and forwards across the area, where the shot had come from. Time seemed to stand still as she waited patiently for something to help her locate the enemy. When it occurred, she nearly missed it. On the right side of the left-hand peak, a flash of light momentarily flashed out, as someone lit a cigarette or opened a door behind the sniper's hide. Looking at the area where the light had come from, she saw several holes in the rock face. Looking closely she saw one was a rectangle like shape.

"They've dug it out and used bricks to make the aperture?" She smiled adjusting her scope. Zooming in, she saw the faintest of movement inside the hole. "Gotcha she smiled. Taking several breaths, she lined up the shadow. Exhaling she paused then slowly squeezed the trigger and waited. At first a quiet settled over the valley, then in quick succession two rounds impacted to her right.

"Fuck there's three of them." She whispered, sliding slowly backwards, into a depression. "No wonder they were zeroed in on my movement?" She cursed crawling to a new position. Sneaking a look she saw movement in a dugout to the right of the one she'd hit. Not firing, she searched for the other one. She couldn't see this one, but she saw the same rectangle slit to the left of the dead one's spot. Aiming at the one moving she fired, before lining up the rectangle. There in the corner she finally saw a fleeting movement, firing again. Not waiting to see if she was on target she moved to a new location.

Like before, silence greeted her, as she scanned the opposite hills. Standing, up she ducked immediately back down again, before running back to Lenore.

"Did you get them?" He asked.

"Yes. There were three of the bastards. I'd say company, will be coming pretty soon?" Marlise replied, watching the hills.

"My thoughts exactly. Let's climb out of this valley into the adjoining one. I think we're in for a hard time from now on," he forced a smile, standing on his splinted leg. "Another couple of days and I will be able to walk without a stick?"

"Well that will make the rest of us happy, you're no lightweight."

"Sorry about that. Anyway, I thought we should shed any extra gear including weapons. Tell the men to smash their spares, only keep the weapon they have ammo for." Lenore ordered as Marlise went to fill in the others.

"I'm killing these men?" He sadly told himself, watching Marlise run to each man. He knew he was slowing them down, as he opened his pack. "Six men, including me. How long till I order them to leave me behind?" He mused, as bending down he dumped most of his gear, taking the bare minimum.

For the next two days, Marlise led her squad through a series of hills ever growing less in stature, as they approached the border with Niger and Libya. Many times they heard the movement of vehicles either behind or to their front. Each time they went to ground, hiding in whatever cover they could find. Now as she lay next to Captain Lenore, Marlise knew cover in the desert country ahead would be at best sparse.

"What do you suggest Sir?" Marlise asked, looking out over the barren ground for movement.

"The squad won't make it carrying me Marlise. It's best you leave me here and come back for me once you reach safety. I'm afraid this is as far as I go."

"We won't leave you, Sir. I suggest you think of another plan." Marlise replied, horrified in leaving anyone behind for the Bedouin.

"It's an order Sergeant. Just leave me any spare water, I can hold up here for several days." Gathering the men in Marlise told them of his plan asking for questions.

"I don't care if I get court-martialled. I didn't carry the Captain this far to have him left behind to be tortured to death. He wouldn't leave any of us behind, be fucked if I'll leave him!" Corporal Benin snapped, the others voicing their support. Approaching Lenore, they told him they weren't leaving him.

"Look men I appreciate it, but there is no cover out there. You'll all die if we're caught in the open. I won't have that on my conscience" Captain Lenore exclaimed, before going quiet.

"There might be another way," Marlise whispered. Getting a nod to continue from Lenore, she continued. "One person with just their weapon could cross the border and bring back help in less than two days. I suggest we send someone." Everyone went silent weighing up the chances of making it alone.

"It's risky Sergeant, although one person could find cover where a squad could not. Any volunteers?" The Captain asked.

"I'll go." Benin volunteered, as the rest remained silent.

"Forget it Corporal; your left leg is fucked, you wouldn't be able to travel fast enough," Lenore answered.

"We're all fucked, Sir. I have a better chance than most here." Benin answered.

"No. I'll go," Marlise replied, causing a chorus of nos.

"Marlise its too dangerous for, I hate to say it, a woman."

"Bullshit I'm fitter than anyone here, you all know that. And sex has nothing to do with it!" Marlise retorted.

"Look at it this way Marlise. If one of us gets captured, it will be a little torture and death. If they catch you, they will keep you as a prize. You know what they'll do to you." Lenore softly answered, the men unable to look at her.

"No one is going to capture me, alive Captain, I can assure you of that. Now if there aren't any other stupid questions, I suggest you all find some shade and dig in." Marlise pointed out, dropping her pack. Grabbing an AK assault rifle from one of the privates, she handed him her sniper rifle. "I'll be back for that Private Guanine. Make sure it's in the same condition, or I'll have your balls," Marlise growled, before smiling.

"We've got five days of water. If you haven't returned in three, we will start across after you." Captain Lenore stammered out, embarrassed in having to let her go alone.

"I'll be back don't worry." She assured him. Without another word, she clipped on a water bottle to her belt and then started out onto the barren desert plain. The squad behind lay silently watching her, until she grew smaller disappearing into the heat haze.

"Do you think she'll make it?" Benin softly asked Lenore.

"She's right Corporal; she's the fittest one here. If she can't make it, no one can," Lenore answered. "Okay men find a shady spot and start digging in and keep watch for the enemy, he's out there somewhere?"

TRAPPED

Mahomet Jundela stood over the body of Captain Bursa. Putting his pistol away, he looked east over the flat deserted desert. Like his commander before him, he had failed, and failure was not an option to Jundela. He had now taken over command of the operation himself, tired of the constant excuses for not capturing the French paratroopers.

"She's out there in the hills Miguel; I can smell her?" Jundela exclaimed, scanning the desert with his binoculars. Miguel beside him sat motionless unable to turn and look. Realising his mistake, Jundela gripped his brother's shoulder. "Don't worry brother. Soon you will see it all I promise you." Jundela smiled, for a brief second seeing merriment in Miguel's eyes, before they again turned black filled with hate.

Four hours after Marlise had left, disaster struck her squad. They had just finished digging in, when a jeep crested a rise behind them. After a quick scan of the countryside, it drove right towards their position. Telling everyone to keep down, Captain Lenore hoped they'd pass by. It wasn't to be, as the jeep came abreast of their position, it stopped. Four soldiers, one equipped with a radio, alighted from the jeep all urinating beside the jeep. One finished, looked casually around before going still. He must've seen one of Lenore's men move. Screaming in Arabic to the others, as he grabbed for his weapon on the back of the jeep.

Every gun they had opened up, spraying the tribesmen. All dropped shot to death in the one sided battle. Hobbling from his cover, Lenore made sure they were all dead, before checking the jeep. Unfortunately, it had taken several hits to the engine; it was useless.

"Fuck that was our ride out of here men," Lenore growled, knowing no one, including himself, had thought to try and leave the jeep undamaged. Looking back the way the jeep had approached, Lenore saw another jeep sitting on the crest of the hill, before it turned rapidly, vanishing. "Now we're fucked." He said to himself, ordering his men to strip the jeep of anything helpful. They then hurriedly moved further back into the hills.

"We got them now!" Jundela shouted out; his men screamed out their support. "Order all units to converge on their position." He ordered his radio operator, before shouting to his men to load up. "She will scream tonight my brother. The wait is over." He smiled, as his driver slammed the jeep into gear heading for the paratroopers' position. By the end of the day, three hundred men had Lenore's squad trapped on a lonely hilltop.

"Do we rush them Jundela?" One of his Officers asked him.

"No. We'll hold them here tonight. Tomorrow we'll have some mortars and a couple of tanks here. I want them to surrender my friend; I don't want the women killed unless we have no choice. Is that understood?"

"Yes, Jundela. It will be as you command."

"And tell your men, if any escape they will pay with their lives, as will you," Jundela warned, moving to his tent that his men were erecting.

Marlise out on the desert heard the shooting behind her. Stopping she considered turning back. It would be useless to go back she sorrowfully realised, knowing without help she could contribute nothing. Increasing her pace, she decided to run through the night risking the unknown. It was coming up to around ten in the evening, when tired she came over a rise to see the outline of two armoured vehicles sitting hidden in the darkness.

Dropping to the ground, she pondered what to do. Total blackness and no noise meant whoever was camped there, were not amateurs. Deciding to give them a wide berth, she crawled away from the enemy position giving them plenty of room. A thought came to her that she should try to steal some water for the next day, having used up her supply.

Leaving her weapon near a small bush, she drew her knife edging her way back towards the vehicles. Becoming accustomed to the night, she saw several forms lying between the two vehicles.

Surprised at the small number of personnel, she played with the idea of killing them all and taking one of the vehicles. Deciding the risk was too high; she edged towards a jerry can, marked water, which sat next to the rear vehicle. Picking it up, she made to move back the way she had come, when a knife touched her throat. Fear touched her, as her failure to not only herself but her squad as well hit her.

"Hey, Peter! Marlise has come for a visit!" A voice barked in the dark, sounding like a cannon going off. Marlise frozen felt the knife move away from her throat, as the shapes on the ground exploded upwards grabbing their weapons. Marlise in shock, started to cry, as it came to her that she wasn't going to die, that Peter had come to rescue her.

"Is it you Marlise?" Peters' voice thundered in the darkness, as he rushed up to her. Silence enveloped the group as Marlise unable to talk, fell into Peter's arms crying uncontrollably. Turning, she looked back at the man who had captured her. At first, she couldn't work out who it was, then turning he walked back into the darkness, as if he was a Ghost.

"Steve is that you?"

"Yes, Marlise it's me. I'll just do another sweep, then we can sit down for a talk," his voice came to her out of the night, as Peter and the others climbed into the back of one of the carriers. Once inside and the door was closed, they turned on a light. Looking around Marlise recognised Turk and Jasmine.

"My God. What are you two doing here?"

"Peter promised us an adventure." Turk laughed, the others joining in. After the group had all caught up, a tap sounded outside. Everyone froze.

"It's Steve," a voice called out, as turning off the light, they opened the door. "Tamal can you keep watch outside?" Steve asked, as Tamal without a word grabbed his weapon and moved outside. Once he was clear, they closed the door and turned the light back on.

"It's good to see you Marlise, where did you leave the others?" Steve asked producing a map. "If it helps, we are here." He added, pointing to the map. Looking at it, Marlise traced a line north.

"Somewhere there, where the hills end." She answered as Steve stared at the map.

"There was small arms fire coming from there earlier this afternoon, and now when it's quiet, I can hear spasmodic fire coming from that direction."

"Yeah, I heard it too. My Captain broke his leg, the others stayed with him, while I went for help. At one stage I nearly went back."

"You made the right decision, although approaching darkened enemy vehicles for water was risky," Steve pointed out.

"Their sentries aren't usually as good as ours," Peter interrupted, the others hiding their smiles.

"You should never think that way, Peter. The enemy is always unpredictable. In the past, I found that out more than once." Steve warned, before lightening up. "Although I am still pretty good." This caused the others to laugh.

"What now?" Peter asked Steve.

"Commonsense tells me that we should cut and run. Your friends knew what they were getting into." Steve answered, seeing everyone look shocked he continued. "Of course we'll ignore that advice won't we?" He smiled, shaking his head at his stupidity in trying to rescue them.

"It could be dangerous. We don't know how many men they have out there." Turk put in.

"Turn off the light and come outside for a minute," Steve asked, as the others not sure what he was getting at complied. As they all emerged from the carrier, Steve asked them all to be quiet and listen. Standing in the darkness, the noise of crickets and other desert creatures came to them over the desert's silence. In the background, a muted squeaking noise travelled on the wind, sometimes fading, other times lasting for a few seconds. It was accompanied by a deep thumping, which although faint, seemed to vibrate through their chests.

"Do you hear it?" Steve asked, breaking the silence.

"Sounds mechanical. What is it?" Peter asked as everyone lapsed into silence again concentrating. When no one else could come up with an answer, Steve filled them in.

"They're a long way off, but there's only one vehicle which makes a noise like that people and it is a tank," Steve answered, as the night grew quieter.

"It could be an armoured vehicle like these?" Tamal put in.

"You're right it could be, but that deep thud you're feeling in your chest suggests something a lot heavier than a carrier. No, I'm sure it a couple of tanks, maybe more." Steve pointed out.

"Where are they heading?" Marlise asked, her voice betraying her fear.

"Towards your friends."

"These armoured carriers are no match for tanks Marlise," Peter warned, thinking a rescue was now out of the question.

"Peter, why do you think I brought those special weapons Aaron had left at the boat?"

"I didn't think much of it at the time. Do you think they will make a difference?"

"Yes, they'll make a difference. The secret is, how do we use them to our advantage?"

Jundela was in a foul mood. After getting up early to finish off the paratroopers, he found the tanks and mortars hadn't arrived. Around him, his small army waited for the signal to attack Looking up on the small hilltop he tried to calm down and tried to see where the paratroopers were hiding. Calling his mobile infantry commanders over, he decided to start the attack. The two commanders were less impressed. Even though the troops were mostly foreigners, not tribesmen, they were still good men. Neither commander, wanted them squandered in an attempt to capture one woman.

There was also the problem that because of the rocky outcrop their armoured carriers were unable to move in close, their only use being to supply cover fire. Despite their concerns, Jundela was about to give the order when several explosions sounded from the desert behind them. All movement stopped as all eyes turned to the east.

"Air attack!" Jundela's radio operator shouted as all in hearing distance looked skywards.

"Disperse your men into the surrounding hills commanders. Leave only enough men to keep the paratroopers bottled up!" He shouted in anger, as knowing staying in the open was suicidal, his mobile troops fled into the hills to seek safety.

Out in the desert, Steve and Peter lowered the two launchers to the ground. The Juvenile launchers were usually used for busting concrete bunkers, having a specially designed warhead for penetrating reinforced concrete. Tanks with their heavy armoured plate were a far different target to crack, except when the crew were driving along in the desert heat with their hatches open.

"The poor bastards didn't even know what killed them," Peter whispered beside him.

"Would you rather have warned them?" Steve asked, a small smile on his lips.

"Okay Turk, send the radio message," Steve yelled across to the first armoured vehicle where he waited. Picking up the mic, Turk shouted in Arabic that planes were attacking his tanks.

"That should do it." Steve smiled, as Marlise and Jasmine on the rise above them, watched in the distance troops on the hill where she left her squad, dispersed.

"Captain Roberts, we've got another column of vehicles approaching from the same direction as the tanks," Tamal warned. Ever since they'd gone into the field, Tamal had started calling Steve 'Captain Roberts'. Steve admitted it made him feel old, but telling him to call him Steve didn't get through.

Steve, letting it go, pulled out his binoculars looking east. There, just coming up on the tanks were three trucks. The first had what appeared to be a mortar set up.

"Reload Peter. Take out the second truck with the radio before it reports." Steve ordered, as he too reloaded. Peter ready first, fired. Unlike the tanks, the soldiers on the trucks saw the missiles rise from the ground. Stopping, they started to dismount, when the rocket hit. Steve firing next, watched his camera screen showing the flight of his rocket. Adjusting the flight, he aimed for the lead truck. As with Peter's, it was on target. Peter by this time had already started reloading. Not waiting, he again fired. Looking at his small TV screen, he watched the missile climb skyward, before steering it down on the last remaining truck.

Through their binoculars, they estimated half the soldiers were down either dead or injured. There was no sign of the radio or its operator.

"Back to the vehicles now!" Steve ordered, as Turk and Tamal lending a hand, carried the launchers back to the vehicles. The men exhausted, then waited for the women to return from the hill. Two minutes had passed before they arrived.

"The main units have fled into the hills as you predicted," Marlise told Steve, placing his headset on, he ordered both vehicles forward.

Captain Lenore with a sense of foreboding watched the enemy units ready themselves for an attack. The day before they'd been forced to move to higher ground, digging in at the crest of the hill. The enemy had tried to dislodge them once, only to be repulsed. Of his six remaining men, two were wounded, one badly, although at the moment, not life threatening. Still, he'd received a nasty wound in his left leg, which would need surgery. All his men could still fight, but running now, was out of the question.

The enemy during the rest of the day had surrounded their position, and Lenore knew any determined attack would breakthrough. As it grew dark, his men had braced for the attack, only to find that except for harassing fire, the enemy seemed happy just to keep them pinned down. Now daytime revealed a strong force preparing to attack. His men readying themselves had laid a small minefield of anti personnel mines in front of them, although no one thought they'd seriously stop a determined attack.

"Where is Marlise?" Lenore whispered, wondering if she had made it. "Well, at least she has a chance." He smiled, hoping she did make it. Lining up a soldier who was edging forward, Lenore was just about to open fire when two explosions echoed out of the desert. "What the shit was that?" he asked himself, when several minutes later, three more were heard. The enemy troops gathered down the hill, suddenly raced to their vehicles, driving towards the mountainous country to the west. Even though this lowered the numbers of enemy soldiers, it still left a large number surrounding them. "Should we try to breakout?" he mused, when in the distance two armoured vehicles came rapidly towards them.

Down below them, he saw the enemy troops turn and stare at the two vehicles. They were part of the group as several soldiers waved to them. Lenore sensed that something was not quite right with the appearance of the two vehicles, as an officer moved out hesitantly, to meet the approaching vehicles. Signalling for them to slow down, he waited while his men held back. The two vehicles immediately slowed, as the enemy Officer and his soldiers now more confident, moved out to greet them.

Lenore watched as an Officer jumped from the first armoured carrier. After what appeared to be a heated exchange, the tribesmen guarding the hills around them packed up, leaving the two armoured vehicles facing them.

"Get ready men; I'd say those two carriers are going to try and take this position." Captain Lenore shouted out, as the two vehicles edged forward.

"What do you mean try Sir? We haven't got anything left to stop them." One of his men yelled back, several others laughed. Lenore thought over what his man had said before answering.

"Okay men. If the mines don't stop them, break for the surrounding hills. I don't think surrendering is an option." Lenore shouted out. His men answering, with Good luck Sir.

"Well let's make them pay," Lenore said to himself, as the two vehicles almost on top of the mines stopped.

"Anyone want a lift?" A familiar female voice yelled out. Around him, Lenore could see his men tense as they all recognised the voice.

"Is that you Sergeant?" Lenore yelled back, still fingering his weapon's trigger.

"Yes Sir and I haven't been captured. Peter is here with some friends." This brought subdued laughter from the carriers. Jumping down from the first carrier, Marlise and Peter's hands in the air came forward. Lenore, painfully climbing to his feet limped forward.

"Don't come any closer. There are mines in front of you." Lenore shouted out.

"Okay, we'll wait here," Marlise yelled back, as Lenore and his men unsure what was going on, slowly climbed out of their holes, before weaving their way through the minefield.

"Captain is everyone okay?" Marlise asked, sounding concern, as the men shuffled forward.

"Yes, Benny and Junee received wounds in our last exchange. Junee will need surgery pretty soon." Lenore told her.

"Let's get them all on board before the Bedouin find out they've been had," Peter suggested, as Lenore overjoyed at being free, hugged him and Marlise.

"Thank you, both. I don't know what to say?" Lenore stammered out, as Peter seeing him start to wobble on his feet, grabbed him, helping him towards the second carrier.

"Then say nothing. Let's go." Peter insisted, as Lenore's men looking relieved, boarded the carriers.

Turk and Steve watched the paratroopers climb aboard. Both saw they were in a bad way.

"I can't believe we pulled it off?" Turk smiled, as Steve closed the rear door, turning the carrier.

"It's the unexpected that always gets you. These tribesmen are so scared of their leaders that they never question an order." Steve replied, accelerating out into the flat open desert.

When Steve had first asked Tamal and Turk to play officers in the Bedouin's army, they had both laughed till they cried. They'd sobered quickly, when they saw he wasn't kidding. Sharing his plan with all of them, Steve saw their growing concern at the plan's recklessness.

"You're putting us in harm's way if the Bedouin question us?" Turk pointed out, during Steve's briefing.

"Yes, I am. Many things could go wrong, although we have the element of surprise in that no one will suspect us until it is too late." Steve answered.

"How will we remain hidden? For your plan to work, Turk and Tamal must exit the carriers and talk to the Bedouin officer in charge. What's to stop the Bedouin looking inside the back of the vehicle and either seeing no troops or worse seeing me and the others?" Marlise pointed out.

"It is a bluff Marlise. The rear door will be left opened to show we fear nothing. None of their men will check because their officers being confused, will not ask them to. Trust me, in any army; orders are orders, it will work." Steve told them all, although even Peter seemed unconvinced. Still, except for fighting it out, the group saw no other options, so they prepared for the mission. First, they had to make Turk and Tamal look like Officers. This was the simple part because the carriers contain the kits of the once owners. The uniform was one thing, teaching a man to act like he was a born Bedouin leader was another.

Turk, because of his experience with these tribesmen, got the feel of it quite quickly, Tamal struggled. Young, with no military training, kept stumbling over his lines when talking to Turk. Peter, in the end, solved the problem.

"Let Tamal be the senior Officer. He can pretend to be above them all; his arrogance can be his cover?" Peter suggested winning Tamal's approval. It wasn't long before Tamal liking his role, as an uppity spoilt relation of the Sheik, developed a constant sneer on his face, accompanied by an arrogant swagger.

"How do I look Captain Turk?" He said with a sneer in rough Arabic to Turk while training.

"Good, but don't get overconfident, this isn't going to be easy, and I'm still the boss," Turk told him, before grabbing him in a bear hug, ruffling his hair.

As Turk had said, it wasn't as easy as they thought. When they had driven up to the Bedouin's position, they saw many of the Bedouin point their weapons towards them. Peter for one thought they might know of the loss of these vehicles. He was getting ready to move the machine-gun around to face them, when Steve stopped him.

"Leave it. We're approaching friendly forces. Would you point a weapon at a fellow soldier?"

"They're pointing theirs." Peter reminded him.

"They don't know who we are that's why they're reacting, give it time," Steve warned. At that, they all settled.

Stopping just short of an Officer who had appeared, Steve opened the rear door. Tamal, his guts in knots, looked anything but confident.

"Get out there and charm them." Steve smiled back at him, as Tamal returning the smile, turned to the door. Putting on his cap, he marched out followed by Turk.

As Steve predicted the soldier didn't bother checking the open door, instead they stood with their Officer. Turk wondering how Tamal would go, nearly lost it, when Tamal ignoring the Officer, walked passed him to stare at the hilltop. The Officer slighted by being ignored had death in his eyes.

"Who are you and why are you here?" The Officer challenged. Tamal waving his hand as if none of them mattered, took another look through his binoculars, before turning to Turk.

"Captain Turk, give them their orders." He sneered, his eyes not leaving the hill. Angrily the Officer and his men turned to Turk. Turk spellbound by Tamal at first failed to answer. The Enemy Officer mistook this for embarrassment at his treatment. Clearing his throat, Turk addressed the Officer.

"Sorry about this, but Jundela himself has ordered Colonel Tamal to take over the operation here." Turk told him before whispering, "He is his cousin."

"What are you whispering Turk?" Tamal shouted, startling everyone.

"Nothing Sir. I'm just passing on Jundela's orders to the Officer only." Turk lied, looking at the enemy Officer who had developed a small smile at his treatment.

"Good, let's get this over with shall we. I want to get back to the coast as soon as possible." Tamal told him, moving towards the hill for a better look. Once he was out of hearing range, Turk spoke again.

"Insolent pup. If it weren't for his cousin, I'd shoot him myself" Turk told the Officer, who tried not to laugh.

"I don't envy you your assignment, my brother." He smiled, before becoming serious. "The French paratroopers are tough, are you sure you don't want us to stay and assist?"

"No, he wants all the glory. We'll attack once you're gone. With these carriers and my men, I don't see a problem in capturing them." Turk answered looking angry.

"I will take my men and join Commander Jundela in the hills. That way I won't have to give an opinion of his cousin." He chuckled, some of his men sniggering too.

Once they had left, Tamal and Turk came back aboard, before closing the door.

"How did it go?" Peter asked.

"I nearly shit myself," Tamal confessed, as the others laughed.

"Even I thought you were the leader's cousin Tamal. No one else would've had the gall to treat a fellow officer like you did." Steve added.

"I thought it was easier than talking. Like you said the tribesmen fear their leaders, more than any enemy." Tamal pointed out. Once the tribesmen had left, Steve ordered both vehicles forward. He then ordered them to stop just short of the paratrooper's positions.

"Okay, Marlise. Grab the loudspeaker and talk to your friends." Steve had asked her, ending the mission.

"Still it was touch and go there, Steve. Jundela could've come back?" Turk pointed out.

"Not with the fear of being bombed by American planes. No, he will be deep in the hills by now." Steve smiled, as Marlise and Captain Lenore approached them.

"Where to now?" Lenore asked after Marlise had introduced him.

"We left a plane about a hundred clicks to the south of here. It will be a squeeze but we should all fit aboard." Peter answered sitting down next to Marlise, as the carrier picked up speed.

After travelling at speed for most of the day, the two carriers reached the intersection where they had acquired the carriers. Steve driving the first carrier slammed the brakes on, turning hard left. The other carrier following behind automatically followed.

"Isn't the plane straight ahead?" Peter yelled from the rear. Steve not answering swerved again entering a thicket beside the track. Stopping, he waited for the second vehicle to pull up, before opening the rear door.

"Get your weapons!" Steve ordered as the others scrambled after him. As Steve left the first carrier, he ran to the second carrier, warning them as well. Once everyone was armed, they positioned themselves around the carriers. Steve still on edge signalled for silence as he disappeared into the surrounding scrub. The others immediately sought cover and waited. Peter watching Steve run in the direction of the river, saw for the first time a thin trail of smoke rising in the distance.

Over an hour had passed before Steve reappeared. He seemed a little more relaxed, as he signalled them all to sit down.

"What's going on Steve?" Peter whispered.

"Did you see the smoke?" Steve asked. Most signalled no, Peter nodded yes.

"When I reached the crossroad, I saw smoke rising from the river. It was from the area where we had left the plane. I travelled towards there just now; there is a sizeable force of soldiers waiting there for us."

"Then why burn the plane and alert us?" Captain Lenore asked.

"I'm not sure they did. I saw several dead bodies on the way there and back; they were dressed in Niger army uniforms."

"That might be part of the joint push north. Before we dropped we heard the Niger and Chad Governments, had allied to push the tribesmen and their allies back," Captain Lenore explained.

"Good for them. How does that help us?" Peter asked.

"It doesn't, although torching that plane saved our arses. What it does is make travelling all that more dangerous, as both sides will do their best to kill us." Steve confessed walking to the carrier. "Everyone into the second carrier. Peter and I will be in the first. You will travel at least two hundred metres behind us at all times. At the first sign of trouble you turn away and head south. Is that understood?" Steve's hard voice, made them all shy away from challenging him.

Jundela stood on the hill where the paratroopers had made their last stand. His anger at being tricked again made his men give him a wide berth. Unlike before he hadn't punished anyone, this one was his fault. He had fallen for the fake air raid warning, ordering his men into the hills. Confused and unaware, the Officer left in charge had only followed what he thought were orders from him. It was only twenty minutes after his troops had left their positions and travelled here, that he learnt the attack on the armour and mortar units was by ground launched missiles.

Instead of blaming everyone he had asked his men in the field to search the area where those two carriers had come from. There they had found the dead crews and later the plane. A brief skirmish with Niger regulars had left the plane destroyed, but at least it meant his prize was still out there somewhere.

"Colonel Fulner. Gather all our forces and sweep along the border with Niger. The enemy must be between here and that plane, let's find them?" He smiled climbing aboard his jeep.

"That will leave our flanks, vulnerable Sir," Fulner replied. Unlike most of his Officers, Colonel Jidel Fulner was not only a capable leader, but also a friend. As children, they had played together and later attended the same University in Egypt. When his father the Sheik had been killed, Fulner had returned from serving with al Qaeda in Syria. There he'd been running the insurgent war against the Kurds, helping their brothers in arms achieve many victories. Jundela wanted to put him in charge of the forces in Libya, but he had declined. He asked first to prove himself taking command of a field unit here in Niger.

For five years he had ruthlessly pushed south, conquering half of both Niger and Chad. If it weren't for France and America sending their Air Forces and military muscle, the two countries would have fallen in less than two months. Undeterred by the setback, Fulner had organised the retreat of their forces to the border, keeping ahead of the two renewed and rearmed forces of Chad and Niger. He had also skilfully worn down the advancing enemy forces, while slowly building their forces up.

In both Niger and Chad, as the retreat was underway, Fulner's militia units whittling away at their enemy's resolve, by attacking their exposed flanks. Now, even with the enemy's use of air power, Jundelas forces were again pushing south. Jundela knew his fixation with capturing the woman who had maimed his brother, had cost them dearly. If he could've foreseen the trouble, it had caused he admitted he would not have done it. Captain Fulner when first briefed on the operation so far had said it all with his eyes.

In front of the other officers he had said nothing, his loyalty to Jundela absolute. In private he had rebuked him for putting the will of Allah, behind his vendetta. Jundela had wept, admitting his vanity and stupidly in the pursuance of this quest. Fulner had embraced him then as a brother, promising to kill these jackals for him before launching their offensive south. Jundela had told him no.

Instead, he gave him complete command of all their forces, while he finished the search for the paratroopers. Fulner reluctantly accepted, knowing the coming offensive was about to begin and couldn't be delayed. Already his best-trained men had crossed the border, travelling in secret to the airfields where the enemy's air forces were based. On his command, they would launch attacks on the fields crippling the enemy's ability to respond.

"Okay, Jundela. Find this woman, but do not take too long. I might need your help if things go wrong." Fulner warned, leaving for their command centre.

"Now all I need is to locate the woman?" Jundela smiled. "We'll have them soon brother. It's only time." He promised his silent brother beside him, as they drove south.

Colonel Fulner watched Jundela go. They had been childhood friends, but Fulner sensed there was something wrong with Jundela. Their cause had always been about securing Africa; now this woman took priority with Jundela.

"His Bedouin tribes' lust for revenge, risked everything we have accomplished," Fulner confessed, as climbing aboard his jeep, he drove back to his headquarters.

The net was tightening as Steve with Peter's help, steered their small group along the border probing for a place to cross. Several times they'd had to hide from both American warplanes and Jundela's Bedouin tribesmen. In the end, they had dug in beside the river. Steve studying the map, worked out they were ten miles east of where they'd first landed in the plane.

"We're stuffed, Peter. They hold all the crossings in this area and soon we'll be out of fuel."

"What do you suggest?" Peter answered, watching a crocodile rise to the surface and give them a look over.

"It's taking a chance, but how about giving Nigel a ring. By now the yanks know the French have been playing them. This build up of Jundela's forces here is not for us; they're going south again."

"Do you think they are going into both Chad and Niger?"

"No, I'd say they're going to concentrate on Niger. The forces facing Chad are just a show of strength for the Americans to think the French are serious about fighting. I think the French are going to sit this one out." Steve put forward.

"I think you're right, but do you think Nigel will believe me?" Peter warned. Steve sat there thinking about it before with a shrug of his shoulder he made a decision.

"Give me your phone." He whispered, clearly not wanting to.

Nigel was sitting with his boss going over photos of the build up of Jundela's forces along the border with Chad and Niger.

"They can't be that stupid. If they cross those borders, our air power will chew them to pieces." Nigel's boss mumbled.

"Could it be a show of strength to get a better deal from the French?"

"You could be right, but would you bet your life on it?" Nigel's phone ringing made them both look at it.

"It's Peter," Nigel told him. Answering the phone, he put it on speaker. "Peter, how are you going?"

"It's Steve Nigel." Nigel shocked, stood up, before sitting back down. His boss beside him stared at him; they all knew Steve's history.

"God Steve, you're supposed to be dead." He blurted out his eyes misting up.

"When the boat blew Natasha was in front of me, she took the main impact. I was thrown overboard. Knowing it was a bomb; I swam under the walkway and escaped. I'm sorry I didn't tell you Nigel, but it would've told whoever did it I was still alive." Steve confessed, his voice trembling.

"What are you doing with Peter?"

"Against my advice, he wanted to rescue his girlfriend. So here we are. And by the way, I was the one who killed the French Foreign Minister, not Peter."

Nigel not knowing what to say sat there stunned.

"Steve. This is Nigel's boss John Carrington. Can you tell us what's going on there?"

"The Bedouin forces are preparing to go south. By the looks I'd say the forces facing Chad are a show of force only, Niger's the target."

"Are you sure, they'll be chewed to pieces by our air force there?"

"These guys are no fools; I'd say they'll hit your airfields first. The border is easy for them to cross here; they most probably have already sent forces south." John Carrington's face went white as a sheet at Steve's words.

"Oh my God you're right. I've got to go," John exclaimed, racing from the room. Nigel alone now came to life.

"What about you Steve. Where are you?"

"We're trapped against the river that flows along the border here. The Bedouin forces are closing in as we speak." Nigel beyond thinking sat trying to work something out.

"Have you got flares?" Steve looked in the rear of the carrier and found some.

"Yes, we have Blue, Red, Yellow and Green."

"I'm not sure if it will help but hang onto the blue. I'll pass along that we have friendlies in the area. I'd say you're in for a plastering."

"Thanks, Nigel any help would be better than nothing."

"Steve, will I tell Lindsey you're alive?"

"No Nigel. It doesn't look good here so don't tell them anything. It would be too painful if I don't make it out." Steve replied, his voice full of pain.

"Okay Steve, but when this is all over, we'll have to talk about what you've been doing."

"No, we won't Nigel. I'm afraid the French won't let us off lightly, after the trouble Peter and I have caused. Goodbye Nigel." Steve ended the call.

After Steve had hung up, Nigel sat at his desk in silence. Steve was again being hunted by a supposed ally nation who'd put their nation's interest ahead of what was right. Getting up from his seat, he walked to the situation room, to find John trying to contact the American force's airfield in Niger.

"General. It's John Carrington from the CIA in Washington." John paused as the General replied.

"What do you want spooky?" The General mocked.

"Look, I've no time for pleasantries General. Put your base on full alert you're about to be attacked." Seeing Nigel, he switched the phones to conference call so Nigel and the other people present could hear the General.

"Look, Mr Carrington, It's nearly lunchtime here, and we haven't seen any rebel troops for months."

"General either put the base on alert, or your replacement will!" John growled into the phone, as on the other end a klaxon suddenly started to blare.

"Well, I hope you're satisfied, Carrington. And I warn you now; you'd better be right.

"Just be prepared for a surprise attack General and get everything that can fly off the ground right now."

"That is already happening. I'll send the majority to bomb the enemy troop build ups along the border. The rest can fly shotgun here. If of course, you agree?" The General added sarcastically.

"Sounds good General. The carrier group, Nimitz, is in the Mediterranean coast. They'll be sending what air units they have, to help neutralize the enemy forces." John ignored the General's attitude.

"Like I said, you'd better be right Carrington." With that, the General hung up.

"Pompous arse!" John yelled, slamming down his phone.

"Well, you warned him, Sir. That's all you could do." Nigel reassured him.

"I just hope your father-in law is right Nigel. If we plaster these guys across the border and the base isn't attacked, we're both going to get shit-canned over it."

"Steve Roberts might be a lot of things, but deceiving us when he's in the firing line isn't one of them. It all fits. The French have been dragging their butts to help us do anything, and someone with state of the art jamming gear is hampering our Comm's. No, on this call we're right."

"We'll know soon enough," John answered watching the satellite image of the border area.

Colonel Fulner stood in Jundela's command centre watching the clock climb towards midday.

"Are our units in position?" He raised his voice as the staff around him all nodded yes.

"Okay. Order them to attack." Fulner commanded, as his radio operator raised his hand, signalling.

"What is it, Captain?"

"Sir. I'm receiving a message from one of our forward units near the American airbase. He reports the Americans are launching their planes."

"Okay, there's no time to waste. All forces attack immediately!"

"Do you think they know of our attack?" The Captain asked.

"Maybe. They more likely decided to attack our forces near the border. They probably spotted them massing there. Radio them to disperse and be prepared for air assaults."

The command centre grew quiet as Fulner, and his staff waited. The radio squawking made them all turn to the Captain near it.

"Sir the commander of our forces near the American airfield reports the attack is progressing well, although the American and Niger troops are putting up stiff opposition."

"So they were ready and knew we were coming. Radio Jundella! Warn him immediately." Jidel ordered as overhead planes could be heard approaching.

"Sir they might pick up our broadcast?" The Captain warned.

"Chance it. We need to let him know that this offensive is doomed." Many in the bunker looked surprised, thinking everything was going as planned. Fulner knew differently. Sure they had damaged the airfields, but the main target, the aircraft, had escaped. They could deploy to another airfield and continue to attack their main forces, as they advanced.

"Captain, have you warned Jundela?" Fulner was worried.

"He can't be contacted, Sir. He left his main forces there after a report of the missing Paratroopers was received."

"Tell them to go after him immediately." Fulner angrily shouted, walking to the bunker's entrance and outside. "Jundela is putting everything at risk for revenge!" He cursed, as in the distance he heard a whistling noise. Looking skywards he saw a flash, as he dived into the croc infested river.

Approaching the border the American planes spread out looking for targets. News from their base informed them of mass casualties amongst the ground crews and support troops including their General and his staff. They all knew that except for a last minute warning, they'd most probably be dead as well. Colonel Bradshaw, the mission commander, thought it time to rally them.

"Okay men. We know why we're here. Let's punish those backstabbers for what they did to our airbase."

Multiple calls assured him his men got the message as many of his pilots dived towards the ground. Watching them, the Colonel saw his threat detector suddenly light up. Looking at the screen, showed someone below them was broadcasting on an enemy command frequency.

"Well, you're all mine, my friend." He smiled. Peeling off and diving towards the signal. Painting the target where the signal originated from, he released two radio-controlled five hundred pound bombs. Pulling up, he watched the bombs continue to dive towards the hidden bunker. This was the sound, and flash Fulner reacted to, as the bombs seconds later, struck the bunker behind him. One minute Fulner was diving into dark water filled with death, the next a huge cloud of debris reigned skywards as the bunker, and Fulner's entire staff were vaporised.

Colonel Fulner, after being flattened on the river's bottom, surfaced in the middle of the river. Clearing mud from his eyes, he saw a huge hole, where the bunker moments before had been located. He thanked God for his miraculous escape, before realising the danger he was in now. Fearfully checking the water around him, he saw it was unbelievably clear of crocodiles, which usually gathered here. Silently swimming to the bank, he climbed out breathing a sigh of relief.

The scaly creatures he guessed had felt the shockwaves from the explosions and were long gone, for the time being. Walking away from the river Fulner knelt down and prayed. Hearing footsteps he slowly again climbed to his feet.

"Commander! Praise Allah; you have survived." Two of the soldiers shouted out, thinking it a sign from God.

"Yes, he was indeed looking after me men. Now let's find some transport and find Jundela immediately!" He ordered, as his men helped him towards where their group of vehicles waited. Once aboard a carrier, he used it's radio, to establish a temporary command centre. Calling all that was left of his army units, ordering them to retreat into the hills, away from the border. Several of the Officers who had come to the command centre seemed surprised wondering if the explosion had rattled him.

"Commander, why are we retreating? The airfields have been neutralised." One of his Bedouin Officers pointed out.

"Yes they captured the airfield, but the planes above us indicate that the enemy's air force is very much alive. We must regain our strength before we go south again my brothers. So gather your men and follow my orders." His voice conveyed he was not going to argue about it.

"What about Jundela? He is still out there somewhere?" Another Bedouin Officer snapped, his hand straying to his sidearm. Fulner's guards immediately pointed their weapons at the Officer, making the situation tense.

"Fire," Fulner ordered, as his guards shot the officer, causing the other officers to lapse into silence, broken at last by Fulner.

"Jundela has become obsessed with the woman and has put our entire army at risk. He put me in command here, because he knew his judgement was being affected by his obsession with revenge. Now follow my orders or join your friend." Fulner growled, cowering the gathered Officers.

"Yes, Sir!" Echoed from them all, as lifting their dead companion from the ground, they turned and left.

"Watch them," Fulner instructed his guard commander, who without a word left the tent. "Now let's get our forces away from the border and fall back to our reserve position." He ordered, his guards leading the way.

"Colonel Fulner. What of Jundela?" His guard commander whispered, not wanting any to hear him question Fulner's decision.

"He has a strong force with him. Sooner or later he will realise the gravity of the situation and join us. Other than that I will not risk more men to find him."

"Very well Colonel. Although I hope you are right in abandoning him."

"I don't give a shit if I'm right. My job at the moment is to salvage what is left of our army. Jundela knew the risk, I will answer to God later." He assured him, before climbing on board their armoured transport.

Jundela with two armoured vehicles and forty men watched the enemy planes pulverise his army. Hidden in a deserted village, away from his army's main advanced positions he had driven his vehicles into the native huts concealing them. Earlier they'd come under attack, losing two support trucks and thirty men.

"Is the radio working?" Jundela asked.

"No Sir. When the enemy plane strafed us, he got lucky and hit the radio."

"It would be good to know what is happening, lieutenant. Do what you can, but I need to know what is going on."

"Yes, Sir. I have sent out some of our men to try to find either replacement parts or another radio. In the meantime, I will try to repair this one."

"Thank you, lieutenant," Jundela replied moving outside to check the skies. It appeared clear of planes at the moment, but appearance could be deceiving Jundela knew.

"Sergeant to me!" He shouted as Sergeant Bola hurried to him.

"Yes, Sir."

"Sergeant pick two of your best men and have them take my jeep and drive my brother back to our stronghold in the desert."

"Do you think our forces are withdrawing Sir?" The sergeant surprised whispered.

"The attack has failed Sergeant. The enemy planes are everywhere, meaning our forces failed to cripple them."

"Do not worry Sir, Miguel will be sent there immediately."

"Thank you, Sergeant. Now tell the Officers from the units near the river, to meet me here." Jundela ordered as the Sergeant rushed away.

"They are good men, I have failed them," Jundela admitted to himself, as the Officers arrived. Once they seated themselves, Jundela started their briefing.

"Are they still near the river Captain Murarrie?" Jundela asked the room silently.

"Yes, Sir. They are dug in, with nowhere to go."

"I have had Officers tell me that before Captain. I hope you are right?"

"They are still there Jundela. I left two of my best trackers watching the only two tracks out of the area. If they left, they swam a crocodile infested river."

"Why not have them watch the enemy's position?" Another Officer asked.

"I tried that twice; I lost six men. Whoever they are, they are formidable soldiers."

"Yes, they are Captain. Which makes their capture all the more important." Jundela replied, making the gathered Officers bristle.

"Jundela killing them would be far easier and cost a lot fewer men." Captain Murarrie pointed out.

"The woman I am after is responsible for my brother's injuries. My Father screams out from his grave for me to avenge my brother. You are not of the Bedouin tribe; you would not understand!" Jundela shouted, spraying his Officers with spittle. Shocked by his anger, the Officers stood stunned, as if turned to stone.

"Then I suggest we go in during daylight. It will take away their skill in the darkness." Murarrie suggested, keeping his opinion to himself.

"Very well. Tomorrow morning we attack. Prepare your men." Jundela barked, leaving them. After he'd left, Captain Murarrie the senior officer there, looked at his fellow Officers. They, in turn, looked to him for guidance. The Officers present were foreign soldiers from all over the Middle East. They had joined the cause with Jundela to bring their hard line view of Islam to Africa. Their commander had just told them that he considered them beneath his tribesmen.

"No one says anything. Just prepare your men. One way or another it will be over tomorrow." He told them, leaving to be with his troops.

Steve lay with Peter overlooking the enemy position. It was clear by their preparations, tomorrow they would be attacking.

"You'd think they'd attack at night? It would allow them to get close."

"They know we're pros. They'd lose more men, and they couldn't guarantee they'd take Marlise alive and that's what this is all about." Steve told him, his eyes never leaving the enemy camp.

"Surely this Jundela guy isn't so stupid that he'd let revenge guide his attack?"

"To him, family honour is everything, Peter. We hurt them badly, killing his father and Marlise left the guy's brother as a constant reminder. We'd have been dead a long time before this, if they'd just tried to kill us."

"Can we use that to our advantage?"

"No, we're trapped by the river. We either win, or we die here. Or worse, we're captured. That I won't let happen." Steve assured him.

"Could we chance the river?"

"We could. Chances are most of us wouldn't make it, as the river is alive with crocs. I'd rather fight than risk it."

"Me too. We'd better get back." Peter suggested, Steve, having one last look agreed.

At the camp, Marlise and the others waited in their prepared positions. A crack of a branch put them on alert.

"Broken!" Turk shouted.

222

"Window!" Peter replied as he and Steve appeared from the dark.

"How did it go?" Turk asked. The look on their faces told them everything.

"They'll be attacking tomorrow. I suggest we prepare." Peter put forward.

"Do we have any other alternatives than to fight?" Marlise asked.

"Only the river and that is close to suicide," Steve admitted. Silence descended over the group as a feeling of inevitability gripped them.

"So unless someone's got something else, let's prepare." Peter put forward as the group prepared to return to their positions.

"I have an idea Sir," Tamal spoke out, his voice a little high pitched with his nervousness.

"Okay Tamal, you have the floor." Steve declared formally, causing the others to smile.

"It's just they seemed to want us alive more than killing us. What if we filled one vehicle with what's left of our fuel and someone alone took off in it. The rest of us could hide here. They'd have to go after it, fearing we were escaping, wouldn't they?" The others sat opened mouthed at his plan. "What is it? Is the plan that bad?"

"No Tamal. Quite the opposite." Peter smiled.

"And you thought my plans were strange." Steve chuckled. The others joining in.

It took several hours to prepare for the coming departure. Steve suggested they stripped the other carrier to make it look convincing. Finished they gathered round.

"Okay. Who is going to go?" One of the Marlise's paratroopers asked.

"We draw straws. The short one goes." Steve put forward. Breaking up some twigs, he held them out for the others to take one. Each member drew one comparing them to their neighbours. In the end, Tamal held the shortest.

"Well it was my plan," he smiled, moving towards the vehicle.

"No Tamal. I will go." Turk snapped, stopping him.

"It is my lot Brother. Let me follow my path," Tamal told him, hugging his brother.

"Then good luck to you Tamal. I will wait for your return across the border." Turk promised stepping back. Behind them, the carrier door closed.

"Wait who closed that door?" Peter warned, as looking around, he saw Steve was missing. Running to the carrier, Peter banged on the side.

"Steve you don't have to do this."

"Yes, I do Peter. I'm the best equipped to survive out there. Go now and set fire to the other carrier, it will convince them we've all left." Steve told him, starting up. Peter with no other choice raced to the other carrier, setting fire to it.

"Everyone to your positions now," Peter ordered, as speechless at what Steve had done, they obeyed.

"Jundela! The enemy is running!" One of his guards shouted out, making Jundela leap out of his bed. Dressing swiftly, he ran to his command vehicle, finding his men frantically packing everything aboard.

"What has happened?" He asked Captain Murarrie.

"One of my scouts spotted one of their carriers heading at full speed east along the border. I sent a squad who found the other carrier burning. Their positions have been abandoned."

"Order every vehicle we have here to pursue them, Captain. They won't get far without fuel?" He smiled, climbing aboard his carrier; the driver immediately drove east after the enemy carrier.

For Peter and the others it was one of the most frightful experiences they had endured. Lying in their holes in the open, close to their prepared positions, they watched the enemy troops arrive. Unaware of their presence, they drove their carriers to within inches of their hidden holes. Peter beside Marlise, prayed that their shallow pit, wouldn't cave in and become their grave, as the tracked vehicle rolled over their hiding spot.

The enemy troops swiftly searched the area, the carriers and their troops departed, heading west. Giving them an hour to be safe, Peter slowly climbed out. Sure it was not a trap; he went from hole to hole, telling his fellow moles they were safe to come out.

"It worked." Tamal smiled, as they all gathered their gear moving to their prepared positions.

"Yes it did, but we're still here." Peter pointed out, hugging Marlise.

"What now?" She asked.

"We send the fittest men along the shoreline until we find a village. Even with all the trouble here there should still be some kind of boat around here somewhere. Once we locate one, we return and ferry everyone across the river. Simple!" He smiled.

"How long before they know they've been had?"

"That's up to Steve and his remaining fuel, I'm afraid," Peter admitted, the others looking around nervously.

Steve meanwhile hammered the carrier racing east. Fuel he knew was dropping to a dangerously low level, but getting distance between him and his pursuers was paramount. The air force he saw had been busy as he passed a group of burnt out vehicles, the bodies of the unfortunate lying around them. As he continued, he saw some vehicles although damaged hadn't caught fire.

An idea came to him, as stopping he turned off the engine. Opening the rear door, he climbed out listening. It was a long way off, but he could hear the noise of approaching vehicles. Seizing the moment he ran to another carrier. Inside he found several jerry cans of fuel.

"Bingo!" he laughed. Lugging two back to his carrier, he emptied them into his thirsty beast. He was about to return for another one, when the noise of his pursuer became much louder. Jumping back in he started up, driving again to the west. Behind him, Jundela's carrier crested a ridge, its driver spotting him.

"Sir! I see him to the east!" The driver shouted. Jundela coming forward, sat next to the driver, as they approached the battlefield.

"Stop the vehicle driver!" Jundela ordered, the vehicle grinding slowly to a stop, as did the others. Climbing out Jundela looked around, wondering why they'd caught up so quickly. Looking at Steve's vehicle's track marks, he saw a wet spot near the two jerry cans. Walking to it, he dipped one of his fingers in the wet spot sniffing it.

"Fuel." He smiled, looking around at his once mighty army's vehicles. To his surprise, he saw one of his Officers, run to a carrier across from him. He realised it was his Comm's Officer. Going to the carrier, he looked inside.

"I judge you're after a working radio?"

"Yes, sir. Since you stopped, I thought I'd look. This one is not working, but the parts I need for ours are all here intact. I should have us on the air in no time."

"Good. As soon as you repair it, find out if we have units up ahead. Not everyone would've left this area yet."

"Yes, Sir." He replied, running back to his carrier.

"These westerners think they're so smart." Jundela smiled to his men. "They don't know what is ahead of them." He chuckled, hurrying back to his carrier.

Steve having curved slightly north into Libya stopped to have a quick look behind him. He saw Jundela had stopped near where he'd found the fuel.

"Funny you'd think they would've kept coming? They must've seen me?" He whispered scanning the area around him. He could see for about ten miles to the east. There seemed to be several areas ahead where vehicles could be seen smouldering after the air attack then nothing.

"What is guarding their flank?" Steve mused, knowing they must've had some units here to block any flanking movements from their enemies. Worried by the nothingness to the east he continued, searching for fuel or a way across the river.

Peter, for the boat search, had sent Turk and Tamal east, while Marlise and a recovered Captain Lenore went west. Peter in charge reluctantly stayed put. The going was surprisingly easy for both groups, as a well-worn track followed the river at a safe distance, meaning villages in better times must have travelled along the river frequently. Marlise with Lenore, many times intersected tracks leading to the river. Checking each one, they found either fishing spots or signs where boats had been moored. Unfortunately, there was no sign of any watercrafts.

"You know except for the constant fear of death; this place is quite pretty." Lenore smiled, making Marlise smirk.

"You're quite the romantic Captain. I for one don't want to see this God forsaken hole again."

"That's pretty hard Sergeant. It's not the country's fault that these murderers seek to control it." Her reply was cut off, when a metallic crashing noise came from up ahead. Crouching down, the two paratroopers guided forward silently approaching the area where the noise had come from. Seeing nothing, they turned onto a side track that led to the river. The scrub here was waist height making approaching easy. Lenore stealing a quick look at the riverbank, ducked back down, signalling for Marlise to move back.

"What is it?" She whispered.

"It's a kind of punt for moving vehicles across the river. The Bedouin must be using it to transport their vehicles across here." Lenore explained.

"How many guards?"

"I saw six; there could be more," Lenore warned.

"Six or twenty, we need that boat." Marlise pointed out, Lenore agreeing.

"Okay. You start at the front; I'll clear from the back."

"Which is the front?"

"Shit. You clear from the west, I'll clear from the east. When I fire you start as well. Okay?"

"Crystal clear. Let's go."

"Pulling out their pistols they both separated moving forward. Coming out through the scrub, they broke into a clearing beside the craft. Lenore spotting his first target fired. Shouts broke out at the first shot. Marlise aiming dropped two men who decided to see where Lenore was shooting from. Two more soldiers appeared on the raised deck above Marlise firing at her. Exposed she fired back hitting one. The other fell overboard, shot by Lenore.

Running up a boarding ramp, Marlise froze as looking into the hull she saw it was full of dead bodies. Getting over it, she charged towards the rear where Lenore was trying to seize control of the bridge section of the craft, where they steered it from. Marlise seeing the two remaining guards were concentrating on Lenore shot them both before securing the bridge area.

"That's all of them, Captain," Marlise shouted out. Getting no answer, she looked down beside the ship, seeing Lenore lying face down on the jetty.

"No!" She shouted, running to him she knelt beside him. Turning him over, she saw two neat red-rimmed holes in his chest. Knowing she couldn't help him, she lowered him back down. "Now what do I do?" She cried out, getting to her feet.

Piloting a boat, especially one like this ferry was out of her league, there were also the bodies. Working out she could run back to where she left the others in about an hour, she stripped off her gear, just taking her pistol. 'What if more solders come here?' she thought, as she jogged along the same track Captain Lenore and she had just explored. "Then I'll kill them too." She growled, running on.

Peter was the first to see her coming. Alerting the others, they watched her approach silently, wondering where Lenore was. Stopping, she knelt down on one knee in front of them, resting, as her breathing continued to come in great gulps. Recovering, she got up seeing the others waited around her.

"What happened?" Peter softly asked as she saw behind him Turk and Tamal. Seeing her look, Peter answered.

"The way east is blocked by a large force of enemy soldiers. Turk couldn't get past them without risking being seen, so they returned." He explained. This meant that despite the enemy's withdrawal from the border, some strategic positions were being held. Nodding she understood, she told them what they'd all already worked out.

"Lenore is dead. He took two in the chest while we were securing a boat." Everyone remained silent, although she could see despite Lenore's death the mention of a boat had galvanised them.

"I'm sorry Marlise. Where did it happen?" Peter asked hugging her.

"I jogged back here in under an hour. Although walking there took four as we were cautious."

"Look it sounds hard, but we need that boat. Are you up to leading Turk and Tamal back there?"

"Yeah although we might need another person, the punt or ferry, is full of bodies. Niger soldiers by the look."

"These Bedouin are just wild animals." Turk exploded, as he grabbed his pack, swiftly readying himself, as did Tamal.

"I can't spare anyone else Marlise. I need the others to protect the wounded if the enemy returns." Peter explained, wishing he could go.

"We'll make do, but we'd better get going." She told them. Swiftly kissing Peter, she hurried back along the river, followed by Turk and Tamal.

"They will be okay Peter. My husband will look after them." Jasmine assured him, as they all moved back to their positions.

Steve was in trouble. Leaving an area where another air attack had taken place on Jundela's forces, he continued east, only to be strafed by a fighter. Remembering what Nigel said, he stopped and popped a blue flare off. The fighter, an F18, was coming in for another run, when it turned away, waggling its wings.

"Thank you, Nigel." Steve smiled. Examining his vehicle showed the steering was shot. "Now I'm fucked!" he yelled out, before calming down. The vehicle although it could still power along couldn't turn. Knowing Jundela's soldiers would be soon here, he wedged his rifle onto the accelerator. The carrier immediately took off continuing east. Steve leaving the driver's seat, opened the rear door. Having no choice, he jumped out the back, as the carrier continued.

"Well, this is just great!" Steve growled, watching his carrier bounce over a small dune charging on. Looking around for an alternative means of transport, Steve dropped to the ground as an explosion erupted behind him. Standing up, he looked east. He saw his carrier on fire, but still rolling forward. That was until another explosion rocked it, sending Steve backwards onto the sand.

Jesus! They've got a minefield out there." He murmured, knowing now why the east flank hadn't been protected. The realisation that he would've been in the carrier if the fighter hadn't attacked sobered him. Getting up dusting himself off, he heard the distant sound of vehicles approaching on the wind. Running back to the battlefield he'd passed earlier; Steve quickly found a suitable spot to hide.

Moments later, Jundela's forces appeared over a dune. Lying hidden beside a burnt out tank Steve watched the Commander of the enemy troops stare at the smoke produced by Steve's burning carrier.

Jundela stood like he'd been turned to stone, as he stared at the carrier, fiercely burning in the distance.

"I almost had her brother." He whispered as a jeep raced past them heading for the carrier.

"They will stop short of the minefield and check the carrier once the fire dies down Jundela." Captain Murarrie informed him, as he too stared towards the east.

"I suppose in a way our family has had its revenge. Dying trapped in the back of a carrier would've been excruciatingly painful."

"Yes, Jundela I can think of nothing worse than burning in one of these metal coffins, which is why we must leave this area, before the American planes return," Murarrie warned.

"Yes. I have been gone too long. Is the radio working?"

"Yes, Sir. The communications officer has contacted Colonel Fulner. He has moved our forces back into the hills. He is waiting for you, at our reserve command bunker." Murarrie informed him.

"I have made many mistakes lately Murarrie, but I was wise to place him in control of the offensive. He saw we were in trouble and withdrew, taking the responsibility for retreating. Not many men would have the guts to make that call."

"Yes, he was right to retreat. With their airpower, our enemies would surely have destroyed all our forces. We have still suffered losses, but we can rebuild with what survived." Murarrie assured him.

"Then let's return to our command centre in the hills, we have been here too long." Jundela pointed out, as with a hand signalled Murarrie order his unit to head east.

Steve happily watched the enemy forces roll east away from him. His only worry was the jeep and its three-man crew to his east, waiting opposite the burning carrier.

"They'll know once the flames die down that there was no one in it." He said out loud, thinking about his situation in the middle of nowhere without transport. Smiling, he looked again towards the three men.

"Maybe there is a solution to both problems." He whispered, moving towards the jeep.

Turk looked towards the ferry, watching the four guards throwing bodies from it. Crawling back to Tamal and Marlise, he told them what he'd observed.

"They must be going to move the ferry away from the shore because of your attack." He concluded, Marlise nodding her agreement.

"Yeah, they would've shit themselves when they saw what had happened to the others. I'd say we could expect enemy reinforcements to turn up at any time now?" Marlise told them, as Tamal nervously looked around. As if the soldiers on the barge had heard them, the ferry's engine burst into life.

"Any ideas?" Marlise asked, screwing on her silencer.

"Yes, but you won't like it Marlise." Turk then told her his idea.

On board the ferry, the four guards hastily prepared to leave the shoreline. Their five-man patrol had been out scouting to the east when they heard the shooting. Returning, they found everyone dead, including one of the attackers. The French Officer by his uniform worried them. They'd heard their commander and the Bedouin leader Jundela, was searching for female French paratroopers, but not why. Fearing that the paratroopers might return and try to cross the river using this ferry, made them nervous. They'd already sent one of their men to gather reinforcements from a village to their north, although until they returned they waited away from the shore.

Disconnecting the lines from the jetty they were just about to leave when two Bedouin soldiers, emerged from the scrub. More importantly to the men of the ferry, they were pushing a half-naked white woman ahead of them. All four soldiers grabbed their weapons, as the small group approached.

"Halt!" Their sergeant shouted, as the two Bedouin soldiers stopped and lowered their weapons, before slinging them over their shoulders.

"We have a prisoner for Jundela." One yelled out, his headgear disguising his features. It wouldn't have mattered anyway, as the four soldiers only had eyes for the woman.

"Who is she?" The Sergeant asked, mesmerised by the woman's athletic body.

"She is the one he has been searching for. Surely you have heard of her?" Momentarily there was a pause as the four soldiers conferred over it.

"We have heard of this woman. Our comrades were earlier attacked, by French paratroopers." The Sergeant replied.

"This explains much. My men were involved in a firefight with some French troops. They came from this direction; it is how we captured her." The same Bedouin soldier told them.

"Then Allah has been kind to us. She and her friends killed our comrades. We will have our revenge with her." The Sergeant snarled, his men eager to have the woman.

"You can do what you like to her, as long as she is alive when she is handed over to Jundela. I can assure you she is a handful." He laughed cupping her breast, which brought a scream from the woman.

"Barack tie off the Ferry." The sergeant ordered one of his men, licking his lips at the sight of the woman's fear. Once the ferry was secured, the four soldiers advanced on the woman.

The two Bedouin moving back laughed, as the woman cowered on the ground.

"Please don't hurt me!" She screamed in French, as the four soldiers surrounded her.

"We won't hurt you much, as long as you satisfy us." The Sergeant sniggered, his men ripping at her remaining clothes. As Barack pulled her pants down the woman's hand appeared from behind her leg holding a silenced pistol.

"Suck on this!" She yelled, shooting Barrack in the mouth, before firing at another soldier. The Sergeant reacting reached for his rifle, only to find Turk's knife at his throat, before it sliced deep. Tamal beside him finished the last guard who tried to run.

"Feel satisfied now you pigs!" Marlise shouted kicking the dead Barack in the head, before putting her clothes back on as Turk and Tamal looked the other way.

"Well it worked Turk, but next time you're the naked bait."

"I'm sorry Marlise, it was the only way" Turk apologised.

"You're right Turk. But it doesn't make me feel any better." Walking to the first rope that secured the ferry, Marlise angrily cut it, while Tamal cut the next.

"Let's get going." She ordered, wanting to be away from this place. Turk having been around boats at the Marina knew how to drive the ferry. At its maximum speed of eight knots, the ferry ambled along, reaching the others in three hours. Peter was over the moon at their arrival. Running to Marlise, he went to hug her, only to be shrugged off, as she walked past him.

"What is wrong Marlise?" He softly asked as they both moved away from the others. Marlise then explained what she'd done.

"I feel cheap for exposing myself and pretending to be just another weak woman to them." She spluttered, upset.

"Turk's idea paid off Marlise. You achieved the mission, and now we can save these men's lives. Get over it. No one thinks less of you." Angry she looked at him before with a sob she collapsed in his arms.

"This is all my fault, Peter. If I had killed Jundela's brother outright, none of this would've occurred. This whole mess here is my doing. Captain Lenore and the others who'd died would never have been in danger if it wasn't for me."

"It has nothing to do with you Marlise. If you hadn't shot that little shit, Jundela, would've still come after us for killing his father. Don't take the blame for this. If anyone is responsible, it's my family for coming after my sister and her husband."

"Let's get back to the others; we need to go?" She pointed out. Peter, wanting to say more, silently accompanied her.

When all their equipment was aboard, Marlise's unit and Peter's group settled in. Most thought they'd just cross the river and be safe in Niger; it was far from the truth. Jundela's army might be stranded on the northern bank, but his rebel fighters held sway along Niger's side of the river. Peter and Turk after discussing the dilemma, decided on heading down the river east towards Egypt. It would, of course, be risky, with enemy forces on both banks, although the river for this time of the year was quite wide.

"If we stick to the Niger side, it will give us a measure of safety and the ability to land when we want to take cover." Turk pointed out to the others.

"It also allows the wounded to keep off their feet and undercover until we reach medical help," Peter added.

"It's no good thinking about it. Let's go." Jasmine suggested, standing with Marlise supporting her. She knew more than anyone there what Marlise was going through. Turk smiling at his wife signalled Tamal to start the engines, as two of Marlise's paratroopers cut the lines to the bank. With a groan they started off.

Back on the bank, unnoticed by the ferry's new crew, one of Captain Murarrie's trackers watched their progress, before running towards the north.

SACRIFICE

The following day Jundela arrived at his reserve command post to find Colonel Fulner had withdrawn their forces suffering unknown losses.

"How bad is it?" Jundela enquired, watching Fulner check on one of their armoured units.

"Not as bad as it could've been if we'd proceeded with the attack. Our troops suffered few losses as they're hard to spot and attack from the air. The armour and transport unfortunately suffered nearly forty percent, either damaged or destroyed." Fulner informed him.

"It is indeed bad, although the armoured losses can be replaced in time. How is the army's morale like?"

"It remains high Jundela. The men support the cause. It will take more than a few air attacks to rattle their beliefs."

"I owe you everything Fulner. Without your quick read of the situation, we could've been wiped out."

"It was the will of God, Jundela. The command bunker received a direct hit, but I alone survived to organise the retreat. Thank him, not me." Fulner smiled, as Jundela overcome embraced him.

"I was so obsessed with revenge for my brother, that I risked everything to capture that woman."

"Is she dead?"

"Yes, although not as I intended. Their vehicle ran over one of our mines on the east flank; no one got out."

"Dead is dead Jundela. Be at peace, your search for justice is over."

"Yes, it is time to concentrate on our cause. Have you had time to work out how the Americans discovered our plan?"

"Our friends the French, have told us that someone named Peter Mustaffer is feeding Intel to the Americans. They have a hit order on him for killing one of their

Government Ministers." At the news Jundela exploded from his seat. "What is wrong Jundela?"

"Mustaffer is the French woman's boyfriend. We had a hit on him as well as his family. He is an Officer in the Swiss Special Forces and killed the entire squad of assassins sent after him. I knew someone was helping the French paratroopers, but not that it was him." Jundela paced backwards and forwards, while Fulner kept quiet. He suddenly stopped. "It was too easy!" He growled his eyes suddenly seeing Fulner standing watching him. "I'm sorry my brother. I just realised I have been deceived again. Contact our units along the river. See if anyone has sighted the French paratroopers." He asked, before dejected, he walked outside.

Fulner seeing his distress, immediately instructed one of his staff to contact their forward units and check on sightings. He is stunned when Captain Murarrie reports that one of his trackers reported sighting the paratroopers on the missing ferry several hours earlier. Grabbing the radio, he contacted the Captain himself.

"Captain, why didn't you inform me of the sighting?"

"Jundela is obsessed with the woman Colonel. I was going to handle it without telling him."

"Then she's still alive?"

"Yes. I fear the armoured carrier was a diversion."

"Do you think this woman's boyfriend is responsible?"

"Maybe. My scouts report an older man and two Libyan men are with him. The older man is the leader and as my scouts tell me a Death Walker."

"Death Walker! What is that?"

"My trackers are from the ancient local tribe which supports us. They talk of a devil that kills in the night with no mercy. That is a death walker." Fulner looked up to see Jundela beside him.

"If you fail Captain, you will hope he gets you," Fulner warned Murarrie.

"I will willingly die to keep Jundela safe Colonel. Try not to tell him." Murarrie warned, signing off.

"So he knew she was alive and didn't tell me. I am ashamed that my men think I am unworthy." Jundela sobbed, Fulner didn't answer. "Don't worry Colonel, Murarrie will not be punished. I will take four men and join him. You in my absence must consolidate our position and start pushing the enemy's troops back. If in two days I haven't caught or killed the woman, I will return."

"As you wish Jundela. Just remember the cause needs you. Without you to lead your tribe, we will fail."

"Where are the three men who were checking the burning carrier?" Captain Murarrie asked Havel, his Communications officer, as their vehicle ploughed along the overgrown track next to the river.

"They haven't been heard of since we left them there yesterday, to check for bodies."

"Then they're dead; it's the only explanation," Murarrie answered, as their lead vehicle ground to a halt.

"But how?"

"The Death Walker must have been the driver and got out before the carrier hit the mine." Captain Murarrie absentmindedly answered, thinking about who the Death Walker was. Several soldiers in their vehicle looked towards Murarrie at the mention of Steve's nickname.

"Best not to use that name Sir, it upsets the men." The Comms Officer whispered, as Murarrie turned and saw his men watching.

"Dismount!" Murarrie shouted, his men swiftly exiting their truck. "Yes, you're right Havel. Superstition is a weapon in itself, something that we must watch amongst our men." Murarrie smiled, climbing down from the truck as well.

By the time Murarrie reached his objective, his men had secured the small bridge. On the eastern side of their position, close to the minefield, the old rusted structure spanned a narrow section of the river. Militarily it had limited use, as it was only wide enough and strong enough to allow a small vehicle to cross. Their rebel forces used it only on foot, but nothing bigger than an unloaded jeep could cross the ancient structure.

"I wonder who built it?" Murarrie whispered marvelling at the vision of someone long ago to build it in the first place. "Probably the British? They liked to do this sort of thing back then." Walking onto the structure, he saw it was in need of serious repair. Looking down, he noticed that he could see through the cracks to the river below. Steel had been used to tame the river, but timber had been used for road treads, being flexible. Many of the original timber beams had long ago fallen to pieces, replaced by trees cut locally.

It made walking or if you were desperate enough to cross in a vehicle, uneven and dangerous to say the least. Several creaks, greeted his footsteps, making him tense as he looked down hesitantly at the timber beam he was standing on. Seeing his men watching him, he straightened, practically marching towards them.

"Are you ready men?" He asked, seeing their unit's two heavy machineguns, had been set up already.

"Yes, Sir. Nothing will get past us." His Sergeant assured him from the middle span.

Good. The enemy shouldn't be too long. Open fire as soon as the ferry appears." He ordered, walking back to his command vehicle beside the bridge.

"Any sightings of the ferry?" Captain Murarrie asked Havel.

"One of our trackers reported it about twenty minutes cruising time from here.

"Obliterate it. I want no one to survive." Murarrie ordered, wanting the woman gone from Jundela's life.

"There you are Captain Murarrie," Jundela's voice sounded from behind Murarrie, making him jump, startled by his commander's presence.

"Jundela! What are you doing here Sir?"

"Just visiting my forward units to see if they're keeping busy. What are you doing on our flank Murarrie?"

"Rebels are believed to be on a ferry heading east. We are going to intercept them here."

"Sounds good. I will stay and watch if you don't mind?"

"Of course Jundela. My scouts tell me it won't be long."

"What is your plan of action?"

"Once they're in sight we will open fire immediately," Murarrie replied, Havel silent beside him.

"No attempt to capture prisoners?" Jundela asked.

"No. Not this time." Murarrie replied, knowing Jundela knew.

"You are in command; it is your decision." Jundela conceded, as walking outside he moved down to a position near the riverbank.

"Captain," Havel started to say when Murarrie stopped him.

"Don't say it, Havel, I know. Pass the word to the men to try and cripple the ferry. If the enemy stops firing, take the survivors as prisoner."

On board the ferry Peter and Turk, looked again at the north bank.

"You're right Turk there's someone following us along the bank."

"If they know we're here, why haven't they attacked?" Turk responded as Peter looked east along the river. All he saw was the river banks merging into a turn to the right.

"Have we any maps of this section of the river?" Peter asked him.

"Yes, although it isn't very accurate." Turk going to a small cupboard returned spreading a map on the bench, beside the steering wheel.

"What is this structure marked here where the river narrows?" Peter asked, seeing a faint line on the map ahead of their position.

"Could be anything from a cable crossing to a small bridge, it's hard to tell."

"Shit it's a trap, they're waiting for us!" Peter warned, turning the wheel towards the southern shoreline.

"You can't be sure Peter?" Turk pointed out, but his eyes went to the curve in the river ahead.

"I'm an idiot. I just considered that with the bombing all the bridges would be gone.'

"You could be right the bridge may have been destroyed."

"It doesn't matter. Even if the bridge is gone, it's a choke point. The enemy knows they can shred this boat as we try to pass." At this point Marlise appeared at the door.

"Is there a problem?"

"Yes. We all have to get off right away. The enemy has been shadowing us; we think they're waiting around the next corner." Peter informed her.

"But if we stop, they'll know we've gone ashore won't they?"

"It can't be helped. At least we're on this Niger side of the river this time." Peter tried to smile.

"Well, it's no good worrying about it let's get everyone off and head south." Marlise agreed, before hurrying off to help the wounded disembark.

As soon as the ferry nosed in, their equipment and supplies were thrown ashore. The injured, went next, Peter leading them away from the shoreline into the dense bushland adjoining it. Turk being up the rear was the last to leave the ferry when Marlise moved past him going back towards it.

"What are you doing Marlise?" Turk asked.

"I'll just turn it around and send it back towards the other bank."

"I can do that Marlise. You go back to Peter."

"No, I'll be okay. Once I start the engine, I'll jump off." She assured him, climbing onto the ferry before he had a chance to dissuade her. Turk watching saw her enter the control room and start the engines as he had shown her earlier. Backing away from the shore she turned the ferry, then instead of jumping, she headed away from the shore.

"Marlise! Don't do this!" Turk yelled, guessing now what she intended.

"Go, Turk! This is my fault; I'll fix it!" She shouted, heading east. Turk not knowing what to do ran after Peter. Catching up with him, Turk, gulping a lungful of air, told Peter what Marlise had done. Peter fearfully started to sprint back to the river, followed by Turk. They were approaching the bank, when the sound of heavy weapons firing came to them, making them both dive to the ground. Not discouraged Peter stood to continue, when Turk's arm seized his leg, pulling him back down, holding him while he struggled.

"She made her sacrifice to buy us time Peter. We have to get the wounded to safety." Turk told him, holding him until he stopped trying to stand. After several seconds he stopped struggling.

"You're right Turk. We'd better go." Peter softly answered; his eyes wet with tears, as Turk letting him go, allowed him to stand with him. Walking back where they'd left the injured, Peter grabbed the end of a stretcher.

"Let's go," He told them, helping Tamal carry the injured paratrooper. Silently the group heading south, the sound of rapid gunfire continued behind them.

On the river, Marlise wounded, tried to control the dying ferry as it started to go down, bow first. The engine, coughing out its last breaths, continued to push the fatally wounded craft forward heading north, broadside to the bridge. How the ferry continued to move forward, she had no idea, as the murderous fire continued unabated.

She had at first thought to let the enemy see her, then cross to the north bank, while her friends on the south bank got away. Instead, the wall of metal had knocked her to the floor. Looking down, she saw she had wounds to both her arms and her left thigh. Groaning with pain, she'd grabbed a field dressing from her backpack and tied it tightly around her thigh wound, being the biggest worry. Sneaking a look outside, she'd fought to guide the ferry away from the murderous fire, as water swirled around her feet.

Kneeling on the floor, she held the wheel, knowing the only reason she was still alive, was the cabin had been built of steel plate, giving her a small margin of protection. With a thump the engine stopped, the boat shuddering as water rose around her. Scared of dying, she noticed how suddenly silent it had come, realising the guns had ceased firing. Looking out the shattered window, she saw the riverbank in the distance, was lined with soldiers.

"Well. I've got their attention." She sniggered manoeuvring her assault rifle to fire out the window. The water level was now to her waist, as she waited, expecting for the Bedouin to rush the boat. "What the hell are they waiting for?" She asked herself. Looking at the murky water, she saw the reptilian scales of a croc, slide below the surface. "That explains why no one is swimming out here." She smiled, looking towards the doorway. Realising the scaly creatures might decide to visit. Shouldering the door, pushing what was left of it closed, she sealed it.

"Now I can drown in peace." She giggled before suddenly stopping. Looking around, she noticed the water wasn't rising. "Bloody hell. I'm on a sandbank." She whispered, trying to see what the enemy was up too. Sneaking a peak brought a storm of return fire, making her duck back down into the water. Tired of being shot at, she aimed and let a whole magazine go, watching the Bedouin either drop to the ground for cover or retreat away from the river. A standoff then began, as the Bedouin stayed out of sight, while Marlise, trapped on the sunken ferry, lay in the water, silently waiting.

"You on the boat. Surrender, and we will treat you as we would any enemy combatant." A voice speaking French yelled from the bank. Marlise knowing what would happen if she surrendered, remained silent. The fact they hadn't just killed her meant that Jundela was out there.

"Very well. Soon we'll have several boats here. Then we will have you at our mercy!" The voice continued, this time not trying to hide his obvious anger.

"Jundela! Are you still pissed over me making your worthless brother into a dribbling halfwit?" Marlise yelled back. The silence stretched out until an assault rifle pounded the ferry.

"When you have satisfied all my men here whore, I will stake you in the desert and slowly roast you alive!" The voice screamed out, as the sound of vehicles approaching, drowned out the voices shouting. Marlise on the ferry shivered in the water, as the sound of trucks, came to her.

Jundela couldn't believe it when the ferry came into sight. Looking through his binoculars, Jundela, saw the woman he had gone to so much trouble for, behind the wheel on the bridge of the ferry. Captain Murarrie's men on the bridge also saw the ferry, firing everything they had at it. From bow to stern the ferry was turned into Swiss cheese, as the ferry turned towards where Jundela was standing.

"Tell them to cease fire!" Jundela yelled to the Comm's Officer, who contacted Captain Murarrie beside the bridge. Murarrie at first hesitated, wanting the woman killed. Knowing Jundela would kill him if he didn't, he signalled his men to stop firing. Like everyone there Murarrie watched the sinking ferry crawl towards the bank, its bow dipping under. Most thought rightly that it wouldn't make it and when the engine finally stopped the ferry looked about to sink.

"The crocs will be feasting soon." One of his men laughed, seeing several in the water near the ferry. To Murarrie's disappointment, the ferry stopped sinking, coming to a halt twenty metres from the shore. Hurrying to Jundela, Captain Murarrie stood beside him looking at the boat.

"Any volunteers to swim out to her?" Jundela angrily asked.

"Not likely Sir, not with those crocs circling," Murarrie answered, amazed Jundela would suggest it.

"Why are they here anyway? That shooting I thought would've sent them packing."

"The woman must have been hit; there's blood in the water. Like sharks, it must draw them I suppose." Murarrie put forward. Suddenly, one of their men opened fire, followed by another.

"Cease fire. What are you shooting at?" Jundela asked.

"I saw movement." One of the men replied as return fire made them all retreat out of sight.

"Anyone hit?" Murarrie yelled out.

"Two men. Both dead. One was the soldier who shot at her. She is a skilled fighter." Havel replied.

"Yes. She is. I'll try to talk her into surrendering?" Jundela smiled.

"Good luck Sir and keep down," Murarrie warned as he started. When he first asked her to surrender Jundela was in control. When she replied shaming him, he exploded. Grabbing a weapon from one of the soldiers, he fired at her, screaming like a mad man. Murarrie, going to him, put out his hand to steady him.

"Sir, calm down. The men are watching." Murarrie warned as Jundela, his blood up, pointed his weapon at Murarrie. The sound of trucks approaching reached them. "The boats are here Sir," Murarrie informed him nervously, as Jundela settling down, lowered the weapon.

"Good, Go get her now!" Jundela growled, walking away. Around Captain Murarrie his men stood frozen by Jundela's behaviour.

"Okay, men lets unload those trucks," Murarrie ordered, his men looking from Jundela to him, before obeying. Walking back to his Havel, Murarrie out of sight of the men sat down wiping the sweat from his face.

"That was close Sir. Jundela's falling apart. I thought he'd kill you."

"So did I Havel, but keep your voice down. I don't want the men knowing we doubt his competence."

"Something must be done, or we're finished." Havel pointed out.

"Maybe when he has the woman he will settle down? I pray to Allah that he does." Murarrie answered, hoping he was right.

Marlise checked her mag's, seeing she had two full ones left and a half load in the one she had fitted now. The boats as the voice said, had arrived and had been moved down to the water's edge some distance from the ferry. She'd fired a few random shots at them, but the range was too great for her assault rifle to be accurate. She'd achieved little except for rattling the boat handler's confidence. Now as darkness approached she feared what was coming. Escape she knew was impossible.

Already she had one visit from her reptilian neighbours. His body floated just outside the door. If she hadn't closed the door earlier, she'd have been his supper. As it was, he'd hit the door with such force; she'd lost her rifle. His demise was caused by his huge girth, getting caught in the steel door frame. By the time he'd thrashed about, trying to reach her, she'd regained her rifle, shooting him multiple times in the head at close range. This had ended his struggle, allowing her to push him back outside and closed the door. Now as she sat up to her waist in water she wished he'd been thinner, ending her struggle.

"No. I don't mean that." She said out loud, thinking about her predicament and Peter. She realised she should have told him that she loved him. She knew that after this, she never wanted to see a gun again. Looking skywards, thinking that she should try to pray at least once before the end came, she saw something. Focusing in the fading light, she saw a hatch. Shocked that she hadn't seen it before, she moved to it. Climbing onto the half sunken steering wheel, she reached for the handle, turning it.

Pushing it up and away from her, she stuck her head cautiously outside. In the gathering darkness, she could see shadows moving along the banks, although there was no sign of the boats yet. Crawling up and onto the roof section of the wheelhouse, which when the ferry settled on the bottom had lent away from the enemy shore, she saw a round cylinder. Although it had multiple holes in it, Marlise realised it was a storage container for an emergency rubber raft. Opening it, she took it out examining it. Four bullet holes were barely visible in the fading light, as she examined the container. Overjoyed, she found rubber repair patches, which she used to repair the holes.

Unfortunately, the pump was long gone, so she took her first big breath blowing into the air hole. Ten minutes found her with a raft, a massive headache and acute dizziness. Resting, she looked carefully around for more scaly creatures, before lowering the raft into the water. If it was killing their brother or because staying in a war zone was bad for their health she wasn't sure, but the crocs had left.

Still fearing their return, she as quietly as possible slid into the raft, pushing off. Letting the current take her, she floated eastward, before something bumped her raft, making her urgently paddle to the shore.

Scrambling up the bank she saw two red eyes staring at her from the water's edge.

"Not tonight boys." She whispered, moving silently inland. She had covered about a mile when a flare lit the sky behind her, followed by gunfire. Knowing what it meant made her move faster.

"She has escaped! That is impossible!" Screamed Jundela. Many of Murarrie's soldiers backed away from their commander, fearing him.

"The woman cannot have gone far. Search the banks!" Murarrie shouted, his men glad to be away from Jundela. It only took ten minutes for the soldiers to find the raft, floating beside the bank, caught in a thorn-covered vine.

"She's close Captain Murarrie. Have all your men start searching immediately." Jundela bellowed, a pistol in his hand.

"Wouldn't it be better to wait until morning Sir?" Murarrie asked, scared of Jundela's present state of mind. At first, he thought by Jundela's stare; he would finish what he started and kill him. Instead, he seemed to calm.

"You are right. Have a third of your men continue searching. Rest the others so they can take over at first light. I will be in my tent if she is sighted." Jundela told him, moving into the darkness. Behind him many stared at their Captain, all wanting to know what he intended.

"As he said, men. Companies two and four will keep searching. The rest of you get some sleep; we will need our strength in the morning. Tomorrow we will be free of this problem men." He assured them, many nodding as they melted away into the darkness.

"You have to do something, Sir?" Havel whispered beside him.

"I know. Let's leave it till tomorrow, shall we?" Captain Murarrie softly replied, putting his pistol back in its holster. When he'd confronted Jundela and asked him to wait for morning, he'd secretly grabbed his pistol placing it in his pocket, preparing to shoot. Now he stood in the dark shaking, wondering what the morning would bring.

"I'm going back!" Peter declared, loading his pack onto his back.

"I'll come with you," Turk told him standing as well.

"Not without me you're not," Jasmine growled as Tamal stood as well.

"Hey! I'm going alone people. You all need to stay here and look after the wounded." Peter barked, silencing them.

Since leaving the river, they had continued south finding no enemy troops. As the sun was starting to sink, they'd found a knoll in the thick scrub giving them a vantage point to watch the surrounding countryside. They'd by luck spotted a company of Niger soldiers patrolling and had cautiously approached them. Telling them they had wounded, the troops had left a medic to help care for the injured until they could get some support vehicles here to move them. They had then continued on, having a mission to complete before returning. In their absence Turk had suggested digging in. Peter seeing the wounded were safe, had decided to return and look for Marlise.

"It's too dangerous on your own Peter?" Turk warned him.

"I've a better chance of slipping past them on my own than with a group Turk. You know that. Please, no more arguing." Peter asked softly.

"Then go after her Peter. We will wait here till you return.

"Thank you. If I can't find her in two days, I'll return. If I haven't, head south with the Niger troops." Peter told them, leaving. Behind him Jasmine moved to Turk holding him.

"She is probably dead my love. I should have gone with him." Turk groaned.

"He must do this alone my husband. He is an elite soldier." She assured him.

"So was Captain Roberts," Turk sadly reminded her, as they stood watching Peter disappear into the darkness.

Two hours of slogging through the scrub found Peter near the southern end of the bridge, where Captain Murarrie's men had intercepted Marlise. Although Murarrie's soldiers had moved north after finding Marlise had fled, a holding force had been left securing the bridge. Peter had just finished cursing himself for coming this way when the roar of a fighter plane made him dive to the ground. An old F4 fighter belonging to Niger's ageing air force had flown the river from the direction of Chad. Turning, it came around having spotted the Bedouin soldiers on the North end of the bridge.

Peter had to admit the Bedouin holding the bridge had guts, as instead of running they sent an impressive amount of small arms fire at the incoming fighter. The plane undeterred sprayed the bridge with machinegun fire before dropping two bombs on the north end. As with most battles the action finished with the stunned silence of concussion, as the shockwaves radiated out, slamming the remaining ground forces. Peter laying a good three hundred metres away covered his mouth with his hand, coughing as quietly as possible, choking on the dust created by the shockwaves. Grabbing his water bottle, he drank deeply spitting out the dust in his mouth and nose.

Standing up trying to orientate himself, he again hit the ground as troops appeared at the south end of the bridge advancing onto the damaged structure. Like Peter the soldier who'd survived the attack, looked confused and bewildered, as Niger troops attempted to cross the bridge. Unlike before when the Bedouin had stood their ground against the fighter, this time they folded, running north. This left the Niger troops in possession of what was left of the structure.

"Who can blame them?" Peter whispered, still shaking from the bombing. Unfortunately, this didn't help Peter much, as the Niger troops holding the bridge, would shoot at anyone who approached the bridge they didn't recognise. Knowing there was no other crossing; Peter decided to wait till morning, hoping he could then approach the Niger troops with a better chance of surviving.

CAPTURED

Marlise's extraordinary run of luck had run out. With the coming dawn, she found herself entering a desert area devoid of cover. Climbing a small ridge, she sneaked a look back in the direction she'd come. There she saw was a long line of soldiers spread out east to west, moving towards her. Checking her weapon, she loaded a full magazine.

"Better save the half empty one for me." She murmured, knowing capture wasn't something to be looked forward to. "Got to find a hide somewhere." She whispered, moving down from the ridge and running west. The move lost her ground, but if they were following her footprints, the move might confuse them slightly, she hoped. Up ahead half buried in the sand, Marlise spotted what she was after. It was a small wadi, which at one time had held water and was surrounded by several torn cover bushes. Running to it treading on rocks to hide her footprints, she began to dig a small tunnel into the group of thorn-covered bushes. It was a desperate move, but given the circumstances it was the only shot she had. Crawling feet first into the hole, she was just about to grab her gear, when a rifle butt crashed into her face, knocking her out.

"We have her Jundela!" Captain Murarrie shouted out, as Jundela out walking with the line of men, rushed to him.

"Who caught her?" Jundela asked, his face lighting up, with an insane smile.

"I sent some of my trackers ahead, to dig in and wait. They saw her digging a hide near them and surprised her."

"This is great news! Bring her here; I will stake her out on the sand after the men have finished with her!" He screamed out, shocking Murarrie and the soldiers around him.

"What about the bridge Sir? My men have been pushed back; we must re-secure it before the Niger troops bring up reinforcements. We are out of time Sir." Murarrie warned.

Jundela seemed miles away staring at nothing, as Murarrie's hand slowly slipped down towards his pistol. He was just about to draw it, when Jundela coming out of his daze, spoke.

"I will take her to my brother at our stronghold Murarrie. He must witness her torture."

"Good idea Sir. You go with your men; I will return to the bridge with mine." Murarrie suggested, as Jundela without another word left for his vehicle, his guards following.

"He is unfit to command Captain. We must inform Colonel Fulner." Havel whispered beside him.

"You are right Havel. I will call him shortly. For now, let's be glad he's gone." Murarrie admitted, ordering his men back to their vehicles.

Peter woke to find it was morning. Cursing himself, he looked towards the bridge, finding it empty. The Niger troops had withdrawn. Getting up, he moved slowly forward reaching the south end of the bridge.

"No wonder they left?" Peter said out loud, seeing the bridge was all but useless. The northern end had been hit by at least one of the bombs. A huge crater meant nothing but a human could cross, and that was extremely dangerous as well. A single steel beam held the bridge intact. Walking to it, Peter looked down to see a crowd of croc's had gathered, hoping some fool like him would try and navigate the twisted beam.

"Do I have a choice?" Peter asked himself, as with a shrug he put his left foot on the beam. It was answered by a groan as the beam protested over his weight being added. Placing his other foot on the beam caused another groan, but the beam held. Backing up, he judged the gap, taking off his pack. Praying that reducing his weight would give him a better chance, he tossed it to the remaining section of bridge on the north bank.

It cleared the gap and then rolled back towards the edge, before stopping. Breathing a sigh of relief, he considered throwing his rifle as well. Deciding instead to strap it onto his back, he moved out onto the beam. There was no groan this time as if the beam had decided to graciously let him cross for shedding his pack's weight.

Feeling better, he edged out onto the beam, reaching the centre. Below his reptilian fans silently watched as if they were privy to some unknown secret. Peter relieved, managed a smile as he approached the northern side.

"I made it. No meal today." He told the crocs, as stepping happily onto the wooden crossbeams, he plunged straight through them.

"Shit no!" He screamed out, as he headed towards the water below. As suddenly as his descent started, it stopped. His rifle had become jammed across the hole in the beams stopping his progress towards the audience below. Scared shitless he tried to figure a way out of his predicament as several crocs snapped at his feet, making him tuck them up under him. Reaching up, he felt for his rifle, using it to pull himself up. After several minutes of pulling and twisting, he managed to wriggle back through the hole. Laying flat on his back, he took several deep breaths before standing up. Beside him stood Steve, making him jump back, nearly falling back into the hole.

"Fuck Steve! You could've said something?" Peter stammered out sweating badly.

"I thought if I yelled out, you would go into the water. Let's go." Steve continued walking to the north end of the bridge. Peter checking his weapon found the barrel bent. Tossing it in the river, he followed Steve. Reaching a depression, which once was the riverbed, until the river changed course, Peter found Steve climbing into a jeep.

"You want to tell me how you got away?" Peter asked him, climbing in beside him.

"There's no time Peter. Jundela's got Marlise." He softly told him, starting up the jeep and driving north. Peter beside him sat motionlessly.

Colonel Fulner sat in the command centre watching the dots indicating their units either move back into Libya or disappear from the map. When they'd first retreated, casualties except in armour had been light. Now the Americans seemed to be concentrating on their infantry units.

"The attack on their airbases has angered them," Fulner said out loud. Several officers in the room nodded their support to his involuntary statement. Realising he had spoken out loud, Fulner moved to the Comm's officer. "Have you contacted Jundela?" He asked the Comm's Officer, who nodded absentmindedly before he saw the Colonel standing there waiting.

"Sorry, Sir. Yes, he has captured the woman and is returning to his stronghold." The Officer stiffly replied. Fulner, of course, hid his surprise, expecting Jundela to come immediately here.

"Some good news men. Our commander will soon be here!" Fulner announced the Bedouin officers in the room cheering. Secretly he was deeply troubled. Captain Murarrie had given him an honest opinion of Jundela and to say the least, he'd been surprised. Murarrie was not the type to exaggerate, and he had been one of Jundela's most loyal Officers. Yet, he thought Jundela should be relieved of command over his single-mindedness in pursuing the woman.

Fulner himself had seen the change in Jundela since he'd learnt this paratrooper was within his grasp, but he'd pretended it didn't matter, now this. Walking outside for some air, Fulner saw his Sergeant assign two of his men to guard him. Ever since he'd had that useless Officer shot, he felt a rift between him and the Bedouin Officers growing. They weren't use to taking orders from anyone other than Jundela, their tribal leader and Fulner although a lifelong friend of Jundela was not one of their tribe.

The Bedouin he knew, considered themselves better than the other fighters here, how would they handle Jundela's removal? Seeing his Sergeant in the doorway, he signalled for him to come to him.

"What is it, Sir?" He asked softly.

"Ask Captain Hares to join me," Fulner ordered him. The Sergeant instantly left, returning with the Captain. He indicated for his Sergeant to stay.

"I have been told that Jundela is unfit to command, which causes a problem." Both men instead of answering nodded for him to continue. "The Bedouin won't like it if we remove him, what do you two think?" Both men looked at each other, before Hares answered

"We outnumber the Bedouin tribesmen two to one Colonel. We also have most of the armoured units, including the reserve tank units under our control. I see no problem."

"I don't want it to come to that Captain. We're being chewed up by the Americans enough without turning on ourselves." Fulner replied.

"Then deploy them forward. Send all their units across the border into Chad. The French have betrayed us and are letting the Americans punish us, while they stand idly by and do nothing. If we hit them swiftly, they won't be ready for it." Hares suggested.

"But the Americans will help them." Fulner pointed out.

"I would say the Americans would be slow to react. They must know by now that we attack only Niger and not Chad. They'll smell a rat." The Sergeant added.

"You could be right Sergeant, and by the time they bomb the units we deploy, they will have severely damaged the French and Chad units along the border. In the meantime increase our men here Sergeant. Do it quietly; I'll contact our Officers myself. For now, let's keep it between us."

"Yes, Sir" Both men replied. As the Sergeant moved off, Captain Hares remained.

"Why include the Sergeant in our discussion Colonel?"

"I want to know if the men are with us, Captain. You would, of course, support my decision even if you thought it wrong. The Sergeant would've questioned me further if he had doubts."

"Good thinking. I will pass on what is going on in person to my Officers. Better that way." Captain Hare told him, hurrying away. Fulner after looking around returned to the command centre.

After discussing the coming offensive with two of his advisors, he made a list of the units to sent south. It took over an hour to work out a suitable plan; all it needed now was for Jundela to approve it. Unfortunately, that wasn't going to happen, so he decided to gather the Officers and make an announcement without asking him.

"Warriors of God. Jundela has ordered us forward into Chad. He has ordered us to punish the French for their treachery. Return to your units and await orders." Fulner ordered as the Bedouin, and the other unit commanders cheered loudly, rushing excitedly out into the darkness. Several however stopped beside Fulner.

"You will pay for your behaviour now our leader has returned." One of them threatened, as another spat at the Colonel's feet.

"I answer to God for my behaviour. Follow your orders!" Fulner warned, as the Officer sneering, walked into the night. Smiling Fulner decided later tonight, to visit his fellow Officers while the Bedouin units began their deployment south into Chad. Once the command room had quietened down, Colonel Fulner briefed his chosen few on what was going on.

"What if Jundela discovers the truth before the offensive begins?" Havel, Murarrie's second in command asked.

"Then we are all in trouble. At the moment Jundela is taking the girl to where his brother is staying. He is in a

Bedouin village twenty miles north of this position. By the time he's finished with the girl, the troops will have been deployed leaving only troops loyal to our cause here. If he does turn up, he will be arrested for his own good."

"Many things could go wrong Colonel. What if the Bedouin find out?" Captain Tupelo a commander of a mechanised unit asked.

"Then I will meet Allah and let him decide my guilt. For now, we proceed with the operation. God be with you all." Fulner smiled as his trusted Officers returned to their units. Alone, Fulner looked up to see his Sergeant at the door.

"Is there a problem Sergeant?"

"There is a report of two armed white men in one of our vehicles in the desert to the north of here. They captured some of Murarrie's men, releasing all except one, who could speak English."

"Does anyone else know?"

"No. One of my men on patrol to the north spotted them, but lost sight of them soon after. Why?"

"There are reports of an older man the trackers call a Death Walker. A younger man was accompanying him. It's some superstitious thing they go on about." Fulner pointed out.

"Yeah, I heard talk of the trackers acting a little shaky lately. Whoever he is, he's got them rattled."

"Well then unless we receive word of an attack by them, we will do nothing for now. He can be Jundela's problem." The Colonel told him, the Sergeant nodding before withdrawing outside. Fulner, wondering what the two men were up to looked up at the clock on the wall of his headquarters. It ticked slowly towards the launch time of the coming offensive.

Steve and Peter lay on a ridge looking down over the enemy's headquarters.

"No wonder, Gaddafi couldn't find the Bedouin's hideouts," Peter whispered, as Steve continued to watch the group of sand covered buildings below.

When Steve had first told Peter that Marlise had been captured, Peter thought Steve was taking him to pick up her body. Instead, they'd driven at speed north to where Steve had spotted her. He'd been driving along the border trying to find a way across when he'd stumbled across the exchange between Marlise and Captain Murarrie's men at the ferry. Unable at first to get too close, he'd finally got to within striking distance of the enemy's boats when he saw one boat arrive beside the ferry. He didn't have to know the language to figure out she'd given them the slip by the shouting.

With the help of a sleeping soldier, he had then dressed as one of Murarrie's soldiers joining in the search. Unfortunately, he arrived there too late. Grabbing several soldiers, he by luck found one who could speak English. He'd persuaded him to tell him where Jundela was heading. What he found interesting was how eager the soldiers were to have him go after Jundela. They appeared to be more scared of Jundela than of him.

He left the ones who couldn't speak English tied up, keeping the English speaking one for an emergency. He was in the process of letting go of his captive at the bridge, when he'd spotted Peter hanging from it. Knowing time was running out, he'd decided the two of them plus the unfortunate linguist would have to do. Several times since they'd started they'd lost the trail. Only dumb luck in the end had helped them. They'd been trying to spot the Bedouin leader's tracks, when an armoured vehicle similar to the ones they'd used earlier, appeared from nowhere. Backtracking they'd found the headquarters hidden in a ravine. All the structures were painted or covered with sand. There were no gaps or streets between the buildings, giving a view from the air of just another sand filled gully.

The place was heavily guarded with only one way in and out, meaning approaching it would be tricky. Signalling to Peter, Steve slid back down the ridge away from the ravine followed by Peter. Sitting down, they ate some rations with their tied up friend, while Steve thought about the coming raid.

"She could already be dead Peter or worse," Steve said, breaking the silence.

"Yeah she could be, but this Jundela didn't go to all this trouble, to just cut her throat and leave her. He wants to stake her out and see her suffer, like they've done for thousands of years to their enemies." Peter replied, hanging onto a straw, as the tied up soldier nodded his head in support.

"You don't seem to like Jundela?" Steve said, loosening the scarf in his mouth.

"I am from Egypt, many of us here came to do God's work, not be slaves to these Bedouin butchers. Jundela is a madman. He puts his family honour before our cause. Because of him, God has abandoned us." The soldier told them. Peter and Steve both looked at each other, wondering how many felt like this.

"Do you think Jundela took the girl to his headquarters?" Steve asked him.

"I wouldn't think so. His brother who is a cripple stays at a Bedouin village to the north; it is hidden like our headquarters. I don't think you will find it easily."

"Thank you, brother, that was good of you to tell us," Peter replied.

"You are a brother in our faith?"

"Yes although I have a different view. I follow the way of peace."

"Yet you're here?"

"The woman Jundela has is my wife to be. That is why I am here."

"Yes. I see your point." The soldier admitted as Steve cut his bindings. "What is this?"

"You've been honest with us. You may go your own way." Steve told him.

"I could betray you to the Bedouin."

"You could, but I don't think you will. Get going before I change my mind." Steve ordered as he and Peter moved back to their jeep. Behind them the soldier walked off back towards Fulner's headquarters.

"He could betray us, Steve?"

"He might, but what does he know. We don't even know where we're going exactly. I'm not killing someone if I can avoid it, those days are behind me," Steve confessed, before turning off the engine. "Peter before we head north, there's something I've got to say. Marlise mightn't be the same person you knew."

"I know. But I've got to try Steve," Peter groaned, knowing what Steve was saying. Steve leaning over gripped his shoulder.

"Then let's go get her son," he smiled, turning the engine on again.

"Thanks," Peter got out.

"Forget it," Steve answered as they drove north.

Marlise was in hell. Awakening, after being captured, she'd been stripped naked and tied on the front of Jundela's truck. They had then driven north showing her off, as if she'd been some animal killed for sport and loaded on the bonnet of a pickup truck. The day had been blisteringly hot, as Jundela silently sat watching her, as she slowly roasted. Severely sunburnt she groaned in pain, causing her tormentor to giggle insanely.

By the time they had arrived at a camouflaged Bedouin village, she was close to death, hoping to die. Taken to a room, she awaited her fate. To her surprise the Bedouin women had bathed her. They then dressed her wounds, before applying cream to her burns. Thanking them caused momentary confusion, before one of them who spoke French, translated what she had said to the others.

This brought laughter from all the women. The translator smiling told her that it wasn't because they wanted to help her. It was so her torture the next day would last longer. Jundela had ordered them to prolong her suffering for as long as possible. Finished, one of the women spat beside her, before they trooped out, some giggling.

With their departure, two soldiers entered. Too weak to put up much of a fight, she was tied spreadeagle to a bed. Standing above, they both stared at her naked body until one smiling spoke.

"You will die tomorrow in great pain." He announced in French, as together they both moved to the door.

"Fuck you goat herder!" She yelled at them, knowing translating those words wouldn't be necessary. One of the guards turned pulling a knife, only to be halted by someone's voice outside.

"You have spirit. I'll say that for you." Jundela laughed, entering. Marlise turning her head saw he was pushing a young man in a wheelchair. Recognition hit her.

"Is that your little brother Jundela? He doesn't say much does he?" Marlise laughed, trying to enrage Jundela. Jundela death in his eyes pulled his knife, advancing on her. When Marlise thought he would stab her to death, he stopped.

"You would like that wouldn't you bitch?" He chuckled. "See my brother; tomorrow will be a day to remember when we slowly cook this whore alive." He shouted, spit spraying over her. Marlise for the first time felt real fear. She'd come to the conclusion, that Jundela was insane. Watching him with a growing sense of desperation, she saw him prop his brother up in his chair next to the bed.

"We have waited for this for a long time," Jundela confessed, his dead eyes matching his brother. Removing his clothing, Marlise saw he was aroused, as he climbed on top of her and commenced to rape her. Doing every despicable, depraved thing he could think of, he did his best to degrade her. Sobbing and humiliated, she lay lifeless on the bed, as Jundela his strength gone, climbed off her. Dressing, he stood looking down at her, an evil sneer on his face.

"I wish we had more time to train you more slut, but alas tomorrow is judgement day for you." He sniggered, turning to his brother. "Justice is ours brother. All we dreamed of for our tribe is about to come true. Allah has blessed us." Jundela screamed, walking towards the door. "Oh, I forgot to tell you Marlise. That's your name, isn't it? Anyway, your agonising death will be filmed, so your boyfriend and the world can see our revenge." Jundela announced, as leaving the room, his insane laughter echoed off the walls, getting distant.

With his departure, Marlise depressed and fearing the worst, thought seriously of taking her own life. Tied to the bed, she looked around for anything she could use to end her life. Angry, she saw everything had been removed from the room, even the blankets and sheets. Cold she lay in the dark waiting, as Jundela's brother sat silently staring at her.

"Are you happy now?" Marlise asked her silent companion. For a moment, she saw a slight twitch at the corner of his mouth indicating the start of a smile. Kicking out she tried to hit him, but he was just out of reach. Surrendering to her fate, she cried, her black-eyed watcher continuing to stare at her, his hatred apparent. She knew no matter what happened tomorrow; she would never be the same again.

Jundela sat with his fellow tribesmen, revelling in his success. He had avenged his brother and would soon, with Allah's blessing, seize both Niger and Chad. This would honour his father's legacy to bring their tribal brand of Islam to their southern neighbours. Only one thing worried him; he was not in control of their forces. He had left Colonel Fulner, his friend in charge.

His Bedouin Officers had complained that he had shot one of his own Officers, without any hesitation. Fulner knew that Jundela's tribe were fiercely loyal to him; he should've left the man's punishment to him. He and Fulner had always been close friends, and Jundela knew Fulner had saved their army from defeat; it was a pity he would have to be killed.

Jundela knew in this; he had no choice. He couldn't have his tribe's loyalty threatened by an outsider no matter how much of a friend he had been. Then there was also Captain Murarrie. He had questioned his orders in front of his men. Murarrie was a good Officer, but like Colonel Fulner he wasn't one of his tribe and had shown disloyalty to him. They would both need to be taken care of quietly so as not to alienate the other foreign fighters who'd joined their cause.

Picking up his Sat phone, he decided to contact one of his Bedouin Officers and tell them of his plans for Fulner and Murarrie. What he heard frightened him.

"You are what!" Jundela exploded into his phone, as Captain Huron one of his Bedouin Officers, jubilantly told him they were advancing into Chad, after wiping out the enemy border units. Huron suddenly realised by Jundela's tone, that he didn't know.

"Colonel Fulner said it was your decision to attack Chad to punish the French?"

"I gave no such order Huron. Which other units are involved in the attack?" Jundela asked, trying to figure out what was happening.

"A great many Jundela. Maybe the Colonel used your name to encourage us." Huron suggested, unsure what was going on. Jundela considered the idea, when a thought struck him.

"How many of our tribe's units are engaged, Huron?"

"All of them I'd say. The foreign troops seem to be in reserve." Huron answered when it hit him. "We have been betrayed. Haven't we?"

"Yes. I think Fulner intends for our brothers to be bled white, while he consolidates his position. Huron can you contact our units and have them stop their advance. We must deal with Fulner immediately.

"I will try Jundela, but we are engaged along the whole front and have advanced several miles into Chad. It will not be easy to pull back."

"You must try or else the Americans will send their planes, and then it will be all over."

"I understand Sir. Best you stay away from Fulner's command centre. He must be preparing to arrest you, Sir."

"Just bring our units back. Then we'll deal with Fulner." Jundela promised, hanging up. Across from him, tribal brothers sat motionless, having overheard the conversation.

"I see it in your eyes, brothers. I made a mistake in trusting outsiders. Who will go with me to our headquarters and deal with Colonel Fulner? Cheers broke out as every man got to his feet.

"Jabir. Take two men and guard the woman with my brother until I return." Jundela smiled, leaving. Once outside Jundela mobilised all the tribal men he could, including their own private armoured unit. It was kept in secret in the desert to the north, for just such an emergency. They'd be outnumbered he knew, but he had the advantage of surprise, and after all, they were Bedouin. By the time he'd rallied his men, it was 2 in the morning.

"What about the woman?" One of his men asked.

"She's not going anywhere. My brother, Jabir and two guards are watching her, let them have their fun." He cried out insanely, as his small army drove out of their stronghold heading south.

BROTHERS FIGHTING

Lieutenant Havel, Murarrie's second in command, had been lent to Fulner to monitor the radio communications during the offensive. He was the first to spot the pull back of the Bedouin units.

"Colonel, we've got trouble?" Havel spoke out, the command centre quietening.

"Let's hear it, Havel?" Fulner ordered, the room now dead quiet.

"The Bedouin units are heading back towards the border. They've changed frequency, although I found them on one of their reserve channels. Jundela's ordered them to crush us."

"Well, we knew this might happen sooner or later. Contact our forward units. Tell them to destroy the bridges and mine any crossing they will use. Order our artillery to deal with the traitors who are running," Fulner commanded.

"They're not running Colonel?" One Officer pointed out.

"To our men at the front they are. Pass the order," Fulner ordered, as Murarrie appeared at the door.

"So it's true. Jundela knows?"

"Yes, it would appear so," Fulner answered, listening to the radio chatter of his units on the border.

"He will come here for blood with whatever he can gather." Captain Hares warned, the command centre again going silent.

"He can't have much. Maybe a thousand men." Fulner suggested, looking at the map, showing the road he'd travelled on.

"There are rumours that he has a reserve of armour hidden somewhere in the desert." Havel put in, having listened to them talking.

"Then let's prepare for the worst. Murarrie take our armoured reserve and your battalion and block the road to this position. If possible, I want Jundela taken alive with as few casualties as possible. He is still the key to our cause here in Africa."

"I see little chance of that Sir," Murarrie replied, remembering that gun in his face.

"Then make it decisive. There can be no power struggle; we must have unity to continue God's work." Fulner told them, as the room emptied.

"Do you think God is still on our side Colonel?" Captain Hares whispered.

"In Syria I did. Now with all the killing of our brothers and the innocent, I no longer know. All I know is Jundela has lost his way. Once we stop this infighting, we can start our campaign again, although I fear we have lost the support of the Bedouin tribes forever.

"Then how can we move south with our rear unsecured?"

"Many of our brothers, who fought Gadaffi, hate the Bedouin tribes for their betrayal. With their elimination many will flock south to our cause. We will be victorious brother; it is just a matter of time." Fulner moving back to the plotting table, watch the Bedouin forces progress.

"What do you mean the crossings have been destroyed?" Captain Huron shouted into his headset.

"It appears our brothers in arms have decided to finish us," Sergeant Salem informed him, as to Huron's front, artillery started falling on his forward units.

"Can we ford the river anywhere else in this area? Jundela needs us, Sergeant."

"There is an old ford to the west. I only know it, as my father brought me here when I was a boy. The vehicles can cross, but the infantry have little chance of making it," the Sergeant told him, ducking down behind his jeep as a round dropped close to his position.

"Tell Lieutenant Peller the fords position. Tell him to order all rear units to cross there immediately Sergeant. It appears the French have woken up." Captain Huron shouted to him,

over the noise of French tank shells screaming past them.
"All forward units retreat," Huron yelled into his mic, as with
a jolt, Huron's armoured vehicle started to move north
towards the border, his tanks firing backwards at the now
advancing French and Chad troops.

"I hope Jundela takes command soon or there won't be
anything left of our army to fight with," Huron growled as
overhead flares dropped. "God help us?" Huron whispered as
wave after wave of fighters roared down out of the dark sky.

Jundela with a growing sense of alarm listened as his
army was cut to pieces by both the French and their former
allies. It was his fault he knew for trusting outsiders instead of
his tribesmen.

"I will spreadeagle them all out in the desert. They will
beg for God's forgiveness for their betrayal." Jundela shouted,
the men in the vehicle with him shouting their support. "How
far driver?"

"Over the next ridge and we will see the command centre
Sir," he yelled above the vehicle noise.

"Order our armour to deploy," Jundela ordered the driver,
as in the distance; multiple flashes erupted from the ridge
ahead. "What is," Jundela started to say, as his vehicle was
hit, grinding to a halt. His jubilant men became rag dolls,
screaming in pain, as the vehicle was cut in half. Jundela
thrown clear lay dazed trying to rise.

"Stay down Sir. Wait till our own tanks reply," a soldier
beside him yelled, only to have his face shot off, ending up on
top of Jundela. Jundela frightened, stayed down. For the first
few seconds' death rained down on Jundela's men, until the
shock wore off. Well practised, their armoured reserve
pivoted to both flanks before firing. Murarrie's units finding
themselves in a deadly crossfire, slowly retreated, back down
the reverse side of the ridge.

Seizing the advantage, the Bedouin armour climbed the
ridge, firing on the retreating armoured units below them.
Jundela hearing the firing had moved away from him, pushed

the body off him. Standing up, he surveyed the battlefield. They'd lost nearly half their armour in those costly few minutes, but so had their enemy. Seeing a tank stopped down the hill from him, he ran to it, shouting to the crew. Recognising him, he was lifted up next to the turret where the tank commander stood looking towards the ridge.

"Are they on the run Captain?" Jundela shouted, over the constant noise of battle.

"It looks like it Sir. But it was too easy; surely they would've fought for that ridge, instead of leaving." The Commander replied.

"Nonsense they are not Bedouin, Captain. The cowards are running! Advance immediately, we must reach the headquarters before our brothers are destroyed across the border." Jundela yelled out, the tank commander. Unsure, yet scared of Jundela, he ordered his tank forward. Clearing the ridge Jundela like everyone else looked down where the headquarters used to be. Like the enemy armour, it was gone.

"Why would they leave?" Jundela asked.

"Because they knew we were coming, Sir. I suggest you get inside now." The tank commander ordered his fear that they'd walked into a trap plain to see. Jundela had no sooner climbed inside, when the tank was hit, grinding to a stop.

"What has happened?" Jundela asked the commander.

"Not a tank shell or we'd be dead. Could be we ran over a mine."

"Tell the other tanks to halt. You were right it was too easy. They've led us into a minefield.

"Done Sir, I suggest we get out before their tanks come back." The Tank commander warned as Jundela agreeing climbed back out. Looking at the tank, they saw the commander was right; the left tracks had been blown off.

"Can you fix it?" Jundela asked.

"Yes, but it will take time. Better you go to the rear of this ridge Sir and marshal our remaining troops. We're going to need them." The Tank commander warned, as, in the distance, the rumble of tanks could be heard moving towards their flanks. Climbing back over the ridge, Jundela found an armoured troop vehicle checking on the wounded. Grabbing the vehicle's radio, he ordered all his troops to rendezvous at his location on the north side of the ridge. Telling his men to dig in, they waited.

Captain Murarrie was worried. His plan had worked, but the Bedouin were still fighting, and this time it was their turn to advance in the open. From his scouts he'd learned that the Bedouin were digging in behind the ridge. Now they had the advantage of the minefield protecting them from a frontal attack. Losses had been high he knew amongst the Bedouin's armoured units, but they'd suffered crippling losses too.

He was sure they could destroy the Bedouin if they attacked, although their own army would be all but destroyed as well. There were also reports of the Bedouin front line units breaking through at several points along the border. Murarrie knew he'd need his force intact to deal with them. Contacting Colonel Fulner, he outlined the situation asking him if he had a solution. Colonel Fulner looked to the north, where Murarrie was fighting.

He'd moved the headquarters as soon as the battle had started, knowing they'd be in range of the Bedouin's tanks once they'd cleared the ridge. Now he felt the battle turning in the Bedouin's favour. The border he knew had started to leak Bedouin units as they crossed in areas thought uncrossable. The Bedouin had been here for years and knew this area much better than his troops did. Despite that setback his troops were fighting well, helped by of all things the French and now the American air forces. They had reacted to the crossing much more swiftly than Fulner had thought possible. This surprised him, considering how far they'd penetrated the border.

"The Allied ground troops are finished." He concluded, knowing that without airpower, Chad and Niger would eventually fall, their armies demoralised by the constant fighting. Maybe not this year or the next, but it would happen, no matter what the Americans or French did.

"It's too bad Jundela lost it." He thought, thinking they could be marching now into the enemy's heartland, except for this absurd search for the girl.

His problem now was how to stop Jundela's forces without losing their ability to wage war. "If only I had an Air Force," Fulner said out loud, before stopping. He did have an air force; it was bombing the Bedouin already.

"Havel! Come here!" Fulner called out, making Havel spin around from the Communications table walking to him.

"Yes, Sir."

"You were saying before, that the Americans are monitoring the Bedouin's frequency. How sure are you?"

"I'm positive Sir. I heard a Bedouin tank commander say he was crossing just south of an abandoned bridge. Moments later there was a report of the crossing being hit by French artillery. That's too much of a coincidence." Fulner nodding pulled out his pen, writing on a pad.

"Good. Captain Hares to me." Fulner called as Hares appeared beside him. Captain, I want you to take a small radio and tune it to the Bedouin's frequency. I then want you to move towards Jundela's army's position. When you're close enough, send this message." Fulner ordered. Captain Hares taking the pad looked at the message.

"Sir this is wrong!" Hares pointed out, as Fulner raised his hand, stopping him.

"Does it matter who pulls the trigger Captain? We must save our army! Do it!" He ordered, as Captain Hares unconvinced left.

Nigel sat in the CIA Operations room looking at the offensive Jundela's forces had launched. At first, they'd driven miles into Chad destroying everything in their path. Now they were heading back north, for reasons unknown.

"Maybe they realised we were going to attack them with our air force as well as the French's?" John Carrington put forward, scratching his chin at the same time.

"It still doesn't make sense, the French had a deal with them," Nigel pointed out.

"No longer I'd say. Could be it was just a show of strength?" Carrington mused.

"An expensive one by the reports. This report even says the enemy is shelling their own troops."

"Could be just confusion on their part? Any chance of contacting Peter Mustaffer again Nigel?"

"I've tried a few times, just can't get through."

"Have it boosted through one of our satellites."

"Are you sure boss? We're not supposed to reveal we can do that unless it's a priority two, emergency." Nigel softly replied as people in the room looked towards them for whispering.

"Get it done. We've got to know what's going on." Nigel nodding left the room and went to the Communications section. Using his ID, he entered. Once inside, he asked the armed guard to give him a sat link. The guard at first hesitated.

"John Carrington ordered it." Nigel softly told him, as pointing to a terminal the guard moved to a phone. Nigel knowing the guard was checking with Carrington went ahead and changed the frequency, allowing Peter's phone to be called. Dialling it, it rang out. Nigel worried rang again.

Peter and Steve lay in a shallow trench as tanks of the same army, fired at each other across the valley they were in.

"What the hell's going on?" Peter asked as Steve beside him watched the battle progress.

"Remember what that soldier told us about the Bedouin treating the other soldier's in their army as slaves? I think the slaves have decided to take over." Steve pulled Peter down, as a shell struck to their right.

"That's unbelievable?"

"I know but look around. What else can it be?" Steve asked. More shells landed as Steve and Peter lay together staying still. Peter's phone ringing made them both look at each other.

"Did you order pizza or something?" Steve chuckled, as a machinegun laid a trail across their trench. "For God's sake answer it, Peter," Steve shouted, above the noise.

"Is that you Nigel?" Peter yelled. Nigel at the other end could hear the battle going on as well as Peter's voice.

"Are you okay Peter?"

"Yeah, there's a civil war going on here at the moment."

"What are you talking about?"

"We think the Bedouin have had a falling out with their supporters. They're going at it tank for tank at the moment." Peter answered.

"Are you sure it's not Niger or Chad troops?"

"No, they're definitely the Islamic forces of Jundela and whoever commands the foreign fighters here. We're in the middle of it at the moment, and we're miles inside Libya."

"Bloody Hell. I've got to go and tell my boss. I'll be in touch." Nigel told him, hanging up. Running back to the operations room, he rushed to Carrington.

"Spit it out. What's up Nigel?"

"It's a fight between the Bedouin and their foreign fighters. It seems they got tired of being slaves." Around Nigel people stood opened mouthed.

"You're shitting me. Are you sure Nigel?"

"Peter and Steve Roberts are caught between the two sides in a tank battle on the northern side of the border. We haven't any units there."

"Jesus it makes sense. That report about them firing on their own troops, it wasn't an accident. That means whoever is in command, sent the units he wanted taken care of south

274

across the border. They found out and are trying to recross and attack the forces left there."

"What about the battle your friends are caught between?" an Officer asked from the side.

"Probably forces loyal to the Bedouin leader are coming south from their bases in the desert there," Carrington guessed.

"It fits. What do we do about it?"

"Nothing. Let them kill each other." Another Officer put in, causing many to smile.

"We got another radio intercept, Sir." A messenger told Carrington, who read it.

"Someone just sent a message. It says they're marshalling their armour at his position for another attack." John Carrington told the room, giving them the location.

"Bullshit Sir that's too far north." An Officer told them, after checking the map.

"Who wants to bet someone's tipping us off to their enemies' location?" Nigel put forward.

"Yeah, but which one?" Someone asked.

"Does it matter? We can take out a large section of their armour in one blow. And you can bet his forces are either north or south of this position." John Carrington answered moving to a phone. "I want the commander of our Strategic Bomber Command in England."

Peter's phone ringing again made him jump. He and Steve had managed to crawl their way out of the battlefield, and were now lying in a ditch beside a busy road. Grabbing it quickly, he softly spoke into it.

"How did you go Nigel?'

"Good. You were right they are killing each other all over the border."

"Why are you ringing back then?"

"It seems someone has let it leak that a force is gathering to the north of the border, we're about to plaster them. Here are the co ordinates," Nigel then read them off.

"Okay. They must be Jundela's forces; they're too far north to be the rebel forces."

"Our thoughts too. We're looking for the rebels armour as well. We think it's south of that position."

"Sounds reasonable why tell us?"

"It's going to be quite a bombing. They're bringing in some pretty heavy ordinance. Might be best if you get out of there."

"Thanks, Nigel we'll keep that in mind."

"Why are you up there anyway? I have reports of several French paratroopers and some of your friends I presume, in Niger at one of our bases."

"That's good news. Unfortunately, Jundela captured Marlise my girlfriend. Steve and I are going after her."

"Peter I don't want to," Nigel began when Peter cut in.

"Don't start Nigel. I know what our chances are, but I've got to try."

"Okay, Peter. If it's any help, we worked out where the Bedouin base in the desert is."

"How did you do that?" Peter asked surprised.

"There are heat blooms from their vehicles moving north and south from the battle. We figured it must be where they're taking their injured."

"That's great Nigel can you give me the position?" Peter exclaimed excitedly. Nigel sending the co ordinates wished them good luck and hung up.

"What do you think Steve?"

"Does it matter?"

"No."

Jundela smiled as he saw the Rebel tanks deploying in the south. His armoured vehicles had already chipped away at the enemy forces, whittling down their precious armour. His units to the south had amazingly crossed back into Libya after suffering heavy losses. That withstanding, they were still fighting and pushing back the rebels.

"We can still win this and destroy these traitors," Jundela whispered watching the enemy.

"They don't seem to be coming any closer?" A tank commander stated, as he too watched the enemy movements. He was the same tank commander, who had saved Jundela earlier.

"Why do think they keep their distance Captain?"

"Something's up. Fulner is a sneaky bastard; he's planned something." The tank commander answered, his eyes still on the enemy.

"Jundela took in what he was saying, thinking it over."

"The message we picked up on our frequency, giving away our location. Did we find out which one of our units broadcast it?"

"No Jundela. No one would admit doing that." The commander smiled.

"If it was us!" Jundela suddenly yelled, startling everyone in hearing. "Have our forces head north now!" Jundela shouted to his Comm's Officer, who immediately transmitted the message.

"What is wrong Jundela?" The tank commander asked.

"Fulner has tipped off the Americans," Jundela growled, running to his vehicle. Grabbing the radio, he contacted Captain Huron.

"Huron I'm retreating, Fulner must've found our backup frequency. He betrayed us to our sworn enemy.

"How could he?"

"I have no answer, my brother. If we don't make it, take command and avenge us." He commanded, as with the others he scrambled aboard an armoured transport.

"God is with you Jundela," Huron answered, cutting the link.

"Drive!" Jundela yelled, as his driver seeing them all aboard closed the rear door and flattened the pedal to the floor. Looking out the side apertures, Jundela watched as his army drove north as fast as the vehicles would go. Above them the bombs started dropping.

Peter and Steve were ten miles further north when the first bomb hit. They'd overpowered a four-man patrol in a jeep, which was guarding an intersection near where they'd been laying low beside a road. Driving north at speed, they'd turned east towards the base's position that Nigel had given them. They were just doing a recon of the area when a rumble started in the south. This was followed by a flash that lit the sky, as shockwaves hit them several seconds later. The first was like a sudden breeze, as Steve sensing what was coming, pulled Peter down, behind their Jeep. Because of the distance it barely shook the vehicle the second explosion that came next, was far different. This one turned night into day.

Peter had heard of fuel-ignited bombs, but he'd never seen one used. These the yanks called 'MOAB' or the Mother of all Bombs. Weighing over ten tons each, they could level an area of ten square blocks. Turning away from the bright light both Steve and Peter had time to scramble into a ditch away from their jeep, when it somersaulted over them, landing on its side. They'd hardly got over the shock, when three others followed in quick succession, sending their vehicle rolling away from them.

Clinging to the ground, they lay scared to death; as shockwaves shuddered through the ground, throwing them into the air, but luckily back down into their ditch again. Several moments had passed before again the horizon lit up, the light slightly dimmer and the shockwaves less intense. Rising timidly from the ditch Steve and Peter covered with sand, stared south at the horizon seeing fires burning everywhere.

"My God those poor bastards," Steve said out loud. Getting out of the ditch, they both shook sand out of their hair and clothing.

"They are our enemies Steve." Peter pointed out, taking a big swig of water from his water bottle, before passing it to Steve.

"No one deserves to die like that Peter. And there are not just soldiers out there. Remember that there's always some poor innocents in the wrong place at the wrong time." He told him, moving towards their jeep. One look told them it was a write-off, as checking their surrounds, they started to walk towards the Bedouin stronghold.

Jundela was dazed, as stared out over the graveyard of his army. He still couldn't hear, which he considered a blessing as around him his soldiers screamed silently, their mouths moving but no sound forthcoming. Looking down, he saw his left hand was nothing more than a stump. His fingers had been burnt off, when he'd escaped their overturned vehicle.

In fear, he had used his hand to pry open the rear, red-hot door. Amazingly there was no blood, his burnt flesh sealing the wounds.

"I am one of the lucky ones," He told himself, as he staggered north away from the smell of burnt flesh.

He thought they'd made it, when the first bomb struck to their south, missing their retreating army. Using his binoculars, he looked at where it had impacted, expecting to see a crater. Instead, he saw the bomb was nothing more than an overgrown flare, used to locate the enemies' target.

"They know we have moved," he said to the driver as the first real bomb hit. The bulk of the Jundela's armour had been thrown around like toys. His own carrier had spun in the air, as in panic his men screamed. Landing on its side the vehicle again was thrown into the air as the next bomb hit, throwing it into a gully. Many thought their ordeal was over, when the sides of the vehicle began to glow.

Screaming, terrified, Jundela like the others tried to keep away from the burning metal, fighting each other to stay on top of the dead or dying. Desperate, the survivors used their bare hands to open the rear door. Out of the twenty men inside, four got out alive, although not unhurt. Like Jundela, they all headed north, not caring for anything other than to get as much distance as they could from the burning desert.

For at least five miles the survivors walked or crawled until they reached a ridge that shielded the desert beyond. Many, upon reaching the ridge looked back and cried. Others stood silently their own pain having drained their voices of sound. Looking around Jundela counted a hundred injured soldiers from their thousand warriors.

"God, what have I done!" Jundela wailed, as in the distance he saw a convoy of vehicles approaching. At first, fear touched him, as like many there he thought the vehicles were full of ghosts, their occupant's garbed in white. As they neared, his fear turned to relief, seeing they were the women from his stronghold. The women fearing the worst had come south, to bring the wounded home.

Jundela, their leader, was carried to a vehicle, where he received first aid for his wounds. Around him his tribal brothers in arms stared at him, their silence saying more than words. Ashamed he hurried to a vehicle, ordering the woman who was near the vehicle to drive him home. Once away from his men he cried like a baby, his shame unbearable.

Turning to the woman, he was about to make her promise never to mention his weakness, when she struck him across the throat, paralysing him.

"Sit back and relax honey. I'm here to take you home." The woman giggled.

Colonel Fulner woke in pain. Like Jundela he'd been burned, although only superficially. His wounds were from shrapnel, from shells exploding around an artillery battery, positioned down the road from his headquarters. Despite his pain, he felt lucky, having underestimated the Americans response to his tip off. Now his entire reserve had been destroyed, suffering crippling losses in the bombing.

Lieutenant Havel, his Communications Officer, was now the most senior Officer he had left. He'd told him to order all forces to retreat east towards Egypt. Captain Murarrie, who Fulner had hoped would rally their forces once Jundela was gone, had been incinerated along with his entire regiment.

Jundela's forces north of his position he knew were gone, although the Bedouin units across the border had escaped. Despite heavy losses they had managed to break out of his trap and cross back into Libya setting up a position in the desert to his west. The newly promoted Captain Havel had suggested finishing them with the forces deployed along the border. They had survived the disaster only suffering light casualties and were all battle ready.

Fulner feeling that his men were beyond caring about the cause had told him instead to move them east as well. They would all rendezvous next to their minefield on their flank, the same one Steve had hit while running from Jundela.

As his headquarters' units limped east, he had another problem. One of his spies had reported that Jundela might have survived the inferno. Chances were he was dead, although if he had survived, Fulner knew he had a major headache ahead of him. To the Bedouin, their loyalty to Jundela was everything. Despite his mistakes, his men would rally to him, prolonging this war. Looking up, from his stretcher he saw Havel leading a soldier wearing Murarrie's unit's insignia on his shoulder tabs to him.

"Who is this?" Fulner asked Havel.

"One of Murarrie's soldiers. He was looking for the female paratrooper with three other men on Captain Murarrie's eastern flank when he was captured. Best he tells you, Sir," Havel suggested, as Fulner nodded for the soldier to start.

"Sir we were on guard when the Death Walker and another soldier captured us," At his words the men in hearing range turned in his direction. The soldier seeing their looks stopped.

"Continue soldier," Fulner told him, ignoring the others.

"Yes, Sir. They let my three companions go, as I was the only one who spoke English. They were after Jundela Sir. One of them is the husband to be, of the woman Jundela captured."

"They must be the ones causing all this trouble for Jundela?" Fulner smiled. "Do you think they went after him?"

"Yes, Sir. Nothing will stop the Death Walker. He knows no fear, I saw it in his eyes."

"Interesting. What of the other man? You said he was a soldier?"

"He is more than that Sir, he is a Muslim brother, although he follows the path of peace."

"Then why is he here killing?"

"I asked the same question, Sir. He said he came for his woman. He is a soldier of honour. When I leave here I will follow his path," the soldier stated, many blinking in surprise.

"You would give up the cause?" Fulner angrily replied.

"What cause? We fight each other. Jundela is a madman yet for years we have followed him. I am tired of bloodshed Sir, I am leaving," He announced turning away.

"Halt, or you will be shot!" Havel shouted, the man flinched, but still kept walking away.

"Let him go, Havel. There has been enough killing already. Anyone who wants to join him can." Fulner shouted out, as Havel lowered his gun.

"We can't afford all the men to leave Sir?" Havel whispered.

"We can't afford to shoot them all if they do Captain. Right now we'd be outnumbered. Best we keep the ones loyal to the cause, I don't want to be like Jundela," Fulner told him. The men around them looked at each other, before resuming their duties none of them leaving. "Thank you, men!" Fulner acknowledged their support.

"What about this Death Walker Sir?" Havel asked, watching the men.

"I hope he finds Jundela. By the sound of it, he might just save us all the trouble of fighting him again." Fulner admitted standing up and walking to his vehicle.

"Let's go men. We've rested enough." Fulner yelled out, many chuckling.

INSANITY

Peter and Steve ghosted into the stronghold of Jundela. Groans and moans filled the air, the ground outside the Bedouin's hospital strewn with wounded soldiers. Helping them were the white covered women, many with red coloured patterns covering their once white clothing. Moving past them, they approached a large building; they took this to be the Sheikh's palace. Carved into the side of the hill its entrance was blocked by huge double steel doors. Pulling out his knife, Steve in the lead reached the door pushing on it.

It gave, opening onto a paved courtyard lit by oversized lanterns. At first, they both thought the courtyard was open to the sky. Instead, they saw the roof of the cave had been painted blue, stars added.

"I'd have thought there would be guards?" Peter whispered, next to Steve's ear.

"So did I. Something is wrong." Steve moved forward inside the building. They found the first guard inside, his throat cut. Further inside they entered a passageway, finding two more guards. By the time they reached the room, where they presumed Marlise had been held, they'd counted ten guards dead. All of them, including these three had, had their throats cut. Unlike the other guards, though, these three had been mutilated; their genitals cut off and shoved in their mouths.

"My God! Do you don't think Marlise did this?"

"Peter. Look around. She's probably been badly treated? There's no telling what she'll do now?" Peter at Steve's words stared at the bed, seeing the bindings for the first time.

"I love her Steve. I don't care what they've done to her, I just want her back," Peter sobbed, as Steve moved to the door.

"Pull yourself together Peter We've got to get moving. She's taken Jundela's brother, and I think I know where she's gone?"

"How do you know that?"

"When we entered the stronghold I saw an abandoned wheelchair near where they parked their vehicles. At the time I thought Jundela took him with him to the battle. Now I suspect when Marlise broke out, she took him with her."

"Why?" Peter replied.

"To get even. She's gone after Jundela."

Jundela woke as the sun started to rise. Realising he was lying on sand, he went to rise, only to find he couldn't move his hands. Struggling, he looked around to see he was tied spreadeagle on the sand.

"Uncomfortable isn't it?" Marlise beside him laughed, seeing Jundela angrily tear at his bindings.

Marlise had given up hope that night. When Jundela had left her, she was resigned to wait for her fate. It was not to be. Jabir and two men arrived shortly afterwards. One look at her lying naked on the bed and the three men swiftly disrobed. While one made sure Miguel was comfortable the other two started. It continued for over two hours, the men laughing insanely at every groan of pain they inflicted. Seeing Marlise was all but finished they stopped, fearing Jundela's fury if she died. Cleaning her up as best they could they moved to a table playing cards, their prize forgotten.

Lying there, Marlise held back her tears, denying them their fun. She knew she was in bad shape, but in their hurry to have their way with her, they'd untied her arms. Curled over as if in pain, she'd untied her legs, leaving them hidden under the filthy sheet they'd covered her with. She was just about to try and rush them when a distant explosion shook the stronghold.

The guards standing in shock looked to the door as if expecting French paratroops to rush into the room. When nothing occurred a wild conversation broke out, as two of them rushed out leaving one to watch her. Once they'd left, she saw the guard look her over, his arousal plain to see. Pulling a knife, he showed it to her as he climbed on top of her. The last thing he was expecting was to have her grab it and drive it into his heart.

"You weren't expecting that?" She giggled, climbing off the bed. Standing, she collapsed onto the floor, her legs giving out. It occurred to her that if it weren't for the explosion, she would've fallen on the floor when she tried to rush them. Trying again, she found her balance, managing to sit again on the bed. Taking several breaths, she cleared her head, trying to get a plan of escape together. Clothes were her first problem and easily fixed by her dead friend. Putting them on was painful, but pain kept her going, her focus completely on revenge.

Looking down at the dead soldier, she cut off his penis, shoving it in his mouth, before realising she wasn't alone.

"Oh, Miguel. I forgot about you." She giggled, approaching the live statuette that sat rigidly in his wheelchair. "Did you enjoy the show? I didn't see you clapping?" She laughed insanely, her knife tracing his neck. Staring into his eyes, she saw nothing except hate. "You'd like me to kill you wouldn't ya?" She smiled turning him a full circle in his chair. "Well, I've got a better idea. You'll love this one." She promised. She was about to wheel him toward the door when she heard footsteps approaching. Moving to the door, she stood up against the wall as the two guards entered.

Both froze as they saw first Miguel facing them and then the dead, mutilated guard. Stopping was their death sentence, as Marlise slashed the first guard's throat, before plunging it again into the second ones. Ripping their clothes off she cut off their penises shoving them into their mouths.

"This could be my trademark from now on," Marlise told Miguel, who for the first time showed some fear in his eyes. "I see you're getting to like me, Miguel. Just give it time." she giggled, wheeling him into the corridor. Leaving had been easy for Marlise. The guards were all facing the other way, all she had to do was leave her friend and kill them, easy.

By the time she'd reached the front door, the stronghold was already loading up their vehicles to help the wounded at the battlefront.

Burrowing a white outfit from a now dead woman, she pushed Miguel into the back seat of a jeep and threw a tarpaulin over him.

"Don't make any noise Miguel," Marlise whispered, driving out into the night, following the other vehicles towards the red glow. They had arrived as the survivors in shock, walked out of the bright horizon down a ridge towards them. Marlise even unhinged, saw the horror of the burned and dying men. Like many others, she brought water to the soldiers leading them towards the make shift hospital. The language here wasn't a problem, as no one spoke, the gravity of the situation making everyone there mute.

In time her reason for being there appeared, as Jundela was lead down to a makeshift hospital. After being attended to, Marlise thought he looked ashamed, as he backed away from his men, moving toward a jeep. Marlise, seeing he was about to leave jumped behind the wheel, knowing Jundela with his arm bandaged, couldn't drive himself. A shout from him was all the prompting she needed, as guessing it meant go, she drove away from the melting pot of flesh.

It was then he started to cry, which made Marlise nearly burst into laughter. Suddenly he stopped. Wiping his eyes, he turned to her angrily yelling at her. Marlise didn't understand a word, but tired of his tongue lashing; she stopped the jeep. A Karate chop, him across the neck, stunned him. It was followed, by hit across the back of his head with the tyre iron, knocking him unconscious. The last thing he remembered was her speaking in French.

"Sit back and relax honey. I'm here to take you home."

Jundela remembering that insane voice, tried desperately to break free. The witch had escaped somehow and now held him captive. It was worse than being dead.

"You will pay for this whore. My tribe will track down your family and butcher them." Jundela warned her. Marlise above him just sat there watching him. "What? You didn't like being raped whore? What will you tell your boyfriend?" He laughed, as Marlise not understanding his language, but understanding his anger, smiled. Sitting silently above Jundela in the jeep, she thought she'd show him her surprise. Starting the engine, she backed up, so he could see what was on the other side of it. There staked out like he was, lay Miguel. Jundela at first couldn't believe his eyes. Sobbing, he turned away ashamed.

"What's wrong Jundela? Don't you recognise your little brother? We've had quite a discussion about you. He thinks this is entirely your fault Jundela. I for one believe he's not being fair. Let's face it, Miguel, you're responsible for your daddy's death, aren't you?" She giggled. Jundela stared at her seeing madness in those eyes.

"Look my brother has suffered enough. I'm the one you want Marlise, let him go." Jundela spoke in French.

"Well, well, well the Bedouin leader speaks French. You even sound civilised. It's just like those shows where they teach a dog to do tricks. You know it's just a stupid dog, but it looks clever? Is that you Jundela, a dog that can do tricks?" Jundela unable to think of an answer lay there staring at the monster he had made.

"You can't win Marlise. Even now my men will be looking for us. It is only a matter of time until they discover your tracks from the hospital camp.

"I followed the other vehicle tracks back towards your village before turning off. By the time they get here your brother, and you will be red raw. I'd say." Marlise told him, as the heat of the sun started to warm the sand around him.

"My God will protect us." Jundela smiled, relaxing.

"Like he did in the battle?" Marlise laughed, as the heat from the sun grew intense.

At the same time, Jundela was talking to Marlise, Captain Huron with his lead company arrived at Jundela's stronghold. His unit had broken through the rebel's lines and finding little resistance had come straight here. Finding Jundela missing and the guards there all dead, he called the hospital. Jundela he was told had left there hours ago, his jeep driven by a woman, yet he had not arrived at the stronghold.

Calling his regiment, which was strung out across the desert behind them, he ordered them to spread out from the hospital where Jundela had last been seen and look for any tracks, leaving the road. He was just about to leave himself and join the search when one of his men rushed into the room.

"What is it Bengali?" Captain Huron asked, seeing the man's eyes looked haunted. Huron for a second thought Fulner had launched another attack.

"Sir. One of our armoured transport vehicles, which was thought to have broken down, has been found. The entire crew of twelve men are dead, all shot." Sergeant Bengali exclaimed.

"Where was it found?" Huron growled.

"About half way between here and the hospital. Do you think it's Colonel Fulner's soldiers?" Bengali asked nervously.

"No. Reports all confirm they have moved to the east. Have our units searching for Jundela, concentrate in that area. There's got to be a connection."

"It's the Death Walker." One of the Bedouin old native trackers called out, making everyone freeze. The Bedouin had always had a close relationship with these natives. They lived along the border area and shared the same ideologies and religion as the Bedouin. Jundela's father had always used them as trackers; their skill at this task was unmatched.

This gave them a voice to speak as equals to the Bedouin tribes.

"Nonsense. It could be many things. There could be rouge enemy units trying to break through to the east for all we know." Huron replied, trying to play down the native's claim.

"It is him, Captain. He is helping the soldier who loves the woman Jundela took. The story is being told up and down the border. They say he kills without fear or mercy; my fellow tribesmen along the river think he is a demon. Already he has killed many trackers, who at the time were fighting for Captain Murarrie." Another old Tribesman called out.

"That is just superstition talking. Death Walker is just a myth created to scare children and old men. Soldiers killed the trackers, not demons. I will hear no more of this blasphemy. God will protect us." Huron shouted, silencing the old tribesmen, who stood like stone, their thoughts guarded. "Now everyone gets out and look for Jundela. We need him to lead us against the rebel traitors." Huron barked, making everyone in the room leave. Outside he saw Sergeant Bengali loading a belt of ammo onto his jeep.

"Sergeant to me!" He yelled, as Bengali left what he was doing and hurried to him.

"What is it, Sir?" The Sergeant asked. Huron looked around before answering.

"This soldier, the old tribesmen, call the Death Walker, I want him found and killed. Take the old ones; they seemed to know this man."

"But you said,"

"Forget what I said Sergeant, just stop him before he gets Jundela. He is just a man although I fear he is an elite soldier. With your team of four and the twenty native trackers, you should have no trouble."

"Yes, Sir." The Sergeant answered, his voice sounding all but confident.

"Good." Huron smiled walking to his command vehicle. Bengali turning saw the tribesmen waiting near his jeep.

"There you are. I was just about to look for you." Bengali smiled.

"He wants us to hunt him?"

"Yes, he does." Bengali answered.

"We will not return." Another spoke out, as they climbed aboard a truck behind Bengali's jeep. Bengali feeling his skin starting to sweat jumped aboard his jeep, signalling his driver to go.

"I'm not dead yet?" Bengali smiled, hanging on.

Marlise sat watching the men cook from under a tarpaulin she'd rigged up above the jeep. It was getting hot, and although she hadn't stripped Jundela and Miguel naked, they were feeling the heat.

"Put your hand up if you want a drink?" Marlise giggled, as Jundela tried desperately to free himself. Miguel, on the other hand, lay motionless. Marlise looking at him climbed out of the jeep and moved to him. Feeling his pulse, she found he was dead. "We haven't been here that long?" She said out loud, making Jundela stop struggling. Examining him, she found because he couldn't blink, his eyes had been burnt out, killing him. "God I forgot about that. Hey Jundela, your brother has gone to whatever heaven you believe in."

"He will be well received by our God. He was a loyal follower of our faith." Jundela cried out, his grief overwhelming him.

"He was just a lowlife murderer like yourself. He'll burn in hell as you will." She growled climbing back under her cover.

"Marlise! It's Peter. Can I come down?" Peter's voice sounded from a small hill above them. Marlise, grabbing a rifle aimed at the hill.

"You just want my body like the others, Peter. Come closer, and I'll kill you." She screamed out, firing wildly at the empty hillside. Giggling, she looked sideways to see the butt

291

of a weapon, before it struck her head. Staggering sideways, she tried to steady herself, as she blacked out.

Steve beside her lowered his weapon and held her upright until Peter arrived. Taking her from him, Peter lowered her to the ground beside the jeep, keeping her in the shade.

"I suggest you secure her hands," Steve told Peter, moving to Jundela.

"Do you think that's necessary?" Peter sounding surprised replied.

"Unfortunately yes," Steve answered. Standing above Jundela, Steve looked across at his brother. "So much for honouring your family?"

"The bitch is mad. Look what she has done? Release me, and you will be allowed to go free." Jundela commanded, his voice grating with thirst. Getting a water bottle, Steve untied Jundela's arms letting him drink.

"Thank you. You will be rewarded." Jundela promised as Steve stood watching him.

"Why didn't you just let it go, my friend? You killed Peter's parents and his friend Aaron and his wife. You then tried for me and killed my wife. Now, this. You have destroyed your tribe and their dreams, plus murdered untold innocents. Do you think your God will be happy?"

"You know nothing Westerner. Honour to my people is everything. I will not stop until you are all dead for what you did." Jundela screamed out, as Steve pulled out his knife.

"I thought as much," Steve replied, stabbing Jundela in the chest where his heart was. "Go join your family Jundela. You have failed." Jundela shocked, took in what he had said. With a groan of sorrow, knowing he had indeed failed, Jundela lay back down and died. Wiping his knife on Jundela's clothing Steve walked back to where Peter sat with Marlise.

"We have to move Peter; they're coming." Peter through tear filled eyes focused on him.

"I love her Steve. I know she's changed, but I love her."
Marlise lay motionless, her eyes closed as if in sleep.

"Did you tie her hands?"

"God forgive, but yes," Peter answered, turning her so he could see.

"Good. Because she's awake Peter." Steve warned as Marlise jumping forward head butted Peter nearly breaking his nose. Steve reacting held her down.

"Let me go, or you're dead," Marlise screamed, as Peter dazed stood up.

"Settle down Marlise. No one's going to hurt you," Steve told her slowly releasing her. Marlise managing to get to her feet stood there looking at them both.

"You're right. I'm so sorry Steve." Without warning she launched herself at Steve, only to find herself back on the ground.

"Stay there," he warned, as he checked Peter.

"Steve," was all he got out.

"It will take some time Peter, which at the moment we don't have." In the distance, a sound of vehicles approaching could be heard.

"We can't fight and watch her. Better to make a run for it?"

"Good idea. Go get the transport and bring it down here." Steve ordered.

"But they'll see me move it."

"I know. I'm counting on it," Steve smiled.

By the time Peter arrived; Steve had loaded Marlise into the back of her jeep after tying her legs together and gagging her.

"Is that necessary?" Peter felt ashamed.

"Yes, it is Peter. She isn't herself, although in time she'll come back. Now climb in and get going!" Peter surprised didn't move.

"I'm not leaving you, Steve."

"I'll follow you in the other vehicle, just get going!" Steve told him.

"You're not coming, are you? You're going to stay behind and give us time to get away?"

"Yes, Peter I am. But it will be for nothing if you don't leave now. Marlise needs help, I'll buy you a couple of hours then I'll follow, but you've got to go now," he warned, as Peter without saying a word hugged him.

"Look after her son. Now go." Steve whispered in his ear, pushing him away. Peter wiped his eyes climbed into the jeep and started it. Not looking back he flattened the accelerator, racing out onto the open desert to the north.

Sergeant Bengali looked down into the ravine where Jundela and his brother lay dead beside an abandoned armoured transport. Around him, the twenty trackers and his team watched for any sign of movement. Through his binoculars, he could see in the distance, the jeep travelling at speed away from them.

"They're getting away Sergeant?"

"Relax we'll catch them. It's down there I'm worried about," the Sergeant replied feeling unsure.

"Death Walker is near." One of the trackers warned, the desert becoming silent.

"They're gone Sergeant let's move," another of his men urged.

"Okay, lets take the vehicles down. You trackers deploy, we'll meet you down there."

"Some of us will die," one of the Trackers growled although they all spread out advancing down the slope.

"Okay men bring the vehicles around to the right, we'll follow their vehicle tracks down."

Crawling slowly forward, they reached the abandoned vehicle, stopping next to it. The tribesmen having come down the slope had already moved up to the end of the ravine. They stood looking at the jeep in the distance.

"Those trackers are a crazy bunch Sergeant?"

"Yeah, but they can fight. Now check the armoured vehicle and then collect the bodies. We'll load them aboard the tracker's transport vehicle for now. While you do that, I'll call Captain Huron. He's going to be angry," Bengali told them as he moved to the radio. He was just tuning in the frequency when he saw his men signal the armoured vehicle was secure. Giving them an okay, they then approached Jundela. Two of them grabbed an arm each, while the third went to grab his legs.

"Check for booby traps!" Bengali yelled out, as two men lifting his arms froze. The other not hearing lifted his legs. One second the three men were standing there, the next they were blown to pieces. "God no!" Bengali screamed running to them, the trackers seeing what had occurred ran back.

Bengali's men were all dead, mutilated beyond recognition. Signalling to the trackers to be careful, he asked them to check Miguel. One throwing a rope pulled him sideways, causing another explosion, but no causalities.

"Those bastards! Let's go after them." Bengali growled.

"The Death Walker is near Sergeant." One of them warned, the others watching the hills around them.

"He's long gone. Now load up. I want this bastard spreadeagled as he did to Jundela before night." Bengali screamed, the trackers unsure, loaded aboard their transport. Starting up his jeep, Bengali lead the way forward out onto the open desert. "I'll get you for this." He cried changing gear and accelerating.

The two vehicles had travelled no more than a hundred metres when Bengali saw the transport truck hit by heavy machinegun fire. Its front wheel disintegrating made it flip over. As the vehicle mortally wounded rolled the trackers in the back, being catapulted out. Bengali looking for the machinegun, saw it up ahead of him. As becoming aware of him, it switched targets, chewing his jeep to pieces. Jumping clear Bengali rolled only to be shot in both legs.

Many tribesmen survived the crash, only to find themselves in the open without cover. They were slowly all mowed down till only the wounded and dying remained.

Sergeant Bengali lay motionless near his jeep. He was in great pain, but he dared not move knowing the enemy was out there somewhere. Sneaking a look, he saw the machinegun sitting unattended beside a group of bushes.

"He's hunting us down," Bengali whispered watching the surrounding desert. A brief movement to his left side made him fire wildly at the bushes. "Did I hit him?" he asked himself. Crawling towards the spot where he'd peppered the bushes he saw a trail of blood on the ground.

"I got him." He said out loud, as a knife cut his throat.

"I wonder what he said?" Steve asked himself not speaking the soldier's language.

Rising from the ground, sure he'd killed them all Steve examined his wound. The soldier had managed to shoot him in the arm and the thigh. Amazingly the thigh wound wasn't too bad, the bullet having passed right through. The arm was different. The artery had been nicked and was bleeding badly. Already he felt nauseous, not a good sign. Bandaging it, Steve took a large swig of water, before heading back to his vehicle in the ravine.

He'd only just reached the armoured transport when the sound of heavy vehicles labouring through the sand came to him. Although they sounded still a few miles off, he knew he'd never be able to outrun them. Thinking about what to do, he decided on a course of action.

Captain Huron gazed out on the small but important battlefield. Jundela's body lay amongst the dead, meaning their Bedouin tribes was leaderless. When they'd first arrived, an armoured transport vehicle had fired upon them. Several of his men were killed in the exchange before the two tanks that were escorting his column blew it to pieces. What was left of a badly burnt man's body, was removed from its wreckage. Searching it, Huron found a Westerner's passport. His name was Steve Roberts.

"He killed over thirty of our men Captain. We should burn what is left of his body to punish his afterlife." Lieutenant Hafar snapped.

"At least I can tell our native trackers that this mythical Death Walker is no more." Huron smiled, his men laughing.

"He is not dead Captain. He is here watching us somewhere?" A tracker answered from behind Huron making him turn.

"The only thing left of the man is laying over there. No one could've survived being hit by a tank round." Huron angrily replied, signalling to his men to prepare to move.

"You are making a mistake Captain. Stop thinking about ruling the Bedouin and help us find the Death Walker!" The tracker shouted out. Turning, Huron drew his weapon and shot the tracker. The surrounding soldiers froze as the tracker collapsed onto the ground at Huron's feet.

"Anyone else want to question my orders?" Captain Huron yelled out, his men speechless. "Good. Now let's get going we have a war to win!" He bellowed moving to his vehicle. Around him, the desert exploded with the noise of engines, as the tanks cranked up their engines preparing to roll. No one heard the shot. One minute Captain Huron was mounting his vehicle, the next he was laying on the sand shot through the head. Running to him, Lieutenant Hafar ordered his men to sweep the area; they found nothing. Worried he approached another tracker.

"Can you see him?"

"See who Sir?"

"The Death Walker." Hafar snapped, angry with the tracker.

"Captain Huron said he is dead. We cannot find whoever fired that shot."

"What, you're saying Captain Huron, was shot by a ghost? How do I know one of you trackers didn't shoot him?" Hafar growled reaching for his pistol.

"I wouldn't do that Sir." The tracker warned, looking around the desert as he did. Hafar understanding let go of his weapon, moving to his vehicle.

"Let's get out of here." He ordered his driver, as the column moved off. In the end, the only ones left were Huron's Trackers. Loading their fallen comrade onto their vehicle, they stood together praying.

"Our alliance with the Bedouin is over," the senior tracker announced, the others nodding their agreement.

"We lost many good men here. Although it appears to be the fault of the Bedouin," another pointed out.

"Although the Death Walker did kill them," another added.

"Does anyone want to try and find him?" The senior asked. Silence followed his question. "Then let us leave this place," he suggested the others climbing onto their vehicle which signified their agreement. The senior tracker was the last to climb aboard. As he did so, he threw his canteen onto the ground behind the truck as it moved off. Canteens of the other trackers followed his, as they disappeared towards the west.

Two days later on patrol, the trackers would find the canteens had been taken.

Peter after two days of looking over his shoulder reached safety in Niger. Travelling south, he reached Djado the northern countries' main city, although it was more like an overgrown town. Going first to the Hospital he explained how Marlise had been raped and brutalised, causing her distrust of men. To his surprise, it was greeted with an unsurprised acknowledgement, showing it was a daily occurrence in this country.

Leaving her, he went to the American Airbase to find news of the others. He'd only just parked his jeep when a familiar voice exploded from a hotel opposite.

"Is that you Peter?" Turk yelled, running across the street to him.

"Yes, Turk it's me. Are the others here?"

"Yes, Jasmine and Tamal are here with me. The French paratroopers have returned to France. They said they would plead your case to their superiors. Where is Marlise?"

"Better I tell you what occurred together," Peter started to say, before breaking down and sobbing. Turk knew that being silent was the best response, helping Peter across the road to their hotel. Entering, Peter saw Jasmine and Tamal sitting having coffee. Seeing him, they stood and started to run to him, only to stop when they saw his eyes. Returning to their seats, they waited for him to start. He then told them what had occurred from when he left them. By the time he'd finished, he wasn't the only one crying.

"So Captain Roberts was still alive when you left him?" Tamal asked amazed by the story of his survival.

"Yes although I don't know what happened after I left. I had no choice."

"No one blames you, Peter. Your first concern was Marlise. How is she?"

"I don't know? There were times when we travelled here that I thought the old Marlise was breaking through. Other times I thought she might break free and kill me. I hope the Hospital here can help her, but they seemed overstretched to me. If they can't I'll have her flown back home; I really think that's the answer."

"Have you contacted Nigel?"

"No. To tell you the truth, I haven't had the guts to tell him yet."

"Now might be the time Peter," Jasmine suggested as the group gave him space, moving away. Peter took out his phone and stared at it for several seconds before dialling.

Nigel and his boss were the pin-up boys of the Agency.

The President himself rang and thanked John Carrington for his work in stopping the terrorists dead in their tracks. It had been a massive coup for the CIA. They had stopped the takeover of two countries and destroyed ninety percent of the attacking forces. Intel they'd received put the Bedouin tribes as no longer a fighting force, relieving pressure on both Niger and Chad. Still, Nigel worried about Steve and Peter. Since the bombing, he hadn't been able to reach him. Nigel found the silence worrying. His phone ringing made him jump.

"Peter how are you?"

"I've been better Nigel." Peter paused then started again. "There's no easy way to say this, but Steve stayed behind to let me and Marlise escape. We were trapped in the desert, and a larger force was closing on us. I took Marlise and ran Nigel. I'm sorry."

"He insisted on staying behind didn't he?"

"Yes, Steve was a good guy. We wouldn't have made it unless someone stayed behind and fought."

"So you didn't see him die?"

"No, but it looked bleak Nigel, and there wasn't much cover."

"He's a hard man to kill Peter. Don't give up on him. I won't."

"Will you tell your wife?"

"No. Not until I know, one way or the other." Nigel confessed not wanting her hurt again. "How are you and Marlise anyway?" Nigel changed the subject.

"Marlise is not good. They worked her over pretty bad. She tried to kill me when we rescued her. Steve stopped her. I'm hoping the doctors here can help her. If they can't, I'll take her home." Peter stammered out. Nigel on the other end didn't know what to say, going silent. Peter feeling the silence continued. "I better go, Nigel. Thanks for your help."

"It is I who should thank you, Peter. You and your friends saved countless lives in Niger and Chad. And by the way, don't worry about the French coming after you. My boss has had words with them; they won't touch you or shit will hit the fan."

"Well, that's something anyway. Again thanks for everything. Someday we'll have to meet up."

"It's a date. Just ring when you're in town."

"Goodbye Nigel." Peter hung up. Sad that this whole affair had cost him not only his parents but a good many friends as well, Peter then went looking for Jasmine. She had gone to the hospital to visit Marlise. He had just reached the hotel foyer when Jasmine arrived in a taxi. Jumping out, she paid the fare and hurried towards him.

"What's wrong?" Peter asked his guts in knots at the look on her face.

"I'm sorry Peter. She's gone."

Jasmine had arrived at the hospital, to find the place surrounded by soldiers. Staff members were streaming out the doors, some crying, others running. Seeing an Officer she'd met earlier when they reached Djado, she approached him.

"Captain Barlee. What is going on?"

"Jasmine. Best you come back another day. This does not concern you."

"One of my friends brought a French woman here for treatment. She had been treated badly by the Bedouin."

"Was she a paratrooper?"

"Yes, that's her."

"Then this does concern you. It's not completely clear yet what happened, but it would appear a male orderly, may have touched her inappropriately. She cut his throat and threatened staff members, before disappearing. We're searching the building for her."

"This is terrible. I can't think of anything worse she could have had done to her. Can I help look for her?"

"If you wish. I for one think she is long gone. Just remember she has murdered someone, we will arrest her." He admitted, obviously not looking forward to it."

"She is a skilled soldier Captain. Best warn your men."

"These men are from one of our best units. They know about what you and your friends have done, if they can, they will not hurt her, although they must defend themselves."

Jasmine spent the next two hours with the soldiers searching for her. Like the Captain had said, she was long gone. Knowing she could do nothing more, she returned to the hotel to tell Peter what had happened.

"So she had gone Peter. As you said she is disturbed, although I too would have killed the orderly."

"Where do you think she will go?" Tamal asked. He and Turk had joined them to hear what had occurred from Jasmine.

"I don't know? Maybe back to Europe if I'm lucky. Best we pack and go home. With her or without her it is time for us to leave," Peter put forward the others agreeing.

CHRISTMAS EVE

Nigel, after the fuss had died down in Africa, wondered if he should tell Lindsey about her father. It was coming up to Christmas and Robin, Lindsey's sister and her husband Patrick, had just arrived and were staying with them for the holidays. He'd noticed they were all grieving still. It was bad enough when they'd thought it was an accident. Now to find out Natasha and Steve had been murdered was heartbreaking.

"Still there'd never be a better time?" Nigel told himself. With both sisters here together to support each other, he could tell them about Steve. The problem was should he tell them he hadn't been murdered, but now he might have died in Africa? Needing a drink, Nigel stole out the back to his garage. His pride and joy sat on the garage floor. He'd bought an old Harley-Davison bike as a project. He'd stripped it down but was having problems putting it back together again.

Smiling, he remembered Steve looking the bike over. He'd told him he should stick to what he knew and keep away from mechanical problems.

"Still trying to get it going?" Patrick asked, from the doorway.

"Yeah, it's a labour of love?"

"Doesn't look it?" Patrick smiled, as Nigel laughed.

"You're right; I hate the thing now," Nigel admitted as they both laughed before going quiet.

"Do you think Steve's really dead Nigel?" Patrick softly asked, making Nigel drop the spanner he was holding.

"Why would you say that Patrick?" Patrick stood looking at Nigel, his years of being news reporter giving him a feeling about people.

"What do you know Nigel?" Patrick asked his happy mood gone. Nigel thinking of an answer took too long.

"Why did you go to Australia? What lead you to think something was wrong?"

"Patrick, back off. I can't talk about it. You know the rules."

"Know what rules?" Lindsey said from the door. With the men's disappearance, the women had come looking.

"What's going on?" Robin asked.

"Nothing's going on. I just came out here for a quiet drink that's all." Nigel answered defensively.

"Are you asking Nigel questions, Patrick? I warned you about that. You know where he works so don't!" Robin snapped.

"Hey. I was asking him about if he thought Steve was dead. I'm still waiting for an answer." Patrick replied. The room froze as Nigel felt the glare of his family upon him.

"He died with Natasha didn't he?" Lindsey sobbed, Robin, holding her.

"His body wasn't recovered. I just want the truth." Patrick asked, his eyes misting up. Nigel knew he was close to Natasha as well as Steve.

"I don't know that Steve's alive now," Nigel answered truthfully.

"Then you're saying he survived the bomb?" Robin put in.

"Jesus! You've talked to him haven't you?" Patrick pounced, seeing Nigel cracking.

"Nigel," Lindsey started.

"Stop it! I can't tell you anymore!" Nigel angrily shouted, shocking them all, as he turned for the door.

"Get off his back Patrick. He's just doing his job!" a voice barked from the doorway in front of Nigel. There in the doorway stood Steve.

THE RETURN

Peter stayed with his three friends at the Marina for several weeks, hoping he would hear something from Marlise. He'd immediately contacted her father once they'd reached Europe, but he'd heard nothing from her. Peter had told him the whole story about everything that had happened. He took it fairly well, although he didn't want to meet with Peter. His last words were, 'bring my daughter home.' These words would haunt Peter for years to come.

Returning to Zurich, he resumed his position as Director of his father's bank. His sister returned from Lebanon with her husband. They'd stayed with him at their parent's home, promising to keep him company until she returned. Peter didn't just wait for her; he hired an army of investigators and his friends to search for her, even at times going out looking for her himself. For the next three years he searched finding nothing, then he received a lead.

Tamal, who he had hired to look for her, had heard from a friend that an ex French paratrooper had joined the Peshmerga in Northern Iraq. Since the unit was made up of women, it had to be a female. She had made a name for herself in attacks on enemy ISIS fighters at night, cutting their throats while they stood watch. ISIS had put a hefty reward on her head. Peter reading the report knew it was Marlise.

Going to his sister Michelle and Hussein, he showed it to her. To his surprise, she started to cry.

"She's too far gone, Peter. She's only there because she's obsessed with killing men. Don't go near her Peter; she'll kill you," she cried her husband, in the end, leading her away. Peter after they left stood alone gazing into the fireplace thinking of what Marlise meant to him. A slight noise behind him made him swiftly roll to the side, coming up with a gun in his hand. Checking the room he found nothing.

"Stop thinking Peter. Go get her!" a voice told him from the shadows.

"I will need a ghost on this one."

"No Peter. You must become the Ghost. I'm too old." Steve replied, stepping into the light.

"How did you know?" Peter asked as he went to shake Steve's hand, to see it was gone. "Oh no, Steve. I'm so sorry. How did it happen?"

"First, I know your Investigator Tamal. He told me what he'd found out. And how I lost my arm? Well, I got careless in the desert. That is why I came Peter. To get close to her you must become the best, I have come to train you."

"I have kept up my training Steve. I am still one of the elite."

"Yet a one armed man came into this room, and you didn't know? Your dad was the unit commander Peter, but I was the scout, I got up close. Let me help you. I'm too old and damaged to go with you."

"Okay Steve, when do you want to start?"

"Ring your bank and tell them you won't be back for some time. We start tonight." Steve told him, opening the outside door. "When you've told them that, come outside and find me. I'll teach you about the dark," Steve chuckled, disappearing into the night.

THE END

www.ingramcontent.com/pod-product-compliance
Lightning Source LLC
Chambersburg PA
CBHW031219120726
47905CB00002B/398